THE SONGS OF SYMERID THREE
BOOK ONE OF THE CELESTRIAD

Marise Morland

THE SONGS OF SYMERID THREE
BOOK ONE OF THE CELESTRIAD

DOUBLE DRAGON

Prologue

Tristell was dead, and Tralvar was very, very drunk. Having failed after three days to attain the oblivion he craved, he left the akron at dawn and walked unsteadily up the hill toward the Lyricon. Soon the artisans would arrive to take down Tristell's statue, which stood forlorn and isolated amid the towering colonnades. Once there had been a whole avenue of statues, each one a celebration of a living singer. Now, there were no more singers. Tristell had been the last.

The stonemasons appeared, duly noted Tralvar's dishevelled presence, and made a show of ignoring him. Such a public display of grief was unseemly. It was no excuse that he'd loved the dead girl, because that in itself had been foolish. Tristell had attracted many lovers, all valued citizens. And what was Tralvar? Untrustworthy, a close ally of Alendis the tyrant, and a failed musician into the bargain.

Tralvar, though he kept his mind closed defensively, was well aware of their attitude. Alone in the great auditorium, he sat at a distance and watched the men begin their work. No-one dared ask him to leave.

Far above, other eyes had spied him. Two women, mother and daughter, regarded him from the window of their apartment.

"I'm surprised he had the nerve to show up," remarked Zenzie. Her youth and prettiness were marred by the scowl on her face and the dark shadows under her eyes. Her white-blond hair was unbrushed.

"Put off your anger, child," Floren said reprovingly. "It does no-one any good, least of all you. Poor Tralvar's probably suffering more than we are."

"Poor Tralvar?" Zenzie repeated scornfully. "He's a good actor, I'll admit, but I'm not fooled and neither should you be. I'm convinced he had something to do with Tristell's death and I intend to prove it."

"If you're right, then harmony help him," said Floren, still gazing at the solitary figure below.

"I don't see why you feel so sorry for him."

"Because...." Floren hesitated, trying to give her instinct some substance. "Because I represent the scolia and I've always believed they let him down. He's a born musician, better than many in the Guild. If they'd allowed him to persevere, he'd have been a very different person today."

As she finished speaking, a young man entered the room. He directed a reproachful look at Zenzie before picking up an embroidered wrap and hastening forward to place it around her. "You shouldn't be up, my little love," he said gently.

"Idenion, it's been five octals since the miscarriage. All this lying around is *making* me tired." She glanced out of the window again. "Or maybe it's the company."

"I saw him arrive," Idenion said quietly. "He won't let me read him; should one of us go down there, Floren?"

"We'll both go. Zenzie, I think you should stay

here."

"With pleasure. Just make sure you send him packing."

Tralvar stood up as Idenion and Floren approached. They paused on the step above him, but his sombre presence was enough to offset his disadvantaged position.

"My compliments, Custodian," he said with a curt nod towards Floren.

"Walk in harmony, First Scientist," she replied pleasantly.

"Greetings, First Poet," Tralvar continued, this time addressing Idenion. He makes it sound like an insult, Idenion thought, flinching very slightly as he recalled what had happened to the previous First Poet.

+Tralvar had nothing to do with that+ Floren reminded him. +He was here, with Tristell and me.+

"Please don't feel threatened," Tralvar said, moving closer. He stank of liquor. "I admit your new title doesn't sit easily with me, but you can blame that on your overblown verses. Now, is it true that the scolia won't play?"

"It's true," Floren said. "They're too dispirited to form a lattice."

"Then they're making things worse. How much longer do you think the administrators can keep Alendis out? There has to be a concert, preferably several. And quickly."

"Tralvar," Floren said sorrowfully, "you of all people should know how delicate the lattice is, and how easily disrupted. A poor recital would be worse than none at all, and unworthy of our traditions

7

here."

Tralvar shrugged. "In that case you'd better start looking for a new home."

"I shall organise a concert," Idenion said suddenly. "For tomorrow."

"And how will you command the scolia?" Tralvar inquired. "An inspirational poem, perhaps? You've done enough damage with those already."

"I regret it," Idenion said candidly.

Floren glanced warningly at him.

"I guarantee that the scolia will play," he continued.

"Pardon my scepticism, but I think the task is beyond you," Tralvar declared. "Scribble a few more odes to Alendis, my friend. Protect your livelihood." With one final insolent look at the poet he stalked off, but Idenion knew his distress and wasn't offended. He watched until Tralvar had quit the main portal, then said: "I shall need your help, Floren, if my plan is to go ahead."

"I'll organise things here; I consider it my duty. But are you sure you're ready?"

"I'm sure." Idenion faced her resolutely. "It's all happened sooner than I expected, but I've studied and prepared. If the scolia have a singer, I know they'll play. And once they've accompanied a true voice, they'll demand more voices, and Alendis will have to give in."

"Ever the optimist!"

"The attempt has to be made," Idenion said stubbornly. "Think of the alternative, and then tell me I shouldn't go."

Floren was silent.

8

"Admittedly," Idenion went on, "Hellas is far from ideal. They have wars, they take slaves. But on the other hand, we've no record of our previous expeditions coming to harm."

"The journey itself is perilous," Floren said quietly.

Idenion laughed. "What? After Tralvar has personally inspected all our spacecraft?"

"He does make mistakes."

"In music, perhaps. In engineering, never." Idenion's tone was emphatic. "I must get a message to Halon. In fact, I'd better go to Communications and see him. The Hellas flight programme has to be found."

"Are you going to tell Zenzie what you're doing?" asked Floren.

"Later," promised Idenion. "I don't want any histrionics just yet. I've some serious writing to do."

"Writing? At a time like this?" exclaimed Floren, but Idenion didn't elaborate. Floren, ever more troubled, watched him hasten away. Her first instinct was to go after him, shake him, remind him that he was not invulnerable. But in the end she did nothing. Poets, after all, weren't renowned for their prudence.

Having delivered his message, Idenion spent most of the day in the city archives, drafting a document which he eventually left there under seal. Then, at twilight, he paid his second visit to the communications centre on the eastern edge of Alda Mexa. The spacefield was unlit, as was the custom when no traffic was expected; but off to one side, lights burned in a white tower. Halon, hopefully

9

alone, was waiting for him. A discreet mindsweep confirmed this was so. Idenion also discovered, with the acuteness of perception he was renowned for, that Halon had not been entirely successful in his search for the Hellas programme.

The entrance doors whispered apart at Idenion's touch, revealing empty reception areas and an elevator to the nine floors above. This building, plain and functional, had neither the history nor the grandeur of the Lyricon; yet, paradoxically, it showed more signs of age. The white stone walls were mottled, the synthetic floor covering was scuffed.

Halon was in the data analysis area on the fifth floor. Despite its officious title, the room looked half-derelict, with a thick layer of dust on the monitor screens and work surfaces. Some of the dust had transferred itself to Halon's hair and clothing.

"Who's upstairs?" Idenion asked, glancing in the general direction of the control room on the uppermost level.

"Jarras. He'll mind his own business," Halon reassured him.

Idenion picked his way across the room to his friend's side. "What's been the problem?"

Halon switched on one of the monitors, which displayed a neat list of galactic coordinates. "This," he said, pointing at one entry, "is the Hellas planet, Symerid Three. And here it is again, further on. Only..." He pressed a tiny switch on the desk in front of him, and a shallow drawer slid open to reveal a trayful of gleaming crystals. "Only it isn't here. At least, not where the index says it should be."

Idenion peered at the date above the entry. "But the list was only revised a few spans ago."

"I suspect it was copied without reference to what's in here." Halon opened another drawer, and another. Inside, the fabric which lined the trays had torn, allowing the crystals to roll about. All semblance of order had long since vanished. "It's years since I examined this store," he continued. "I should have known it wasn't being looked after. To identify the contents I had to run each crystal through a simulator, and I didn't have time to check many."

"But you did find something," Idenion persisted.

"Two programmes, almost identical, which can take you to the right planet. But neither of them has the precise coordinates for Hellas. From what I know of the place I can think of two possible reasons: either it was so popular that directions weren't necessary, or someone put a ban on landing before the visits ceased altogether. The latter, I'd say. Conditions on the ground could have deteriorated." Halon smoothed his mop of fair hair, redistributing the dust. "If things stood like this alone, I'd be crazy to let you go - "

"You *have* to," Idenion said, regarding the jumbled crystals with near-resentment. It was this kind of thing, wasn't it, that Alendis had railed against - technology discarded and left lying around to rot?

"Aldacite crystals don't rot," objected Halon.

11

"They just need someone to tidy them up, that's all. Now stop looking so miserable and sit down. There's something else you should see." He slid his chair along to the next monitor and set it in operation. "My tutor, Elos, was concerned about the age of these programmes. So, each time one of them was successfully used, he noted it in this register. Someone went to Symerid Three only seventeen years ago."

Idenion stared. "To Hellas?"

"It's a possibility. They went into geostationary orbit, and that's all it says. I'll put the details on your flight plan."

Idenion continued to frown, and Halon grew slightly annoyed.

"The important thing is, they got back again. Just be thankful the programme was tested so recently. I'm sorry I can't tell you where Hellas is, or if these people made landfall, but I couldn't find any trace of a flight log."

"Forgive me. I'm being unreasonable." Idenion looked contrite, then worried. "It's just that everything's beginning to seem so difficult..."

Halon smiled. "You're being realistic at last." He took Elos' file from the reader and replaced it with another crystal. "This ought to resolve a few difficulties."

Idenion gazed in half-recognition at a series of architectural drawings. Pillars, porticos and friezes etched themselves into existence and just as suddenly disappeared. Halon showed him how to change the perspective, to travel round, through and over each structure until he began to feel giddy.

12

"It's from the Hellas scrolls," he said slowly. "Where did you get it?"

"It's mine, from my student days," said Halon. "Essential background. From an engineering point of view, this stuff's brilliant."

"And will this - stuff - guide me to Hellas?"

"With a little perseverance. I'll put in into a seek-and-locate format and show you how to use it tomorrow."

"What time should I report to you?" Idenion asked eagerly.

"Let's see... no earlier than dawn-plus-two. Your transport will be in the maintenance bay for pre-flight checks. I'll download all the information while the bay is sealed off - that way no-one will see what's being planned."

"More checks?" queried Idenion. "You've been over everything once. Why make more work for yourself?"

"Because," said Halon with exaggerated patience, "our biospheres are getting old. Treva isn't supplying any new ones. There are a few incomplete 'spheres in the vats, but nothing seems to get finished off these days." He paused and regarded the younger man gravely. "I fear for you, Idenion. You know so little of space travel - of transposal - "

"Transposal," Idenion repeated softly. "The progression across. Do *you* understand it?"

"I don't think anyone does. But I do know how to navigate home, should my sphere emerge in the wrong quadrant. You couldn't begin to do it, so I'm making sure you don't have to try."

"Nothing will go wrong. I won't allow it!" Idenion assured him. "And tomorrow night we'll have the best concert ever."

"Tomorrow night?" Halon echoed. "But you can't!"

"And why not?"

Halon sighed. "Explorers wrote these programmes, Idenion, and sightseers used them. This one makes a tour of Symerid's outer worlds before it goes anywhere near Hellas. You'd never get back in time even if you started now!"

+There's something you're not telling me+ Idenion's keen, slightly irreverent thoughts took him unawares.

"I...."

+Come on, out with it+

Discords, thought Halon, why does he make me feel guilty for keeping to the rule book? It's his life at stake. But I can't hinder him now, and he knows it. No wonder Alendis dotes on him.

"Well, Halon?" Idenion prompted. "The other programme..."

" ... goes straight to Symerid Three," Halon said resignedly. "Oh, Idenion, did you have to make that stupid bet with Tralvar? I want your plan to work, but how can I sanction the use of an untested programme?"

"You said they were almost identical."

"Yes, but -"

"And they've both been in use before?"

"At one time, yes." Halon stretched his tired limbs. "Look, I'll tell you what: I'll compare the vectors in detail and see where they differ. I'll stay here all night if I have to. Logically, you'd be safer not trailing around a strange solar system; and if I decide that's the case I'll let you take the shorter route."

Idenion, smiling broadly, stood up to leave.

"That wasn't a promise," Halon added. "Don't treat it as one."

"Of course not," Idenion said.

***

The following morning, technician and poet stood side by side in the maintenance bay annexe. Idenion was taut with impatience. "I told you it was no use being early," Halon said. "I can't open the airlock or the roof until the chamber's fully pressurised. You'll just have to wait."

Two assistants wandered past, pausing incuriously for a moment. Idenion contrived to relax until they had gone.

"Now," Halon continued, "about the untried part of the programme. You'll lose transposal well above the plane of the ecliptic, so you'll be clear of the asteroid belt and its rubble. Nevertheless, as soon as you've defined your quadrant, you must follow the safety procedures I've detailed in the flight plan."

"All right," Idenion said absently. He was feeling rather wretched, having just quarrelled with Zenzie. Where in the name of discord had she acquired such a temper? She certainly hadn't absorbed it from Floren. Incandescent, wilful girl, with a spirit too bold for her frail body. Five octals

15

ago she had stormed into Alendis' presence, reviled and condemned him - and with good cause....

But he didn't want to think about First Poet Relto. Not in here.

Subsequently Zenzie had miscarried. And Idenion was made First Poet in Relto's place - a doubtful honour, but one which he'd dared not turn down.

"Well, get going," Halon said, pushing him; and he found himself walking trancelike across the service bay. Above, the roof began to slide ponderously open. A bright sliver of early morning sunlight cut into the near-darkness and dazzled him. Suddenly, a small, determined figure darted across the gloomy recess and planted herself firmly between him and the waiting spacecraft.

"Dena!" he exclaimed. "What are you doing here, little sister?"

"Zenzie's just told me what you're up to," said the girl breathlessly. "Did you think I'd let you go alone?"

"But, Dena, I can't involve you. I'll come back safely, I promise."

"And will you also promise," she inquired, "to bring back someone who can sing in tune?"

"Well - I..."

"Exactly. You need me. Besides, I told Zenzie I'd keep you out of trouble."

That, under the circumstances, was so impossible that Idenion decided not to comment.

Chapter One
Cheveney, West Berkshire, 30th July 1966

"Laura! Hey, Laura!"

Laura Gilcoyne stirred fitfully at the shout. A moment later the cry was repeated, accompanied by the sharp crack of a pebble on the window-pane. She opened her eyes and looked at the alarm: 5.50 a.m! Perturbed, she slid out of bed and opened the heavy curtains, admitting a wash of grey daylight. When she'd finished blinking, she looked down and saw a familiar red-haired figure aiming another pebble.

"Jimmy!" she called, opening the window hastily. "Whatever's wrong?"

"Come down," Jimmy replied. "I have to talk to you. I'm going to London."

He must mean Wembley, thought Laura. It's today, isn't it - the World Cup Final? She ran a comb through her tangled brown hair and dressed swiftly, wondering what on earth couldn't have waited until tomorrow. When she opened the front door, her sense of foreboding increased. Jimmy, who was seldom nervous, looked more ill at ease than she'd ever seen him.

"Is your uncle at home?" he asked.

"If he had been you'd have woken him with all that yelling," she returned. "What's wrong? Why are you here?"

Jimmy fidgeted. "To say goodbye," he said after a pause. "I'm not going to the football. I'm going for good."

"Going?" she repeated blankly. "You mean - leaving? Leaving Cheveney?"

Jimmy turned away from her stricken eyes. "I knew you'd look like that. I nearly went without seeing you, but I didn't want you to worry."

"But where are you going to live? Do you have any money?"

"Don't know, and no," said Jimmy lightly. "Now don't fuss - I'll be all right. I'll sell my World Cup ticket."

"Who else knows about this?" asked Laura.

"Tracey," said Jimmy, shamefaced. "I didn't intend telling anyone, but she got it out of me."

"I bet she did," Laura said sarcastically.

"There you go again!" Jimmy said. "You never wanted a relationship, so why get jealous of Tracey?"

"And if we'd *had* a relationship, would it have made any difference? Of course not. You'd have run off just the same."

"Laura." Jimmy gripped both her hands; they were cold. "I can't spend the rest of my life in this dump. You may think I'm letting you down, but perhaps this is what you need to get your own life sorted out. I'm setting you an example."

"What example?" Laura's grey eyes flashed with anger. "You're being irresponsible and thoughtless."

Jimmy grew angry in turn. "What was I supposed to do, Laura? Stick around until you decided to grow up?" His voice was over-loud in the still morning air. "You've hidden yourself here," he continued after a self -conscious cough, "and what worries me is that you'll hide for too long. Don't forget I've seen the real you - the girl who can dress up and walk on stage and sing her heart out. Are you willing to let all that talent be stifled?"

"I'm not that good."

"But it's *in* you, Laura. It's your heritage. You've always said so." He glanced at his watch. "I have to go - I've a lift arranged. Promise me something?"

She looked at him miserably. "What?"

"If someone offers you the chance to get away - a chance to go somewhere decent, I mean - you're not to hang back. Okay?"

"Okay," she said expressionlessly.

"Right. Look after yourself, angel. Bye." He traversed the lawn with his familiar loping stride and set off down the lane.

"Will you write?" she called.

He waved, pretending he hadn't heard. A soft drizzle began to fall.

Laura stood at the front door long after he was out of sight. Then, feeling numb and empty, she shut the door firmly and went to make a mug of coffee. Sitting in the cool quiet kitchen, with its outsize wooden table and rows of willow pattern china, she pondered what Jimmy had said. *Was* she hiding?

Laura had come to Cheveney in 1962 as a shy, bewildered twelve-year-old, newly discharged from hospital after the car crash which had killed both her parents and left her with a disturbing gap in her memory. She was to stay with Nathaniel, her father's elder brother, whom she hardly knew.

19

Nathaniel, a bachelor in his mid-fifties, made it clear that he'd acted from duty rather than compassion. He'd sent her to a prestigious boarding school in the area and detailed his part-time housekeeper to look after her in the holidays. His work as a financier took him to London for days on end, and consequently he was almost as remote now as when Laura had first met him.

For companionship Laura had Mrs. Moffat and Jimmy Stretton. Mrs Moffat, the housekeeper, was an honest uncomplicated soul who doted on Laura. As a mother-substitute she was the best choice that Nathaniel could have made, though he was irritated by her attempts to mother *him*. Jimmy was two years Laura's senior, a bright but disaffected youth with an unappreciative family. He'd been drawn to Laura by her tragedy and they'd soon become very close. At first she'd been woefully insecure, always needing his approval or reassurance; later, as his family situation worsened, he'd needed hers just as much. But she'd kept their friendship platonic, saying the time wasn't right for anything more, knowing instinctively there never would be a right time.

And now he'd gone, turning his back on his home. Dear, safe, unprepossessing Cheveney. How rustic it had seemed to her at first, and how small. But the little community, and the ancient forest that surrounded it, had soon endeared itself to her. Nathaniel's house, Windbourne, had once been the vicarage. It had a rambling garden, a conservatory adjoining the study, and an air of genteel decay. Not even Nathaniel had been able to impose his personality on this house; it had stood too long and forgotten too much. Laura had been strangely comforted by its indifference to human affairs and had settled in at once - perhaps a little too well.

"But I'm not hiding *now*," she said aloud.

The sudden click of the back door latch made her start. Mrs Moffat bustled in, beaming.

"Just off to Newbury, love, but I won't be long. Roll on three o'clock, eh?"

Laura looked up blankly. "What?"

"The World Cup. Don't tell me you'd forgotten!"

"Er ... no," said Laura, putting down the cold coffee.

Mrs. Moffat scrutinised her more closely. "Have you been crying, pet? Come on, tell me what's wrong."

Laura didn't mention Jimmy. If anyone caught up with him, she'd get the blame. "I just feel so aimless," she extemporised. It was true, anyway. "It's been a fortnight since school broke up and I still don't know if I want to go back. My exam marks were terrible except for music."

"That's Nathaniel's fault," Mrs. Moffat declared. "He should've sent you to an ordinary school." She inspected her perm in the mirror over the sink. "What about learning to type? There's lots of jobs for typists."

"I'll think about it," said Laura.

"You've done too much thinking already, my girl. Why not come to Newbury with me? Get your hair done or buy a new dress. You need taking out of yourself."

21

"No, not today, Aunt Margaret," said Laura with a watery smile. "I have to practice my singing."

"Are you rehearsing for something?"

"No, but I still have to sing. My voice would seize up otherwise. And besides, this is my last chance before Uncle Nat comes home. You know how he hates it."

"Well, if you're sure." Mrs Moffat gave her a peck on the cheek and went out. Silence, profound and dispiriting, eddied back.

Laura made herself a fresh mug of coffee, but had only taken a few sips when she saw a blonde head peering over the privet hedge at the end of the drive. Tracey! Instantly, Laura threw the bolt on the back door and scurried upstairs to her bedroom. Tracey had come to talk about Jimmy, or probably to gloat about him. Well, she wouldn't get the chance. At least, not yet. Laura sprawled face down on her bed and waited for the unwelcome visitor to stop wandering around outside - and the next thing she knew, two hours had passed and the sun was out.

The extra sleep had improved her spirits. She exchanged her crumpled dress for a blue t-shirt and jeans, and hunted out her favourite medallion - a souvenir from Athens with an image of the Parthenon etched into the wafer-thin gold.

Fifteen minutes later, she was at the piano. After running through some warm-up exercises she began to sing Voi Che Sapete from the Marriage of Figaro, accompanying herself as best she could. She wished, not for the first time, that Nathaniel could have been persuaded to pay for piano lessons too. But he'd made her choose, and there had been no mistaking his disappointment when she'd chosen singing. She'd given up asking why.

At two o'clock she made herself some sandwiches and carried the plate into the study. Nathaniel's books were mostly in Greek and Latin, but surprisingly he also had a number of scientific romances which Laura liked to delve into. She took up an ancient paperback, removed her marker and began to read intently.

It was after 3.30 when she re-entered the drawing-room to try one last song. On one of her occasional forays into the loft, she'd discovered a wind-up gramophone and a cache of 78s which Nathaniel didn't want her to play. Naturally she'd disobeyed, and found a song which delighted her: Nuits d'Etoiles by Debussy. She was now in the process of memorising it from sheet music.

The room had become stuffy. Her fingers, disobedient, allowed errors to stray into the accompaniment. Irritably she ceased playing, stood up and opened the window wide. Then she started again, striking the keys painstakingly and omitting any chords she wasn't sure of. Her young soprano voice rang out confidently and accurately, and her introspective mood added just the right touch of ennui to the lyric.

She'd scarcely completed the song when the telephone shrilled a peremptory summons from the next room. It was, of course, Nathaniel.

"Yes, uncle," she said mechanically. "Yes, of course I'm here. Where else would I be? No, I

23

haven't looked for a job yet. I wanted to talk it over with you first."

The terse voice uttered some predictable admonitions. " - and I shall expect to see a tidy house," it continued. "No music scattered about, and no dirty cups left in my study. And I shall only give you careers advice if you promise to be guided by me. No more nonsense about the music business."

"No, uncle," said Laura wearily. "See you later." She dropped the heavy black receiver into its cradle, picked up her dinner plate and took it into the kitchen. The table had a generous scattering of crumbs; she wiped them up carefully, then wandered about the house looking for anything else that might offend Nathaniel's eye. Her music, as he'd guessed, was strewn across the drawing room floor. As she began to retrieve it, the sound of low-flying jets rent the afternoon silence and shook the ornaments on the mantelpiece.

"Get lost!" Laura muttered. She continued to sift through the manuscripts, pausing now and then to re-read the pencilled comments made by her tutor, or to take quiet pride in a difficult piece she'd mastered. I'm *not* going to give this up, she declared to herself. A minute or two later, she paused and looked suspiciously at the window, quite expecting to see Tracey's impish face grinning at her. No-one was there, but she still had the sensation of being watched. Seized with sudden hope, she hastened to the front door and flung it open. "Is anyone there?" she called. "Jimmy? Jimmy, is that you?"

At that moment the jet fighters made another pass overhead. She turned to glare at them, and a second later realised that she did after all have company. "Hey, you two!" she cried wrathfully. "Get off the flowerbed!"

And waited, arms folded, for an answer, never suspecting that it would change her life.

***

Mindful of Halon's advice, Idenion had remained extra vigilant during the final part of the journey. And thus, when a warning siren shrilled and the soft overhead lighting turned a threatening crimson, his hands had slammed down on the instrumentation almost before he knew what was happening. But the guidance system wasn't used to such clumsy treatment. Idenion's lack of skill had sent the craft hurtling, out of control, toward the asteroid belt and yet more danger.

Idenion forced himself to work methodically, reducing speed by careful degrees, trying to re-establish a course for Symerid Three. He tried not to look at the gyrating starscape on the viewscreen, telling himself that he wouldn't, couldn't, panic. There was a clear, cold anger in his mind - anger with Alendis and all that had made this desperate journey essential. He drew on that anger, using its coldness to sharpen his wits and steady his shaking hands. And at last, after what seemed a small lifetime, the controls responded and the cabin lights reverted to their normal subdued pink. For the moment he and Dena were safe.

"What was in our way?" Dena asked. Her small perfect features held an expression of fatalistic calm. Idenion was momentarily surprised, then realised that she didn't fear sudden death half as much as being hurt or stranded. Nor as much as being in space to begin with - a fear she'd bravely overcome in order to be with him. He consulted the instruments, still unsure of what the obstacle had been, and gasped when he saw what a narrow escape they'd had.

"It was a dustcloud with nasty lumps of rock in it," he reported, "situated well above the plane of the ecliptic in an area which was supposed to be free of such things. Remind me to let Halon know. And, Dena, I'm sorry to have given you such a scare. I should have checked for anomalies when we came out of transposal. But when the constellations matched, I thought the rest would be all right."

"Another time, run the checks," she said wanly. "Are we nearly there?"

"Won't be long now," Idenion said, still concentrating on the panel display. "I should have Symerid Three on the screen in half an astal. Then all we have to do is find Hellas."

Dena sat bolt upright. "You mean you don't know where Hellas *is*?" she cried.

"I'll find it," Idenion declared, aggrieved. "I know it's in the northern hemisphere and has islands nearby. Or it may be *on* an island; the surviving reports were a bit muddled."

"Not as muddled as your head," said Dena forlornly. "What are we supposed to look for?"

"Architecture," he answered confidently. "Our Lyricon was modelled after their temples. The computer knows the basic shapes: it'll scan the surface and help us choose the right locality. I don't intend to put us down just anywhere, Dena. The rest of the planet's none too..." He stared hard at the viewscreen. "...civilised," he finished almost inaudibly.

Dena, unused to viewscreen images, didn't immediately see what had startled him. Symerid Three was a large blue-white crescent, rapidly looming larger, its one moon a pale cratered blotch in the background.

"Look at the night side of the globe," Idenion said.

Dena obliged, and gave a little cry. "Lights!" she whispered. "Cities! Idenion, how old is the Hellas programme?"

"I don't know. I didn't think it was *that* old."

"We'll have to go back," Dena said. But Idenion's eyes were dancing rapturously.

"Go back?" he repeated. "This is even more promising than I'd hoped. The Hellenes were always fighting - "

"You didn't tell me that."

"...and eventually we left them to it, or so the story goes. We thought it was an arrested society, that they'd never apply themselves to practical science. Obviously we didn't recognise their potential." He moved to the communications panel. "I'm going to try the radio. Perhaps they...." A blare of sound obliterated the rest of his words and he hastily reduced the volume to a bearable level. The transposal modes, he noted, were significantly empty; but the entire radio spectrum was crammed with transmissions of every kind. Codes, callsigns, conversations; voices shouting, talking, chanting...and singing. There was an abundance of music: some discordant, some quite beautiful. The automatic tuning, accustomed to dealing with maybe three broadcasts at a time, was unable to cope with the input and began vacillating wildly from source to source.

For the first and only time, Idenion felt a stab of real doubt. Oh, discords! he thought to himself. There's so much of it, so many of them. But he didn't speak aloud, nor communicate his misgivings to his sister. The moment passed and his resolve emerged unscathed. He was not going to crawl back home empty-handed. These people weren't psi-conversant, so naturally they'd use radio extensively. There were singers here, and he'd choose one.... somehow. Three times he curtailed the reception range until comparatively few frequencies were being searched. But far from bringing clarity, the results confused him.

"They have more than one language," he stated.

Dena was going to ask how he knew, but decided against it. Idenion had great skill with the spoken word, so it was only fair to assume that in this case he could hear what she could not. If he could, it would more than make up for his other deficiencies. Had their mission not been so serious, she would have been vastly amused at the idea of her tone-deaf brother trying to find a singer.

"Can you tell which language is the right one?" she asked.

"Not without seeing it written down," Idenion said abstractedly.

"That's what I thought. Well, why not check for telecasts? You might find a clue that way."

"My clever sister!" Idenion declared, and hugged her briefly. "I knew I'd be glad I brought you. Telecasts, yes; they're bound to have them. Now let's get this right... " He tapped hesitantly on the computer console and the planet's image disappeared from the viewscreen in a shower of static. He checked to make sure the sphere was in an orbit geosynchronous with the coordinates suggested by Halon, then waited.

"Can't you hurry it up?" said Dena, fidgeting.

"Sorry. I don't understand computers well enough."

"Then what instruction did you just give it?"

"The problem-solving one, of course," Idenion said. "From chaos to order; from dissonance to harmony. That usually does the trick."

The screen relit in a dull monochrome and a picture began to build, strip by narrow strip in a horizontal scan. The delineation, now that the formula had been established, was swift, but not swift enough for the fretful Dena.

Soon, as with the radio, the mechanism began its rapid switching from subject to subject. After a few moments of perplexity, Idenion chose a broadcast at random for an in-depth study; but he was still unable to make sense of what he saw and heard, other than to reassure himself that he and Dena could pass as natives. Once some writing appeared, each line moving jerkily up the blurred picture to disappear off the top. The symbols were not those he'd memorised. He was busy

29

pondering the significance of this when Dena said:

"Admit it, Idenion. You're as confused as I am."

"Afraid so," he said sadly. "It all looks wrong. But I can't give up yet - something has to make sense. Will you keep watching it for a moment or two? I have to run some course checks."

"All right," Dena said passively.

On screen, an announcer began an animated but incomprehensible monologue. Idenion ignored him and began a painstaking inspection of the flight display. No more alarms had sounded, but there was something registering that shouldn't have been out there. "Discords," he muttered involuntarily.

"Is there a problem?" Dena inquired, ever anxious.

"Just a slight one," Idenion said. "I'm going to have to move closer in. There's a bit of debris up here and it would be just our luck if something hit us now."

"More meteors?" Dena sighed.

"I expect so," Idenion said non-committal, hating himself for the lie. No, not meteors. The density was all wrong. And at least one of these "meteors" was relaying television programmes. Symerid Three's inhabitants weren't just scientifically accomplished, they were *emergent* - exactly the type of civilisation he was supposed to stay away from. In stubborn disregard of that edict, he extended his hands to the panel - then paused irritably.

"Dena, what's that noise?"

"People," she replied.

Idenion completed the course correction,

verified that the sphere had settled into a lower orbit, then decided to set Halon's architectural scan in operation. He was no longer sure of finding Hellas by this means, but it would do no harm to try. Finally, he returned his attention to the Symerid telecast. A huge exuberant crowd, armed with banners and flags, filled the screen. Another roar of sound ricocheted about the tiny cabin; he flinched and switched to vision only.

"Any idea what they're shouting at?"

"It's a contest with a ball," Dena said. "Their priestess is up on those terraces somewhere. The athletes lined up behind some musicians and dedicated the ball to her."

Idenion's interest deepened. "Could it be an Olympiad?" he asked.

"I don't know," Dena said. "Would they be wearing clothes, if it were?"

"I'm not sure," Idenion admitted. "Did you get a look at the stadium from the outside?"

"Yes, just for a moment," Dena said, giving him a mental image of what she'd seen. Her portrayal of the alien structure was clear and meticulous.

"An ellipse with two towers at the portal," Idenion said, half to himself. "Distinctive."

"Only to us, perhaps."

"Perhaps," Idenion repeated. "But it's worth taking a chance." He turned back to the computer, and Dena gave a little squeal.

"Idenion, don't! Don't fool with it - you don't know enough. You'll delete everything and we'll never get home!"

31

Idenion looked at her reproachfully. "Try to have a little more faith in me. If I ruin anything, it will only be Halon's temple surveys - and I somehow don't think we'll miss those. Time has tricked us, my sister. This game we're watching is probably our best hope of finding Hellas – if it still exists."

Dena looked unconvinced.

"What have we got to lose?" Idenion persisted. "I'll put the outline of that sports-place into Halon's programme. I'm sure I can do it. He left it open-ended in case we needed to add things."

Dena curled up miserably in her chair, refusing to watch his uncertain efforts at the keys. Instead, she stared at the tiled floor, until she suddenly remembered the Drive was under there and averted her gaze superstitiously. Very few people could repair a defective stardrive any more, least of all Idenion. She looked up at the viewscreen's silent scurryings just in time to see the hurtling ball hit one of the players in the face. After that, she simply closed her eyes.

"All done," Idenion announced, "and nothing's been lost. If you get a command wrong, the computer just ignores you and lets you try again."

"And how did you find that out?" inquired Dena.

"I ... well, that's what just happened," Idenion confessed. He manipulated controls airily, and the grey of the telecast gave way to the bluish outline of the continent below. "See those islands?" he continued, pointing to the left of the screen. "I'm going to resume the scan there."

32

Dena blinked. "Why?"

"The game's being televised there too, and the topography seems more like Hellas than this sprawl."

"*Someone* must have landed here," Dena said.

Idenion looked uneasy for a moment. "We don't know that," he said at last. "Now, I'm assuming that the sports ground, wherever it is, will have a television transmitter near it. I'm going to study the land around each signal source, starting nearest the continent and working north." He reactivated the scan, then leant back gratefully in the pilot's chair. "The programme's running. Now we wait."

"This is going to take for ever," Dena declared. But she was mistaken. In less than half an astal, coordinates flashed triumphantly across the visual display; and the viewscreen, at the limit of its magnification, could just discern the mass of people through a haze of shifting air.

"You see?" said Idenion softly. "I was right." He took a deep breath, wondering why he suddenly felt so calm. "This is it, Dena. I'm taking us down."

"You can't land *there*!" cried Dena, aghast.

"Don't worry, I won't. But I have to look for a quiet place. How am I supposed to do that from a distance?"

"Someone will see us!" wailed Dena.

"They have to see us sometime," Idenion said reasonably, busying himself with the panel.

Patchy grey cloud drifted by the sphere as it descended. The Olympiad, if it *was* one, disappeared from the screen and the terrain came clearly into view for the first time. A city. An

33

ill-assorted mass of buildings caught in a tangle of roadways. In the distance the buildings were taller, greyer, more forbidding. Idenion realised he was holding his breath and exhaled slowly. He still felt vulnerable - nothing was going to change that - but no matter how daunting the sight, he knew there was something valuable to be gleaned from this world. The numerous moving dots of ground traffic signified unwarranted haste, but energy and purpose as well. For some reason, Idenion thought briefly of Tralvar.

"What's that?" asked Dena, pointing over his shoulder at a circle of crimson light which was flashing imperiously.

"Nothing," Idenion said unhelpfully.

"But that colour means danger," Dena persisted.

"It means I'm flying without a programme," replied Idenion, guilty at having lied a second time. Dena wasn't trying to read him - why should she? He'd never lied to her before. My apologies, dearest sister, he thought to himself. If I told you what that light really meant, you'd get into a panic and want me to take you home. And I can't do that, not yet.

"Oh, look," said Dena, her gaze shifting to the visual display. "Halon's idea worked. There's a temple."

The dimensions of the building were logged and stored, and the scan continued.

"This must be Hellas after all," Dena said brightly.

Idenion had begun to doubt it. The architecture didn't seem to follow any set pattern, so the temple

34

was probably a copy. Again he said nothing to Dena, hoping to preserve her fragile optimism while he found a less populated area. He changed direction, heading away from the city centre, adjusting course almost immediately to avoid overflying a landing zone where large, graceful air vehicles ascended and descended in orderly precision.

"They're not spacecraft, are they?" Dena asked dubiously.

"Don't be silly," said Idenion. "They're too big." And as the sphere continued westward and the city was left behind, he found the key which deactivated the tell-tale crimson light.

Dena kept her eyes on the viewscreen as if it would miraculously point out somewhere safe. At their present low altitude their speed was all too apparent, and she winced a few times. At last Idenion brought the sphere to a near standstill as he prepared to examine the sounds at ground level - a final precaution before landing. The habitations had thinned out, replaced by a neat patchwork of fields and hedges.

"Apparently the sound-sweep doesn't work too well," he said half to himself. "But we should be able to hear a fight, for instance..."

"Look! Animals!" Dena exclaimed. "Idenion, don't land near any animals."

"They don't appear dangerous," Idenion objected. "Especially not those white fluffy ones. Anyway, I can deal with animals. I've seen them on Myrma."

"Deal with them how?"

35

"Communicate," Idenion said wisely, "as with alien people."

"I think I'll leave the people to you," Dena said. "I've never spoken with nonconversants."

"Then here's your first lesson - don't call them nonconversants. They always take exception to that. You must say 'not telepathic'."

"I won't know how to speak with them," Dena insisted.

"You *will* know, as I did," Idenion predicted. "Oh, discords - there's another town coming up. I'll head for those woodlands instead. We'll need some cover when we land."

Dena shivered. Dark treetops filled the viewscreen, perilously close. "There won't be anyone here," she commented. But, as she spoke, a few houses became visible - a tiny settlement half encircled by the wood.

"Perfect!" Idenion enthused. He engaged the sound-sweep, but heard nothing except twittering birds. Perhaps he'd failed to scan in line with the houses. He circled, tried again; still nothing. "I must be doing this wrong," he murmured. Then, borne upon the breeze that danced at ground level, came the sound of beautiful singing. Dena raised her head in wonder.

For a moment the wistful melody hung in the startled silence of the cabin, then faded in mid-phrase. With a gasp, Idenion scrambled to correct the sphere's drift. The song returned.

"That voice," whispered Dena. "It's - it's like the bell of Alda Nima..."

"As clear and pure as crystal," breathed

Idenion, and his fingertips fled across the controls in ecstasy. The sphere hit the treetops, veered upwards momentarily, then plummeted into a clearing and bounced twice before coming to rest. Its spin slowed, then ceased.

"Oh, Idenion!" Dena said reproachfully.

"I was distracted," Idenion said, unabashed. "You heard her, Dena. A real voice."

"Yes, I heard."

"My plan's going to succeed. It really is." He cut the power to the console, then stood up and took Dena's hands. "Well, are you ready, little sister?"

They stepped outside, their movements rendered momentarily graceless. Symerid Three's gravity was significantly stronger than anything they were used to. The air was sultry and full of strange odours. Dena wrinkled her nose, but experienced no ill effects. Beside her, Idenion sneezed several times, walked down the short ramp and found he couldn't stop descending. With a slightly bemused expression, he sank to his knees in the damp undergrowth. Dena, alarmed, hurried to help him up.

"Sorry," said Idenion with one final sneeze. "I wasn't ready for that."

"Should I fetch the bioshells?" Dena asked.

"No, no." Idenion waved an arm vaguely. "The atmosphere's within acceptable limits. I should have introduced the changes into the life support, gradually."

"You must try and remember these things," Dena admonished, brushing some twigs off his tunic.

37

"I didn't forget," Idenion objected. "I was trying to save time. We shouldn't stay here any longer than we can help."

Dena agreed, with much fervour.

Idenion regained his balance. Resisting the urge to lean on the sphere, he tapped out a careful code on the pressure plate beside the open hatch. It closed with a soft rippling movement, blending seamlessly into the rest of the hull. Through the trees he could see the gaunt grey walls of the singer's dwelling-place. Her mind, the strange, enclosed consciousness of a nonconversant, enticed him with its quiet preoccupations. But first, the sphere had to be placed in cloud cover.

Halon had given him a remote control device - a small square object not unlike the hull sensor. Idenion hadn't known such things existed. He wondered what other half-forgotten artefacts lay rusting in the Communications tower.

"Don't look so tragic," he said to Dena. "I won't endanger the sphere. Halon showed me exactly what to do." He made a few small adjustments to the unit. The sphere didn't budge.

Before he could try again, a sound like distant thunder made him look up sharply. In the time it took to draw one breath, the rumble became a searing roar. Two aircraft - smaller, sleeker and unmistakably more threatening than the ones he'd seen over the city - swept low across the forest and were gone. Suddenly, placing the sphere in cloud cover didn't seem such a good idea.

"Why don't we just leave it here?" Dena suggested. "We could keep an eye on it then."

"I daren't do that, much as I'd like to," Idenion said soberly. "Our spacecraft has to be kept away from these people. Halon was most insistent about that, and he was thinking of a much lower level of technology. I don't know how high those machines can go, but just to be on the safe side I'll opt for maximum range. That's beyond the atmosphere ... I think."

This time the control unit functioned, and Dena gazed miserably after their means of transport as it suddenly whisked into the sky. If Idenion couldn't retrieve it..... no, such a thought was unworthy of her. She trusted him that much; she only hoped he wouldn't crash-land it again in front of the singer.

Idenion had refocused his attention on the house, was reaching out with his acute perception to read the nature of the being whose help they sought. As always, Dena marvelled at the subtle sensitivity he displayed - a talent which had almost sent him into the ranks of the relayists, until they discovered that he couldn't actually project a thought very far. His skill was all in the nuances. Dena had been vastly relieved at the guild's decision. Her brother was so involved with life; it would have been a tragedy to set him apart from all he wished to experience.

"Her name's Laura," Idenion said at last. "She's an orphan - that seems important to her - and she's very lonely. Lonely for something she cannot yet define." He closed his eyes in concentration. "She's just lost a friend - a boy who despised the parochial way of life in this village. He's run off to that awful city. Her guardian spends most of his time there too..."

"Look," interrupted Dena. "She seems to be aware of you now."

Laura had opened the door. She looked about her and spoke a few plaintive words.

"That settles it," Idenion said, taking Dena's hand firmly. "Come on."

They began to walk toward the house with as much dignity and calm as they could muster, stepping over a sagging wooden fence and picking their way through rows of plants. Laura was gazing in the opposite direction.

"I'll have to use vocal transference," Idenion announced. "It may upset her but we don't have time to be circumspect. She has to *believe*."

Just then the two aircraft reappeared, as noisy and threatening as before. Caught in the open, Idenion and Dena clung to each other in sudden fright. And before they could regain their composure, Laura turned and saw them. She yelled something that sounded positively hostile to Dena.

"Straighten up! Smile!" Idenion whispered. "I'll sort this out." Then, marshalling all his faculties, he addressed the girl's mind. His name.... an impression of his voice.... a reassurance....

It was enough. Laura gave a little scream and disappeared into the house. But after a moment she crept out again, as Idenion knew she would. And as he'd hoped, there was no disbelief.

"She fears us," Dena whispered.

"No, my sister. You misunderstand." Idenion was suddenly worried. "She's not afraid *of* us - she's afraid *for* us."

40

Chapter Two

The instant she'd slammed the door, Laura regretted taking flight. That's you all over, she told herself fiercely. Hiding again. Head in the sand. There's something amazing right on your doorstep, where nothing amazing has ever happened, and if you turn your back on it – on *them* – you'll kick yourself later. Besides, they looked so scared. Maybe they're lost. You can't let them wander off.

When she re-emerged, she found they hadn't moved. Greatly daring, she beckoned, then silently watched them approach.

To calm herself, she focused on the mundane. She remembered thinking - a small lifetime ago - that they looked rather sweet. She still thought so. They were about her age, or maybe a little older. The girl was small and dainty, with an elfin face and grey eyes. The young man was taller, with the same delicate features. They were both very pale, with shoulder-length blonde hair. Their clothes were unremarkable: loose-fitting trousers, rope sandals, long-sleeved tunics in soft pastel colours.

They halted in front of her and waited for her to speak. The innocent trust in their eyes was enchanting, and at the same time alarming.

"Your voice – your thoughts," she stammered at last, addressing the boy. "Why did you *do* that?"

"It was necessary," he answered, speaking aloud with slow deliberation. "We wanted you to know the truth about us."

"But why me?" Laura asked reproachfully.

"Are you always so free with the truth? You know nothing about me!"

"I know a great deal about you," came the quiet reply.

Only Laura's stage experience prevented her from blushing furiously. "This isn't fair," she muttered.

The youth's earnest gaze held hers apologetically. "Let us start again," he suggested, "beginning with our names. I am Idenion and this is my sister Dena. We need your help."

High overhead, Laura glimpsed a vapour trail. "Those jets," she said suddenly. "The ones that buzzed the village. They were looking for *you*, weren't they?"

"I believe so," Idenion said. "Someone tracked our spacecraft when we were over London."

Dena gave a small cry. Laura's was louder.

"London? What were you doing *there*?"

"We saw the Olympiad on your television broadcasts," Idenion began.

"Olympiad? But it's the wrong year," Laura said, baffled.

"The game with the ball," Idenion supplemented helpfully.

"The World Cup," said Laura, more puzzled than ever.

At that moment Dena made a sudden dart forward and grabbed at her pendant. "Lyricon!" she exclaimed, then backed away shyly.

"It's the Parthenon, in Athens," Laura told her gently.

"Athens," Idenion repeated to himself.

"Athens... Athinai?"

"Look," Laura said, "I don't want to sound rude or anything, but you're not making much sense."

Idenion looked pained. "Am I speaking the language incorrectly?"

"No, but...." Laura faltered to a stop. Every time he spoke, she had the strangest feeling of dèjá-vu, as if he'd said the words twice over.

"I'm afraid that's my fault," he informed her. "In order to converse, I have to convey my thoughts to you on a subliminal level. You subvocalise what I've said, I read your mind and say your own words back to you. When I've learnt more of your speech I will not need to do this."

Laura gaped at him. "You don't know English," she said slowly. "Oh. Well. Why should you?"

"May I say something?" Dena ventured. Idenion stared at her in surprise.

"I may not be good at this but I will try," Dena went on . "Idenion is our First Poet. He loves language and words. But sometimes he doesn't get to the point."

Laura looked at her hopefully.

"We need a singer," continued Dena. "We have chosen *you*."

"We heard you from the air," Idenion elaborated hastily. "We think your voice is very beautiful."

"You'd better come inside and explain this from the beginning," Laura said, more severely than she intended. These gentle, vulnerable people - she couldn't quite bring herself to think "aliens" - were here because of *her!* Her voice had lured them,

43

though she couldn't imagine why. Clearly, her first instinct had been right: she had a duty to protect them, whatever that might entail. For the moment all she could do was get the two of them out of sight.

She took them into the study with its single window overlooking the conservatory. Dena sat down incuriously, but Idenion began to make a thorough exploration of the room. His eyes lit up when he saw Nathaniel's books.

"The language of Hellas!" he cried, seizing a copy of Aristophanes from the shelf and waving it triumphantly. "Laura, I can *read* this!"

"Idenion," Dena said warningly.

Reluctantly he put the book aside.

"You mentioned your spacecraft," Laura said tentatively. "Where is it? Are there more of you?"

"No, just us." Idenion beamed proudly. "Our sphere is safely in high orbit, away from prying eyes and jets. When we are ready I can summon it with this." He held up what appeared to be a small white tile.

"May I see that?" asked Laura, and he unhesitatingly handed it over.

"It's blank," Laura said after a moment. Idenion reached out and applied a firm pressure to the edges of the tile. Before Laura's startled eyes, a split appeared in the centre. Then the surface rolled - no, *flowed* - back to the corners, revealing a tiny colour coded panel.

"It looks alive!" said Laura apprehensively. "Here, take it."

Idenion let the surface trickle shut and pocketed

the device nonchalantly. His attention strayed back to the bookcase.

"What's your planet called?" asked Laura hurriedly, interposing herself between him and the books.

"Slestr'a," Idenion replied.

"Celestra," said Laura, mishearing him. "What a lovely name."

"No, it's Slestr'a," Idenion corrected her. "At least, it *was*; I like your version better. Slestr'a just means 'homeworld'. In combining our two languages, the meaning changes from 'homeworld' to 'beautiful world in the sky'."

"Idenion!" cried Dena, exasperated.

"Oh, I'm sorry," Idenion said, smiling disarmingly at Laura. "Dena thinks I'm wasting time. But language is a marvellous thing, isn't it?"

"I suppose so," said Laura feebly. She found his smile almost as overwhelming as his thought-transference.

"I shall certainly rename my world," Idenion continued airily. "From the moment I return, it shall be known as Celestra."

"Just like that?" queried Laura.

"I am First Poet," Idenion stated as if that clarified everything. "I can make this change. And now, I'd better explain our mission before Dena loses her temper with me." Despite his flippant remark his expression had suddenly grown very serious. Expectantly, Laura sat down at Nathaniel's desk, rested her chin in her hands and listened.

"Many years ago," Idenion began in his light, pleasant voice, "my people found they were losing the ability to sing. The precise reason was never discovered; our vocal chords had been compromised, perhaps, due to our reliance on telepathy. With each succeeding generation the problem grew worse, and by the time Dena and I were born, there were only three singers left. Now there are none."

"Oh, how awful!" Laura exclaimed. To be prevented from singing, as she was likely to be, seemed bad enough; but to be physically unable to utter a note ...

"Making music is very important to us," Idenion continued. "The best musicians enter a guild, the scolia, and devote their lives to the furtherance of harmony. Dena works with the Lyricon scolia, the most accomplished in the world."

Dena took up the story. "Our last singer, Tristell, died only a few days ago. Since then, the scolia has been unable to play. You could remedy that."

"One concert," Idenion said eagerly. "To revitalise the scolia and save our lovely theatre, the Lyricon."

Laura blinked several times, but could think of nothing to say. Idenion went on to describe their space voyage, their near-calamity with the dust cloud, and their amazement when they realised how the "Hellas planet" had evolved. Throughout the narrative, Laura became more and more tense.

"You're angry," Idenion said at last, mildly concerned. "Please tell me why."

"Don't you know?" Laura asked, with a return

to her initial embarrassment.

"When you're not actually speaking, your thoughts are undisciplined," Idenion returned with brutal honesty.

Laura, instantly defensive, found the courage to shout. "Why are you being so thick? Don't you know what kind of a world this is?"

"Yes, I suppose I do."

"Then why didn't you turn around and go home when you didn't find Ancient Greece? Why did you risk getting mixed up with an - an - "

"Emergent."

"An emergent species. When I think of some of the places you could have landed...! You could've been shot at, arrested, interrogated, maybe even tortured. And your ship could have been shot down, or impounded and taken to bits. *You* could have been taken to bits."

Dena began to cry bitterly.

Idenion looked stunned by what he'd heard, but recovered enough to ask: "Laura, will you come with us? We can't possibly make another search after what you've just said."

"But you *will*, if I say no," Laura accused.

Idenion was silent.

Dena's sobs grew louder, and after some hesitation Laura went forward and put an arm round the girl's delicate shoulders. "Dena, don't be frightened. You're safe enough here."

Just then, the back door crashed open and a stentorian voice yelled: "We won the Cup! WE WON THE CUP!"

Dena bounded off her chair and tried to hide

47

under the desk. Laura pulled her out.

"In the study, Aunt Margaret," she called.

Mrs. Moffat hastened in. "Oh, there you are! Sorry, I didn't realise you had visitors."

"I am Idenion and this is my sister Dena," Idenion said, gliding forward with one of his devastating smiles.

Goodness! the woman thought. I always reckoned I could look anyone in the eye, but not this young man. "Nice to meet you, Denny, Tina," she managed to say. "Er - didn't you see any of the match, Laura?"

"Afraid not. We've been talking."

"Haven't you offered your friends tea?" Mrs. Moffat asked, looking quizzically past her at Dena, who was dabbing her eyes with her sleeve.

"They didn't want any," Laura said hastily. "That is, they don't have time. They've got a show organised but their principal singer's been taken ill. Someone told them about me and they, um, came to audition me at short notice."

"Laura has a lovely voice," Idenion said warmly.

"That she does," said Mrs Moffat, approaching Dena and patting her kindly on the arm. "Now don't be upset, poppet. I'm sure Laura will do all she can to help out."

Laura came to a swift decision. "Yes, I will," she announced.

A look of pure joy transformed Dena's face, and Mrs Moffat smiled benignly back at her. "There, what did I tell you?"

Idenion, noticed only by Laura, slumped

48

momentarily against the desk - whether from relief or tiredness, she couldn't tell. But in a couple of seconds he had recovered and was addressing her in business-like tones. "Now that you've decided, we should leave at once. Come as you are - we'll provide everything you need."

"I think you ought to wait for Nathaniel," said Mrs Moffat doubtfully.

"Oh, *no,* Aunt M!" Laura protested. "He'd stop me - you know he would."

"Please let her go," Idenion added.

Under his intense gaze, Mrs Moffat's objections fled. "Oh, well, where's the harm in it?" she heard herself say. "Off with you then - but mind you look after her!"

"I promise," Idenion said gravely.

Laura hesitated just once. "Will you stay here, Aunt M, and explain to Uncle Nat?"

"Leave him to me," Mrs Moffat declared. It was only after the three young people had disappeared down the lane that she realised she'd no idea where Laura was going, nor for how long. She went outside, but there was no sign of them; no sign of any car, either. She did, however, meet the ubiquitous Tracey Wyatt.

"Where was Laura off to, Mrs M? Who was that boy?"

Mrs Moffat sighed. "I wish I knew, Tracey. I wish I knew."

***

It didn't take Laura long to realise that she was

leading the way, and that Idenion and Dena were following obediently. She halted; so did they. "I don't know where I'm supposed to be going," she announced.

"I have to call the sphere down," Idenion reminded her. "I can't land where I did before."

"And where was that?"

Idenion pointed back along the lane, and Laura raised her eyebrows. "It's a miracle you weren't seen," she said, then gave a shamefaced grin. Miracles had nothing to do with it. The World Cup did. "How did you avoid hitting the trees?" she added.

"Our spacecraft is quite small," said Idenion, neatly evading the question.

"In that case I know just where to land it," Laura stated. "It's called Wickens Clump. This way." She began to walk briskly.

"Someone is watching us," Idenion said as he hastened after her.

Laura glanced round, saw Tracey in the distance, and grimly strode on. "Hurry!" she called, turning off the lane into a thicket. A barely perceptible track led deeper into the wood; she traversed it with the ease of long familiarity. Cracking twigs and rustling leaves told her the others were close behind, but after a minute or two the sounds ceased abruptly.

"Wait!" cried Dena, her voice high and childlike in the green gloom.

Laura retraced her steps. Idenion was leaning on his sister for support, his right arm crooked against his side. He looked up apologetically, but

50

seemed too winded to speak.

"He has a stitch," Dena said. "The gravity is strong here. It tires us."

"Oh," said Laura guiltily, remembering how exhausted he'd seemed back at the house. "Idenion, you should have explained."

"There was too much else to explain," he said with a wan smile. "I'll be better in a moment. But do slow down!"

"We're nearly there," Laura said encouragingly. She set off again at a more leisurely pace, looking round frequently to make sure they were keeping up. She wondered why Dena wasn't having any problems with the environment.

"She's a dancer," Idenion said laconically. "She's in better shape than I am."

Soon, bright patches of sunlight began to dapple the path ahead. Laura held a large branch to one side and motioned her companions through.

Idenion, stepping past her, uttered a small cry of pleasure. Before him the track widened into a shallow bowl, completely surrounded by dense greenery but with nothing underfoot save last year's fallen leaves. Ancient trees framed a section of sky.

"Will this do?" asked Laura.

"Just about," Idenion replied, peering upwards.

"Jimmy loved this place," Laura added. "We'd sit and talk for hours. He called it the Cradle of the World."

"Then he was a poet too," Idenion declared. The accolade pleased Laura, and she realised - with a pang of wonderment - that she'd expected Idenion to know who Jimmy was, and hadn't minded.

The control unit reappeared in Idenion's hand and Dena promptly retreated into the wood. Laura thought she'd better follow her example, and thus she never saw the spacecraft's descent. There was a swishing sound, a thud that jarred her ankles, and an indignant fluttering as several dozen startled birds took to the air. Idenion was standing where she'd left him, smothered in leaf mould and looking so chagrined that she felt an urge to giggle. Trying to spare his feelings, and well aware that she couldn't, she turned to study the object nestling in the glade.

Idenion had called it a sphere, but hemisphere would have been more accurate. It was white and featureless, surprisingly small - about eight yards in diameter as far as she could judge - and looked about as substantial as an eggshell. Idenion, trying not to sneeze, slid down the gentle slope and tapped lightly on the hull. Laura wasn't surprised to see a rift appear in the hitherto seamless alloy.

"Why didn't he burn his hand?" she asked Dena. "Aren't spacecraft supposed to heat up on re-entry?"

"Ours don't. They're made of theridolyte, the most harmonious of substances."

A section of the hull had folded downwards to form a walkway. Idenion disappeared inside, Dena close on his heels. Laura followed hesitantly. The aperture melted eerily shut behind her and she stood staring at the curved wall, biting her lip. This was getting much too weird. The enormity of what she was about to do had finally caught up with her.

"Laura." Idenion was beside her, his hand clasping hers reassuringly. "This is a daunting moment for you. If you need longer to prepare, I could open the hatch again."

Hatch, not airlock, Laura thought. I suppose there's no need for one, the way that stuff seals itself up. "No, don't open it," she said resolutely. "If you did I might bolt. And I mustn't. We both know why." Then, with a determined smile: "You chose me and now you're stuck with me."

Idenion gave her an approving look, then turned and led the way across the pink-lit cabin. "I have to plot a course round that dust cloud I told you about," he announced, seating himself in a large comfortable chair and activating the controls in front of him. A small screen flickered on, displaying a shifting stream of alien symbols.

"Is that your computer?" asked Laura, peering over his shoulder.

"Yes," said Idenion absently, intent on his task.

"Can it talk?"

"Talk?" Idenion looked bewildered. "Why should it?"

"Come, Laura." Dena uncurled herself from a second chair near Idenion's. "Let him complete his work. I will show you round our vessel."

Laura followed her to the cabin's perimeter.

"We carry provisions," Dena announced, unsealing a panel which opened downward to form a shelf. Inside, covered beakers stood in a rack. Cold air wafted from the compartment. "We didn't bring any food on this journey, but there is water, wine or liman."

"Or - what?"

"Liman," repeated Dena, opening a beaker and

handing it to Laura. It looked like coconut milk, but its taste hinted at vanilla. Laura, after a few cautious sips, drank it all. She'd been very thirsty. Dena took a cup to Idenion, then resumed the tour. There were several more compartments set into the white walls: the doors, to Laura's relief, all had visible edges. She was no longer sure exactly where the hatch was.

Next, Dena opened some of the lower wall panels and unfolded a sizeable bunk. "For long voyages," she explained. "There is extra seating also."

"Somebody likes pink," commented Laura. The chairs in the control area, and the fabric of the bunk, were a vivid cerise.

"Trevans have no sense of the aesthetic," Idenion remarked over his shoulder.

"Treva is the town where spheres are built," Dena explained. "We will not be going there, but to our capital."

The next compartment contained four space-suits, or as Idenion called them, bioshells.

"You're not concentrating!" Dena rebuked him when he'd interrupted for a second time.

"I've finished!" he retorted, and disappeared into the next cubicle along. A moment later, his grubby clothes flew out of the door and landed at Dena's feet. She ignored them and continued to explain, laboriously, that the bioshells were not used much as inhospitable worlds were seldom visited. "And besides," she concluded, "who would want to wear such an ugly garment?"

"What if the sphere needs repair while you're in

space?" asked Laura.

"That is done from the inside," she said, her gaze straying rather unhappily to the centre of the floor.

Laura had already noticed that the floor was tiled. The central tiles each carried an angular yellow symbol, plainly a warning of some kind.

"The Drive," Dena said in a low voice. "If you want to ask about that, or other aspects of our journey, you'll have to wait until Idenion finishes his shower. And, yes, the hygiene unit is in the shower cubicle. I will show it you later."

"Thank you," Laura said, pleased to have her thoughts answered so tactfully. "Dena, shouldn't we be on our way? Anyone could come through the wood and see us."

"But we *are* on our way!" Dena said, surprised. "Idenion took us past the dust cloud, and the rest is automatic."

Laura swallowed hard. "So much for second thoughts," she said, doing her best to grin. It was a logical enough mistake – there was no sense of motion and apparently no way to see out.

"We do have a viewscreen." Dena pointed to a blank panel above the instrumentation. "Idenion left it turned off because he didn't want to alarm you. Or me," she added ruefully.

"Then - could you turn it on for me now, please?"

"I think so." Dena went forward and touched a key. The large, elevated screen lit dramatically.

"It's beautiful," Laura breathed. "So many stars.... Dena, what's the matter?"

"It frightens me," she whispered, hanging her head.

"Don't let Dena spoil it for you," said Idenion from across the cabin. Laura turned to speak, but instead gave a startled cry and put a hand over her mouth. Idenion was wearing nothing but a broad smile. He was so completely unselfconscious that Laura managed not to turn away, although the colour of her face must have matched the chairs.

Idenion's smile faded. "Forgive me," he said, grabbing a clean set of clothes from somewhere amid the bioshells and setting them swinging madly. He dressed in haste, retrieved his sandals from under the pilot's chair and sat down to fasten them.

"It's all right. Really," Laura said tentatively.

"No, it isn't," Idenion contradicted. "I've embarrassed you. I'll try to be more perceptive in future."

"Surely," Laura ventured, "it's up to me to fit in with *your* way of life?"

"You are our guest," Idenion said solemnly. "Your customs will be observed."

"Whenever possible," Dena put in. "Sometimes people forget themselves during sciesha."

Laura looked mystified.

"Sciesha does not translate," Idenion added. "So let's ignore it for now. When I came out of the shower, you were about to ask me how long we'd be in space. If you give me your watch, I'll try and make the conversion to your units of time."

Shortly thereafter, Laura discovered that an astal was approximately six minutes, and an ild

56

about fifty minutes. The journey to the newly-named Celestra would take two and a half hours.

"It is not good for anyone," Dena pronounced, "to carry the time on their arm. Seek your own tempo, Laura."

"The time-piece may be damaged by transposal," Idenion commented.

"What's transposal?" inquired Laura.

"Our home is light years away," Idenion said matter-of-factly. "At our present speed it would take several lifetimes to complete the journey. So, we transpose."

"Several lifetimes?" echoed Laura. "Are you teasing me?"

"Of course not," said Idenion with a hint of impatience. "Where do you think we're going - Saturn?"

Laura looked blank.

"You read a book about Saturn today," Idenion reminded her. "Pirates of the Nine Moons. Actually, that's not right. I can't quite remember what our charts said, but it has at least sixty moons."

"If you say so," said Laura dubiously. "Well, how far *is* it to your planet?"

"I'd like to study that book sometime," Idenion reflected. "Such beautiful words - effulgent, diurnal, sidereal - "

"Idenion," prompted Dena, "answer Laura's question."

"I was about to," he said airily, turning back to the console. "Using Earth's year, since ours is far longer, it's ... three hundred and fifty-four light years."

"Surely not!" protested Laura. "I really don't think that's right, Idenion."

"It *is*," he insisted. "Why the disbelief? You've accepted everything else!"

Laura spread out her hands helplessly. "But the sphere's so little!"

"It has to be. Large objects can't sustain transposal."

Laura gave up. "Okay, okay. You know best. But – what happens during this process? Shouldn't everyone be sitting down?"

"The viewscreen deactivates," Idenion said, "and everything goes quiet. Otherwise, nothing changes - at least, not in here."

Dena gave a delicate shudder. "No-one ever sees what's outside," she explained. "It's a safety measure."

"We'll spend about six astallen in transposal," Idenion added. "After that we have to decelerate, which takes twice as long. All very tedious, once you've grown used to looking at stars."

"What do you use for fuel?" Laura asked, still preoccupied with the smallness of the craft and the vast distance it had to travel.

"Particles," Idenion said vaguely. "The Drive absorbs them. I'm not sure how."

"Well you ought to be," Laura declared. "Suppose something went wrong with it?"

"I often suppose that," Dena said dolefully.

"Nobody understands the Drive except a few scientists," Idenion said defensively. "It's ancient technology - it was old before Hellas. This particular sphere is probably a hundred years old."

58

Just then, the viewscreen blinked off. The panel lights changed their pattern once. Laura, putting a hand to the floor, thought she could feel a slight warmth. But there was no vibration, and no sound except the faintest hint of something like laughter. This suggestion of sound did not emanate from the floor, nor from any other visible point. It just *was*.

Into this strange silence, Dena said, "Sing to me, Laura."

She stared. "What, now?"

"I need to know if the scolia can read you. If I can sense the correct harmonies as you sing, they can do likewise, and you will have a fine accompaniment."

And so, bravely setting aside her doubt and incomprehension, Laura sang.

***

"A word with you, technician."

The voice was soft, well-modulated, even gentle, but Jarras leapt up as if he'd been scalded. If there had been anywhere to run to, he would probably have done so; but from the top floor of the Communications tower there was only one exit, and it was currently being obstructed. So he stood his ground, and spoke as calmly as he could.

"What brings you here, Alendis?"

"I seek an explanation," the other replied after a measured silence. "I gave orders that a sphere should be kept in readiness for me at all times. Yet the field is empty and so is the bay. Enlighten me, if you please."

"I can show you the orbital flights in progress," ventured Jarras, "just as soon as I've re-aligned the scanner. And if you'd care to examine today's schedule - "

Alendis strode forward impatiently and swept the document from his hand. "Don't dissemble, young man. Someone arrived at this facility, probably at short notice, and took my spacecraft. I see you've been scanning deep space. Perhaps you're awaiting the return of that someone?"

Jarras said nothing. His head began to throb with the effort of shielding his thoughts. And, dazzled by Alendis' charismatic presence, he had to fight an impulse to blurt out his disloyalty and beg forgiveness.

"I'm sure you're aware," Alendis continued, "that I don't tolerate insubordination?"

"Jarras is not to blame," said a voice from the direction of the elevator.

"Halon!" exclaimed Jarras thankfully.

"Idenion wanted the sphere and I allowed him to take it," Halon said deferentially. "Since he has your favour, I assumed you'd sanctioned his request."

Alendis sighed. "The boy grows presumptuous. Very well, Controller Halon, I'll overlook this matter for now. Have Idenion report to me when he returns." He paused, his keen and supercilious gaze returning to Jarras. "You must be Tralvar's trainee."

"Yes, First Citizen."

"I've heard good things about you. But why are you not at Treva, preparing new spheres?"

"I'm not qualified to work unsupervised," Jarras

said hesitantly. "So while Tralvar was - sick..."

"Drunk," Alendis corrected him.

"During that time, I was deputised as a monitor."

"I see. Industry comes to a halt whenever my chief scientist takes to his cups." Alendis abruptly turned on his heel and stalked out. The two technicians exchanged relieved but bewildered glances.

"Now he'll go after Tralvar," Jarras said unhappily.

"So? They're as bad as one another," Halon muttered.

"And Idenion will suffer too," Jarras went on. "I know you were only trying to help me, but - "

"Idenion said that at the slightest sign of trouble, we were to name him," Halon stated firmly. "I only hope his good standing with Alendis is enough to see him through this."

"Do you really think he'll bring back a singer?" Jarras asked wonderingly.

"He was determined enough this morning," Halon said. He touched a sensor on the wall and the opaqueness of the windows began to dissolve, letting in the late afternoon sunlight. "If he wants to put on a concert tonight he'll have to hurry up!"

Jarras gazed down toward the base of the tower. The diminutive but imposing figure of Alendis was walking toward an equally diminutive aircar. "I nearly betrayed our friends," the youth said sadly.

"He has that effect on me too. But we have to resist him, Jarras. Never lose sight of that."

"I shall keep reminding myself of his cruelty,"

Jarras vowed. "The other day, Tralvar showed me some rooms in the akron basement. The doors have restraints on them to stop people getting out."

"If you hadn't been based in Treva you'd have known about the detention suite long ago," said Halon. "Alendis is very proud of it."

"Someone should try and stop him," murmured Jarras.

"If we tried, we'd end up like Relto," Halon countered. "Your precious Tralvar might do better, if he weren't so busy helping him."

"But he doesn't - " began Jarras.

"He's in charge of the detainees," Halon said heatedly. "And he designed those locking mechanisms. That's help enough."

Jarras was nonplussed. Tralvar had been unfailingly kind to him, so it was hard for him to share Halon's dislike; yet he had to admit that his mentor often made him nervous. Just then a new voice, bright and impatient, dispelled the unhappy silence.

"Hey! Control tower! Is everyone asleep?"

Halon was at the transposer in an instant. "Idenion! I thought I told you to use the callsign first?"

"I've been sending the callsign for at least an astal. Don't you ever look at the screen?"

"Alendis was here," Halon said brusquely.

"Discords, I hope you didn't tell him anything!" Idenion's confident tones faltered.

"Only that you'd taken the reserve sphere. He didn't seem too worried."

"He's going to be," said Idenion grimly.

"You mean you're bringing someone?" exclaimed Halon. "In harmony's name, what do we do *now*?"

"You're the Controller," Idenion reminded him.

Halon paced distractedly in a circle, aware that Jarras was staring at him in expectation. "All right," he said at last. "We have to maintain secrecy as long as we can. Therefore, make this your only communication. You'll soon be too close to use the transposal mode, and the other frequencies will almost certainly be monitored from the akron."

"I know that," Idenion said indignantly.

"Secondly," continued Halon, "your... er.... guest must not be seen at the spaceport if we can help it. Can you take the sphere directly into the maintenance bay?"

"I'd rather not."

"Discords, Idenion! Can't you land a spacecraft yet?"

"Not that well," said Idenion cheerfully.

Halon sighed. "In that case I'll have a flitter standing by, and you'll have to effect a swift transfer."

"Could someone notify Floren?" Idenion asked. "Go and see her, I mean?"

"I'll send Jarras," said Halon, still sounding far from happy. "I can't believe you're actually doing this." Then, as curiosity overcame trepidation: "What's the singer like?"

"She's called Laura," Idenion said proudly, "and she's very nice."

***

"Now we're no longer in transposal," Idenion said, "I must speak with my friend at the spaceport and let him know I've been successful."

Laura didn't answer; an alarming thought had suddenly crossed her mind. Idenion resisted the urge to pre-empt her and waited till she'd vocalised her misgivings.

"If we've been travelling faster than light," she ventured at last, "will years have gone by when I get home?"

"Absolutely not!" Idenion declared. Then, when she still looked doubtful, added: "I'm no scientist, but I do know that transposal isn't any kind of a speed: it's more like an altered state. I promise you, this round trip's only taken half a Celestrian day." He jabbed impatiently at a panel near his head. "My signal's being received, but they're not answering. Can there really be no-one on duty?"

"Isn't there a time-lag?" asked Laura hesitantly, afraid this question would sound as silly as her last.

"Not on this equipment," Idenion replied. "The signal's transposed by us and retrieved by the ground station. If anyone's listening, that is!"

"Maybe you should have tried them sooner," Laura remarked.

"We can't call anyone while we're in transposal ourselves," Idenion explained. "Nothing gets through."

"Another of your safety devices?"

"No, something to do with physics. It's just the way things are." He smote the panel again.

"Laura." Dena was at her side, looking

64

concerned. "You should rest your voice. You've sung three songs and talked ever since!"

"I'm nervous," Laura admitted.

"We all are," said Dena.

Laura capitulated and sat down, leaving Idenion to fidget with the communication controls. She'd temporarily run out of questions, anyway.

"Would you like some of our wine?" Dena continued. "I can water it down for you. Tristell used to say it soothed her throat."

"Did you know Tristell?"

"Everyone knew Tristell."

"Could she sing better than me?"

"Tristell was a fine performer, dedicated to her work," Dena said. "But she could not sing as well as you."

Laura, only half reassured, agreed to try the wine.

Idenion was trying to make voice contact with the spaceport. Laura sat quietly, sipping the sweet purple drink and listening to the sibilant phrases he uttered.

It soon became clear that something was amiss. Dena gave a frightened gasp and nearly dropped the cup she was holding. Idenion seemed more displeased than dismayed, and launched into a rapid conversation with his distant colleague. Laura heard her name mentioned once; then, the transmission completed, Idenion swung his chair away from the panel and sat staring into the middle distance.

"What's wrong?" Laura ventured at last, and to her surprise a vestige of guilt crossed his face.

"Laura," he began apologetically, "there's

something we haven't told you. Do you remember me saying we had to save the Lyricon?"

"Yes, I remember. I thought it was going to be pulled down."

"And I let you go on thinking that," Idenion said unhappily. "The real problem is Alendis, our First Citizen."

"The ruler of your country?"

"There are no separate countries on my world. Alendis rules it all," Idenion said. "And he wants to make the Lyricon his home - to pollute it with his hatred of music."

In sorrowful tones he continued his vivid word-portrait of the First Citizen. Alendis: eloquent, persuasive, revealing his thoughts but rarely. He'd dazzled his impressionable listeners with clever rhetoric, had sailed swiftly and effortlessly through the administrative ranks until he'd attained the position he sought. Once in charge he'd voiced his dream of conquering other worlds, and issued strange new edicts concerning the advancement of science and the winding down of the arts. And when his wishes were ignored, had begun to exile or imprison his subjects. He'd promised that the Lyricon could remain in public hands as long as there was a singer to occupy it - and then Tristell had died.

Laura listened with resignation. How right she'd been in thinking these people were too vulnerable to wander the Earth, and how typical that they should allow a dictator to take control of them.

"That's an oversimplification, Laura," Idenion said. "I know there were unscrupulous leaders in

Hellas, and I see from your thoughts that there have been many since. But Alendis is the very first of our kind to act in this way, so we had no forewarning."

"Can he force these changes?" Laura asked.

"I don't see how. We're not an acquisitive society - we've never had wars, we don't even have weapons. We could never become what he wants us to be."

"Well, then," said Laura dismissively, "kick him out and elect another ruler who's more sympathetic."

"We can't do that," said Dena.

"Why not?"

"We'd fail." Idenion spoke with such finality that Laura knew she'd risk angering him if she pressed the point.

"Why didn't you tell me about Alendis?" she asked. "Were you afraid I'd be put off?"

"No. You'd already decided we needed protecting." Idenion managed a wry smile. "I kept you in ignorance for a similar reason. When Alendis looks into your mind - and he surely will - he'll see that you were unaware of his existence and innocent of all conspiracy. I originated this plan, and I've already confessed it in a formal document."

"All for the sake of your theatre?"

"While there are singers, the Lyricon is ours," Idenion declared.

"Alendis did not say the singers had to be Slestr'an," Dena put in.

"Celestrian!" Idenion corrected her sternly. She gave him an apologetic look.

Laura continued to frown. "Aren't you being a

67

shade too literal? If you get on the wrong side of him – "

"My brother will come to no harm," Dena interrupted. "Alendis respects him."

"He respects no-one," Idenion contradicted. "But he indulges me, as I've written many poems in praise of his character."

Laura stared. "But I thought you hated him!"

"Not at first," Idenion said, and was about to elaborate when he was interrupted by an imperious chime from the control system. The cabin lights deepened briefly to crimson, then returned to normal.

"The programme's ending," Idenion explained. "I have to take over now." Unhurriedly, he settled himself in front of the panel. Dena scurried to the other chair, planted herself in it firmly and gripped the armrests. Laura perched uneasily on the pink bunk, wondering if she should follow Dena's example and hold onto something.

"That won't be necessary," Idenion pronounced. "Both my Earth landings were poor, but I wasn't used to the conditions. The gravity's weaker on Celestra - and on Myrma, the only other world I've visited."

"Is this Myrma hundreds of light years away too?"

"No, only about seventeen. It's a jungle planet with many beautiful flowers."

"Are there people?"

"Indeed there are. They're friendly, but primitive - we trade with them a little."

"Can't *they* sing?"

"Not in any disciplined sense. They don't even have a proper language, so it's difficult to communicate with them. Although - " and he gave an impish grin - "it can be fun trying."

Laura looked puzzled for a moment, then said "Oh!" rather self-consciously. At the same time, Idenion fell into an aggrieved silence and began to examine the controls with great interest. Dena's face was a study in disapproval.

She's told him off, Laura thought. Poor Idenion! He's certainly a free spirit, as Jimmy would have said. But is that so bad? They really mustn't try to hide these things from me.

Once she stopped being amused, however, she felt a pang of inadequacy. How often did they use telepathy? How many times *hadn't* she noticed? Then Idenion smiled warmly at her, and the uneasy moment passed. She had a talent they envied, and that gave her a measure of equality. Didn't it?

From the viewscreen came an intense burst of sunlight, rapidly extinguished as Idenion made a course correction. When Laura had banished the afterimages, a planet had appeared in place of the nameless stars. It was already so close that only an anonymous portion of the globe could be seen. A fleeting puff of whiteness denoted the cloud layer. A mountain range hove into view, all jagged peaks and snowcaps; then it too was gone, replaced by an expanse of ocean. And the sphere was falling swiftly, very swiftly, toward it. Expecting the worst, Laura closed her eyes tightly - and opened them again just as Idenion made the lightest of touchdowns on what appeared to be a lawn.

"Is that it?" she asked incredulously.

"We're here," Idenion confirmed cheerfully. "You don't seem convinced."

"It's just that...." Laura paused, trying to articulate her doubts. "I don't feel I've travelled anywhere. I've seen stars on a screen, a landscape on a screen – half of me believes we're still sitting in Wickens Clump. You could at least have given us a bumpy landing!"

Dena was already at the hatch. It flowed open, admitting clean fresh air and the pearly gleam of natural daylight. Laura stood up, and nearly overbalanced. She'd acquired a strange buoyancy, as if she'd stepped onto a trampoline.

"What's wrong with me?"

"Careful," Idenion warned. "Remember what I said about the gravity. You'll feel lighter."

Hell's teeth, Laura's thoughts said. It's real, all of it. I'm on another world.

"You certainly are."

"The gravity wasn't – different – in here," she said plaintively.

"I simulated Earth's. I didn't want you feeling sick."

"Oh."

"You'll adjust very soon," Idenion promised. "Would it surprise you to know you've been breathing our air? Dena insisted on it. She was worried it might affect your singing."

"So that was why my breath control was all over the place," Laura remarked. "Don't pretend you didn't notice!"

"I'm not an expert," Idenion said gravely.

"Come on!" Dena called from the ramp. "Halon's on his way."

"We'll be taken by flitter to the city centre," Idenion explained.

"Flitter?"

"That's how it translates. A small aircraft." Idenion was suddenly all eagerness. "Oh, I almost forgot – welcome to Celestra! We have to hurry now. Can you manage a few steps?"

He offered his arm, Laura took it, and together they walked out of the spacecraft.

Chapter Three

Laura's first glimpse of Celestra was disappointing. A square windowless building faced her across the strip of grass she'd seen earlier. The grass itself (broadbladed and slightly the wrong green) was unkempt. The top of a tower loomed in the distance, seeming to tilt. Before she could ask where they'd landed, the aforementioned flitter arrived: an oval six-legged craft, settling to the ground with a gentle whirr. It looked reassuringly slow. The hinged canopy swung open, and the pilot – fair and unsmiling - motioned them forward. He gave Laura a vague nod, but didn't speak.

"This is Halon," Idenion said. "He's shy."

There were two pairs of seats in the flitter, and a large storage space in the back. Laura, still unsure of her footing, scrambled past Halon and took the seat behind him. Dena came to sit next to her. Idenion, in front, began giving Halon directions, and in no time an argument had sprung up.

"Halon wants to take you straight to the Lyricon," Dena explained, "but Idenion must go to the archive first."

"Why?"

"To register the planet's new name," Dena said placidly.

"A new name, a new era!" Idenion proclaimed.

Halon, abandoning the dispute, took off with a lurch. They flew over the windowless building, and Laura immediately saw where Idenion *should* have landed - an immaculate green field with a carefully defined perimeter of white posts. The tall tower was adjacent to it. The field was completely empty - there were no spheres to be seen, nor any other flitter craft. Laura would have asked why, but there were too many other distractions. The sky, streaked with green and gold in the region of the setting sun; the sun itself, a diminutive orb of white fire; the horizon, no longer dominated by the spaceport buildings, looming disconcertingly close.

"Our planet is smaller than the Earth," Idenion said, anticipating her question. "Our sun's name is Alda, and our capital city is Alda Mexa. This literally means city of the sun, but it can also mean a place of enlightenment. Look, Laura! It lies before us."

Laura craned over his shoulder, wondering how she could have failed to notice a capital city. A moment later, she knew why. Alda Mexa was not the gleaming metropolis she'd envisaged, but a pleasant, white-walled town which at first glance wouldn't have seemed out of place in Italy or Greece. Its houses rose in level terraces around a central hill.

"Why, it's only - " she began, but the words caught in her throat. Her gaze had reached the summit of the hill, and there, through a sunset haze, she glimpsed the lines of a magnificent, breathtakingly familiar building.

"Is - *that* - the Lyricon?"

"Yes, Laura," Idenion said with quiet pride.

"But it's just like the Parthenon!"

"Not exactly, as you'll see," Idenion replied. "But now you'll realise why Dena was so interested in your pendant."

Laura subsided into her seat, grasping the gold medallion as if it were a talisman. Silently she wondered what type of theatre the colonnades hid - and more importantly, what size.

The flitter banked, following the terraces, or laterals as Idenion insisted on calling them. "The archive is on Lateral Three," he informed her. "We number the laterals in descending order."

"The Lyricon being on Lateral One, I suppose?"

"The Lyricon *is* Lateral One," Idenion said with a laugh. "I've asked Halon to make an aerial tour on the way there."

"Shouldn't we just get this over with?" Laura ventured.

"I want to show you my home," Idenion said obstinately. Dena, who knew that tone well, gave him a beseeching look which he ignored. "It's what you'd like," he added.

Laura couldn't deny it, despite Halon's taut silence and a tiny sigh from Dena. Trying not to let their anxiety intrude, she fixed her attention on the streets below.

Any resemblance to a Mediterranean town was purely superficial, evoked by the stone walls and red tiled roofs. These buildings were tall and narrow, and the odd placement of the windows made it difficult to tell how many storeys they had. Rows of spindly trees cast a degree of shade.

The laterals curved round the hill in lazy circles, connected by steep paths and flights of steps. Along one lateral the houses had multi-coloured roofs, which from a height resembled a bright snake coiled around the hillside. Laura wondered who would appreciate the display, since no other flitters were in the air. She did, however, see several of the craft lined up in paved parking areas. There was no ground traffic and little sign of industry, although from time to time she noticed single-storeyed buildings that could have been small factories. There were no shops, or none she could identify. Further on, the clearly defined laterals almost disappeared in a maze of balconies and bridges.

"This is the student quarter," said Idenion. "Every young person is encouraged to spend some time in Alda Mexa, to round off their education."

"Every young person from this region?" inquired Laura.

"No, from anywhere in the world. Of course, they don't all come here."

"It must still get very crowded," began Laura, but just then Dena leant forward and spoke to Halon in soft urgent tones. He promptly changed course and accelerated the craft toward the city centre.

"Floren is summoning the scolia," explained Idenion. "I'm not of the scolia and neither is Halon, so we can't hear the call."

Dena sat for a moment, her face rapt. "They echo the call throughout the city," she said at last. "They're joyful. They will play well today."

"*Why* can't you hear it?" Laura asked Idenion, who merely shrugged.

"It isn't our usual form of mindspeech," said Dena. "There's no meaning, no message. It's more like chords sounding in my head. From the cadences I can tell the mood of the scolia."

"We'll finish the tour another time," Idenion promised. "We need to reach the Lyricon ahead of your audience!"

"Floren should have waited till we arrived," Dena said.

"She trusts my expertise," Idenion laughed, and Dena gave him a withering look.

Halon brought the flitter to rest near an ornamental garden, presided over by a dilapidated, creeper-covered building which Laura presumed was the archive.

"Philosophers meet here to discuss - " began Idenion, but Halon released the canopy and pushed him out. Then they were on their way again, skimming the rooftops as they headed for the Lyricon.

***

Tralvar, breathless and dishevelled, stormed noisily into Alendis' private rooms at the akron. The dictator was at his writing table, and glanced up briefly as Tralvar flung open the double doors. Then he returned to his work, setting down several more phrases in his neat, elegant handwriting before turning to confront his visitor.

"Well?"

"You've been in my workshop!" Tralvar accused. "Where's the device? Where *is* it?"

Alendis' cool aloof eyes regarded him disparagingly. "Really, Tralvar, I do wish you

76

wouldn't go about looking like that. You make the place untidy."

"Never mind what I look like. You've been picking over my research while I was resting – "

"While you were drunk, Tralvar. Drunk, paralytic, catatonic. I borrowed your key and returned it to you. It's hardly my fault if you forget to secure your apartment."

"I need the device back, Alendis."

"I don't have it."

"I'm sick of your games," Tralvar said wildly. "You took the prototype - didn't you realise that? The other one is flawed."

"That's the story of your life, isn't it?"

"I need to study the original," Tralvar persisted, tight-lipped. "You had no right to take it."

"No right?" Alendis' voice became very quiet and his eyes narrowed. "Correct me if I'm in error, but I commissioned this work. Therefore, it belongs to me. Now if you were to ask calmly and reasonably, I might consider lending it back for a while."

"I will not beg," muttered Tralvar.

"Then be polite. The results could amaze you. I might even forgive this Tristell episode."

Tralvar stared. "*You'll* forgive *me*?"

"For being such a poor judge of character." Alendis stood up lazily in a swirl of silver, and paced toward him across the opulent room. "Try to be more resilient, Tralvar. Why torment yourself over a vain stupid girl?"

Tralvar looked about him as if trapped. Under the critical, faintly mocking gaze of his ruler, his anger shrank and retreated. He felt dull, apathetic, tired. Not even the slight to Tristell's memory could revive his brief fury. "Don't," he whispered involuntarily, although nothing had been done to him. He knew, only too well, what Alendis *could* do.

"That's better," said the despot conversationally. "Now, since you're here, I may as well inform you of your next task. One of the satellite relays needs repair - the one serving Alcine and the south."

"Don't send me into space," pleaded Tralvar.

"Don't worry, I shan't expect you to retrieve the satellite. In fact, I had planned to assemble a crew earlier today, but when I went to the spaceport I found that Idenion had taken my sphere. I must have words with him about these trips; he shouldn't need the stars for inspiration when he has such an attractive little wife. I found your trainee, Jarras, working at Communications. It seems he ... Tralvar, what ails you?"

Tralvar had moved aside and now stood with his head raised as if listening. His face suddenly looked less careworn. "The scolia!" he murmured. "I'm called!"

"But you're not *of* the scolia," Alendis reminded him with exaggerated patience.

"I can still hear the call. I must go to them."

"What for, may I ask?"

Tralvar gazed at him with a measure of triumph. "That's something you can never understand."

Alendis looked thoughtful. "So the wretches are

going to play, are they? Well, if you insist on being there, find out what's changed their minds and report back to me personally."

"If I must," said Tralvar, and departed in haste for the Lyricon. He already knew the concert would be meaningful, not just a vain attempt to keep Alendis at bay. The scolia had purpose again - and so, for a while, did he.

***

The Lyricon stood in solitary grandeur on the crown of the hill, not isolated like the Acropolis but the focus of a multitude of paths ascending from the lower laterals. And hastening up these paths, almost keeping pace with the flitter on the last lap of its journey, came eager groups of citizens. They poured into the square which fronted the colonnade, some of them disappearing through the pillars into the Lyricon itself. Others, more perceptive, waited to see who had arrived.

"Laura." This was Halon, speaking very diffidently. "May I attend your concert?"

"Yes, of course," Laura said awkwardly.

"Thank you," said Halon, and blushed.

The Celestrians clustered round the flitter as it landed. The last rays of the sun cast gold lights over their uniformly fair hair and softened the outlines of their pale, angular limbs. Half the gathering wore pastel-coloured garments embellished with beads and rope belts. The rest weren't wearing much at all - just a type of shift, sleeveless and gossamer-thin. Many pairs of eyes watched intently as Halon helped Laura to disembark. She endured their gaze stoically, keeping her own eyes downcast and trying to avoid looking at the near-naked young men.

Several of the scantily clad people greeted Dena as she emerged. "I must speak with my friends for a moment," she said. "Don't be embarrassed, Laura! They're dancers - they've been rehearsing for the Peisistrata."

Whatever that is, thought Laura wryly.

The lithe, diaphanous figures closed around Dena as she went forward. Laura took one or two hesitant steps toward the Lyricon, and suddenly found herself confronting an older man with lank brown hair and a drab grey tunic. His gaze, quizzical at first, turned rapidly to astonishment. He glanced once at Halon and Dena. Then he retreated toward the edge of the square, turning several times to look back at Laura.

Halon, suddenly very agitated, tugged her arm to regain her attention. "The flitter's in the way here. I must remove it." And without waiting for a reply, he leapt into the craft and was gone.

Dena dismissed her entourage and returned to Laura's side. "There, that's all arranged," she said. "They'll provide entertainment while you get ready."

"Who's that man?" Laura asked, pointing. "The scruffy one."

Dena frowned into the sunset. "It's Tralvar, our First Scientist," she said resignedly. "I might have known *he'd* turn up."

"Halon was afraid of him."

"Tralvar is feared almost as much as Alendis, because he's in his employ," Dena explained.

"I thought Alendis ruled alone," said Laura, taken aback.

"No, he has two allies - Tralvar and Strephin," Dena said. "Don't let Tralvar worry you - he won't act against the scolia." She turned and began to forge her way through the spectators. Laura followed hastily, trying not to push anyone, very aware of how sturdy she was compared with these people.

Beyond the two rows of pillars was a solid wall with a huge golden door. It stood ajar, and many of the citizens were hurrying through it. Dena, however, went to a less spectacular door near the corner of the massive building. Inside, a featureless flight of stairs led upward, lit by a multitude of slits in the stonework. The glass in the tiny windows was tinted, creating a prismatic effect.

Laura wanted to know more about Tralvar, but while she was climbing the stairs, the thin air of Celestra left her no breath for talking. And by the time she reached the top, she'd decided to let the matter rest. If Dena wasn't afraid of the man, there was surely nothing to worry about.

***

Tralvar descended to Lateral Three as fast as he could, annoyed that half the population of Alda Mexa seemed to be coming in the opposite direction. He wished he'd been quick witted enough to take Halon's flitter. The alien girl's unshielded mind had told him where Idenion had gone, and once closer to the archive, he determined that the First Poet was quite alone. Just as well, he thought sourly. *It saves me having to throw everyone out. I need to talk to Idenion in private.*

The musty air of the archive made him cough a little, as it always did. Tralvar disliked the place: it reeked of stagnation and decay, of things best forgotten. The soft artificial lighting did nothing to dispel the aura of decrepitude. There was no sign of movement amid the stacks of paper and scrolls, although he did notice several treatises flung aside as if the readers had left hastily. Then Idenion emerged from a secluded corner, carrying an ostentatious-looking document.

"Ah, just the person I wanted to see," he said with his ready smile. "This has to be witnessed by someone resident in the akron. I think you qualify."

Tralvar scowled. "What is it?"

Idenion explained.

"That's just typical of you, changing the planet's name at a time like this," Tralvar declared as he scrawled his signature. "There. Now get back to the Lyricon this instant."

"Why? What's wrong?"

"What's *wrong*?" echoed Tralvar. "I was going to ask whether you enjoyed living dangerously or whether you were just plain stupid. Now I know."

"You're a fine one to talk about living dangerously," retorted Idenion. "You've walked the edge of eternity ever since you threw in your lot with Alendis."

"I'm used to it - you're not," Tralvar snapped.

Then, more quietly, "I realise why you've brought this girl here, and I have to admire your audacity. But how could you just abandon her, leave her with Dena and that clod Halon? She trusts you, harmony help her, and it's your responsibility to see that she's safe. You're the only one with any measure of influence over Alendis."

"Do you really think there's danger?"

Oh, discord take me, Tralvar thought wretchedly. How can I ever give you proof?

"Tralvar?"

"I don't know what he'll do," the scientist said at last. "But whatever it is, I won't be able to stop him. You know that."

"In that case," said Idenion quietly, "I'd like you to take something to him. Before I went to look for a singer, I wrote a declaration and lodged it here. It exonerates everyone else from blame. Now where's it gone?"

He swept a pile of papers from the chief archivist's desk and located a small scroll with a ribboned seal. Tralvar gave it a troubled stare.

"Are you sure you want him to have this? It's redolent of premeditation, of a plot. Far better to let him think that you did everything on the spur of the moment."

"That didn't help Relto, did it?" asked Idenion, and Tralvar flinched.

"Relto had spoken against him for a long time. You have no such reputation."

"If you're alluding to my odes of praise, I've disowned them. I wish I'd never written them."

"Is that what you've put in here?" Tralvar

nudged the scroll with one finger. "Then take my advice and burn it."

Idenion's mouth set in a stubborn line. "I have to shield Laura," he said. "If this is what it takes ... so be it."

Reluctantly Tralvar picked the scroll up.

"There are some flitters in the nearest park," Idenion added helpfully.

"I'll pretend there weren't. You'll need time to get the concert under way."

"Thank you, Tralvar!" Idenion was genuinely pleased. "Do try to hear some of it. Laura has a wonderful voice."

"I was afraid of that," said Tralvar.

***

Laura emerged from the stairwell and looked cautiously about her. She and Dena had reached the top of the colonnade and were standing on a narrow walkway set slightly below the pediment. To the right was a stout wall and a panoramic view of the city; to the left, another higher wall and a discreet row of casement windows.

"Do people *live* up here?" she asked incredulously.

"Yes, *I* live here," said Dena with a smile. "These apartments are reserved for the custodian and other Lyricon staff."

"Don't you get tired of climbing stairs?" inquired Laura, still breathless.

"There is an elevator to each dwelling," Dena said disinterestedly.

"What? Then why didn't we use one?"

"They can only be reached via the auditorium, and there are crowds of people in the way. This was quicker."

"Only just," Laura muttered, leaning on the wall to recover.

Below, silvery street lights flickered into life around the plaza. I suppose this is where Alendis wants to govern from, she thought. Monarch of all he surveys. Brr! It's a bit draughty though. I bet it's freezing in winter.

"In Alda Mexa, freezing doesn't happen," Dena said seriously. "This way, Laura. Floren's waiting." And, grasping Laura's hand, she hurried her along the balcony.

Laura couldn't help glancing up at the colossal stone pediment, daunted by its bulk against the sky. To her surprise, she glimpsed something incongruous perched above the heavy slab - something which, in the fading twilight, looked like a campanile with no bell. But before she could ask about it, Dena had clicked open one of the casements and motioned her through.

"Now I must leave," she said. "I have to organise the dancers. Floren will look after you."

Floren was a graceful woman in early middle age. She wore a gown of pale green and a silver circlet in her hair. Around her neck was a tiny key on a chain. "Welcome, Laura," she said. "I am Floren, custodian of the Lyricon. Enter and be at ease."

Laura took a few shy steps forward. The room was bright and airy, with panelled walls, a soft white carpet and dainty wooden furniture. The light came from a vertical column which extended from floor to ceiling. Before she could fully examine her surroundings, a young woman in a shawl hastened through a connecting arch and confronted her silently. The newcomer's gaze was openly resentful.

"Zenzie!" exclaimed Floren. Then, to Laura, "You must forgive my daughter. She worries about Idenion."

Laura noted the sudden surge of colour to the girl's pale face, and guessed that Idenion meant a lot to her.

"Of course he does!" Zenzie said indignantly. "I'm his wife."

"Oh!" said Laura, startled. "I didn't know. I mean, he never said. He brought Dena..." She stopped in confusion.

"They're twins," Zenzie stated. "So, they're in accord."

"The only living pair of twins," Floren added.

"Idenion has put this ... foolishness before our personal happiness," Zenzie continued. "He ignores the risks. I cannot support him in this." Then, at a soundless reproach from Floren, she turned sadly away.

Perturbed, Laura watched her depart. She hoped that Zenzie's apparent dislike was only due to concern for her husband. It was obvious why he'd chosen her, for she was very pretty - and not in a childlike way, as Dena was. Zenzie had the type of beauty Laura had always aspired to - high cheekbones, elegant nose, wide grey eyes. But that didn't quite explain why Idenion, the free spirit, had married so young.

"Our marriages are not like yours, I think," said Floren after a significant pause. "Come, Laura. You've not yet seen the performance area." She led the way through the long narrow apartment. Laura tried not to stare into the rooms they passed, thinking it impolite; but she did notice that each one was lit by one of the vertical tubes. As they walked, the buzz and chatter from the auditorium grew louder, until finally Laura was ushered onto a private balcony above the waiting crowd.

Her knees shook and her mouth went dry. So this was what Idenion had meant by "not exactly like the Parthenon"! The Lyricon, or all she'd hitherto seen of it, was an elaborate shell surrounding a great amphitheatre cut into the side of the hill - the side which Halon hadn't had time to show her. Two rows of colonnades, dark shapes against an indigo sky, bordered the terraces. Ahead of her, beyond the distant stage, the lights of the town twinkled.

"I can't," she said piteously. "I can't do it!"

"You think your voice will not carry," said Floren, unruffled. "Wait and listen."

The stage was lit, though not brightly. Musicians carrying stringed instruments were taking their positions on one side, and a few dancers wandered about at the back. Then Dena appeared, tiny yet unmistakable. She made some kind of announcement to the audience, and her little voice carried perfectly to where Laura stood. The dancers took up their positions and Laura could hear the scuff of their bare feet on the ground.

"That's fantastic - " she began, when bright strips of light suddenly flared in the sky overhead. A pulsing blue grid, in the shape of a dome, settled over the auditorium and stage. The crowd seemed quite unconcerned. Gradually the spaces in the grid began to fill with the same clear blue until the semblance of a summer day had been created.

"It's a weathershield," Floren explained. "At one time it could generate many colours, but blue was our favourite, and now it won't change. Sometimes it won't start at all. Now, shall we go back inside? The leading members of the scolia are coming to see you."

"What do they want?"

"More knowledge of your music, of course," Floren said.

"I don't know much theory," Laura confessed. "I just sing."

They went back into the reception room, where they found Zenzie nibbling on a small yellow fruit. Laura immediately felt hungry.

"I know it isn't a good idea to eat just before a performance," she said, "but I've had no food since - " She automatically looked at her watch and found it had stopped at 6.20. The precise moment, she recalled, that the sphere had achieved transposal. "- since lunchtime on Earth," she concluded somewhat inaccurately.

"I'll see what I can find," Zenzie said, and hastened off with more speed than was necessary.

Laura ignored the snub and carefully rewound her watch. It started obligingly enough, and after a brief cogitation she turned the hands forward two hours.

"This is important to you?" queried Floren.

"Yes, it's sort of reassuring," Laura admitted. "I suppose you don't approve - Dena didn't. She told me to follow my own tempo."

"That is good advice," Floren said gravely.

Laura was about to examine the discarded fruit when the scolia players arrived. A subdued whirring sound caught her attention, only just audible above the various noises coming from outside. Then one of the wall panels slid open, revealing the elevator Dena had mentioned. Obviously the crowd had deferred to the scolia and made way for them at ground level.

Two men and a woman emerged from the silvery cage. They carried no instruments; their garments were dark brown, unadorned by any of the usual beads and accessories, and their expressions were sober, almost reverential. The woman murmured something to Floren, who said to Laura: "I will speak for them. Please demonstrate the range in which you will work."

Laura obligingly sang two major scales.

"Is that the only mode?"

Laura sang a minor scale.

"What is the smallest interval?"

Laura sang a few semitones. Further questions followed concerning key changes, cadences and harmony. Laura quickly realised that their art, not she, was the cause of their reverence. And they expected her to be equally dedicated. In the midst of her demonstration, a wide-eyed Zenzie peeped in and was waved away by Floren. Finally the questions came to an end; the trio turned as one, re-entered the lift and were gone. Just as the panel closed, the woman smiled at Laura and said something encouraging.

"She's pleased with you," said Floren. "She says if you were telepathic you could petition to join them."

"I didn't know her harmony questions," Laura said dolefully.

"Never mind," Floren said consolingly. "You've given them enough to work with. They'll be able to guide the others."

"How many musicians will there be?"

"Eight. There are always eight."

"That's all right then," said Laura, who had envisaged a whole orchestra arriving to accompany her. "Won't any of them be able to talk to me? Do they have to remain apart in some way, like a religious order?"

Floren frowned. "I know of religion," she said. "Our spacefarers told of it - it makes whole species unhappy. We have no use for such a thing. To answer your question: the scolia has its disciplines, but does not practice seclusion. You'll find that many people can't communicate with you, because they've had no experience. Few of us have Idenion's gifts."

"But *you* do."

"Not really. Zenzie and I, and Dena to a lesser extent, have to welcome tourists from all over the world. We have only one basic language, but there are regional variants, and we like to converse with our visitors in their own dialect. Without this activity, I doubt if we'd have had the mental dexterity to speak your English."

"I appreciate - " began Laura; then, realising her words weren't being heeded, lapsed into a fidgety silence.

"Sorry about the distraction," Floren said after a moment. "I'm wanted downstairs - there's a dispute over who will sit in front. Zenzie will attend you from now on."

Zenzie had in fact just entered, carrying a small tray.

"Don't worry, Laura," Floren added. "I think you'll find her more amenable now."

Zenzie set the tray down and Laura went to inspect what was on it. "I've brought you cereal and cake," Zenzie said. "And liman, which I perceive you've tried already. You can have some of the fruits if you like. They're called pilif, and come from our orchards to the south."

Laura looked at her quizzically, wondering why her attitude had changed.

"I heard your voice," Zenzie replied simply. "I didn't know what a real singing voice was."

"Surely you heard Tristell sing?" Laura asked, puzzled.

Zenzie laughed. "Tristell couldn't sing like you! She could only pitch her voice to a few different levels. And if she did it too much, she couldn't speak for days!"

"Oh," said Laura, taken aback.

"No-one, not even our oldest citizen, has heard a voice like yours. Didn't Idenion tell you that?"

"No. Dena dropped a few hints, now that I

91

think about it, but nothing specific."

"Maybe I shouldn't have said anything," Zenzie mused. "They wanted you to sing your best."

"I'll *still* sing my best!" Laura said indignantly. "People will know what to expect. They may not have heard a living voice but they'll have heard records."

"Records," Zenzie repeated blankly.

"Yes, of your singers, before they died out."

Zenzie didn't answer. Laura turned her attention to the food, and after some initial caution began to eat rapidly. The cereal was soft, crumbly and in need of some sugar; the cake was more to her liking, especially the tiny thread of yellow syrup in the middle of each slice. Zenzie peeled one of the succulent little fruits and offered it to her.

"I'd better not," Laura said. "I might drop juice down my shirt."

"That wouldn't matter," said Zenzie airily. "You'll need to change anyway."

"Do I *have* to?"

"Yes, you do. If you go on stage wearing blue, you won't show up against the weathershield. Floren says you're to have one of Tristell's dresses. As soon as you've finished eating I'll take you to her apartment, which will be yours for tonight."

Laura looked doubtful.

"It's traditional for a First Singer to use it," Zenzie assured her, then paused and frowned. "Discords! Floren says you're to be ready in five astallen. We must hurry. Come on, it's only next door."

Walking into Tristell's apartment was like

entering a sea cave. Green and blue drapes as thin as veils were suspended from the ceiling and walls, half concealing the radiant columns which lit the unoccupied dwelling.

"Isn't it a bit wasteful leaving those on?" asked Laura.

"Not at all," Zenzie replied. "They use solar energy. The collectors on the roof discharge themselves overnight, whether the units are switched on or not." She went briskly into the sleeping area, leaving Laura to follow.

Tristell had chosen to sleep nearest the amphitheatre, beneath a picture window overlooking the stage. The weathershield cast its incongruous form of daylight into the room. Laura wandered slowly in Zenzie's wake, gazing with troubled eyes at the many personal effects strewn about. Scarves, jewellery, cosmetic pots with their lids astray - and on a delicate table beneath a mirror, a hairbrush with several golden strands trailing from it.

"Do those things bother you?" asked Zenzie, in a tone that suggested surprise. "I'll take them out later. I didn't think we'd be playing host to another First Singer!"

"You shouldn't call me that," began Laura, then stopped as she was confronted by a large erotic mural above the gold-draped bed. "Did this, um, orgy scene belong to Tristell?"

"No," said Zenzie muffledly from the depths of a vast wardrobe. "It belongs to the Lyricon. We've always sought to promote sciesha."

"Idenion said sciesha didn't translate," Laura

93

said hesitantly. "Is it something like free love?"

Zenzie ceased rummaging. "No, although free love is often the result of sciesha," she replied bafflingly. "Now will you please choose a dress - or must I decide for you?"

Tristell's dresses were amazing. A multitude of colours met Laura's eye, blue being significantly absent. The styles ranged from the simple to the ostentatious, and the lengths varied accordingly. All were of the same delicate material, which Zenzie called firi: and all had been created for a very slender person.

"Zenzie, I can't get into *any* of these," Laura pointed out.

"Let me worry about that. Just choose."

Laura sifted through the clothes, noting the faint floral perfume which rose from them. "They're all lovely. I'd prefer a long one, I think. What about shoes?"

"No shoes," Zenzie said adamantly. "Not on the Lyricon stage. They make too much noise."

Laura took out a green dress and studied it. "The neckline's too daring," she said at last, and put it back. "Can you really make these fit me?"

"I designed these gowns, and I can make them fit anyone," said Zenzie. "Tristell was always asking for changes at short notice. Now, since you can't make your mind up.... " She took a pale yellow dress from its hanger. It had short, filmy sleeves, a band of ruched material at the hem and a tracery of gold leaves on the skirt. "What about this? It was the last one I made her, and the spare material's still here."

94

"All right then," said Laura, not entirely at ease with the choice. It was a gown for someone with presence, with charisma.

Zenzie, if she sensed these thoughts, took no notice. She whisked off her belt, a long plaited rope with occasional beads, and proceeded to measure Laura with it. Then she went to an alcove in the adjoining room and wheeled out a wooden trestle. Picking up a small bale of the yellow firi, she spread it carefully over the table and, using the measure and a tiny pair of shears, began to cut. She worked in silence for a moment. Then she said:

"You were quite wrong, you know, about the recorded voices. There aren't any."

"Why not?"

"Because we don't know how to record sound."

"What? But that's crazy!" Laura exclaimed. "You can travel all over the galaxy and yet you can't record sound?"

"I'm not a scientist, so I can't give you technical reasons," Zenzie said. "But I do know about music, and how most of our pleasure comes from performing it or being at a performance. A recording, or the concept of a recording, would be scorned by the scolia. There'd be no immediacy, no rapport with the public. A whole dimension would be lost."

"It sounds like you've had this discussion before," Laura ventured.

"I have. With our First Scientist," Zenzie replied with a curl of her lip.

"Tralvar?"

"Oh, you've seen him, have you? Yes, he

wanted to record Tristell, and some of the others before her. But he couldn't get it right." Zenzie stood up. "Bring the dress over, would you?"

Laura obeyed, then watched curiously as Zenzie eased the dress over a large hollow cone until it was stretched taut. Then, using an object like an oversized fountain pen, she stroked the material with a transparent liquid. Much to Laura's concern, it began to dissolve. Separating the two halves carefully, Zenzie took one of the pieces she'd cut out and placed it against the original fabric. Using the other end of the pen, she repeated the anointing process until the new material was joined invisibly to the old.

"That's brilliant!" Laura enthused. "I was wondering why I couldn't see any seams."

Zenzie started on the next segment. "When this is finished, we must go downstairs," she warned. "Why don't you get those ugly things off and have a wash? And comb your hair while you're about it." She'd begun to look a little nervous.

Laura's own nervousness had subsided, mostly due to Zenzie's revelations about recorded sound, and despite a recent look out of the window at the packed auditorium. They all love this place, she thought. Well, it's down to me now. I've got to help them keep it.

Almost before she knew it, she was dressed and ready. She pulled a face as she caught sight of herself in a tall mirror. The gown fitted, but she still looked like an awkward schoolgirl.

"You'll do," declared Zenzie, sounding a little like Tracey at that moment. "Come on, into the elevator."

"Dena wouldn't go through the crowd," objected Laura.

"Neither would I if the scolia weren't playing," Zenzie said. "There'll be no commotion now."

"How do you know?"

"Because," said Zenzie, marching her into the lift. "During a performance, the musicians' minds are linked," she continued as the cage began its smooth descent. "This link has a specific pattern known as a lattice. It's the height of bad manners to do anything which might disrupt the lattice."

"Then let's hope everyone remembers their manners," Laura said dubiously.

They emerged at the back of the crowd. Zenzie turned to the right, following a curved wall; Laura followed, hitching up her long skirt. She noticed a few turned heads, a few stares, but mostly the audience was quiet. They were of all ages, Laura noticed, from dignified old people to drowsy children. Because the young adults had reached the portals of the Lyricon first, she'd assumed she was to sing for them alone.

Zenzie reached a door in the wall and opened it to reveal a broad, well-lit corridor with a downward slope. "On Earth, you have music for specific age groups?" she inquired.

"We certainly do."

"That isn't good," pronounced Zenzie. "Divided music causes division."

Their route took them through a repair shop where several of the lozenge-shaped stringed instruments lay on benches. Most had damage to the

97

strings and tuning pegs.

"Is this the only type of instrument you have?" asked Laura.

"No, but it's the most popular," Zenzie replied. "It's called a strelsis, and as you can see, there are three sizes."

After another section of corridor, they passed through a large basement area filled with debris - props, masks, costumes, lengths of cloth, old furniture.

"If you think *this* is a mess, you should see the city archive," remarked Zenzie cheerfully.

Laura was just starting to get breathless when the corridor took an abrupt left turn - and she was face to face with Floren, Idenion, Dena and several other people she didn't know. They fussed over her, apologised for the length of the walk, made her sit down and offered her a drink.

"I'm fine, really," she said, trying not to blush. They continued to fuss.

"Are you prepared? Shall I tell the dancers to stop?" asked Dena eventually.

"Yes, please do," said Laura. "I'd like to get on with it." She stood up and straightened her shoulders.

"Now remember, Laura - start singing and the scolia will follow you," Floren said. "They cannot start without you."

"I understand."

"And don't forget, I want you to sing Nuit D'Etoiles," Idenion put in.

"I'll do it," Laura promised.

"Shoes!" yelled Zenzie, and she hastily kicked

98

them off. The dancers, exuberant and beaded with sweat, rushed down the gentle slope from the stage.

Idenion gave her a tiny push. She turned, smiled at him, then walked purposefully up the slope: up toward the blue artificial sky and the surrounding colonnades, until at last she set foot on smooth, cool stone, in full view of the audience. She went forward, resisting the urge to pick up her skirt again, and halted centre stage. There was absolute silence. Blessing whatever genetic quirk had endowed her with perfect pitch, she took a careful breath and began to sing.

"Early one morning, just as the sun was rising...."

At the end of the first line she heard the gentle ripple of strelsis-strings accompanying her, and gave an inward sigh of relief. Everything would be all right now. Everything.

***

For the second time that day, Tralvar found himself outside Alendis' suite on the top floor of the akron. This time his entrance was less forcible.

"So you've decided to honour me with your presence, o pretender to the scolia," Alendis said coldly. "My relayist has been busy collecting news: can you tell me anything I don't already know?"

"Idenion brought back an off-worlder," Tralvar said reluctantly.

Alendis' expression did not change. "And he chose a female, of course; Idenion is always consistent. But what is she, Tralvar? Her origin is still unclear. If you've seen her, show me her image."

Tralvar tensed visibly. "Do you expect me to *invite* you into my head?"

Alendis sighed in exasperation. "You need fear no harm, Tralvar - yet. At the moment, I'm only concerned with Idenion and what I should do about him. What planet did he trawl to find this... singer? If she's one of those Myrmian degenerates - "

"She's as intelligent as we are," Tralvar interrupted.

Alendis' eyes gleamed in anticipation. "You read her mind! Well done. Now let me share this revelation."

Tralvar obeyed with an involuntary shiver. He felt as if something private and precious was about to be demeaned. Alendis held the contact longer than necessary, studying every detail of the silent encounter with Laura. Then he smiled fractionally and said: "So."

Tralvar stepped back, sweating.

"And now you'd better give me the scroll," Alendis said mildly. "Come on, stop dithering. Get rid of the responsibility."

Reluctantly, Tralvar fished the slightly crumpled missive from his pocket and handed it over. "I - er - don't think you should take too much notice of this," he ventured. "Idenion's young - he gets too dramatic sometimes..."

"Shut up, Tralvar," Alendis said in a bored voice, and broke the seal with a deft flick of his thumbnail. As he read his face grew white, suffused with emotions Tralvar had never expected to see there. Shock, dismay, even sorrow. Idenion's diatribe had obviously found its target.

"So," Alendis said again, but this time he did not smile. He walked slowly toward his desk, where a tiny, perfumed candle burned, and held a corner of the scroll to the flame. When the paper was well alight he dropped it to the tiled floor and watched, motionless, until it was consumed. Then, very deliberately, he crushed the charred fragments beneath his sandalled foot. Tralvar watched, hardly daring to breathe.

"Such sentiments, if published, could do Idenion's career much harm," Alendis remarked in neutral tones. "Fortunately, this need go no further than me. I shall speak to him." Then, with a return to his normal acerbic self: "Well, what are you gawping at? Get back to the Lyricon and stop that concert."

"I don't think I can," Tralvar said lamely.

"Nonsense! Who else can disrupt a scolia performance with a single thought?"

"I mean," said Tralvar, "I don't think it's appropriate for me to do so."

Alendis regarded him balefully. "Do I hear a refusal?"

Normally, Tralvar would have given way before that look. He desperately wished he could. But older, deeper loyalties - to music and the scolia - proved stronger for the present. "Yes, I refuse," he said quietly.

Alendis remained very still. Tralvar, after a moment's hesitation, turned to leave. He took three steps –

101

- and he was in space, his lifeline broken, tumbling helplessly toward the planet beneath him -

A vision lasting but an instant, but vivid and utterly terrifying. A wave of vertigo assailed his senses; he swayed, and would have gone crashing to the tiles if Alendis hadn't caught him and hauled him to a nearby sofa. Released, Tralvar slid into a prone sprawl. He couldn't regain his balance, couldn't even raise his head from the soft ticklish upholstery.

"Poor, foolish Tralvar," Alendis said softly. "Did you really think I'd allow you to walk out? When will you learn that you cannot disobey me? I know your every weakness, my friend; everything that can be turned against you. Far better, don't you agree, to do as you're told *when* you're told?"

Tralvar endured this litany in miserable silence. The only alternative was to beg Alendis to stop - and he would not beg. Finally, something cool and calming touched the back of his neck - or maybe the inside of his head - and the universe slowly stopped its wild spinning. He sat up shakily.

"You're unwell, Tralvar," said Alendis with mock solicitude. "My little trick shouldn't have affected you to that extent. You must take better care of yourself. You're extremely valuable to me."

"I know," Tralvar said tonelessly.

Alendis gave a winning smile. "Then let's forget this incident and return to the matter of the concert. You've walked an appreciable distance today, have you not? To avoid tiring you further, I shall requisition a flitter for you and have it brought to the basement entrance. In the meantime, go to your apartment and smarten up. Try to find a tunic without any holes. Since you'll be representing my authority, the least you can do is look tidy."

"And where will *you* be?" Tralvar inquired sullenly.

"Preparing to follow. I intend to deal with Idenion personally; you may tell him so. I also wish to see Floren." He motioned Tralvar to stand and gently propelled him towards the door. "I shall be there, never fear. It's good psychology to keep them waiting."

Tralvar paused on the threshold. "What of Laura?" he asked, a little too casually.

"She'll be sent home," Alendis said without much interest. "After she's seen Idenion humbled, of course. And Tralvar - I don't want you hanging around while I settle this. Deliver your message, then leave."

Tralvar departed, a bowed shabby figure amid the akron's finery. When he reached the broad winding stairs he began to run: doubtless, opined the watching Alendis, due to an urgent appointment with a strong drink.

Then the autocrat retreated into his private residence and closed the doors. His proud demeanour fell away, and for a moment he looked almost as weary as Tralvar. He went slowly to his desk and stood contemplating the litter of charred paper on the floor.

"Such an adroit betrayal," he said softly. "You've wounded me, Idenion. But rest assured, you'll be repaid in kind."

103

Chapter Four

When Tralvar stepped through the Lyricon's doors and set eyes on the stage, he thought for one painful moment that Tristell stood there. But although the dress was Tristell's, the able young voice was not. Laura was singing in a language which was neither his nor hers, singing of night and stars and love lost. Her mind was a still node at the centre of the most perfect lattice he had ever encountered. He almost wept. And he knew that he could never sabotage anything so beautiful.

Having made up his mind not to interfere, he felt calmer and more able to enjoy the song. He strolled into the back of the auditorium, ignoring a succession of apprehensive glances, and began to make his way toward the stage. He did not follow the same route as Zenzie and Laura, but kept to the mezzanine level in order to see and hear what the performers did.

The last notes of the song died away, and a collective sigh arose from the gathering. Nothing more, for noise would disturb the lattice. It was clear that Laura had been told this, and equally clear that she was not at ease with it. For she could not sense the pleasure of the crowd – could sense nothing. Tralvar tried to imagine what that was like, without much

success. The lattice was poised receptively, tremulous as an insect's wing; and at last Laura led the scolia into a song of homage to a bird, in which her trilling melody lines were echoed by the fluting notes of the pyxis.

Tralvar wondered how long she could sustain such an output. If she showed any tiredness, it would at least give him a chance to wind the proceedings up neatly. Otherwise he had two unpleasant alternatives - destroy the lattice, or let Alendis arrive to find the concert still in progress. The former, he'd already decided, was out of the question. The latter he preferred not to think about.

Reluctantly he forsook the delicate grace of the music and descended to the basement. Skirting the area where Floren and the others waited, he approached a walled-off section directly beneath the stage. The generator for the weathershield was located there, its presence denoted by faded warning symbols and a subtle vibration in the air. A rusting metal door stood ajar; inside, a lone technician stood before an array of screens and switches. Tralvar strolled up to him, pausing briefly to examine one of the displays.

"How's it going, Lydion?"

"Beautifully," replied the operator. "No breakdowns, no problems."

"Why's the temperature setting five points below normal?"

"I didn't want anyone fainting," Lydion answered drily. "That's a capacity crowd out there."

"I'd noticed." Tralvar gave a brief smile. "Is projector four all right?"

"It went slightly out of phase to start with, but soon settled down."

"Don't let it overheat." Tralvar knelt to check some machinery near the floor.

"Watch out!" warned Lydion. "That's filthy."

Tralvar stood up again, absently brushing at some smudges on his tunic. "Did you warn the power station to expect a heavy demand?"

"Er...no," said Lydion. "I forgot."

"Oh, well, it's little more than a courtesy anyway," said Tralvar. "If their reserves run low, they'll close us down regardless. In fact, I wish they would."

Lydion gave him a quizzical stare.

"There's trouble on the way," Tralvar said, and went on to explain his dilemma.

To his credit, Lydion didn't panic or bolt as Halon had done earlier. "I could create a malfunction," he offered. "It seems rather a shame though. The girl's singing so well."

"And how did you discover that?" Tralvar demanded. "You didn't leave the shield unattended, I hope?"

"Just for a while," Lydion said, unrepentant.

Tralvar looked exasperated for a moment, then smiled. "Very well - I suppose it *is* a significant occasion. I'd have done the same if I'd been stuck down here. Now, how are we going to...."

"What's that noise?" Lydion interrupted edgily.

Tralvar could hear nothing but the steady hum of the shield. "Don't worry, it isn't going to fail."

"No, not that - something outside. A kind of - yell. There it is again!"

This time Tralvar heard and identified the sound. "Stay there," he advised Lydion, "and be ready to cut the power on my instruction. This could be the opportunity I need." He hastened out, no

106

longer worried who he encountered offstage. And possibly because he was *not* worried, he found only Floren and Idenion. Again, the cry which had so startled Lydion resounded through the auditorium.

"Lau-ra! Lau-ra! Lau-ra!"

"They won't let her go," Floren said tensely without turning her head. "Those students in front started it. I had trouble with them earlier."

More and more people joined in the chanting, and Tralvar groaned inwardly. There was no hope of pretending he'd stopped the concert: the crowd's noise would easily carry as far as the akron.

Laura tentatively put up her hands and made a pushing movement. The noise diminished. She then began to sing again, but it was obvious to the backstage watchers that she was tired and troubled. The lattice was still intact, but barely.

"What *is* that song?" muttered Idenion irritably. "She mentioned a deity. I distinctly told her not to sing about gods or death."

"Let her be," snapped Tralvar, rounding on him. "You're so pedantic at times. She's done all you've asked of her."

The song was extremely short. As soon as the last chords faded, the uproar broke out afresh, dissolving the lattice. Floren looked helpless.

"Leave this to me," Tralvar said, and marched forward. Avoiding Laura, he went to the edge of the stage and planted himself in front of the students Floren had indicated. Gradually, without a word or thought from him, the chanting began to peter out.

"The concert's over, or hadn't you realised?" he inquired, addressing the now crestfallen students.

The excellent Lyricon acoustics took his words and conveyed them to everyone present. "Are you just going to sit there till Alendis arrives?" he continued. "He's on his way and he'll be looking for someone to blame. You, perhaps? Or you... ?" The terraces erupted into movement. Tralvar watched without satisfaction for a moment, then instructed Lydion to turn off the shield.

The canopy of blue light collapsed upon itself and was gone. A chill wind whistled across the amphitheatre, scattering the audience even faster. Laura scurried for cover, holding onto her billowing skirt. Tralvar followed more slowly, pausing to gaze at the scolia, who only now were beginning to pick up their instruments and depart. They looked haggard but exhilarated; it would be several ilden before the effects of the lattice wore off. Tralvar felt the old envy stir in him, and prudently decided to go and help Lydion cool the projectors. He'd almost reached the generator room when he was confronted by an anxious Idenion.

"So Alendis is coming here?"

"You heard," Tralvar answered laconically.

"It's me he's after, I suppose."

"You, and Floren to a lesser extent. It seems he wants to deal with you in front of a select audience."

"That doesn't sound so bad," Idenion said, and managed a half-hearted grin.

"Idenion!" Floren came hurrying up, with Laura trailing behind her. "Laura can't find her shoes. Would any of your sandals fit her?"

"Too big!" Idenion extended one bony foot to

demonstrate. "Ask one of the girls. Where are they, by the way?"

"Don't you ever listen to Zenzie?" Floren remonstrated. "She went to have a rest. And Dena's off somewhere with Melor." She flitted away, Laura doing her best to keep up. Idenion started to follow, but Tralvar grabbed him.

"What does Melor want?"

"Scolia business, I suppose," Idenion said evasively.

"That can only mean Laura," Tralvar surmised. "Now listen to me, Idenion. You've made your point with this concert, so be satisfied with that. Don't get her involved with anything else. Take her home."

"You're hurting my arm," Idenion protested.

"I'm warning you, you featherbrained - " Tralvar stopped abruptly, aware of Lydion's disapproving presence in the background. "If you can't be concerned for your own safety," he continued in a low voice, "then at least be concerned for Laura's. Alendis hasn't yet seen her as a threat. Don't wait for him to change his mind."

"Dare I ask what that was about?" inquired Lydion when Idenion had hastened off. "Does he have more plans for the girl?"

"He's concocting something with Melor," Tralvar said, staring down the empty corridor. "I'm worried he'll start something he can't handle."

"He's already started something," said Lydion quietly. "I've never known such joy, such hope, as I sensed in that audience. They won't forget tonight in a hurry. There'll be some changes made."

"I never knew you were such an idealist,"

Tralvar said witheringly.

"Scoff if you like, but I'm right," Lydion declared. "We're already different people, Tralvar - you and me and everyone else who heard that glorious voice."

***

Laura stood bemused, watching her audience run away. She'd done it. She'd really done it. She'd sung well, even by her exacting standards, and the Celestrians had cried her name over and over and refused to let her leave the stage. She'd been on the edge of panic, realising she couldn't control them. Tralvar had stopped them though. He'd said just a few words - threatened them with Alendis by the sound of it - and they'd taken off like a swarm of butterflies. He was still out there, making sure they all went.

Laura wondered if she should go and thank him, but hesitated. She wasn't entirely sure that he'd had her welfare in mind. And the people were certainly afraid of him, just as Dena had said. The scolia, however, seemed unperturbed. They were still sitting in their cluster, ignoring Tralvar as they had previously ignored the crowd.

"Thank you, it's over," Laura said to them. They didn't seem to hear. Then the weathershield cut out, and she fled.

Floren was alone backstage. She put a wrap around Laura's shoulders and handed her a mug of water. "Not too much at once," she cautioned.

"Where *is* everyone?" asked Laura after a

lengthy swig. "Did Tralvar frighten them away too?"

"No-one of the Lyricon fears Tralvar," Floren said softly. "You have nothing to fear either. He came to hear you sing, and he defended you to Idenion."

Laura looked mystified. "Why? Have I done something I shouldn't?"

"Idenion wasn't too pleased about your encore," Floren explained.

"That was my school song," said Laura, abashed. "I Love All Beauteous Things. What didn't he like about it?"

"You mentioned a god," Floren said seriously. "He said you'd promised not to."

"Oh, honestly! All this fuss!" Laura exclaimed, depositing her mug with a clatter. "You should have heard him on the sphere. Don't sing this, don't sing that, don't mention death or religion. Or money! Now why didn't he want me to sing about money?"

"I don't understand," began Floren, but Laura wasn't listening.

"Where are my shoes? Did Zenzie move them?"

"No; I saw them here after she'd gone," Floren said.

They searched further along the passage, with no success.

"I'm so sorry, Laura," Floren said at last. "There were some spectators here earlier, and I think they must have taken your shoes as souvenirs."

"It doesn't matter," said Laura, thankful that her Parthenon pendant was safely round her neck.

"I'll find you some sandals," Floren went on. "Some of Idenion's, perhaps."

"Where did he go?" Laura asked a little plaintively. "Why didn't he wait for me?"

"He went after Tralvar," replied Floren. "Alendis is on his way here and Idenion wants to know what to expect."

"I'd like to know that too," said Laura uneasily. "Does Alendis often send Tralvar to pave the way for him?"

"Unhappily yes," said Floren.

They found Tralvar and Idenion near the powerhouse. While Floren talked with the poet, Laura caught Tralvar's eye and smiled brightly. She was promptly subjected to a long reproachful stare. What have I done *now*? she thought, and was somewhat grateful when Floren hurried her off. In the distance she again heard Tralvar's voice raised in anger, and this time the name on his lips was not Alendis' but her own.

"I'm causing trouble, aren't I?" she said dolefully.

"We always knew there'd be trouble," Floren replied, none too reassuringly.

"I - think there was a pile of shoes in the props department," Laura said after an awkward silence. "May I look?"

"Quickly, then," said Floren.

Laura was correct. Discarded in the dusty basement were several pairs of tattered but dainty slippers, pale green with clusters of paper flowers on the toes. To her relief, one pair fitted her.

"What's the matter?" she asked Floren, who

was looking doubtful. "These will do, won't they?"

"For now, I suppose," Floren conceded.

Just then Idenion caught up with them. He looked askance at the slippers, but offered no comment. Suddenly too drained to make conversation, the trio walked back toward the apartments. As they neared the elevators Laura spotted someone loitering behind a pillar, but her unease soon turned to delight when the figure emerged from the shadows.

"Halon! You came back!"

"How could I not?" said Halon diffidently. "Thank you, Laura, for what you've done today. Idenion - " He reverted to his own language for the rest of the sentence. Then having delivered his brief accolade he departed, following the last few stragglers out of the building.

"What did he say?" asked Laura.

"He says he's glad to have been involved," Idenion told her. "You see - already my venture has a following. Alendis *has* to listen. He has to let us keep the Lyricon."

"We'll soon find out," said Floren.

***

They assembled in the custodian's suite: Idenion, Dena, Zenzie, Floren and Laura. Laura had made a quick dash into the next apartment, scrubbed her feet and returned wearing her own clothes. The borrowed slippers looked silly with her jeans, especially as the grubby paper flowers were beginning to crumble, but she tried to ignore that.

113

In the silence, the drone of the ascending lift was clearly heard. Everyone stood up, perhaps as a mark of deference. Laura, who'd been standing already, folded her arms and tried to look nonchalant. Then the door clicked aside and Alendis stepped into the room. By Earthly reckoning he was, Laura estimated, about thirty-five. He wore a black tunic trimmed with silver, plain black hose, neat ankle boots and a short cloak. Collar-length golden hair framed a noble, beautiful face. Laura felt no surprise. Of course the tyrant would have the face of an angel: all the better to further his schemes.

Alendis walked slowly round the little group. No-one moved except Laura, who pivoted cautiously to keep him in view. When he reached his starting point he paused and favoured her with a cold smile.

"You've just taught me a valuable lesson," he commented in English. "Never turn your back on an enemy. Don't look so perturbed, Laura. Idenion isn't the only one with a gift for languages." His gaze swept coolly over the rest of the gathering. "For the duration of my visit, we will *all* speak this language. I want Laura to understand everything, and I don't have time for tedious translations."

No-one objected. Alendis took off his cloak, but did not sit down: neither did anyone else. Idenion tensed as the dictator's be-ringed hand grasped his shoulder.

"So, my friend, you've exercised your prerogative and changed the name of our world. Cel-es-tra. Yes, I like it. Perhaps a polyglot name

114

will encourage its people to be less insular. Is that your hope too, First Poet?"

"Don't trifle with him," Floren said angrily.

Alendis turned to her in mild reproof. "Dear Floren," he drawled, "always so concerned for others. Perhaps it would be better, selfless one, if you worried about your own skin for a change. Your conduct in this matter has been far from exemplary. Now, since you're all so keen to see the back of me, I'll get to the point. Idenion!"

The poet's troubled gaze met his.

"Idenion," Alendis repeated more gently. "What am I to do with you? You've broken our most important law - not to fraternise with emergent races - and already the citizens are calling you brave, fearless. To castigate you would be to deny the qualities I've been trying to encourage in them." He glanced at Laura. "Is her planet still as pestilence-ridden as ever? You don't know, do you? I trust our protections are still working."

"Of course they are!" Idenion said indignantly. "I'm living proof of that."

"So you are," Alendis said placidly. "All your sojourns on Myrma, land of swamps. Well, it seems you haven't risked anyone's health. That leaves just one more charge to be answered."

"What?" Idenion looked genuinely puzzled.

"Ingratitude," Alendis stated. "I trusted you, Idenion. I nurtured your career, indulged you, publicised you, promoted you. In return you've slandered and rejected me - and in so doing, displayed the baseness within your nature. Your odes were lies, designed to win my approval and

115

advance your position."

"No!" protested Idenion. "No, you're wrong!"

"Everything you wrote was a lie," repeated Alendis in a bitter monotone. His eyes never left Idenion's.

"I meant every word of my poems!" Idenion cried. His voice was shrill, as if there were hands at his throat. "You know that! And you know why I changed my mind."

"I want to believe you," said Alendis, his voice ragged with some undisclosed emotion. "If your grievance is temporary, we may yet come to an understanding."

"I will not relent," said Idenion.

"For the moment, perhaps not. But the storms of youth are soon over. Grant me one favour: let me confirm your past sincerity. Permit me to read you."

"Don't do it!" warned Zenzie.

"Peace, my dear," Alendis returned smoothly. "Your partner's freedom depends on his co-operation. If he refuses I must assume he's deceived me, and act accordingly."

"My thoughts are open to yours," Idenion said expressionlessly.

"Thank you." Alendis' whisper was barely audible.

Silence returned to the room. The three Celestrian women drew together as if for mutual protection. Alendis and Idenion stood an arm's length apart, confronting each other and, Laura supposed, having a meaningful talk. Or were they? She edged sideways for a better view, and as soon as she saw Idenion's look of frozen dismay she

116

realised that Alendis had tricked him. And in some unfathomable way, trapped him.

"Let him go!" she yelled, tugging at the dictator's sleeve. He brushed her aside.

"Do shut up, Laura. It's bad enough having to route all conversation via your head, without having you squalling at me. Idenion has to take his punishment, so I suggest you stay calm and watch what happens next."

"Leave him alone!" screamed Zenzie, unable to remain silent while her loved one was threatened.

"Discords, I'm surrounded by screeching women," Alendis declared. "You want him returned to you, is that it? Very well - take him!"

Idenion gave a single sharp cry, staggered back as if he'd been struck, and fell. He didn't get up. Alendis sauntered toward him and rolled him over with a deft flick of his boot.

"Will no-one tend the miscreant?" he asked mockingly.

Floren, Dena and Zenzie all sprang forward as if galvanised, but Zenzie was swifter than the others. She dropped to her knees, stroking Idenion's clammy brow and tearfully calling his name. Then, having failed to revive him, she suddenly launched herself at Alendis and beat at him with her tiny fists. He held her off, laughing.

"Isn't she splendid?" he remarked to Laura. "Such fire and fury! She's wasted on a mere poet."

"Zenzie, that's enough!" ordered Floren, and the girl ran away sobbing. Alendis gazed after her appraisingly.

"What did you do to him?" asked Laura

117

shakily. She wanted to go to Idenion herself, but somehow felt excluded.

"He'll soon regain consciousness," said Alendis, evading the question. "But he'll find his thought perception severely impaired."

"For how long?"

"Long enough to scare him, I hope," Alendis said flippantly. "And that, believe me, was the least damaging thing I could have done. Despite his recent foolishness, I'm very fond of him."

"You've a funny way of showing it," Laura commented, watching anxiously as Floren and Dena carried Idenion from the room. She'd started to feel light-headed, probably due to hunger. She hoped Alendis hadn't noticed. But of course, such hopes were in vain.

"Floren!" Alendis called.

She came running.

"Floren, this girl is starving. Is this the way you treat a valued guest? I shall take her to the kitchens and see that she's properly fed."

"The kitchens will be closed by now," ventured Floren.

"They will not be closed to me," smiled Alendis, retrieving his cloak. "Please don't agitate yourself, custodian. I'll look after her. This way, Laura."

She hesitated.

"My dear Laura," said the dictator with exaggerated patience, "I've had ample time to do you harm, if that had been my intention. These good people couldn't have protected you. Now come along!"

And because she was so very hungry, she went. In the elevator she stole a surreptitious look at his handsome profile, and resolved not to let his appearance blind her to the fact that he was unscrupulous and cruel. Alendis studied her in turn, more openly, causing her to blush a little.

"Interesting choice of footwear," he commented. "Do you wish to take part in our fertility rites?"

"*What*?" The colour drained from Laura's face as quickly as it had appeared.

"Did no-one explain? Those shoes are worn during the Peisistrata, our street festival, by girls wishing to choose a mate."

She would not, Laura decided, be embarrassed. It was what he wanted.

The kitchens were in the basement below the entrance hall. Everything looked strangely old-fashioned, from the stone flags and wooden tables to the row of huge ovens set into the wall. No-one was about.

"Perhaps it *is* too late," suggested Laura.

"Nonsense," said Alendis, and in no time there was a flurry of activity, an upsurge of warmth, and the smell of something savoury being cooked.

"They'll do their best with what they have," Alendis informed her, escorting her to a corner table. "The food is delivered fresh each morning, but there were enough vegetables left for a meal. I think I shall eat with you - the akron food has become dull of late."

A nervous girl brought a jug of water, two mugs and two spoons. Alendis favoured her with a dazzling smile. She remained nervous.

Laura fidgeted with her spoon. It didn't seem right, somehow, to be dining with Alendis while Idenion lay injured.

"When you return he'll be awake," Alendis assured her. "If you like, I'll ask the cook to take him some soup. I doubt if he's eaten much today."

"Thank you. I think he'd appreciate the gesture," Laura said politely. Then, with some hesitation: "You've done that before, haven't you? Struck at someone with your mind?"

"And what brought you to that conclusion?"

"You knew what the side-effects would be," said Laura reasonably.

"Once or twice, I've been provoked into such an act," Alendis admitted. "But I assure you, that does not make me a monster. Any Celestrian, given tuition, could use their mind in such a way."

Laura looked doubtful.

"It's obvious that Idenion has spoken against me," Alendis went on, a tinge of unhappiness in his voice. "That's why I'm glad of this opportunity to set the record straight. I want to tell you my side of the story."

"Do you care what I believe?" asked Laura.

"I care," said Alendis, and would not elaborate.

The meal arrived: two large bowls of stew, and a round loaf that Alendis soon decided was stale. Laura began to eat a portion anyway, dipping it in the gravy. She tried to see what the vegetables were like, but they were too thinly sliced. The stew lacked salt - just as, earlier in the day, the cereal had lacked sugar; but it was palatable, and she ate

120

rapidly.

Presently, Alendis pushed aside his bowl and began to talk. He told her that Celestra had once been the home of a vast civilization, with colonies throughout its solar system and possibly beyond. "We can only guess at their achievements," he went on sadly. "They are gone, wiped out by a meteor strike which devastated their homeworld - *this* world. No-one can say what happened next, of course. My own theory is that the colonists managed to survive until the world became habitable, then came home to try and rebuild things. They didn't succeed, and their descendants - my distant ancestors - reverted to the primitive. We have legends, re-told every Peisistrata, of how the survival of the species once depended on one man and seven women." He smiled faintly. "And for centuries that was *all* we had - myths, tales, a vague race memory of some cataclysm. Until we ventured once more to the nearest planets and found what awaited us.

"There had been no attempt to preserve anything systematically – it was simply the flotsam of a desperate, dispirited people, returning home for the last time. But there was enough to give us back our past, and accelerate our progress toward a new era. We found spacecraft, some with their transposal drive intact. We had been given the stars!" He paused, his eyes shining with fierce pride, and Laura realised that she'd been sitting with the spoon halfway to her mouth. He was a wonderful orator. She glimpsed two or three kitchen staff in a far corner; they had crept in to listen, even though he

121

spoke in a language alien to them. Clearly, they were fascinated by him.

"Those were incredible times, Laura!" he continued. "We explored the galaxy, impatient to discover what was out there. Wanting to know, wanting to learn. We came to Hellas and admired the Parthenon, newly built. Which of my ancestors could have dreamt that two thousand years later, only the Lyricon would remain as tribute to Celestra's age of adventure?"

"Is that why you want to live in it?" Laura inquired.

He stared at her sourly, annoyed at having his speech interrupted. "Partly. But mostly because a lot of agile minds waste their time within its walls. If I were present, I could do something about that."

Laura finished her meal and folded her hands tidily, knowing he would continue.

"You were surprised, were you not," he pursued, "to find Alda Mexa was so small and quiet."

"Yes," said Laura. "Very surprised."

"And doubtless there were some other things that puzzled you? Things that didn't meet your concept of a spacefaring nation?"

"Well," Laura said, "now that you mention it, there were no other spacecraft on the landing field and no other flitters being used. I thought that was a bit odd. And I haven't seen a television or a radio, except on the sphere."

"We do have radio," Alendis informed her. "In fact, there's one in this room." He glanced round at the spectators; one of them stooped toward some hidden mechanism, and presently the hiss of a carrier wave filled the air. The silence was broken at intervals by a series of test tones, almost like a tune. Over and over the tonalities sounded, monotonous and somehow sad, until Alendis signalled for the receiver to be turned off.

"We have radio," he repeated. "And an array of satellites to encompass the world. And what does the world hear? That callsign, except when I decide to make a speech. Do you see what's happening, Laura? This planet is in a decline. There are perhaps sixteen operational spacecraft left. I'm trying to rectify that - to make the people realise that their Celestra is becoming a dull pastoral backwater. Naturally I'm unpopular! But I have to maintain this course for the good of us all." He leant forward confidingly; his firm cool fingers closed over Laura's hand, and his expression was one of gentle earnestness. "I hope I've convinced you that Idenion was wrong in what he did. Our singing voices are lost forever, and it's unhealthy to dwell on this aspect of the past. I want you to tell him that you will not perform again."

"But," stammered Laura, "he said there'd only be one concert."

"That wasn't what I heard," said Alendis grimly. "He'll ask you to do more. It's important that you refuse."

"It isn't that simple," began Laura, carefully extricating her hand. "If I tell him I won't sing, he'll go looking for someone else and put himself in danger."

"Let him," said Alendis dismissively, giving

123

Laura a glimpse of his innate selfishness.

"You're very plausible, Alendis," she said frostily, "just as Idenion said you'd be. I don't see that music and concerts, or the lack of them, have anything to do with restoring Celestra's greatness. You just want your own way all the time."

He raised his eyebrows at her audacity.

"If you gave up your claim to the Lyricon, Idenion would have no further use for a singer," Laura continued. "Wouldn't that solve your problem?"

"Don't try and make bargains with me, young lady!" Alendis snapped, sounding very like Nathaniel. "I am not relinquishing my claim, and *you* are not singing one more note here nor anywhere else on this planet. Idenion is to take you home tomorrow. He'll be well enough by then."

"And what happens if I don't go?"

"Laura, Laura." Alendis sighed and ran his fingers through his immaculate hair. "Why are you being so difficult? Do I have to threaten you?"

"What with?" asked Laura, surprised at her own impudence. She'd begun to resent the manipulative nature of this man. She felt sure that the Nathaniel overtones were deliberate rather than inadvertent, designed to make her feel guilty.

"You're forcing me to be unpleasant," Alendis declared. "You're right in thinking I can't use your mind as I used Idenion's, but I have other less subtle ways of enforcing my will."

"There aren't any weapons here. Idenion said so."

"Did he indeed?" Alendis gave a mirthless

laugh. "True, there were no weapons in the past, but what makes you think I don't have any? Do you want to put it to the test?"

Laura eyed him dubiously.

"I'm offering you this chance to leave," he went on more quietly, "for the sake of Hellas, favoured by my ancestors. And because you came here in all innocence. But this will be your *only* chance. Tomorrow morning, a sphere will be made ready for you. If you're still here at mid-day, you'll have cause for regret." He rose in a fluid, graceful movement and strode out. The heavy wooden door thudded shut behind him. Laura looked for the caterers, but they were nowhere to be seen - probably frightened off by the incipient quarrel. Now that the tension had passed, she felt extremely tired. Her watch told her it was nearly midnight, and however inaccurate that was, it certainly meant she'd been awake too long. Force of habit made her stack the dirty crockery and carry it from the dining area: then, abandoning the bright warm basement for the near-darkness of the auditorium, she fumbled her way back to Floren's elevator.

Floren hugged her when she reached the apartment. "You did well," she said.

"Oh, good. You know what went on," said Laura, suppressing a yawn. "That saves me having to tell you. How's Idenion - can I see him?"

"He's in his room," Floren said. "You can go in for a moment, but be prepared to leave if I ask. He won't be able to converse with you, and that could distress him."

She led the way to a dimly-lit chamber near the

private balcony. Idenion was reclining in bed amidst numerous pillows, a tasselled shawl around his shoulders and a cup of liman in his hand. His eyes were closed. Dena sat at the bedside, watching him intently.

"Hello!" Laura called softly.

Idenion opened his eyes and attempted a smile.

"How are you?" Laura asked.

Dena replied for him. "He says don't worry. He has a splitting headache, but his perception is correcting itself."

"Silly," Idenion muttered.

"More than anything, he feels silly," Dena elaborated. "He thought he was exempt from Alendis' punishments. Now he knows better."

"Come, Laura," said Floren at her elbow. "Let him rest."

Reluctantly, Laura followed her out. "Why isn't Zenzie with him?" she asked when they were back in the reception area.

"He needed a calming influence and Zenzie couldn't provide it," said Floren candidly. "He and Dena, as twins, have a bond which doesn't rely on personalities."

"Then where *is* Zenzie?"

"Next door, preparing your bed and making you some night garments," answered Floren. "She wanted to keep busy."

"Oh, I see," said Laura. She wondered if she should ask what plans were afoot for the morrow, but decided not to. She didn't want to face the prospect of another concert just now. Floren, for her part, remained silent on the matter. Instead, she remarked:

"You gave me some uneasy moments earlier. I thought Alendis might turn you against us."

"He's very persuasive," Laura admitted. "And I thought he had a point about the radio. Why isn't it being used?"

"We prefer our music live," Floren said, neatly paraphrasing Zenzie's speech about recorded sound.

"But what about news?" asked Laura. "How do people know what's going on?"

"Our relayists tell us," said Floren. "They're our most dedicated telepaths, usually young men, trained to gather and circulate information. And that is *all* they do."

"It isn't much of a life," added Zenzie, who had just entered. "Your clothes are ready, Laura, if you wish to retire. I'll come with you to make sure they fit."

Zenzie looked desperately tired herself, so Laura bade Floren a swift goodnight and headed for the First Singer's apartment. Outside on the chilly walkway, she immediately noticed the absence of background light. Most of the city streets were in darkness, their silvery lamps extinguished.

"It's to conserve electricity," Zenzie explained. "The solar tubes aren't powerful enough to use as street lights."

Laura closed the casement door thankfully and went through to the bedchamber. Not for the first time, she wondered how the apartments stayed warm. For now, it was enough that they did.

Zenzie had been thorough. Most of Tristell's scattered possessions had disappeared, and the gold bed coverings had been replaced by pale green ones. A white ankle-length robe lay on the bed, together with an elegant wrap in the same green as the coverlet. Laura undressed methodically, pleased that the robe was made from something more substantial than firi. It fitted snugly, and felt luxurious. The wrap was cosy but light, reminiscent of silk.

Zenzie had not followed. Laura went back to the outer chamber and found her standing with her head on one side, a wistful look in her eyes.

"I was listening to the relayists," she said. "They always start about this time. It's easier for them at night: less background chatter."

"What are they saying?"

"It's just lists. Provisions for tomorrow and where to deliver them."

"Won't it keep you awake?"

"Oh, no! Just the opposite. When I was a child I'd wake up crying, then hear the relayists at work and drift back to sleep again, knowing all was well." Zenzie smiled wearily. "These days I'm not so easily reassured. And now, since the nightwear fits you - and suits you, I might add - I'll be on my way."

Laura glanced at herself in the room's full-length mirror. To her surprise, she looked quite regal.

Before she left, Zenzie showed her how to dim the light-tubes to a mere glimmer. "Don't turn them off completely," she advised. "The darkness would be absolute."

"I'm not afraid of the dark," said Laura automatically, but realised she'd be better off with

128

the night lights. If she woke for any reason, she might need reminding where she was.

Zenzie paused at the door. "If anything troubles you, remember we are close by," she said.

"I'll be fine," Laura replied steadily. Then she was alone. She went to the picture window and looked down at the auditorium, but it too had been blacked out. Only the colonnade was faintly visible against a background of unfamiliar stars. There was no moon. Laura was used to dark country nights, but not the profound silence which now surrounded her. In Cheveney there was always the scuffling and rustling of small animals, owls hooting, even the occasional nightingale. Here, there was nothing save the tick of her watch, loud in the stillness. She took it off, wound it and placed it on a table.

With one final look at the giant mural with its frenetic bacchanale, she removed the green robe and climbed into bed - a warm, welcoming bed, with soft fragrant sheets and comfortable pillows. Her one regret was that she couldn't stay awake long enough to appreciate it.

Chapter Five

Drifting awake after a long refreshing sleep, Laura was surprised to find it was still night. The light-tubes sputtered fitfully, their energies almost depleted; and when she slid out of bed, the room was noticeably colder. Perhaps the mysterious heat source relied on solar power as well.

Her watch, when she retrieved it, said half past eight. Which meant it should have been daylight, except that she had no idea how long Celestra's day - or night - was. Recalling where the sunset had been in relation to the Lyricon, Laura donned her wrap and went to the apartment door. Peering through the glass, she could just make out a patch of light blue on the horizon.

Having established that morning was on its way, she decided to take a bath - provided there was some hot water. The oval, sunken bath had tempted her yesterday, and although there had been no chance to use it, Zenzie had demonstrated the faucets and the row of outlets which "rippled" shut.

The water temperature was perfect. The room was tiled throughout, with ornamental vases set into alcoves, and on a shelf at one end of the bath was an assortment of soaps and flasks of oil. When she chose a flask and shook some experimental drops into the water, a pleasant floral perfume was released - the same perfume she'd come to associate with Tristell. Disappointingly, no foam appeared - she'd been hoping for a little camouflage in case anyone walked in. The bathroom door had no lock, and neither had the door to the walkway. Last night she'd been too tired to care, but this morning it perturbed her a little. "Free spirits," she said to herself ruefully. "Well, something tells me I'd better not sing in the bath! Not if I want to be left in peace." And, leaving her nightrobe where she could grab it, she slid gingerly into the scented water.

She remained there a long time, drowsing, trying vaguely to make sense of everything that had happened the previous day. She didn't succeed, of course; there was still so much she'd yet to see, and so much she'd never understand even when she *had* seen it. Why had the Celestrians lost interest in space travel? How had this peaceful, pleasure-worshipping society ever produced someone like Alendis? And more importantly from her point of view, did she have any further role here? The concert had been a triumph, but the Lyricon was still at risk. In her opinion, the Celestrians needed a different kind of help altogether. That worried her, as did the thought that Idenion might go looking for it. Finally, when the sky outside the one high window had turned to soft indigo, she stirred herself and padded across to a small antechamber where concealed vents wafted warm air over her until she was dry.

Slowly, the city was coming to life. Laura could hear the soft drone of a flitter punctuated by the persistent squawk of a bird. She dressed and went quietly outside, taking the shawl Floren had given her after the concert. The sky was gradually turning from indigo to palest blue, with a pink blush on the horizon. There were a few clouds, thin and

131

feathery. Winter clouds, winter colours; but the air was temperate, as in high summer, and presently she put aside her shawl.

For several more astallen she leant on the wall and watched the subtle changes in the sky. She thought of another dawn not long ago, when she'd played a record of Ravel's Lever du Jour and watched the sun rise over Cheveney. This time there could be no music, except what she carried in her head. Alda Mexa would meet the day as it always did... in near-silence.

There was a soft footfall behind her, and Zenzie joined her on the balcony. She said nothing, merely gazed soulfully into the distance.

"You shouldn't be awake this early," Laura ventured.

"I worry," replied Zenzie simply, and continued gazing. A flitter, possibly the one Laura had heard earlier, passed close by. It settled near the Lyricon and the two-man crew began to unload some metal urns and carry them in the direction of the kitchens.

"Liman," said Zenzie.

Laura, who was beginning to want breakfast, hoped a food delivery would soon follow. 'Why couldn't you sleep?" she asked. "Is Idenion still poorly?"

"He's sleeping like a baby," Zenzie replied. "I don't know how he managed to recover so fast. That was a hurtful thing Alendis did." Then, before Laura could speak: "No, not when he struck him. Before that. To allow someone to probe your memory is an act of trust, and in ransacking Idenion's thoughts, Alendis mocked that trust."

132

Laura tried to look as though she understood.

"It's not easy to explain," Zenzie went on. "Idenion felt... diminished, shamed. He made light of it of course, but I know exactly what he suffered. And yet there are plans for you to sing again!"

"What, here?"

"No. Dena was approached by Melor, a respected musician and tutor. He runs masterclasses for young players who have just entered the scolia. His pupils, like the Lyricon scolia, are experiencing problems in forming the lattice."

"And he thought I could help?"

"Melor suggested a musical evening in Tivenne, his home town. You'd only be singing for about sixteen people."

"But you don't want me to do it," said Laura.

"Of course I don't want you to do it!" returned Zenzie, a strange edge to her voice. "I'm afraid for Idenion - so very afraid. Since Alendis murdered my father, I've known he'll stop at nothing to achieve his aims." She paused, noting Laura's wide-eyed stare. "Is it any wonder I can't sleep?"

"Alendis murdered your father," repeated Laura slowly. "Is there anything else I should know about?"

Zenzie said nothing.

"Answer me! What else has he done?"

"When he first came to power, his elder brother tried to oppose him in some way," Zenzie began. "Alendis pushed him from a high window. At the time, everyone thought it was an accident. Later, some of his critics just... disappeared."

"Thank you for telling me," said Laura grimly.

"Idenion will be angry. He says this is different - that it's art, not politics." Zenzie tilted her chin resolutely. "But I think it's all the same."

"Your father," Laura persisted. "What happened - was there a quarrel?"

"Not exactly," Zenzie replied. "Do you see that?" And, turning, she pointed up at the empty campanile.

"I noticed it last night," Laura said. "It looks like a bell tower."

"It housed the bell of Alda Nima," Zenzie said reverently. "For generations, that bell called the citizens to the Lyricon. There are many accounts of its beautiful sound."

"But no recordings."

"Of course not," said Zenzie impatiently. "Long ago, one of the custodians grew careless. He didn't check the fixtures in the tower, and the bell fell down and shattered. No-one could make another to rival it, so the campanile remained empty. To this day, each custodian must wear the key to the tower. It's a tradition." She drew a deep breath before continuing. "Alendis recently designed a flag for himself - a mark of his leadership, he told us. It's bright red, and I hate it. He's got several stuck all over the government building, and I've heard he even uses one as a bedspread. Anyway, he brought one here and hung it from the campanile. It was an outrage! Relto, my father, tore down the flag and burnt it where we're standing."

"And then what?" asked Laura in a near-whisper, expecting to hear that Relto had been thrown over the parapet.

"Alendis is more subtle these days," said Zenzie. "That evening, Relto went on an errand and didn't return. No one could locate him. The next day, he was found dead at the spaceport. He'd been shut in a vacuum chamber."

Laura didn't know what to say. She was shaken, not only by the disclosure, but by the casual way that Zenzie had described Relto's death. She'd seemed far more emotional about the bell and the flag.

"Relto was First Poet before Idenion," Zenzie added as an afterthought. "Now let's not dwell on this further. Look - the flitters are here with the provisions. We can have breakfast now."

"I don't understand you," said Laura unhappily. "How can you just shrug this off? Alendis won't go away, Zenzie. Someone has to stop him!"

Behind her, a door opened with a sharp click. Floren stepped onto the walkway. Laura paused guiltily, thinking she might have spoken out of turn; but the custodian was approaching with her usual serene dignity, the early morning sun glinting on the silver key at her throat. "What a beautiful sunrise!" she said. "Normally there are mists at dawn. I think it will be hot today." Her calm grey eyes met Laura's. "Now that my daughter has explained our tragedy, do you wish to leave? Or will you sing for Melor?"

"I don't want to go home," Laura admitted. "Not yet. But Alendis said I must."

"He just wants you out of the Lyricon," Floren assured her. "At least, that's the impression I had last night."

"If you're sure, then I'll stay," Laura said.

Zenzie looked miserable.

"As long as Idenion doesn't get the blame," Laura added.

"Melor will take the responsibility," said Floren. "The welfare of the scolia is very important to him."

"It must be," Laura said thoughtfully. "I hope I'll be able to do more good than I did here. The concert was a lovely idea, but I can't help thinking that you - or rather Idenion - went about things the wrong way."

"What should we have done?" asked Floren.

"Well," said Laura, ignoring a glare from Zenzie, "since Alendis persecutes the individuals who stand up to him, you should have tried a mass protest of some kind. Something spontaneous with no apparent ringleader." Suddenly her face lit up. "I know! You could hold a sit-in. It isn't too late. Occupy the building - he wouldn't want to move in then."

"I think we'd better go and eat," Floren said, forestalling Zenzie's objections. "Dena is already downstairs, and Melor will be there shortly. Shall we join them? Then you can tell us all about your sit-in." She paused and smiled. "And by that time, Idenion should be awake."

***

They had overpowered Tralvar before he realised what was happening. One moment he'd been walking through Alda Mexa in the bright

136

sunlight, the next he'd found himself struck down and lying dazed and semiconscious on the flagstones. Two men had approached from behind, moving swiftly and purposefully. One was Alendis; the other Strephin, his loyal accomplice. Laughing, they hauled Tralvar to his feet and began to drag him along. He could see the familiar contours of the communications centre ahead of him, and beyond that the square bulk of the maintenance block. And suddenly, sickeningly, he knew where they were headed and why. He tried to speak, to call out, but no words came. His mind clamoured for help but there was no response from the passers-by. Why didn't anyone stop? No-one was even looking at them.

"But of course they're not," Alendis' mocking voice said in his ear. "They don't care what happens to you. They don't even fear you anymore. They simply don't care."

And now they were beside the vacuum chamber with its sturdy airlock and plain white walls. Still laughing, they thrust him inside. He heard the doors close ponderously. Weakly, he tried to raise himself from the floor, but a fresh wave of nausea washed over him and he lost consciousness.

Then came Alendis' voice in his head, beguiling and soothing. +Wake up, Tralvar. This is all a bad dream. Wake now. These things didn't happen+

Confused, disoriented, he sat up, expecting to see the familiar walls of his apartment. Instead he found he was still in the space simulator, with nothing and no-one present but himself. There was no sphere on test. He turned, extending his hand

137

toward the airlock control: it was disabled from without, and to accompany this realisation came the muted drone of the equipment he'd personally operated many times - the pumps which extracted the air from the chamber. The pressure indicator next to the airlock began to fall steadily.

Panic-stricken, he ran toward the compartments which contained the bioshells. He wrenched open the door to the first - it was empty. He moved on to the second. Also empty, as was the third. The fourth held a suit: he snatched at it frantically, only to find the material cut to ribbons.

The insidious whine of the pumps seemed to be getting louder. No suits, no sphere to take refuge in, and soon, no air. The walls were soundproof, so it was useless to shout. Was Alendis still outside, savouring the fate of his latest victim? Tralvar tried to send pleas for clemency, but it was as if the insulation blocked his thoughts as well. There was no contact with anyone.

Increasingly terrified, he hammered at the airlock, knowing such efforts were futile. A tightness began to assail his chest. Invisible fingers constricted his windpipe, stopped his mouth. He sank to his knees, sobbing for breath. The pressure gauge fell and fell; the pumps whined. His senses swam, his vision clouded over, and the artificial lights became a seething, crawling blur. His hands clawed emptiness. With his last scrap of consciousness he ransacked his mind for something, anything which might save him - and suddenly, through the fear and claustrophobia, came one vagrant thought:- "This was Relto's fate, not mine."

And he saw, beyond the white walls of the chamber, another image superimposed. Something which seemed of little consequence and which he scarcely recognised. His own apartment door, locked and bolted.

Seemingly unbidden, his fingers sought for the release mechanism, which responded instantly to his touch. The bolt resisted him, but he managed to draw it back. Then the walls of his prison dissolved, leaving him in a circle of airless nothingness.

Vaguely he realised that someone had seized him by the shoulders and was shaking him. A female voice called his name. A hand slapped his face, hard.

"Tralvar, listen to me," the voice said. "You're hyperventilating. Keep on like this and you *will* pass out. You're awake! Breathe normally; there is no danger."

He tried to obey, awareness returning to him in disjointed fragments. He was lying half in, half out of his apartment doorway, his night-robe drenched in sweat and plastered to him. Instinctively he tried to struggle free of the intrusive grasp, then relaxed with a thankful sigh as he identified his rescuer. It was Rietta, once his nurse, now an akron servant - and one of the few people he still trusted. She'd been bringing him his breakfast. With an ease that belied her anxiety, she helped him back to bed and placed the coverlet around his trembling shoulders. Then she retrieved her tray and offered him a drink of liman. He waved it aside.

"Resnay," he ordered hoarsely. Rietta frowned but took a flagon from a nearby shelf and poured a measure of the strong alcohol. Tralvar downed it in one swallow and held out the glass for a refill. Even more disapprovingly, Rietta complied.

"Are you recovered?" she inquired after a moment, removing the empty glass from his clenched hand.

He ignored the question. "Was I screaming?"

"Not you," she replied. "Silent as ever, just as you were the first time I ever saw you. A frightened, injured child, so anxious not to be any trouble."

"And I've been nothing *but* trouble," he commented wryly.

Just then Alendis' amused thoughts cut into his consciousness.   +Well   done, Tralvar. I'm improving, am I not?+

+Stay out of my sleep, you parasite+ Tralvar managed.

+Certainly, if you obey my orders+ Alendis replied curtly. +Oh, and just as a matter of interest, *you* created those remarks about no-one caring. Very enlightening. I shall remember them. And now I must bid you farewell for a time. I'm off to frighten Laura+

"How does he do it, Rietta?" Tralvar asked wretchedly. "Hardly anyone can read dreams, and yet he's able to restructure mine. Surely it couldn't happen if I didn't somehow allow it?"

"That's foolish," Rietta said sharply. "Healers are trained to reach comatose minds, no matter how difficult or inaccessible, and Alendis would have been a fine healer had he not decided to invert his knowledge. I should know - I helped train him."

Tralvar wanted to believe her. But Alendis had

hinted at an unwilling compliance - and Tralvar, his self-esteem already in tatters, had fallen prey to the lie. If it *was* a lie.

"You can't let this go on," Rietta said. "Leave, I beg of you, before something worse happens."

"Alendis wouldn't hear of it," Tralvar stated. "I've made myself indispensable and he's never going to stop resenting me for that. I'm trapped, Rietta."

***

Breakfast at the Lyricon was a social event. The canteen was crowded with people Laura vaguely knew - dancers, musicians, caterers - and the air was filled with lively chatter. No one seemed to be exchanging thoughts.

"It's difficult in a crowd," Floren explained.

Laura spied Dena at one of the side tables and made her way toward it, pausing to acknowledge various greetings. A group of men, more robust than most, rose to let her pass.

"They're stonemasons," said Floren in response to her unasked question. "The Lyricon needs constant minor repairs. It's a very old building."

One of the men smiled affably and spoke. Laura smiled back politely.

"This is Cyphos, their overseer," said Floren. "He says, the Lyricon itself sang with you."

Laura thanked him a little awkwardly, wondering if this was flattery or some obscure metaphor.

Dena looked bright and alert, despite her

sojourn at Idenion's bedside. Melor, gaunt and silverhaired, spoke briefly to Laura in English. "I'm glad you're coming to Tivenne, First Singer. My home is at your disposal." Then he turned to Floren and began to speak earnestly and at some length. Dena listened attentively.

There was one other man at the table. His light brown hair and sinewy build reminded Laura of Tralvar, albeit a younger and more tidy version. He introduced himself, haltingly, as Lydion. "I know Tralvar," he went on. "He teaches me and others to run weather-shield. This I do. Miss most of concert."

Laura decided she liked him. He had an uncomplicated air, and he didn't fawn on her. And Lydion, despite the racket in the room, seemed able to read her quite well.

"You think, I not from this town. That is right. I come from Atris, far away. In this place, brown hair find often."

"Does Tralvar come from Atris?" asked Laura.

"Where from, Tralvar not know," he said sadly. "Always he wonders. Find out one day perhaps."

The food arrived at last, and Lydion encouraged Laura to try a little of everything. First there was porridge, doubtless made from the same bland cereal she'd already tasted; but there was syrup and some tiny fruits to sweeten it. Then came warm fresh bread with an assortment of spreads, and as always, liman to drink. Lydion kept Laura amused with his droll use of English. When Floren eventually asked her to explain what a sit-in entailed, she was sorry to turn away from her new

142

friend.

"Laura," said Zenzie when she was about to start on her fifth slice of bread, "you can't go to Tivenne in those shoes. Come with me to the market and I'll choose some sandals for you. And some clothes like mine, if you like."

"What market?" asked Laura with her mouth full.

"I'll show you," said Zenzie, getting up. Her place was instantly taken by a young musician wanting to speak to Melor. Laura hastily finished eating and said a reluctant goodbye to Lydion, who gave her a laconic wave and turned back to his meal.

Zenzie was waiting by the stairs. "Sorry we neglected you," she said, "but we don't often see Melor. He and Floren have a lot to discuss."

"She'll be with him all day, won't she?"

Zenzie stopped walking. "Floren isn't coming to Tivenne. Neither am I. Dena will go with you, and Idenion too I suppose."

"Oh, I see," Laura said uncertainly.

"Floren's place is at the Lyricon," Zenzie added.

"And what about yours?" inquired Laura.

"I've already made my views on Tivenne clear enough," said Zenzie. Then, changing the subject: "You seemed attracted to Lydion. Take care. He has an appetite for women, and has visited Myrma."

"Myrma? Isn't that where Idenion - " Laura stopped hastily.

Zenzie chose to ignore her. "You are not like Myrmian girls," she said. "You might have to explain that to Lydion."

They stepped from the shadow of the pillars into the sunny square. There, to Laura's surprise, was the market - about twenty little stalls with brightly coloured awnings. Traders were unpacking goods from large, covered baskets, and potential customers were already gathering. Only textiles, clothes and fashion accessories seemed to be on offer.

"Are the stalls here every day?" Laura asked.

"No, only when there's a need," replied Zenzie.

And they'd know, of course, thought Laura.

The market afforded her a first glimpse of Celestra's leisurely way of life. No one seemed in a hurry to finish displaying the stock, and the customers seemed not to mind. While they waited, they chatted to one another or sat on small benches provided by the traders. Zenzie found a shoe stall and chose some sandals for Laura to try on.

"You should have some boots as well," she suggested. "It's bound to rain soon."

Laura, when she'd found her correct size, kept the sandals on and left the green slippers under a bench. She then, with Zenzie's assistance, chose a yellow tunic and trousers in the loose-fitting style favoured by most of the townspeople. To this, Zenzie added a pair of ankle boots and a hooded green cloak.

Once the vendors had overcome their initial reserve, Laura found herself showered with necklaces, belts, scarves and a huge bunch of white flowers. Zenzie, unconcerned, was inspecting some bales of firi.

"Zenzie, I can't let you pay for all this," Laura

144

protested at last.

"Pay?" repeated the girl blankly.

It was only then Laura realised that no one was paying for anything. All around her, clothes and lengths of material were being folded, placed in cloth bags and handed with a smile to the customers, who merely smiled back and wandered off.

"You don't use money, do you?" she exclaimed. "That's why Idenion wouldn't let me sing about it!"

"That is a form of trade, I presume," said Zenzie after a brief study of Laura's memory. "Although I don't understand why such tokens have value. What do you find strange about our methods? All citizens provide a service of some kind - just as you have done. In return, their needs are met by the city."

"What kind of service does Alendis provide?" Laura couldn't help asking.

Again, Zenzie ignored her. "Let's go in. I think Idenion's awake."

Laura took the lift to the First Singer's apartment and deposited her new clothes on the bed. Then she hurried next door to see how Idenion was faring. He was indeed awake, as evidenced by the raised voices coming from the direction of his room. Zenzie was displaying her famous temper once more, and Idenion was doing his best to placate her. Laura was about to make a tactful exit when Dena came tiptoeing out with a tray containing the remains of a hearty breakfast. She smiled apologetically when she saw Laura.

"I thought I'd better get rid of this before she

threw something," she said. "Idenion's quite recovered, as you may gather, and impatient to leave for Tivenne."

"Is that what they're quarrelling about?" Laura asked.

"Zenzie's trying to dissuade him, having failed with you and me," Dena said.

Zenzie raged on.

"Where's Floren?" asked Laura uneasily.

"With Cyphos, inspecting some repairs to the auditorium. And Melor's gone to look for a flitter. We're supposed to leave as soon as he returns." Dena paused, noting Laura's tension. "Don't worry - Idenion will calm her down. He always does."

"But what started her off?" asked Laura. "I thought we had it all settled."

"With Zenzie, nothing is ever settled," Dena said resignedly. "She thinks we're in danger from Strephin, Alendis' other follower."

Laura recalled the name.

"Strephin lives in Tivenne," Dena went on. "But two days before you arrived Alendis sent him to inspect a mine on the other side of the planet. To keep him out of mischief, so we believe. He'd become unruly, and styled himself the First Citizen of Tivenne. That isn't the kind of support Alendis wants."

"Bit of a liability, is he?" remarked Laura. "So where does the danger come in, if he's been sent away?"

"He won't be away for long," said Dena soberly. "Zenzie thinks Idenion has left himself open to attack. Strephin has been known to punish

146

dissidents."

"Punish them how?" queried Laura.

Zenzie had stopped shouting. There was silence.

"How does he punish them, Dena?" Laura repeated. "With his mind, like Alendis does?"

Dena gave a nervous little laugh. "Oh, no," she said. "Strephin can't do that. Anyway, there's nothing to worry about. Alendis still values Idenion and wants to win back his loyalty. He won't let Strephin jeopardise his plans."

"Doesn't he realise that Idenion *can't* be won back?" asked Laura.

"He doesn't want to believe it," Dena said seriously. "And if you'd read Idenion's odes, you'd know why."

Laura glanced once more at Idenion's room. The silence was profound. "I take it they don't want to be disturbed?"

"No, although they probably wouldn't notice," Dena answered primly. "Before Idenion has another chance to embarrass you, I'd better explain that bonded couples enjoy a special, deeply personal sharing of thoughts."

"Is that why they've gone so quiet?"

"They haven't," said Dena, and blushed a little.

"Is this something else that won't translate, like sciesha?"

"It does translate, and it is not like sciesha," Dena stated. "It's called total unity."

Laura started another question, but Dena swiftly picked up the breakfast tray and summoned the elevator. "You must find your explanations

147

elsewhere. I know little about men."

"Oh," said Laura. Then, irrepressibly: "Why not?"

"Because, like you, I'm not ready to know." Dena sounded rather defensive. The elevator door whisked shut, concluding the conversation. Not wishing to confront the lovers by herself, Laura opened the casement door softly and went outside.

A flitter was just alighting in the paved area between the market and the Lyricon. Maybe that's Melor, she thought, and paused on the walkway to see who emerged. For a long time no-one did. Then the canopy swung up and a lithe golden-haired figure stepped from the cabin. Even from a great height and with the sun in her eyes, Laura instantly recognised Alendis. So, too, did the marketgoers; their chatter was stilled at once.

Laura presumed that Alendis had come looking for her, to ensure she went to the spaceport. She didn't try to hide, believing it to be futile. But Alendis seemed in no hurry to approach her. Instead, he remained where he was and stared up at the Lyricon as if studying it. Then, abruptly, he reached into the flitter's cabin and lifted something out. It looked like a length of pipe, or a telescope. Or -

Alendis raised the device and took aim. The hollow tube spat green fire.

Belatedly Laura ducked behind the wall. A flare, virulent green, hissed over her head and smashed into the pediment, where it continued to burn and spit. Wisely, she kept her head down. An instant later the tiny projectile exploded, showering

148

her with rubble and sharp stone chips. The flitter took off with a self-satisfied whine. Dusty and dishevelled, Laura peered gingerly over the wall to see the market in disarray and people fleeing in all directions. In no time the square was empty, save for a lost child who stood amid the collapsed stalls and cried piteously. Someone, greatly daring, rushed back and snatched it up.

Rapid footsteps sounded on the walkway and Idenion's worried voice said: "Laura! Laura, what happened?"

"Alendis happened," she said shakily. "He had a rocket launcher or something. There was a sort of - green fireball. It lodged up there - " she pointed at the scarred stonework - "and then it exploded. Oh Idenion, this is *my* fault. I really thought he hadn't any weapons, and I told him so. He had to show me I was wrong."

"There's dust in your hair," said Idenion, and gave her a swift hug.

Dena's head appeared round the apartment door. Idenion beckoned to her. When she saw the damaged pediment, her little face grew set and angry. "Alendis says he loves the Lyricon, but he's willing to wreck it just to prove a point," she remarked.

Zenzie didn't come out. Laura somehow didn't believe that fear was keeping her away. Disgust, maybe - or despair.

Floren was next on the scene, accompanied by Cyphos. After Laura had repeated her description of the green fire, the stonemason inspected the damage as closely as he could without a ladder. At length he

149

made a few brief comments which visibly cheered Floren. Dena looked happier as well.

"It's going to be all right," Idenion told Laura. "Cyphos says it's not too bad, that he'll soon have it fixed."

"And what if Alendis takes another pot-shot? He might, you know, if he gets a taste for it."

"He won't," Idenion said positively. "Not with therite - it's too volatile. It could injure him."

Laura looked stunned. "You mean - you know what this explosive *is*?"

"Yes: it's therite. You described it very well. It's used when quarrying for stone and raw minerals, and as I said, it's none too safe."

"You told me there were no weapons," Laura accused.

"There weren't."

"But surely you realised Alendis would use therite to make some?"

"No," Idenion said, blandly infuriating.

"Well you should have!" Laura shouted. 'Why didn't you think? I could've been killed!" And she stormed past him into Tristell's suite. Idenion followed helplessly; the others kept their distance.

"Laura, don't be angry. Don't you understand that we never think as you do?"

"Maybe not. All I know is, this therite stuff was just lying around waiting for Alendis to pick up. And there might be dozens of other potential weapons that *he* knows about and *you* haven't thought about!" She seized her new clothes and headed for the bathroom. "I'm going to wash my hair and put these on. *Don't* follow me in here!"

Obediently, Idenion turned away.

When Laura emerged, calmer and ready to apologise, she found Melor sitting quietly amid Tristell's filmy draperies.

"Oh - I - thought Idenion would still be here. I wanted to say I was sorry."

"He knows," Melor said. "He blames himself for not realising the significance of therite. We have much to learn from you."

"Melor, I...." Laura fidgeted with the hem of her tunic. "I hate to let you down, but 1 really don't think I should sing after this. Alendis would get to hear of it, and then..."

"That's what I thought you'd say," Melor admitted. "That's why I asked Idenion if I might see you alone. Would you consider talking to my students? Just talking?"

"What good would that do?"

"You'd refresh their minds with the music in yours," Melor told her. "Your thoughts, your memories, are interwoven with music - it's always with you on the edge of your consciousness. And this morning, just as the sun rose, you gazed across Alda Mexa and recalled the most glorious melody. I was awake nearby and had no choice but to listen. If the relayists had still been awake I'd have asked them to give your music to the city, but sadly I was the only one to hear it. I've been trying to memorise it for my class, but it's fading now."

"Is my mind really like that?" Laura asked wonderingly.

"To anyone with scolia training, yes. Floren, Dena, the Lyricon scolia - all are aware of your

151

musical spirit."

"What about Idenion? Can't he sense any of this?"

"His perception differs," Melor said gravely. "He's a good communicator and a wonderful poet, but alas, tone-deaf."

"Something tells me today's going to be full of surprises," Laura said with a light laugh. "All right, Melor, you've convinced me. I'll come to Tivenne."

The skies were beginning to cloud over as the little party left the Lyricon. Melor had deposited his flitter on the far side of the square when he'd seen the panic in the marketplace.

"You're lucky it's still here," Laura remarked, having deduced that flitters were common property.

"Then I'd have found another," Melor said mildly. "I have no rigid schedule to maintain."

Does anyone? thought Laura.

"Dena warned me you were a slave to time," observed Melor. "Our system works, believe me. If there's a real need for haste, such as a medical emergency, our relayists can secure a craft at once."

Some subdued stallholders had begun to retrieve their scattered goods. Of their customers, there was no sign. As she walked, Laura couldn't help glancing at the place where Alendis had stood.

"Wait, everyone - look over there!"

"Why?" asked Idenion.

"There's something on the ground. I think it's the therite launcher."

"Surely not," said Idenion, trying to steer her past.

"It *is*." Laura broke away from the group and

went cautiously toward the object. "I think it's broken."

"Leave it, Laura," pleaded Dena. "It could be dangerous."

The narrow pipe looked ancient and corroded, its surface peeling off. Laura nudged it with her foot, creating several large cracks. "No wonder he threw it away!" she exclaimed. "Come and see!"

They obeyed, not venturing too close.

Laura kicked the pipe harder. It broke into several pieces, displaying an interior blackened by intense heat. "It isn't a gun at all - it's a kind of detonator," she said. "One shot and it's ruined. Very inefficient!" And then she remembered these people knew nothing of wars and weaponry. Inefficient it certainly was, but a significant first attempt.

"Tralvar will be flattered to hear it," said Melor rather coldly.

"Tralvar? Do you think *he* made this?" asked Laura, taken aback.

"I know he did," pronounced Melor. "Alendis is not an engineer. This is Tralvar's work." Then, seeing Laura's dismay: "What did you expect? He's no friend of ours, despite his obsession with the scolia. He is First Scientist, appointed by Alendis. Now let's put this distasteful matter aside and be on our way."

Laura and Dena obediently boarded the flitter, but Idenion hesitated, staring back toward the Lyricon.

"What is it?" asked Mclor.

"For a moment I thought we were being studied. It's nothing. Today, I'm nervous of shadows."

Melor scanned the area, but could sense no interlopers. "We're all overwrought," he agreed. "And I, for one, will be more at ease once we've left the city."

Chapter Six

Strephin sauntered into the Lyricon and paused at the back of the auditorium. He was half a head taller than anyone present, with hair of white-gold and pale eyes which seemed to reflect the sky. But his expression was indolent, his mouth sulky. The Peisistrata rehearsals were about to start, and he was half tempted to settle down and watch the girls. For once, however, there was something else on his mind.

Rumours of events in Alda Mexa had reached him halfway around the world. He'd promptly cut short his dull tour of inspection and taken a sphere to the capital. He had little interest in music, but plots against Alendis - especially those involving a First Poet - were always worthy of attention. By the time he'd reached the Lyricon, Alendis had dealt his therite bolt and departed, and life in the square was slowly returning to normal.

"So," said Strephin in unconscious imitation of his master. He was annoyed at having missed all the excitement. He'd seen the weapon demonstrated once already, but somehow, watching Tralvar firing therite chips at a rock face in the middle of nowhere hadn't caught his imagination. Strephin had an abiding contempt for Tralvar and his musical aspirations. No need to wonder why he hadn't wielded his invention today. He wasn't about to knock holes in his precious Lyricon.

Strephin was amazed that Alendis had risked handling therite. The off-worlder must have worried him profoundly. And the vexatious girl was not, Strephin opined, about to depart in the sphere reserved for her and currently being fussed over by spaceport technicians. Therefore it seemed only right that he should stay put and learn what she was up to.

Appropriating someone's cushion from a nearby terrace he slouched into a seat, focusing his mind on the First Singer's apartment. His ill-trained perception had let him down on many occasions, but with this nonconversant female he could be as unsubtle as he liked and she'd never know. There, he'd found her. Talking to... to... discord's dreams, it was Melor!

Strephin couldn't believe his good fortune. Not only was Laura planning to remain, but she was going to stray right into his territory. He remained where he was, idly tracking the company as they crossed the square, his concentration already drifting. But suddenly he was alert again. They'd found the therite launcher, Laura was talking about its limitations, and the image in her head was of something streamlined, deadly and re-usable. She knew about weapons. Her planet had many such weapons -

And then Idenion was onto him. Strephin closed off the contact so suddenly that pain flared behind his eyes. He waited, hunched and guilty, until he was sure Melor's flitter had gone; then, pulling himself together, he walked slowly but purposefully into the square.

He intended to seek out Alendis at once. He had to persuade the dictator to keep Laura here until they'd discovered all she knew about armaments. Surely Alendis would see it was in his own best interests?

Abruptly Strephin stopped walking. What if Alendis wouldn't be convinced? His leader could be most intransigent when he wanted – stubborn enough to let this opportunity slip away. In that case, he, Strephin, owed it to his planet to make some contingency plans. Changing direction, he descended to the next lateral. Despite the importance of his errand he didn't hurry, but strolled in the manner common to most citizens. His leisurely pace wasn't an attempt to be unobtrusive, merely evidence of his laziness. First, he'd take a late breakfast at one of the many bakeries in this quarter. Then he'd find a flitter. Then he'd return to the spaceport.

***

Melor's flitter travelled east, flying low over a series of orchards which paralleled the range of hills. The glint of water in the distance soon resolved itself into a narrow, briskly flowing river which Idenion called the Lisir. Alongside it, nestling in woodlands, was a complex of circular white buildings - Alda Mexa's generating station.

"Hydro-electricity?" asked Laura.

"Yes," Idenion confirmed. "There's just sufficient for Alda Mexa's needs. But sometimes, if the river level falls, we have to economise."

"Couldn't you use coal?"

"We could. But there's no justification when we

have the Lisir."

"We nearly lost our world once," Melor put in. "Now we look after it." And certainly, Laura had the impression of a young, burgeoning planet, rather than one with a history of near-destruction.

They were now overflying fields of tall green shrubs. Soon, apart from the river, there was nothing else to be seen.

"Liman plants," Idenion explained. "We need a lot of them! There are eight processing farms serving Alda Mexa alone."

"It's our most useful plant," Dena added. "It provides us with our staple drink, cooking oil and fertiliser. We can even make a sleeping draught from the roots."

The craft flew unhurriedly on. Below, the river had broadened: tawny, inelegant waterfowl splashed in the shallows or preened on the banks. Presently Laura noticed another line of silver amid the greenery, and when the liman crop finally gave way to open fields she realised she was looking at a monorail track.

"Where does that go?" she asked.

"From Alda Mexa to Tivenne, and on to Treva," Idenion replied.

"Then wouldn't it have been -" Laura was going to say "quicker", but suddenly remembered Melor's admonitions about time and changed her mind in mid-sentence. "Wouldn't it have been less effort," she continued, "to use the train?"

"It isn't working," said Idenion.

I might have known, thought Laura.

"It's Alendis' fault," Idenion added, slightly

158

huffed. "All the people who could have repaired it were ordered to work at Treva, on spheres. The liman farmers had to start using boats to shift their produce. These lapses aren't always the result of indolence or lost science."

"All right, you've got an excuse this time," said Laura, unabashed.

A dense forest now loomed in front of them. They were no longer following the river, but now and again the monorail glinted reassuringly through the trees, showing they were still on course.

"Are there animals in that forest?" Laura asked, peering into the gloom.

"There are no animals left on this world," Dena informed her quietly.

"Did the meteor wipe them out?"

"I'm not sure," said Dena.

"We believed so until recently," Idenion elaborated. "However, animal fossils have been found above the geo-chemical layer left by the impact, so some of them must have survived it."

"What other species do you have?" asked Laura. "Just birds?"

"Birds, fish, some small reptiles - and insects of course," Idenion replied. Then, calmly: "Our ancestors must have slaughtered everything else. For food."

"What, everything?"

"They were primitives, unable to work the land," Idenion reminded her. "And who can tell what state the land was in anyway? All I know is, the animals are gone." He paused, then added: "There's so much about the past we don't understand."

After that, there was a long silence. The forest was behind them now; Melor guided the flitter across a landscape of scrub and bushes that looked much as it might have done in prehistoric times - except for the silver ribbon of the monorail. Something, mused Laura, wasn't right. Where *was* everyone?

If the other three detected her thoughts, no-one ventured to enlighten her. She was about to vocalise the question when a few scattered homesteads came into view. They were approaching Tivenne.

***

Jarras, kneeling inside the sphere which had brought Laura from Earth, replaced the Drive casing and stood up. "There, that's finished," he said thankfully. "Do you need any help, Rillan?"

"No, all's well," Rillan replied. "One can always tell when Idenion's been using the logic systems, though."

"Yes, he's very - idiosyncratic," said Jarras, ever tactful. "Come on, let's eat. We've done all we can here."

Rillan responded with an anticipatory grin. The two young men left the maintenance bay, sealing it carefully behind them, and set off through the dimly lit annexe. The outer door was standing open, admitting a haze of sunlight. As they neared the exit Jarras slowed his pace.

"I still wish Tralvar had inspected the Drive," he fretted. "It was such a distance to the Hellas

160

world. There could be all kinds of hidden stresses -"

"Do stop agonising," said a new voice. "That sphere isn't going anywhere - at least, not today."

Strephin had appeared noiselessly from the shadows, and now stood silhouetted in the doorway. Jarras halted, extending an arm to keep Rillan by him. "What do you mean?" he asked suspiciously.

"Our songbird has already flown," Strephin informed him smoothly. "In the company of Melor, no less. By now they should be in Tivenne – where I shall shortly go."

Whatever possessed them? Jarras thought. Then, aloud: "Did Alendis send you here? If you're looking for Halon, you're too late."

"Should I be looking for Halon?" inquired Strephin. "What has he done?"

"I - er - thought that was why you'd come back," Jarras said, flustered. He'd seen Strephin storm through the spaceport a few ilden ago, and was dismayed to see him again so soon. Rillan, new to Alda Mexa, looked a little bewildered. "We had a message from Alendis this morning," Jarras went on hurriedly. "He wanted to know who'd supplied Idenion with the Hellas programme. That was Halon, so... he went to the akron. To own up."

Strephin snorted. Trust Halon to turn himself in. "How noble," he remarked with an unpleasant smirk. "If he's been detained, I must pay him a visit."

"Since Halon isn't here," Jarras pursued, "I don't think we have any further business."

"On the contrary," Strephin said, still barring the way. "My business is with *you*."

"What could I possibly - " began Jarras, but Strephin had turned his attention to Rillan.

"Where are you from?"

"Corayn," said Rillan, still looking puzzled.

"And in Corayn, do people not know the name of Strephin?"

"Others may, but I do not," Rillan replied candidly.

"I see," Strephin's tone was menacing in its neutrality. "What should I do, Jarras, to ensure this lad remembers me in future?"

"What do you *want*, Strephin?" Jarras asked with a calm he didn't feel.

"That's better," Strephin said amiably. "I want a duplicate of the Hellas programme. You have the necessary skill to produce one. I also want a full transcript of the flight log."

Jarras hesitated for one moment only. Alendis would soon have the same information, so there was no point trying to withhold it. "I can have a programme ready by tomorrow," he replied, "but the contents of the log may take longer. It has to go to Treva for processing."

"And you'll take it there, won't you?"

"If you insist."

"I do. Now get back into that sphere and disconnect the programme crystal."

"But I - "

"Do it." Strephin gave him a push. "I'll keep Rillan company till you return."

"I need his help," Jarras said. It was such a transparent lie that Strephin laughed.

"Oh, I think you'll manage. Now run along

162

before I forget you're Tralvar's helpmate."

Jarras, with extreme foreboding, obeyed. He sprinted, rather than ran, back to the maintenance area. Strephin was, Tralvar had once remarked, somewhat like therite - his unpredictable and explosive temperament had to be treated with extreme caution at all times. Rillan was scarcely aware of this, and could easily utter something which might offend. Breathless, Jarras re-entered the sphere and reactivated the control systems. It seemed an age before the equipment was ready to accept commands. While he waited, he gingerly sought Rillan's thoughts - taking great care not to impinge on Strephin's mind. It was a reflex action, like avoiding a filthy puddle.

Rillan had come to no harm - yet. Jarras swiftly keyed in the code that released the crystal, slid it carefully from its niche and placed it in a carrying pouch. Then he hastened out. As he was closing the bay doors he heard a sound he'd been dreading - a sudden shriek echoing through the quiet building. He pelted toward the exit, ready to take issue with Strephin if he had to. But when he reached the spot he found Strephin gone and a dismayed Rillan kneeling by a prone newcomer.

"Strephin hit him," Rillan said tearfully. "To assist my memory, he said. Why does he do such things, Jarras?"

"There's a rumour that he absorbed something terrible as a child," Jarras said, gently helping the dazed technician to sit up.

"Oh," said Rillan, wide-eyed. "What could it have been?"

163

"I don't know," replied Jarras sadly. "I simply don't know."

***

Tivenne was a town about half the size of Alda Mexa, with buildings of pale pink stone. Like the capital, its terraced streets ascended a hillside; but unlike Alda Mexa, the laterals petered out halfway up. The greater part of the town occupied a broad valley. Melor landed the flitter in one of the main streets and led the way to his home - a modest two-storeyed dwelling with a flat roof. To one side was a small courtyard leading to rehearsal rooms. Melor quickly ushered Laura indoors, but not before some passers-by had stopped to stare.

"Hello," Laura ventured. They continued to watch her, serious and silent.

Inside, she was introduced to Melor's wife and two daughters. Essi, his wife, was much younger than Laura had expected - clearly not the mother of the elder daughter. Blushing and smiling, she greeted the travellers warmly and handed round wine and cakes.

"Do not take the wine, Laura," advised Melor. "You must keep your mind clear."

"Melor has called the scolia," Dena added. "They'll be here shortly. If you're in agreement, I shall join them."

"I'd like you to be there," Laura said. "I suppose Idenion's being excluded from all this?"

"Well - not necessarily," Dena said with a quick glance at Melor.

"Very well, he can attend," Melor said. "But he'll have to curtail his perception if we decide a lattice is needed."

Telsa, Melor's elder daughter, had remained apart from the gathering. She seemed nervous, even a little hostile, and Laura was reminded of Zenzie's initial behaviour. Telsa's drab brown tunic signified that she was of the scolia; typically, she spoke little, and then only to her father. Laura wondered if she genuinely couldn't address the language problem, or simply didn't wish to.

The other girl, Tioni, was very different. Still a child, she was dressed in a multi-coloured tunic adorned with ribbons. She darted excitedly amongst the visitors, flirted innocently with Idenion, and finally attached herself to Laura. She stared at her intently, putting out a hand to tweak her hair and touch her face. Then, unexpectedly, she said:

"You are grown up, like Telsa."

"Yes," Laura admitted.

"Then why haven't you tried to make babies?"

Laura blushed. She was saved from having to answer by the sudden arrival of a thin, sharp-eyed man. Telsa took one look at the newcomer and marched out of the room.

"That's Asterion, my uncle," Tioni said. "He doesn't visit much."

"Telsa doesn't seem to like him," observed Laura.

"Oh, they had a row," Tioni said airily. "I don't know what about, but I think it was to do with - " she lowered her voice - " sciesha. I'm not old enough to take sciesha, but Asterion says I'll soon

165

be ready."

"Tioni," said her father reprovingly, and she skipped off.

The young scolia players were beginning to arrive. They drifted through the courtyard in twos and threes, eager but silent. As they had no instruments with them, they obviously knew the purpose of the meeting.

"They are assembled," said Melor, and Laura found herself being guided toward the little hall, Idenion and Dena close at hand. Asterion, after a short confab with his brother, attached himself to the party. Telsa did not reappear.

Seated amidst the students, looking at their bright, expectant faces, Laura felt her mind go blank. It was easy enough to conjure up music when she was alone and daydreaming, but to summon it on demand, in front of a crowd of people, was another matter.

"I can't think of anything," she said lamely.

"Don't agitate yourself," Melor said soothingly. "We'll help you. Tell us of your home, your past, any scenes which involve music. We'll focus on the music and augment it."

Laura complied as best she could, wondering what sense these ascetic young musicians would make of her childhood memories. All her early years seemed dim and remote, as if she were struggling to see them through layers of thick glass. Only the music still lived.

She was on surer ground when she turned her thoughts to Cheveney: a church concert, the discovery of Nuit D'Etoiles, a record session with

166

Jimmy. Gradually she ceased speaking aloud as her recollections became more vivid. Always there seemed to be rain - lashing the little church, dripping from the eaves of Windbourne.

The rain wouldn't leave her alone. It spattered loudly on the car windscreen, obliterating the steady drone of the wipers. A hand, not hers, turned up the car radio. Grieg's Piano Concerto. She looked out into the dark, saw the opaque night sky and the fleeting skeletons of trees caught in the headlights. The music played on remorselessly. The car moved inexorably through the night. She could change nothing.

"No!" she cried suddenly, and stood up, overturning her chair. Twenty worried faces stared at her.

Idenion was soon at her side. "What *was* that?" he asked. "What frightened you?"

"It was a long time ago," Laura said evasively.

"Perhaps we should halt the session," suggested Melor.

The disappointment was palpable.

"No, don't do that," Laura said hurriedly. "I'm all right now. Shall I sing instead...just a little? I don't want to let your students down."

There were cries of delight, and a scramble to fetch instruments. There followed a ferocious argument as the hitherto taciturn musicians vied for a position on the lattice; and Laura realised, with a sinking heart, that they would never accept "just a little." Melor spoke sternly to his pupils and selected a group of eight to play first. The others, anxious for their turn, remained close by.

167

They asked her to reprise her concert, and she reluctantly agreed. Halfway through Early One Morning, she noticed a press of bodies at the opposite windows and realised the little courtyard was full of people. She also caught sight of Asterion trying to elbow his way out.

"Not everyone likes my singing," she remarked lightly to Idenion while the scolia was being reorganised.

"Almost everyone," Idenion maintained. "The street's full of people too."

Laura's smile vanished. "That's just the sort of thing we didn't want to happen. I shouldn't have offered to sing. I never intended to..." But if she didn't sing with the remaining eight students, there would probably be a riot. Reluctantly she began Nuit D'Etoiles, and after a couple of lines the song beguiled her into complacency. She had little doubt that news of her defiance had reached Alendis by now, but according to Floren, he only wanted her out of the Lyricon. Surely he wouldn't care what she did in a little place like Tivenne?

***

In one of the akron's audience chambers, Strephin confronted a strangely distracted Alendis.

"Tivenne," the dictator muttered, clenching his hands.

"Why am I forbidden to enter your quarters?" Strephin complained. "Tralvar always gets permission. Anyone would think you didn't trust me!"

168

"Tivenne," Alendis repeated almost inaudibly. His face was pale but composed, his fury damped down. "Why did she have to go *there*? The masterclass was untainted - they'd never formed a lattice for a singer. By now, Laura will have ruined all that promise. Discord take her!"

Strephin modified his bid for attention. "And of course Idenion is with her," he commented. "Such disobedience. How can you tolerate it?"

"Idenion went because he finds the girl attractive," Alendis returned irritably. "Melor is the culprit this time."

"I think you should know," Strephin went on hastily, "that Laura's people have many weapons. She has knowledge of them -"

"Yes, yes." Alendis made an impatient gesture. "I should have dealt with Melor sooner. I allowed him to retain command of the best minds on the planet and this is how he behaves. I shall punish him, Strephin. Today."

"How?" Strephin asked breathlessly.

Alendis told him.

"An excellent plan, but Tralvar won't do it," Strephin declared after a pause.

Alendis raised an eyebrow. "If he does not, I shall seriously begin to doubt his loyalty. Perhaps he should no longer be my second in command. Perhaps - someone else should."

"I?" queried Strephin with just the right blend of eagerness and modesty.

"Let us see what Tralvar does," Alendis said with a lofty smile. "If he disobeys me, we shall renew this conversation."

169

"Shall I return to Tivenne?"

"Not immediately. I want you to follow Tralvar after I've given him his orders, and radio me if he fails to carry them out."

"Couldn't I give the orders?" Strephin asked.

"I believe that's *my* privilege," Alendis returned coldly. "Take care, Strephin. At the moment, Tralvar still outranks you. And now you must excuse me - I'm informed I have a guest waiting upstairs." He hurried from the stateroom in a swirl of green.

Strephin, well used to such abrupt departures, wandered curiously into the main hall and gazed up the spiral stair. He could just see the entrance to Alendis' rooms - and the pale beautiful girl who waited outside. Zenzie.

"Probably going to pick another fight," he thought to himself. Much as he would have liked to stay and observe - he'd heard many tales concerning Zenzie's previous visit - he reluctantly forbore. He knew when to keep his distance. It would also have been amusing to find Tralvar and annoy him - but again, caution restrained him. He'd stepped out of line once too often in the past, and Alendis..... no, he wouldn't dwell on that. But he did wonder where Tralvar found the strength to be perpetually at variance with the First Citizen.

And now, what could he do until given leave to depart? Suddenly he was inspired: Alendis hadn't told him to stay away from the detention rooms. Of course, it would mean getting hold of Tralvar's keys, but somehow he didn't think that would be too difficult. As he neared the basement, he cast about

170

for his rival's presence and, finding nothing, halted in front of the appropriate door. It opened at his touch.

"Oh First Scientist, are you there?" he called softly. Then, louder: "Where are you, Tralvar? Asleep? Dead?" Still nothing. Belatedly, he recalled that Tralvar only locked his apartment when he was inside. Stepping disdainfully into the untidy room, Strephin removed one of three labelled keys from a nearby peg and departed, leaving the door ajar. The first of the cells was almost opposite; he unlocked it with a flourish and marched inside. The prisoner looked up, startled. Strephin smiled in a cold, predatory fashion.

"Hello, Halon," he said.

***

"Zenzie!" Alendis greeted his visitor with genuine warmth. "'What brings you here, my incandescent one? I suppose you've come to berate me for my mistreatment of the Lyricon?"

"It can be repaired," she answered steadily.

"Idenion, then. You're still angry about last night." He paused quizzically. "If you'd just stop shielding your thoughts, this interrogation could be avoided."

She remained aloof and troubled. "I *am* here because of Idenion, but not only because of last night. By now, I'm sure you'll know he hasn't taken Laura home."

"Yes, I know. They've gone off to Tivenne, I believe. Are you jealous, Zenzie dear?"

171

"A little," she admitted. "But Idenion has always been intrigued by unusual women."

"Aliens," Alendis supplemented.

"If you like." Zenzie's colour rose for a moment. "You understand his temperament, anyway... so it shouldn't be too difficult for you to overlook his disobedience. Please, don't punish him anymore."

"Your loyalty is commendable," Alendis remarked. "As it happens, I've already decided that Melor is to blame for this current escapade. It's he, not Idenion, who shall answer to me later."

Zenzie had scant sympathy for Melor. She thanked Alendis briefly and turned to leave.

"Wait." Alendis laid a gentle hand on her shoulder. "Now that you're here, I'd like to talk to you."

"What about?" she asked suspiciously.

"Please - not in such a public place." He opened the doors to his apartment and stood aside for her to enter.

Zenzie obeyed slowly, unhappy at the invitation but not wishing to anger him after his magnanimity toward Idenion. Alendis closed the doors carefully and went to stand by one of the heavily curtained windows. He didn't speak immediately. Zenzie remained near the doors and scuffed at the edge of a rug with her foot.

"What do you want to talk about?" she repeated.

"You," the dictator replied simply. "I watched you closely yesterday, and it saddened me to see you so frightened. You shouldn't fear me, Zenzie."

172

Zenzie threw him a look of outrage. "How can you stand there and say that, after the things you've done?"

"I did *not* kill Relto." Alendis paced the floor restlessly. He seemed nervous, which was disconcerting in itself. Hitherto he'd always been the epitome of supreme confidence. "See the truth in my thoughts, if my word isn't enough."

She declined. "You wanted him dead. It's the same thing."

"While you continue to shun me, how can you tell what I wanted?" Alendis asked reasonably. "His death set many people against me, including yourself. Do you think I wanted that?" He paused, and when she said nothing, continued: "But I have to admit your rage enchanted me. You were a creature of fire that day, vowing to hate me for ever. If I'd thought you meant it, I would have been grief-stricken."

"I meant it," said Zenzie in a small, strained voice.

Alendis ceased his pacing, and a stray sunbeam outlined his profile as he turned toward her.

Does he never stop acting? thought Zenzie. Discords, how vain he is. And how undeservedly beautiful.....

"Look into your own mind, Zenzie." The dictator's voice became soft, persuasive. "Face the truth. You don't hate me. You hate yourself for being unable to hate me. Will you not recognise that? Will you not admit you desire me?"

Zenzie spun on her heel and lunged at the door. Somehow, incredibly, he was there ahead of her.

173

"Don't run, my little love. Don't run."

"Let me out!" she cried. "If you touch me I'll let the entire akron know about it. Oh, why am I such a fool? *This* is how you plan to punish Idenion, and I've given you the perfect opportunity. Does that amuse you?"

"You're so wrong." There was such genuine reproach in his voice that Zenzie paused in her tirade. Very cautiously, he took her by the shoulders. "I didn't plan this," he said. "Neither am I trying to hurt Idenion. Indeed, I've long avoided you out of respect for him. But now he's forfeited my respect, and I'm free to speak. As for your apprehensions, I cannot coerce you, nor any other woman, into total unity."

Zenzie gasped. "I - didn't think you meant - "

"A forgivable assumption. Lechery's more in keeping with my public image, isn't it? And Strephin certainly seems to derive something from it. Unfortunately for me, my true desires are quite normal." He released her and moved away from the door. Zenzie remained where she was. "I see that I've aroused your curiosity, if nothing else," he added.

Zenzie was more confused than curious. Alendis had always claimed to despise the Celestrian mentality. It hadn't occurred to her that inherent needs could prove stronger than such prejudice. "I may have misjudged you," she conceded at last. "So I won't try to run away. But I'd like your permission to leave, all the same."

Alendis ignored her request and scrutinised her with a slight frown. "You're getting too thin," he

174

remarked.

"I was expecting Idenion's child," Zenzie replied, wondering why she felt obliged to explain. "I miscarried."

"Oh. I'm sorry."

"Why should *you* be sorry?"

"I'm not without sentiment, especially where the future of our race is concerned." His eyes never left her. "Be my partner, Zenzie. Let me prove that I'm still capable of love."

"Why choose *me*?" Zenzie's voice was a nervous squeak. "There are plenty of women who idolise you. Whenever you make a public appearance you're surrounded by them."

"True." Alendis moved across to his desk and picked up a small wooden box. "Would you like one of these confections? I have them made specially for me by the Corayn herbalists. Crystallised pilif flowers, fortified with liman root."

"That's addictive," Zenzie blurted. "You shouldn't..."

"You fear for my health. How delightful." Alendis popped one of the bright yellow sweets into his mouth and munched it appreciatively. "You were saying? Ah yes - my female followers. Those dull-witted shallow creatures who gravitate to me. They're of no consequence."

"That's unkind."

"No, just truthful. They cannot aspire to me. Once or twice, I offered total unity; and each time my partner was too dazed, too overwhelmed to sustain it. But *you* could match me - I'm sure of that."

175

"You've no right to say such things," Zenzie declared.

"Have I not?" He smiled, but his eyes remained cold. "You force me to ask you once more: whom do you hate, little flame? Me - or yourself?"

"It's my belief," said Zenzie carefully, "that to nurture hatred is poisonous to the spirit. Therefore - "

"I didn't invite you in here to quote Idenion at me. Those are *his* thoughts, not yours. Tell me your own thoughts, girl, if you have any."

A faint blush rose to Zenzie's cheeks. "I *should* hate you," she answered. "I should, but I can't."

He made as if to speak, but she lifted a slender hand to silence him. Amazingly, she had taken control of the situation. "And because I don't hate you, you expect me to love you," she went on. "You're so conceited, Alendis. You think you can always get your own way. I'm gratified to be the one who shows you otherwise. Now let... me... go."

She paused, expecting more of his sarcasm, but Alendis merely turned his back on her. "As you please."

Halfway out of the door, she hesitated. "I'm sorry if - "

"I suggest you leave before I strike you."

Zenzie retreated in haste.

Outside, before she'd even set foot on the stair, a voice said: "Don't go, Zenzie. I must speak with you about what happened in there."

Turning, Zenzie beheld a handsome but careworn woman who had obviously been lingering outside the suite. "You listened?"

"Yes. His thoughts were unshielded and I hoped there would at last be a chance to put things right."

"What do you mean?"

The woman took her by the arm and drew her down a neighbouring corridor. "He may punish me for what I'm about to say, but I think it will change your attitude. I'm Rietta, his sister. And I'm the only one who knows the truth about him."

***

The instant Zenzie had left, a dramatic change came over Alendis. He picked up the box of sweets and hurled it at the wall. Then he directed his enraged thoughts beyond the granite walls of the akron toward a small blastproof building which squatted a discreet distance away.

+Tralvar! Get in here!+

Tralvar duly appeared, unkempt as ever. One glance at Alendis told him he'd better not protest at the mind-scorching summons, even though he'd narrowly missed putting a blade through his hand.

"I've a job for you," Alendis announced, and rapidly outlined what he wanted him to do.

Tralvar blanched.

"Remember, your target is Melor," Alendis added. "The Tivenne scolia is not to be harmed. Neither is Laura. I have plans for her."

"Alendis - "

"I wish you a successful mission."

Tralvar was realistic enough to know that with Alendis in his present mood, no refusal was possible. Not without immediate and terrible retribution. He felt sick.

"Before you go," the dictator said sweetly, "a word about Strephin. He's to observe your prowess and report to me with his findings."

"Why tell me?" asked Tralvar, suspecting a trick.

"Strephin has been presumptuous today, so I've decided to curtail his fun. I'll ensure that he's late arriving at Tivenne. He was so disappointed at having missed my little demonstration this morning. Now he'll miss something better."

"Strephin's *here*?"

"Indeed he is. To be precise, he's in one of the detention suites tormenting Halon. Naturally, I did not give him my permission."

"Then why don't you stop him?" cried Tralvar.

"In a while," Alendis said disinterestedly.

"If you don't, I will," Tralvar declared.

Alendis smiled unpleasantly. "No you will not, Tralvar. You will return to your workshop, collect whatever you need, and go. The sooner you leave, the sooner I can send Strephin after you. And Tralvar...."

"Well?"

"Don't disappoint me. You're considering, are you not, ways in which you can fail without apparently having disobeyed. A deliberate miscalculation, a slip, a mishap.... No need to look so dismayed, my poor friend. Your defences are adequate enough; I cannot read you. But I do *know* you."

Tralvar hung his head, and Alendis playfully

178

ruffled his tousled hair.

"So, what's to be done?" the despot continued. "Should I scold you? Coerce you? No, your recent concern for Halon gives me a better idea. To be honest, I didn't know what to do with him when he turned up, but now he has a purpose to serve. He'll be held here as surety, and if you fail to perform your task well, *he* will take the punishment."

"Alendis, please....."

"Did I hear you beg?" Alendis' voice was soft, mocking. "And you vowed you never would. Odd: I always thought you disliked Halon. Since you've discovered a kinship with him, perhaps you'd nominate another party to suffer in your stead? That useful young man Jarras, perhaps?"

Tralvar swallowed hard. This time he would not be provoked into an outburst. "You're treading a lonely path, Alendis," he commented. His voice was surprisingly steady.

The chance remark struck home. Alendis suddenly looked tense and tired, much as he'd done when reading Idenion's scroll. "Spare me the philosophy," he snapped. "Why are you still here, anyway? Get going!"

And Tralvar, thankful he'd been let off so lightly, made for the stairs.

"One thing more," Alendis called after him in a normal, pleasant voice. "When you return, we must have a little chat about your.... allegiance."

***

"It was the year of the great forest fire," Rietta

179

began. "I was a trainee nurse and Alendis was still an infant. He was a lovely child - intelligent and good natured. I was looking after him and his little friend Strephin when a summons came from the hospital. Several more casualties had been flown in, and they needed me there at once. I found my younger brother Vitorr and told him to mind the children. He was annoyed about that, but there wasn't much I could do about it - our parents had relinquished us and we were still without an allocation. I hadn't pressed for one, to be honest, because I didn't want to lose touch with Vitorr and Alendis.

"When I came home from my shift there was no sign of Vitorr and the others. No-one knew where they were. I wasn't too worried; I knew they hadn't gone near the fire zone because there were no flitters to be had. And what other danger was there?

"It was morning before they returned. The two little ones were exhausted, so I put them straight to bed. They were so quiet and biddable they hardly seemed like the same children. When I went back to Vitorr he was sitting in the same chair he'd fallen into when he came in. He looked up at me, tears streaming down his face, and for the first time I realised how frightened he was. His mind was closed as if against some massive threat. He kept saying he'd been wicked, very wicked, and for several astallen that was all he'd say. I finally persuaded him that he had to share his trouble, and little by little the enormity of his misdeed began to dawn on me.

"Vitorr had been intrigued by space travel ever

180

since Controller Elos had given a talk at his school. He'd taken Alendis and Strephin to the spaceport, perhaps hoping to find Elos. On the way, he happened across another stray child who promptly attached himself to the expedition. Not surprisingly, the spaceport was deserted. So Vitorr, out of pique and bravado and discord knows what else, chose a flight crystal at random, herded the children onto a sphere and took off for an unknown world."

Zenzie looked sceptical. "Why didn't you make this known at the time? "

Rietta sighed. "I was trying to protect Vitorr. Worse, I connived at covering up what he'd done. Let me give you my thoughts, share with you the images I've guarded since my poor wretched brother confided them to me."

Zenzie acquiesced a little nervously, allowing Rietta to begin the transfer of memories. She started with harmless ones: the theft of the crystal, the illicit journey, and a beautiful ringed planet Vitorr had admired - a near neighbour of the world that had so traumatised him. There was, Zenzie realised, nothing of Rietta in this. She had encapsulated Vitorr's recollections, somehow keeping them apart from her own.

"A relayist's trick," Rietta said. "It helped me live with this. Now, Zenzie - prepare yourself."

Crowds, noise, excitement, and the biggest procession Vitorr had ever seen. It was this display, more than any other factor, which had made him land the sphere and mingle with the enthusiastic people thronging the long straight road. Machines, their purpose unknown to him, crawled by.

181

Motorised vehicles. Marching men. And everywhere flags, bright and exultant, each with a proud emblem on a scarlet background.

In sheer joy Vitorr threw his mind open to the crowd - and froze in disbelief. The procession was dedicated to war - the machines were instruments of destruction, and so too were the uniformed men. The people awaited their leader, who had made their country strong and ready to fight. Their collective consciousness, nonconversant but powerful, enticed him even as he tried to break free of it.

He realised, then, what he had done. The infants of his world were open to all thoughts and impressions until they learnt to focus their minds. His charges could not screen anything out, as he was doing. They would absorb it all, and their personalities would be irrevocably changed. And what of the sphere? It was only lightly concealed. What if this warrior race found it?

Even as he gathered the children about him and prepared to flee, a man accosted him, uttering a stream of words in his brusque alien tongue. Vitorr understood that some kind of moving picture image was being made, to record the day for posterity. He was being asked - no, ordered - to take the little ones and stand in the front row. Their appearance, their pale eyes and blond hair, seemed to be the cause of this unwelcome attention. Strephin, sensing danger, began to cry. The man uttered some epithet, slapped him and shoved him in the required direction.

And so they took their place and waited, trapped, while the people prepared to welcome their hero. Presently Vitorr saw the approach of more vehicles and a figure standing within the leading car, acknowledging the crowd's wild cheers with a nonchalant wave of his arm. Nearby, the recording apparatus shifted and prowled, surveying the spectators with its dispassionate glass lens.

"Smile! Look happy!" Vitorr urged his young companions. "Do as the others do."

The hero had alighted from his car, flanked by his officials. He was slowly making his way toward the little group, frequently pausing to exchange greetings or grasp someone's hand. Vitorr knew he would have to confront this man. Resolutely he composed his features into some semblance of calm, put his arms protectively around the children, and waited.

Zenzie gave a shiver and opened her eyes. The contact had been light, deliberately so, but the sinister pageant had still unnerved her. "Was that all?" she asked Rietta shakily. "Did the tyrant speak to them? "

"I don't know. Vitorr couldn't, or wouldn't, tell me. I've no idea how they got away, either."

"The planet.... was it the Hellas world? Laura's world?"

"I never knew which planet it was," Rietta said. "It was best that I didn't. At my insistence, Vitorr went back to the spaceport to destroy the evidence. He got rid of the flight log and put the programme crystal back where he'd found it. No one saw him."

Zenzie's eyes suddenly blazed. "How could he have been such an idiot?" she cried. "Those poor babies ..."

183

"Do you see, now, why Alendis became the way he is?" asked Rietta softly.

"Yes. Discords, yes." Zenzie sounded infinitely sad. "Those flags. He tried to copy them."

"Subliminally. The device isn't the same, but he was close."

"And Vitorr's death? Did Alendis kill him to protect his secret?"

"Alendis has no conscious memory of anything that happened. When he first became obsessed with conquest, Vitorr and I confronted him and tried to remind him of the truth. He accused us of sedition and flew into a rage. Vitorr tried to calm him down, Alendis pushed him and he fell backwards. The window was behind him." Rietta paused. "So there you have it: two ruined mentalities. Alendis wants a race of conquerors and doesn't know why; Strephin offers violence because violence was done to him. And there still remains the matter of the third child. I've never discovered who he was, nor how he was affected."

"Tralvar was the third one, surely?"

"No," said Rietta emphatically. "Tralvar was in hospital at the time, and I was his nurse. He'd burnt his hand rather badly."

"In the forest fire?"

"No, some domestic incident. He was very accident-prone as a child."

"Well, if you're sure he wasn't the one," began Zenzie dubiously.

"I *am* sure. Don't be misled into thinking that Tralvar's like the others. He simply wanted to create new things, and Alendis took advantage of that."

184

She paused again, deliberating. "Tralvar regrets what he's done, but Alendis won't let him go. You might be able to effect his release."

Zenzie looked up searchingly. "Does Tralvar confide in you often?"

"As often as he dares."

"Does he ever mention Tristell? Does he know anything about her death?"

Rietta fought down a flash of anger. "Tralvar hasn't spoken of Tristell since she died. If you suspect a plot, Alendis is the one to enlighten you."

Zenzie stood up abruptly. "I'll go back to him."

"Because of Tristell? Have I given you no other motive?"

"Do motives matter?" countered Zenzie. "I'm going back. That's what you wanted, isn't it?" Then, more quietly, "I'll try and get through to him. I promise."

Alendis sat at his desk, head bowed, fists clenched against his forehead. Zenzie, Tralvar, Strephin - it seemed he'd had verbal battles with everyone today, and the morning was scarcely over. His head ached remorselessly. One of the scattered pilif sweets had rolled into a corner of the desk; he retrieved it and chewed it slowly, feeling his tension lessen somewhat as the liman extract took effect. His despondency, however, did not leave him. For once, his dream of a strong heroic world began to seem hopeless.

"Zenzie, my little flame," he whispered. If only she'd accepted him! With her at his side, he could surely have succeeded. The people would have loved her and, for her, unlocked the power that had always been theirs.

An errant droplet trickled down his cheek and fell with a gentle splash on the document he'd been writing. Absently he watched as the ink began to run. For a little longer he maintained his dignity; then, at last, gave up the unequal struggle and surrendered to the luxury of tears. And it was in this state that Zenzie found him when she tiptoed back through the ornate double doors. Instinctively, compassionately, she offered her thoughts, intending only to give comfort. But after the initial contact she was lost, overwhelmed by impulses she couldn't define. Total unity was established almost before she realised it. Her promise to Rietta was forgotten, so was Idenion, so was everything except the bizarre and fascinating mind of Alendis. There was no way to describe, even to herself, this enigma; this, the nucleus of all his ambitions, a vision at once beautiful and terrible. Beautiful because his infant self had encountered splendour as well as corruption, and terrible because of the chill of loneliness - the knowledge that he, whatever power he might wield, was unloved.

The bond suddenly dissolved. Physically, they hadn't even touched. Zenzie knelt by his side, her head uplifted like a flower seeking the sun. "No!" she cried. "You're not alone, not anymore."

"So," said Alendis quietly, "it would seem." His expression was cold, despite his tearstained face, and Zenzie felt a momentary dismay. But she now knew there was latent good in him. She'd try to bring it forth: she had to try.

186

Chapter Seven

After Laura's fourth song, Melor sensibly dismissed the scolia; but far from being despondent, they trooped into the street and struck up an impromptu dance tune for the patient spectators. Laura thought she could hear traces of "Lo Here the Gentle Lark" in the melody. The crowd at the window had swiftly dispersed, hastening after the music, and the courtyard was empty again. Dena pushed back the folding doors to admit air into the hall, dispelling the accumulated stuffiness and the odour of sweet sticky instrument polish.

"I don't seem to have made such an impression this time," Laura commented.

"You may think that, but you don't know these people," Dena replied earnestly. "It's been so long since they absorbed music at its best. Naturally they'll follow it. *You* inspired the students to regenerate the lattice, and no-one will forget that."

Laura went to the archway which led onto the street, and looked out. The merrymakers had assembled in a nearby square, but her view was partially obscured by more arches. There seemed to be a type of country dance in progress, with the participants - all girls - unfurling colourful streamers.

"A homage to harmony," Dena explained. "It's part of our open air festival, the Peisistrata."

Laura would happily have ventured closer to the dance, but Tioni appeared and announced that Essi had prepared a meal. "It's one of Asterion's recipes," she added.

"Is that good?" Laura asked Dena.

"I think you'll approve," Dena replied. "Asterion likes to experiment with herbs and odd flavourings. It isn't altogether to my liking, but since you think our food doesn't taste of anything - "

"I never said that!"

"You thought it," laughed Dena as they re-entered the house.

Asterion had not returned. Telsa was absent as well, preferring music to food, or so Essi remarked. "I hope this recipe is successful," she added. "Asterion was supposed to help me with it, but he disappeared. Shall we go to the roof garden? We can watch the dancing from there."

Essi had set a table in a little arbour of climbing plants, where the diners could enjoy a view over the town and still be sheltered from the breeze. True to Dena's prediction, the food was indeed to Laura's liking. The vegetables, sliced thinly, were probably identical to the ones she'd eaten the day before, but rendered exotic by a delicious sauce and served on a soft pastry shell. Even the liman had something tangy sprinkled onto it.

Gazing across at the hills which concealed the tell-tale horizon, Laura could half believe she was back on Earth - on the Mediterranean, perhaps. But the trees were too narrow, too slender, fragile branches straining toward the pallid sky. The music had a timbre all its own. And the conversation which ebbed and flowed about her was a constant affirmation of her alien surroundings. She listened without comprehension, intrigued by the sibilant grace of the language, already noticing some recurrent words. But there's no point trying to learn any, she reminded herself. I won't be here long enough.

After the meal she ventured into Melor's library, which spanned the upper storey of the house. Idenion came with her.

"Not much here to interest *me*!" he said cheerfully. "History of the scolia, history of music, design of instruments. Boring! But fascinating to you, of course."

"It would be, if I could understand it," Laura said ruefully, and contented herself with examining the fabric of the books. It was paper of a sort, but with a slightly metallic sheen. She found some illustrations: not photographs, but stylised drawings which looked as though they'd been hand tinted. The print itself reminded her of shorthand, all lines and hooks.

"Don't you have photography?" she asked Idenion.

"Oh, yes," he answered after a pause to clarify the word. "We can do that. But it isn't art!" He paused again. "We don't put much value on trapped images. They're only part of the truth."

"Like recorded sound," Laura commented. "Speaking of sound, what's happened to the music? It's gone all quiet out there."

Idenion wasn't listening - at least, not to her.

"Something's wrong, isn't it?" Laura persisted.

"Tralvar's here, in a spacecraft," Idenion said, mildly perturbed. "He's frightened the scolia - told them to stay put where he can see them. They haven't, of course. They're scattering. Here comes Telsa."

Laura looked out of the small dusty window just in time to see the girl dart through the courtyard and up an outside stair to her family. "Why would Tralvar pick on the scolia? Dena said he'd never harm them."

"He wouldn't; he just has this habit of scaring people," Idenion replied. "He was probably looking for us."

"Surely he knows where we are?"

"He does now." Idenion began to climb the steps to the roof garden. "Come on - we'd better show ourselves."

We're being rounded up, Laura thought. It had to happen, I suppose.

She emerged onto the roof and looked about swiftly. The family was clustered in a tight knot by the stairwell. On the table the cloth was askew, and an overturned sauce boat dripped its dregs onto the tiled floor. A short distance away, scarcely at rooftop height, a sphere was hovering. As she watched, it began to move slowly toward Melor's house.

Curiosity outweighed her nervousness. She'd not seen a sphere in flight before, and hadn't realised they rotated - not that this one was spinning very fast. As it approached, she noticed a patch of colour on the hull - possibly on or near the hatch. It was the same yellow symbol she'd seen on the Drive access plate, but this time with an oblique blue line through it.

"That means it isn't spaceworthy," Idenion said,

beside her. "I remember that sphere. Tralvar often used it in the past, to travel between cities -"

"Up to no good, of course," Melor put in sarcastically.

" - and then it vanished," Idenion continued. "I assumed he'd scrapped it."

The sphere reached their position, paused, then made a swift curtsey and rose high above their heads.

"What's he doing? There's no room to land here," Laura said, her voice a little shrill. No-one answered. As she gazed up at the innocuous white shape an opening appeared in the base, dilating like the pupil of an eye. Then a hand suddenly yanked her sideways, and she realised she was alone on the roof apart from Idenion.

"Downstairs and outside. Hurry!" he ordered. "Didn't he give you a warning? No, of course he didn't. He never goes offworld, so he probably can't speak to you."

Laura stumbled down both flights of stairs in his wake. The others were already in the newly-deserted street. Essi's eyes were brimming with tears. Melor's expression was unreadable.

"What...?" Laura began faintly.

"He has another of his therite devices," Melor told her. "He plans to cast it from the sphere and destroy my home."

"You mean he's got a bomb?" cried Laura. "Oh, Melor, this is all my fault!"

"No, it's mine," he replied wearily. "Now you'll see where Tralvar's loyalties lie!" Then, almost to himself: "I can't believe this. The instruments ... my books..."

"Idenion, talk to Tralvar," Laura urged. "He'll listen to you, won't he? "

"I doubt it," Idenion said without much optimism.

Tralvar's reply was raw with agitation. +Do you think I *want* to do this? My instructions were to bomb the house with Melor in it+

+Then stop this *now*!+

+I can't. If I do nothing, Alendis will harm Halon and Jarras. I'll give you one astal to clear the area+

Idenion articulated this for Laura's benefit.

"This is so unworthy of him," lamented Dena as they retreated into the next street.

"He has made his choice," stated Melor.

Essi dried her eyes and tried to speak brightly to Tioni, who clearly had no idea what was going on. Only Telsa said nothing.

Laura, feeling more guilty than ever, tried again. "Are you just going to stand here and let him wreck your house?" she demanded. "Alendis can knock people unconscious by an act of will, and he's only one man. There are six of you. Surely if you linked your minds together, you could drive Tralvar away?"

"You mean, form a lattice?" asked Telsa. It was the first time she had used English.

"Yes!" Laura replied, although she wasn't at all sure what she *did* mean.

"I will conduct this," Telsa said calmly. "To help my father."

"She's calling the scolia!" Dena whispered in

192

amazement. "They're forming up - they're going to do it!"

"But they're not here," Laura hissed back.

"They don't have to be," Dena said. "Their minds are with her."

"We have contacted Tralvar," Telsa announced. "He is angry but he cannot force us away. What should we do next?"

"Er... tell him to drop the bomb in an open space," Laura suggested.

Telsa didn't waste time on a spoken reply. An eerie silence fell.

To Laura, everything had assumed a dream-like slowness. The leisurely way Tralvar was preparing to deliver his incendiary device; the Celestrians' oddly muted reaction to the threat; the scolia's unheard and unseen challenge. It seemed so unlikely that severe, studious Telsa could summon a counter-attack. It was unlikelier still that she'd even try. But Laura had reckoned without the girl's contempt for Tralvar and the scolia's loyalty to Melor. Slowly Tralvar's vessel moved away, back the way it had come, until with a suddenness that startled them all - even Laura, who believed she was prepared for it - the underbelly of the sphere spat fire and something fell twisting and moaning into the scrublands at the edge of the town. The explosion tore the air; a medley of echoes rebounded from the hills.

Telsa, however, did not flinch. She seemed unaware that the bomb had detonated. Her eyes were half-closed, her face a furrowed mask. A dark red blister was appearing on her lip where she'd bitten it.

"They haven't let him go," said Idenion, perplexed.

The sphere was returning.

"Watch out - he's coming back!" Laura shouted.

"The lattice is enticing him," Dena said dreamily.

The sphere swooped over their heads and back again, ever descending. Its rotation had become erratic. It tried to hover, then tilted dangerously.

"He's losing control of it!" gasped Idenion. He turned swiftly to Telsa and shook her hard, then, when that didn't work, slapped her. Dena and Melor gave protesting cries as the lattice fell apart. A mutual wail signified the scolia's distress, and everyone save Laura winced.

Freed from the numbing effects of the lattice, Tralvar did his best to land the stalled craft. He tried to reach the square where the celebration had been, knowing it was now deserted. But his vision kept blurring over and his hands were leaden on the controls. He came in at an angle, falling short of the square and smashing through an arch to reach it. Still spinning, the sphere skittered across the flagstones, demolished an ornamental fountain and came to rest embedded in a low wall.

The dust slowly settled in the square, and a few bedraggled streamers blew about the craft and its attendant debris. After a moment, one of Tralvar's own safety features caused the hatch to unseal. Of Tralvar himself, there was no sign.

***

194

"Well, Zenzie?" asked Alendis lazily. "Have you learnt anything today?"

"How to see myself through your eyes," she responded, gazing upward. Her own image stared back from the huge mirror above Alendis' bed.

"You don't sound entirely happy about it," he observed.

"I'd rather see myself in your mind," she admitted. "All these mirrors.... it's a bit daunting."

"If you're going to be my partner, you'll have to get used to it," said Alendis, stretching luxuriantly and watching himself doing so. "Cherish your own beauty, my little flame."

"I still don't think I'm beautiful," Zenzie confessed, ill at ease with such overt hedonism. She tucked some folds of the bedspread around herself, trying not to notice the design on it - the same as on the flags, albeit gold and silver to match the decor. A spiral galaxy, Alendis had explained: a symbol of hope for their race to aspire to. A convincing story - except that she knew otherwise.

She glanced sideways at his quiescent form. From the moment they'd entered into unity, he must have known about her meeting with Rietta. Why didn't he care?

"Rietta talks the silliest nonsense," he said lightly, perceiving her unshared thought by some arcane means. "But it brought you to me, so I've decided not to be angry.... this time."

"When shall we register our pairbond?" asked Zenzie, changing the subject. Alendis was so long in answering that she began to wonder if, after all, she'd merely been a diversion.

"We'll visit the registry soon," he assured her after a second prompting. Then, deliberately: "First I must ascertain whether you're still Idenion's wife, or his widow."

"*What*?" Zenzie bounded upright, losing the bedspread. "You promised he'd be safe! If anything's happened to him I'll never forgive you!"

"I don't suppose he'll forgive *you*, either, for what you've just done." The merest hint of a smile touched Alendis' lips.

"Are you teasing me?" Zenzie demanded tearfully. "You are, aren't you? I'd have seen it in your thoughts if you were planning to harm him."

"Would you?" Alendis inquired coolly. "Did you perceive all of me, then, while delirious with unity? I think not. Especially when you shied away from aught concerning Idenion."

"I didn't," Zenzie protested.

"Oh, but you did. Guilt, perhaps." Alendis gave a self-satisfied smirk. "However," he continued, "I suspect you have nothing to worry about. I sent Tralvar to deal severely with Melor - as severely as a cargo of therite would allow - but I doubt if he's carried out my order."

"Why would he disobey you?"

"Why indeed? He's grown rebellious, dear girl. It's impossible to trust him anymore. In fact, I regard him as a potential menace."

"Might this have something to do with Tristell?" ventured Zenzie.

"It might." Alendis gave her a challenging stare.

Zenzie didn't feel quite bold enough to pursue that line of questioning. "Tralvar can't be that much of a threat to you," she opined.

"You don't know him as I do," said Alendis, suddenly uneasy. "He's a driven man, and I believe he'll try to oust me."

"What will you do about him, then?" asked Zenzie.

Alendis hesitated a moment before answering. "There's but one course open to me," he said at last. "Much as I'll regret losing him, Tralvar must die."

***

Laura raced breathlessly toward the crashed sphere. No one followed: she doubted if they'd seen her run off. Idenion's sabotage of the lattice had disoriented the entire group, with the exception of Idenion himself, who was busy comforting Telsa. As she ran, Laura saw a few stealthy figures peeping round corners or out of windows, but no one ventured near the crash site. They were still too scared of Tralvar, she supposed. When she neared the open hatch she slowed her pace to a walk, wary of fire or further explosions. But nevertheless, she went on. It had been her idea to use the lattice as a weapon. If Tralvar was hurt, she had to help him somehow.

She soon realised the sphere was undamaged. Its smooth surface gleamed through the rubble and brick dust, confounding all her notions of fragility. She stepped carefully through the tilted aperture, and for a moment could see little, but then the familiar pink lighting revealed a silent instrument panel, a blank viewscreen, and one or two odd gaps in the floor tiles. More importantly, it revealed a morose dishevelled figure hunched in the pilot's chair.

"Tralvar?"

No reply. She edged closer.

"Tralvar, are you all right?"

He lifted his head. She had endured his reproachful gaze once before, at the Lyricon: the look he now gave her was ten times worse. "Have you any idea what you've done?" he demanded.

Laura supposed she hadn't.

"You should never have come to Tivenne," he continued. "You're interfering in things you know nothing about." His words were accented, but readily understandable.

"So you *can* talk to me," Laura observed. "Idenion didn't think you knew how."

"I may not have been off-world," he retorted, "but I've been everywhere on *this* one, starting at a very early age."

"You don't sound as if you enjoyed it," said Laura impudently.

"Perhaps I didn't. And now, since you've assured yourself I'm in one piece, you'd better go back to your friends. They're looking for you."

Dismissed, Laura took a couple of steps toward the hatch, then thought better of it. "Are you just going to stay in here and sulk?" she inquired.

Tralvar looked as though he might give way to wrath, then forbore. "I'm taking the sphere away as soon as I feel able," he said quietly. "I'm not

198

welcome here. Melor detests me. He..."

There was a scuffing sound from outside; someone had missed their footing on the loose bricks. Laura turned, expecting to see Idenion. In that instant Tralvar darted forward and, with a sweep of his arm, sent her sprawling across the cabin. She landed painfully on one elbow. Something small and deadly smashed into some panelling near her former position.

"Stay down!" yelled Tralvar, just as another missile spanged against the sphere's hull. Laura watched in alarm as he leapt to the hatch and discharged the contents of a small silver handgun at a fleeing figure.

"He got away," he commented, returning to Laura's side. Belatedly she began to tremble. He raised her up and put an arm round her awkwardly. "It's all right. He only had two shots."

"And you're the expert on such things," said Laura shakily, pulling away and regarding him with an air of mistrust.

"Laura, this isn't what you think. I haven't gone round handing out weapons, and I wasn't carrying this one in case I failed with the therite. I made them, yes, but someone stole the prototype from my workshop. I hid the other one on the sphere for safekeeping."

"And used it at the first opportunity," said Melor from just inside the hatchway. His voice shook, as in anger or fear.

"He was protecting me, Melor," said Laura earnestly.

"Is that what he calls it?" responded Melor in

199

the same ragged tone. "Come away from him. Come away *now*!" And he grabbed Laura by her sore arm, dragged her outside and thrust her at Idenion.

"I didn't need rescuing!" she shouted at them both. Idenion pointed wordlessly; she followed his gaze and was instantly silenced.

A little way off, Essi was kneeling by a small be-ribboned bundle. Tioni. Melor reached his wife's side and extended an ineffectual hand to touch her shoulder. Tralvar stumbled across to the group and tried to examine the inert child. Melor pushed him away.

"Don't look too closely, Laura," Idenion murmured. "There's nothing we can do. Tioni's dead."

"Oh, Idenion - did Tralvar ...?"

"He had the means," Idenion said grimly.

Some spectators had at last ventured out in twos and threes. Most of them were staring at Tralvar in shocked surmise. He railed at them, to little effect; then, almost in desperation, turned to Laura.

"It wasn't me!"

She eyed him doubtfully.

"Chaos, girl, I'll prove it!" He propelled her toward the ruined arch, Idenion in wary attendance. "I fired in *this* direction, and both shots hit this wall. Here, and here. Look, you can see the bullets." He prised one loose; it was round, like a musket ball. "Tioni was killed by a ricochet," he added. "From the other gun."

Faced with this evidence, Laura relented. "Then who fired it, Tralvar? And - " she swallowed hard -

200

"were they aiming at me?"

"I didn't recognise him, only the weapon," answered Tralvar, ignoring the second half of her question.

"It was Asterion," said Idenion. "I saw him running away. Tioni must have followed him here."

"Asterion?" repeated Laura, mystified. "Did Alendis force him to do it?"

"If he did," said Tralvar quietly, "it makes no sense."

They watched as Melor lifted Tioni onto a makeshift litter. He and another man began to carry her away. Essi, dry eyed, walked beside them.

And this is all that will happen, thought Laura. No one's going to be arrested or punished. That little girl will just be forgotten – like Relto and Alendis' other victims.

"She will not be forgotten," Idenion corrected her. "Her death will be listed in our central registry and at the furnace house. We grieve for her, though you don't sense it."

"But no-one's crying," protested Laura, looking as if she might cry herself. "And *you* - you're not even upset!"

"Laura, you're swamping us with emotion," Idenion said irritably. "Tioni is gone; so if we weep, we only weep for ourselves. And that is poor discipline."

The little cortége passed close to them on the way back to Melor's house. The body had not been covered, and Laura had a brief unnerving glimpse of the child's face, vacant grey eyes staring at the sky. She turned aside, too late to prevent a mental flashback to a night of rain, wind-lashed trees, and something else she'd never been able to confront.

Essi's angry voice sounded, close at hand. She had paused to hurl some bitter epithet at Tralvar, who uncharacteristically bowed his head and said nothing.

"She said, 'Dwell in discord, murderer'," Idenion reported. "I told her that Asterion was the criminal, but she took no notice."

"That's not fair," objected Laura.

"Isn't it? Tralvar made the weapons," Idenion replied. "He's partly responsible, and he knows it."

Incredibly, someone laughed. Laura whirled to see a tall, dazzlingly fair man, his looks marred by lines of dissipation, leaning on an undamaged piece of wall.

"Strephin," Idenion said resignedly.

The newcomer addressed Tralvar in a light, amused voice. "You've really excelled yourself this time, First Scientist. What a glorious mess. I love it."

Idenion translated this for Laura, omitting Tralvar's reply. Strephin scowled, strode forward and gave Idenion a punch on the shoulder.

"Silence, poet. When I want an interpreter, I'll ask for one."

Lout, thought Laura, guessing what he'd said. Instinctively she bunched her fists. So this was what Dena had tried to warn her about! Well, she'd always stood up to bullies, and this one seemed no different from his Earth counterparts. She wondered if anyone had tried hitting him back.

Strephin, prudently perhaps, took no notice of

202

her. "And where, First Poet, is sweet little Dena?"

"She's at the rehearsal hall with Telsa and some of the scolia," Idenion replied. "They're trying to rebuild their strength and screen out the effects of this tragedy."

"Summon her," Strephin ordered. "We're going back to Alda Mexa."

Laura, hearing the names, understood thus far.

"I'd rather not interrupt their meditation," Idenion said.

"Then go and fetch her," Strephin said testily. "Yes, take the brat. Wait for me at the flitter bay."

Idenion took Laura's hand and hurried her off. Tralvar and Strephin faced one another, guardedly neutral.

"There was no need for Laura to go," Tralvar commented. "Was she making you nervous?"

"Of course not," Strephin replied a little too hastily. "But she did wish to fight, and Alendis wouldn't have been too pleased if I'd returned her in a damaged condition. He's putting her on retrace. My idea, actually. The others will be questioned about Symerid Three and its technology."

"And what about me?" asked Tralvar. "Get to the point, Strephin - I know you only came to gloat. What trouble am I in?"

"None, amazingly," Strephin replied. "Naturally Alendis wants to know all about the lattice and how it overpowered you, but as for the other matter - "

"Well?"

"He was quite pleased with the end result. He wanted to stop Melor being a nuisance and I think you've achieved that!"

"Not me. Asterion," said Tralvar, tight-lipped. And as if on cue, a voice behind them said:

"Strephin! I beg a favour."

Tralvar made a furious grab at the interloper, but Strephin blocked the move.

"Now, Tralvar, don't be so impulsive. This citizen has petitioned me."

"That citizen," retorted Tralvar, "stole my gun and killed a child."

Asterion, unrepentant, produced the gun and tossed it to the ground. "Here, take your useless toy. It isn't *my* fault it doesn't shoot straight. Perhaps if you'd followed my specifications more closely - "

"*Your* specifications?" repeated Tralvar, startled.

"Did you think Alendis could devise a projectile weapon? It was my design, and that's why he gave it to me." Asterion straightened his shoulders defiantly. "For years I've worked for him in secret - advancing his plans, unmasking dissenters. From today I shall support him openly."

"Why did you try to kill Laura?" Tralvar demanded.

Asterion was silent.

"If you want that favour you mentioned, you'd better answer him," Strephin suggested. "Alendis needs the girl alive. You must have known that."

"She's dangerous," Asterion said at last. "More dangerous than you can imagine."

"She's a nonconversant primitive," Strephin declared. "What harm could she possibly do us? You'd better put aside these notions, friend - at least until Alendis has finished with her. Now, what exactly did you want of me?"

"Take me to Alda Mexa with you. I can't stay here."

"Is there a shortage of flitters today?" Strephin inquired. "I've three passengers already."

Asterion looked dejected.

"Oh very well, come on. You can tell me more about your secret career. Tralvar, it looks as if there's no room for you."

"I have to salvage my sphere," Tralvar replied. "But don't worry, Strephin, I'll reach the akron ahead of your party." His tone was casual, but his gaze could not be met by either man. "I'll *always* be ahead of you, Strephin, whatever else you've been told."

Chapter Eight

It had all gone terribly wrong. Laura huddled uncomfortably in the storage area of the flitter, trying to balance on the webbed slings that normally held cargo in place. Idenion had offered to ride in the back, but she'd wanted to put some distance between herself and Asterion - even though he no longer had the gun. Asterion, for his part, seemed more ill at ease than she did. Strephin was the only one who seemed relaxed. Laura kept a wary eye on them both.

Idenion was dismayed that his scheme, initially little more than a prank, had ended so badly. Dena had her own concerns about the scolia and the damage it had suffered. Once on board, neither of them had spoken much. Laura tried her best to be positive. Alendis wanted to know more about Earth, and until he had his information she'd be in no danger from him. But after that?

"I'll get you home, Laura. I promise," Idenion assured her.

Strephin sniggered unpleasantly.

Halfway back to the city they ran into a squall. Rain sluiced down the viewports, dangerously reducing visibility. Strephin, unconcerned, touched a control, and suddenly the rain ceased to pelt against the craft. A myriad droplets danced by without seeming to touch it.

"Does the flitter have a weathershield, like the one at the Lyricon?" Laura whispered to Idenion.

"Nothing so elaborate," he smiled, heartened by

her unquenchable curiosity. "A shield would create a wall of water and we still wouldn't be able to see out. This is just a repeller. It won't stop us getting wet when we land."

Laura wished she hadn't left her cape and boots in Tristell's apartment.

By the time they reached Alda Mexa, however, the rain had ceased. Strephin set the flitter down a short distance from the akron - a large grey slab of a building with rows of identical windows and a disproportionately large entrance. Above the portico, Alendis' flags drooped damply against their poles.

Laura pushed open the cargo hatch and alighted awkwardly, trying to avoid a large puddle. Now that she'd seen the uninspired nature of the akron, she wasn't surprised that Alendis preferred the Lyricon.

Flanked by Strephin and Asterion, she walked with Dena and Idenion toward the gaping portal. As she crossed the threshold a set of inner doors parted soundlessly. Inside, the place seemed more attractive: the spacious entrance hall was tiled in green and gold, with numerous arched passageways leading off it. A wide spiral staircase, carpeted in soft green, led to the upper floors. People on various errands transited the hall and galleries, paying such little attention to the new arrivals that Laura wondered if they'd been ordered not to. Glancing behind her, she saw that Asterion had absented himself - something he seemed rather good at. Strephin, smiling broadly at some private joke, began to usher his three charges up the stairs. Laura steeled herself for another meeting with Alendis, hoping he wouldn't lash out at Idenion as he had before. Strephin spoke briefly to the poet and laughed loudly, causing several heads to turn.

"Don't worry," Laura urged Dena, who had started to tremble. "*You* haven't done anything wrong."

"Whereas I have, I suppose," Idenion said, trying to be flippant. "Strephin says Alendis has something special in store for me. Now what do you think it is? A sojourn in the cells, perhaps?"

As they reached the first landing, Laura felt her arm seized. It was Tralvar, still grimy from his exploits in Tivenne.

"You're to come with me," he said: and despite her protests she was parted from the others. Tralvar marched her along corridors and down flights of back stairs into the lower levels of the building, finally halting outside a nondescript door.

"Wait there," he ordered, dashing inside and returning almost instantly with an oversized key. He proceeded to unlock an adjacent door with it, while Laura, who hadn't expected to see locks *or* keys, peered nervously over his shoulder.

"Idenion said there were cells. You're not going to put me in one, are you?"

"I might, if you don't behave," Tralvar replied laconically.

"Why, it's just an ordinary apartment!" Laura exclaimed as the door swung open. "I thought it would be - "

"I know what you thought," Tralvar cut in swiftly. "Just *stop* thinking it. If Alendis finds out - "

"I can't help what I think," began Laura heatedly, when a querulous voice called her name and Halon appeared in the cell doorway. He looked ill and tired. There was a large bruise on his cheekbone and his right arm hung uselessly at his side.

"Halon, what happened to you?" Laura gasped.

"Strephin broke my arm," he replied dully.

Tralvar spoke to him solicitously and received an answer which displeased him. He all but spat a reply. Halon ducked past him and fled down the corridor.

Laura directed her best quizzical look at Tralvar.

"Sorry," he muttered. "He always manages to annoy me. I offered to free him and he said I hadn't the authority to do it. So I told him to clear off or I'd break his other arm."

"Are you the jailer, then?" asked Laura.

"I have that privilege."

"Will you get into trouble for letting Halon go?"

"Strephin won't be too pleased," Tralvar admitted with a trace of weariness.

"Somebody ought to do something about Strephin," Laura commented.

"Not me!" Tralvar's vehemence startled her. "I think I've done enough today," he added more quietly; and, gripping her shoulder firmly, steered her away from the cell and back to the other door. "This is my apartment. After you, First Singer."

His use of English was still hesitant, but the sarcasm was unmistakable. Laura gave him an icy glare and stepped inside. What a mess! she thought involuntarily.

"I wasn't expecting company," Tralvar retorted.

"Then why am I here?"

"Alendis' idea of a joke. I don't like it any more than you do, but I'll try to be civil if you'll do the same. Sit down."

"Where?" asked Laura.

Irritably, Tralvar swept a pile of crumpled clothes from the nearest chair. The topmost garment had several scorch-marks on it, plus some oil and dirt. The tunic he was wearing hadn't fared much better. He disappeared into the next room with the bundle.

Laura moved the chair fractionally and discovered a bottle underneath it. Greasy colourless fluid swirled in its depths. When Tralvar returned she had unstoppered her find and was sniffing it cautiously. "Ugh, what's this? It smells like turpentine!"

"Give me that." Tralvar snatched the bottle and drained the meagre contents. A little colour crept into his sallow cheeks.

He must still be pretty shaken up, thought Laura, to drink something so revolting.

"I drink it all the time," Tralvar said, a shade defiantly. "It's called resnay, and I have it imported from a city near the south pole. I'll have to order some more."

"I'm sure it isn't doing you much good," Laura said primly.

"Don't nag," he admonished. "Now believe it or not, I don't enjoy being grubby, so I'm going to wash and look for something clean to wear. Can I trust you not to meddle with anything in this room?"

"If I did, you'd know - wouldn't you?"

"Not necessarily." Tralvar's tone was guarded. Laura bridled, expecting to hear something derogatory about her thought processes.

"Did it not occur to you," asked Tralvar with exaggerated patience, "that my inexperience with your... thought processes might have something to do with it?" He waited until Laura was sitting down, then deserted her with some reluctance. "Stay put!" he directed over his shoulder.

For a while Laura did as she was told, wondering how Idenion and Dena were getting on upstairs. She wasn't unduly worried about her own situation, believing that Idenion would somehow come to her aid. If Alendis were really mad at me, she thought, he wouldn't have allowed me so much freedom.

The sounds of distant splashing went on and on. Finally Laura gave way to temptation and began to explore the room, stumbling over discarded papers, miscellaneous pieces of metal, defunct light-tubes and more empty bottles. It could, she decided, be quite a pleasant apartment if it were tidied up. It was large and surprisingly well lit, the daylight streaming through a series of high narrow windows. Beneath one window stood a mysterious piece of furniture under a heavy sheet; she lifted a corner and to her surprise discovered a dainty keyboard instrument. It had a transparent lid and two rows of uniformly spaced keys. Leaving the sheet flung back, she progressed to a large bookcase full of tumbled volumes and tattered scrolls. On the top shelf was a sealed jar containing a beautiful blue liquid. She held it up to the light, scarcely noticing a small flat stone in its depths.

Suddenly, soundlessly, Tralvar was beside her. She jumped violently and would have dropped the jar, but he had already grasped it. He replaced it carefully on the shelf, then rounded on her in anger. "I told you not to meddle! That's therite."

"That blue stuff?"

"No, the stone. That blue stuff, as you call it, is the only thing keeping it stable."

"If it's so dangerous, what's it doing in here?" Laura inquired. To her surprise Tralvar turned away in silence, giving her a chance to notice his changed appearance. His hair, freshly washed and still damp, had a hint of gold in it, and he wore the brown garb of a scolia player. Instead of the usual lack of adornment, his robe had a contrasting green sash.

"Green is the mark of a novice," he explained. "And I'm still entitled to wear it, whatever Melor says."

"Do you play that?" Laura pointed to the instrument.

"I used to."

"I'd like to hear you play."

"I'd like to hear you sing."

Laura ignored the request. "You haven't told me why that explosive's sitting on your bookshelf."

Tralvar looked slightly embarrassed. "To be honest, I don't know. After Tristell's death I drank myself stupid. I don't remember bringing the therite here, nor what I intended to do with it. And because of recent events, I haven't had a chance to get rid of it." He drew a deep breath. "I remember thinking that I had to save the Lyricon, stop Alendis somehow, but at the same time I knew I'd do nothing. Then *you* arrived, and your concert gave me fresh hope. But Laura - " his voice faltered - "did you *have* to wear Tristell's dress?"

Laura thought she at last knew the reason for his reproachful stares. "Were you in love with Tristell?" she asked.

"Yes." Tralvar seemed relieved at having admitted it.

"I'm sorry - no one told me," said Laura contritely. "The dress wasn't my idea. Zenzie chose it."

"I should have known."

"Was there anything special about the dress?" Laura went on. "I mean, was it a present,   or - "

"Not the dress. The material."

Laura looked puzzled.

"I invented firi. For her," Tralvar explained. "Well, not invented exactly. I found the chemical means to modify an existing fabric. The weavers and dressmakers did the rest."

"Was Tristell grateful?"

"She wore the dresses," said Tralvar simply.

"And so did everyone else," said Laura, thinking of the amount of firi that had changed hands in the market. "Weren't you rewarded for your discovery? If you made something like that on Earth you'd be a millionaire!"

"Explain."

213

"You could have anything you wanted," Laura elaborated carefully.

"You mean like Alendis does? I don't think I'd care for that," remarked Tralvar. The two little firearms lay where he'd thrown them on the way in: he scooped them up and placed them, with an ironic flourish, near the therite jar. "No-one remembers who created firi," he continued bitterly. "*This* is what the name of Tralvar means to people. Bombs and guns."

Laura watched rather sadly as he began rummaging through the discarded bottles in search of more dregs. "Did you make every single weapon? Didn't anyone help you?"

"No, I worked alone. The only kind of help, if you can call it that, came from Alendis - he gave me some sketches for the handgun. I always thought they were his designs, but today I discovered they were Asterion's."

"Where did *he* get the idea?"

Tralvar thought he knew, but said nothing. Airing Rietta's theories in front of Laura would hardly be wise.

Laura gingerly picked up one of the guns, glancing at Tralvar to make sure he didn't object. On studying it she could see the marks of a file on the metal. Every segment had been hand finished and polished to smoothness. How long had he laboured in solitude, knowing the device would ultimately cause people to hate him? "You made the barrel too short," she commented.

Tralvar abandoned his search for resnay and came to stand beside her. "So you *do* know about

214

these things," he said, frowning. "I'd hoped Strephin was wrong about that. Who is this man pictured in your mind, cleaning a weapon at a table? Is he your sire?"

"He's just someone I know," answered Laura, wishing she could banish the image of Mr Moffat lovingly polishing his shotgun. "He's a gamekeeper. And my uncle belongs to a gun club. He took me with him a few times."

"To what end?"

"To widen my social circle – and it didn't," said Laura dismissively, putting down the tiny pistol and taking several paces across the room. "Why are you interrogating me? Did Alendis put you up to it?"

"I was curious," Tralvar replied candidly. "Alendis will be more thorough, I imagine."

Laura fidgeted, conscious of his scrutiny even though her back was turned.

"You can't fathom me, can you - First Singer? Do you really think I wanted this career? I was taken in, just as Idenion was. Just as we all were, by Alendis and his pretty speeches."

"He's very gifted in that respect," Laura said cautiously.

"Tried to charm you, did he?" Tralvar sounded resentful. "Doubtless he had a perfect command of your language. Not like me."

"You're doing very well," Laura said, then could have kicked herself for being patronising. "So if you hadn't been tricked into working for him," she went on hurriedly, "what would you have chosen to do?"

"All I ever wanted was to join the scolia,"

215

Tralvar said. "Anything else would have been second best."

Laura lifted the lid of the keyboard instrument and struck one of the keys. The sound was thin and subdued. "What's this called?"

"A zirid."

"I'd really like to hear you play."

"What you'd really like," said Tralvar, "is to know why the scolia wouldn't have me. So let us make a bargain: you sing for me, and I'll explain my failure. Then I might play for you if I think you can stand it."

"All right," said Laura. "But I'll need a drink first. Something nice," she added pointedly.

"I don't keep wine," Tralvar informed her. "I've no tolerance for it." However, Rietta had brought him some fruit juice that morning after he'd been unable to eat breakfast. It resided, untouched, in the cold store. He brought Laura a generous measure and waited, still as a statue, while she drank it. "Now will you sing?" he asked plaintively as soon as she'd put the cup down.

"Do you want the Lyricon songs again?" inquired Laura.

"No. Something different. Something new to this planet."

Laura didn't take long to decide. She thought of the Lyricon, still under threat; and of Tristell, the last singer, whom Tralvar had worshipped. Then she began to sing "The Last Rose of Summer."

***

216

Alendis greeted Idenion and Dena with rare good humour, inviting them to sit down and offering them wine. The poet instantly became suspicious and shielded his mind.

"Your apprehension is justified, perhaps," Alendis remarked, "after my rude treatment of you yesterday. But you need have no concern - I've no wish to delve into your thoughts again. It's an effort, even for me."

"I thought you wanted to know more about the Hellas world?"

"I do, but it can wait until tomorrow. In the morning I shall introduce Laura to the retracer, and by late afternoon - hopefully - I shall have the flight log transcript from Treva. Then I'll decide what, if anything, you can add to this information."

"In the meantime we'll be detained?"

"*You* will. You've been rather a nuisance lately."

"Must you put Laura on retrace?" Idenion went on. "She'll be frightened. Couldn't you just talk to her?"

"Strephin thinks not," Alendis said with a glance at his deputy, who was exploring the room.

"Since when did Strephin start making your decisions?" Idenion inquired sarcastically. Dena tugged at his arm warningly, but Alendis overlooked the remark. So, fortunately, did Strephin. "Laura cannot teach you anything," Idenion continued more quietly.

"In the eyes of her race she is without guile or strength," Dena added.

"And yet," mused Alendis, "she's had us

217

running in circles from the moment she arrived. That alone is worthy of more attention."

Idenion abandoned his protest. "If you don't want to hear about Laura's world, why haven't you locked us up?" he demanded. "There's something going on. You're playing with us."

"Now why should I do that?" asked Alendis, all injured innocence. "I simply want to know what happened in Tivenne. I had one radio message from Strephin - a very hasty one. Now I want details and personal impressions. Yours too, Strephin, if that's not too much trouble."

Strephin had just discovered a fresh case of pilif sweets. "What about Tralvar's impressions?" he queried with his mouth full.

"Or Asterion's, if you can find him," Idenion added.

"Asterion is in the kitchens, of course," said Alendis. "He thinks I'm angry with him. I may decide to be, later. As for Tralvar, he's just been through a unique and taxing experience and needs to recover. But by all means let us study his part in the proceedings. He arrived when the scolia was performing, they read his intentions and defended themselves. Correct?"

"Not exactly," said Idenion. "The performance was over and we'd gone up to the roof garden. Tralvar warned us to leave."

"He... warned you," repeated Alendis, exchanging glances with Strephin.

"Twice, actually," Idenion continued. "We ran into the street and he told us again to get clear. Then Laura said we should pre-empt him somehow - "

"So the lattice was Laura's idea?"

"Yes, I suppose it was."

"Alendis, what did I tell you?" exclaimed Strephin. "She can command. Wasn't I right to insist that you studied her?"

Alendis exhaled slowly. "Yes, it would appear so. I shall have to give more credence to your opinions in future. Now, Dena, I need some information."

"Dena can add nothing to what I've said," Idenion interposed swiftly. "She was with me."

"She was not," Strephin contradicted. "When I arrived she was with the scolia, trying to settle them down. Idenion told me that himself."

"And it's the scolia I want to talk about," said Alendis, subjecting Dena to the full intensity of his gaze. "If I'm not mistaken, Melor has twenty musicians in his masterclass."

"Yes," Dena said timidly.

"But presumably only eight of them formed the lattice against Tralvar. I want their names."

"I don't know," said Dena.

"I don't want to punish them," Alendis went on.

"She says she doesn't know," said Idenion tersely. "Leave her alone."

Alendis noted the rise of defensive anger with interest. He'd always been curious about the bond between these twins, even though he'd never thought of a use for it. He didn't really care whether Dena gave him the names or not - there were other, less confrontational ways to find out - but it amused him to see Idenion so discomfited. Only wait, First Poet, he thought with grim amusement. There's

219

worse to follow. "Don't be tiresome, Dena," he said after pausing just long enough to unsettle her. "You were with them, ministering to them."

She caught Idenion's eye and was silent.

"Then if you won't tell *me*," Alendis pursued, "perhaps you'd like to tell Strephin."

Instantly Idenion was on his feet. "How dare you threaten my sister! I won't tolerate - " The sentence ended in a cry of pain as Strephin seized his arm and, with an expert twist, forced him to his knees.

"Alendis!" cried Zenzie from the door of the bedchamber.

"Ah, there you are," Alendis said cheerfully. "I thought that would bring you out of hiding."

"So it *was* just a ploy," Zenzie said resignedly. "Well, here I am; so you can put an end to all this shielding and bickering."

"Whatever you say." Alendis gave her a condescending smile. "Are you ready to tell Idenion why you're here?"

Zenzie came forward resolutely. She was calm and composed, wearing the same modest tunic she'd worn that morning. Idenion, released, stood up slowly and turned to Alendis in stricken reproach.

"Was this the price of my safety?"

"Obviously you believe I coerced her," Alendis responded coolly. "A natural assumption, but quite wrong." He laid a friendly hand on Idenion's shoulder, and the younger man shivered. "You know her so well, Idenion. Look at her. You don't even have to read her - you can see the truth in her eyes."

Idenion gazed disbelievingly at Zenzie, seeing what Alendis knew he would see. At last he uttered one single agonised word.

"*Why?*"

"The usual reasons," she said evasively. "I'm sorry this has to be so public. I'd rather have seen you alone."

"You can't do this," Idenion said desperately.

"You surprise me," she retorted. "Did you really think we had a lifebond? We fought too much. To say nothing of your escapades on Myrma."

"I'm not talking about you and me. My only concern is you, and the risk you're running. For your own sake, Zenzie, have nothing more to do with this man. He'll destroy you."

"I don't agree," she said stubbornly.

"Idenion, take care," Dena advised.

"Take care what I say in his presence?" Idenion went on recklessly. "Why should I? He knows what I think of him - I wrote it all down." He turned back to Zenzie. "Have you registered the pairbond yet?"

"No."

"Then don't. Think of today as an aberration."

"Why should I? It's what I want," Zenzie replied. Idenion detected a note of pathos.

"You want to reform him. That's it, isn't it? How can you be such an imbecile? He'll never change. And if you go on with this, you'll absorb the very things you're trying to negate."

"Am I so weak, then?" she demanded tearfully.

"No, just vulnerable," Idenion said softly, brushing a strand of hair from her face. "Our unity has been very precious to me. *You* are precious to me. But if you let Alendis taint your mind, I'll never unite with you again. And neither will anyone else."

"Speak for yourself," remarked Strephin.

"Enough." Alendis signalled for silence. "Zenzie, it seems you have a choice to make. Relinquish me and save your inner self for any dullard who takes your fancy, or prove to Idenion and everyone else that you've put your trust in me. Let us go to the registry. I wish to affirm our bond."

She blinked. "Now?"

"Now. If you'll have me."

"I'll go with you," she said, avoiding Idenion's gaze.

"We will *all* go," Alendis pronounced. "Strephin can be my witness, and Idenion yours." His look of triumph was unmistakable.

"Please.... that's cruel," Dena protested. "Let *me* do it."

"On second thoughts, Dena," Alendis continued as if she hadn't spoken, "there's no need for you to accompany us. I'd like you to create a dance in honour of my new partner, to be performed at the next Peisistrata. Go and see your troupe and explain what is needed."

"I'd prefer to stay with my brother," Dena ventured.

"I'm sure you would," said Alendis patronisingly. "Unfortunately, I'm not giving you the choice. Now, if we're all quite ready?" He took up a cloak, placed it about Zenzie's dainty shoulders and escorted her toward the exit.

"What's Floren going to say?" Idenion called

after them. It was one last, hopeless attempt to make Zenzie reconsider. The law was immutable: no-one could forbid the pairing of an unrelated couple, no matter how great the personal objection, if the woman was of childbearing age. Very rarely, an unforeseen blood tie was discovered; but Alendis would doubtless have checked the records in advance. Nothing was going to stop Zenzie.

"Come along, First Poet," Strephin grinned, giving him a jab in the ribs. "Let's do our duty."

Idenion scarcely heard him. All he could think of was Zenzie and the fate she'd chosen for herself.

"If it makes any difference," Dena said hesitantly, "I think he really does love her."

"Perhaps," Idenion conceded. "But that won't help her. She'll still be lost - to me and to us all."

***

Tralvar, Laura reflected, was certainly a man of surprises. After hearing one verse of "The Last Rose of Summer", he had accompanied her on the keyboard, confidently and accurately. The message in the words hadn't escaped him, judging by his set expression, and Laura had quickly offered to sing something else. He'd requested something more elaborate, with a tune he could embellish, and she'd swiftly chosen Voi Che Sapete – the song she'd last performed to an empty room at Windbourne, just before Idenion had discovered her. It seemed a lot longer than a day ago.

She finished the piece and watched, vastly impressed, as Tralvar launched into a series of variations on it, gradually introducing the harmonies and rhythms of his people, but never quite losing the original melody. Then, quite suddenly, he stopped in mid-phrase.

"There, that will have to do."

"But Tralvar, that was brilliant!" Laura exclaimed. "You're really good. Why did the scolia turn you down when you can play like that?"

"Because I can only perform as an individual," he replied sombrely. "When I was young I believed I had a vocation; I studied all the disciplines for years, and entered the scolia at novice level. No one could fault my musicianship, and I was elated when Melor offered me a place at his academy."

"And then?"

"And then, disaster. You know by now what the lattice is, how important it is to a performance. I simply couldn't integrate my mind with the others - and worse, I put everyone else off when I tried. Eventually Melor had to dismiss me, and he's never forgiven me for that. I'm his only failure." He folded his arms and regarded her intently. "Your mind's full of music, Laura. Whatever you're speaking about, it's always there."

"Melor told me that," Laura said quietly.

"You've absorbed so much melody," Tralvar went on. "It's incredible just how much you've had access to. I kept telling everyone that recorded sound could change their lives, but they weren't interested."

"I heard about your experiments," Laura said.

"Failed ones, of course," remarked Tralvar, closing the zirid with a snap. "I did make some

224

recordings, but couldn't play them back. Every substance I tried just vibrated to bits."

"But surely now *I'm* here, you can solve the problem?"

"In different circumstances, I'd be happy to work on a recording device with you. But do you honestly think Alendis would let me?"

Laura found what was left of her fruit juice and finished it, unpalatable though it was at room temperature. "I still don't understand why Alendis is so anti-music," she said.

"Isn't it obvious? Alendis wants the scolia to be his army. He's convinced the lattice could be a powerful weapon, far more effective than anything I could make. Take this afternoon: Melor's students were raw, untested, but they still managed to overwhelm me."

Laura felt a stab of guilt. "You asked me if I knew what I'd done. I've given him proof, haven't I? About the lattice?"

"You certainly have." Tralvar gave one of his mirthless grins.

"I didn't realise," Laura began lamely. "Oh, Tralvar, I'm sorry. They were supposed to drive you away, not make you crash. It must have been awful!"

"Awful? No, quite the opposite. The lattice was beautiful - so beautiful I wanted to be held in it forever." He stood up and tentatively patted her shoulder. "Don't be too upset. They aren't likely to try it again in a hurry after what it did to them."

"Tralvar, I - "

"Continue."

"I don't think it was your fault about Tioni."

He read her sincerity, and his expression softened. "Thank you. It helps a little. But it could just as easily have been *my* shot which killed her. I fired the gun in anger - something I believed I'd never do." Then, abruptly: "This discussion's gone on long enough. I'm supposed to be organising dinner. Alendis made me promise I wouldn't forget to feed you, as Floren did."

Laura supposed it must be time to eat. Her watch had stopped once again, and she'd given up trying to reset it.

"The akron doors are closed at dusk, and so is the refectory," Tralvar explained. "We still have time to go there, but we'd be stared at. Shall I have something sent in?"

"I think that would be best," Laura said, noticing that the daylight was beginning to fade. Rather to her surprise, Tralvar opened a panel near the apartment door and made his request via an intercom. Were the kitchens beyond the range of his thoughts?

"No, they aren't," he informed her, "but there are protocols. You don't bawl across other people's conversations - unless you're Alendis, that is."

The meal duly arrived. Tralvar seemed unwilling to let anyone see Laura. He went outside to meet the caterer and reappeared pushing a sturdy wooden trolley. Laura began lifting lids from the various bowls and discovered soup, a casserole, and a fruit salad. There was bread, as usual; and two large earthenware jars, each covered by a weighted cloth, containing liman and wine.

"Apparently Asterion's been annoying the cooks," Tralvar said. "He's preparing a special feast for Alendis, and won't let them help."

"Much as I hate to compliment him," said Laura, "he does have a talent with food." She tasted the soup and pulled a face. "The others could learn from him."

"Don't you like it?" inquired Tralvar. "I could ask for something else."

"It's all right," Laura said hurriedly. "It just needs more salt."

"Salt," repeated Tralvar. "Say that again, and think of the taste."

Laura obeyed, puzzled.

"I thought so," Tralvar said mysteriously, delving into the clutter on a large table and handing her a crumbling white cube wrapped in paper. "Try this."

She complied. "It *is* salt! Why are you hoarding a block of salt?"

"This is tala, and I stir it into a glass of resnay sometimes. It heightens the effect."

"Masochist!" said Laura, and grinned. "Come on, let's clear some of this junk out of the way and set the table. I'm going to enjoy my dinner after all!"

They ate and chatted, mostly about music. Tralvar merely picked at his food. But the wine, which he initially approached with reluctance, vanished rather fast. His command of English deteriorated somewhat, and Laura couldn't help remarking on this.

"Of course it's the wine," Tralvar admitted testily. "My perception's getting fogged."

Laura didn't complain too much. He was still coping amazingly, considering what little practice he'd had.

"I've had plenty of practice," he insisted. "I have to work with engineers from all over the planet, and I can hardly understand the way some of them speak. So I end up reading them, when they'll let me. It's far easier to read *you* - and a lot more entertaining."

"Are you trying to insult me?" asked Laura, only half serious.

"What? And spoil our evening?" Tralvar returned.

Laura wasn't sure how to treat this, as he wasn't even looking at her. He was peering at the bookcase, and the jar of blue liquid which sparkled in the artificial light. "Must get rid of that," he muttered. Then, before she had a chance to reply: "Therite sounds like an Earth word? It should. It's named after Thera, that volcanic island of yours. Why? Because it went boom, just like therite does. Boom!" He reached for the wine jar, but Laura snatched it away.

"Don't drink anymore," she pleaded. It sounded like an order.

"It won't catch on, you know," he said thoughtfully.

"What won't?"

"Idenion's new name for our world. Alda Mexa will take it up, of course, but elsewhere it'll still be Slestr'a. Such an idealist, our First Poet. But he'll learn. He'll learn."

"I bet his poems are wonderful," Laura said

228

wistfully. "Have you ever tried setting them to music?"

"Now *there's* a sobering thought." Tralvar poured himself some liman and held it up as if it were some rare vintage. "Frankly, I've always disliked Idenion's poems. No, not disliked; that's too mild. I can't stand them."

"Why? What's wrong with them?"

"Well...." Tralvar spread out his hands expressively. "All those *words*!"

This sounded so droll that Laura couldn't help laughing, and to her surprise Tralvar joined in. Just for a moment, Laura saw him transformed. If he'd never been ensnared by Alendis, she thought, this is how he'd look. And as if on cue, Alendis drifted into the apartment, stilling their laughter instantly.

"Sorry to intrude on such an idyllic scene," he said to Laura, "but I need Tralvar's keys."

"Is Idenion here?" asked Laura eagerly.

Alendis raised an eyebrow. "Dear me, how fickle. And I thought you and Tralvar were getting along splendidly. Oh well - he never did have much luck with singers." He chuckled with more amusement than the remark warranted. "You'll find Idenion moping in one of the cells. Don't be surprised if he's a little.... unforthcoming."

Laura darted into the corridor. Alendis turned his attention to Tralvar, levelling a disdainful stare at his attire. "You haven't told her about the retrace, o pretender to the scolia."

"Are you still determined to go ahead with that?" asked Tralvar. "It hardly seems necessary when she can be read so easily."

229

"I need her knowledge on record," Alendis declared. "I want our world to have irrefutable proof that the people of Symerid Three are emergent, yet still make war on their own kind. It will demonstrate how vulnerable we are at present."

Tralvar had to concede this point.

"Also," Alendis went on, "I want to know how she persuaded the scolia to attack you. For years they've been feeding me moral objections about the misuse of the lattice. It seems they've different ideas now." He paused to brush some dust from his sleeve. "So I shall expect you at the retrace laboratory, with Laura, at sunrise tomorrow. Everything will have been prepared - just see that you prepare *her*. I don't want any scenes. You could soothe her with your music, perhaps." He smirked. "By the way, I gather you've been releasing prisoners again. Make sure it doesn't happen with Idenion."

He took one of the keys from its peg and went out, returning in a few moments with a mutinous Laura in tow. "Until tomorrow," he said, tossing the key at Tralvar. Then he was gone, hastening back toward the upper levels.

"No prizes for guessing why he's in a hurry," Laura said caustically.

"Prizes?" asked Tralvar, preoccupied.

"He's just married Zenzie. Don't tell me you didn't know."

"These things happen," said Tralvar noncommittally.

Laura was outraged. "Don't you *care*? Poor Idenion's heartbroken. Alendis even made him attend the wedding supper."

"Alendis likes to gloat," Tralvar admitted. "But bear in mind Zenzie went to him of her own free will."

"Is that supposed to make Idenion feel better? Oh, I nearly forgot - he wants some writing materials."

"Does he now?" Tralvar laughed harshly. "Then we needn't waste too much sympathy on him. He's going to convert his romantic disappointment into verse. Another triumph for the First Poet!"

"Don't be so cynical!" protested Laura.

Wordlessly Tralvar snatched up a fistful of crumpled paper and a small tray of writing implements, and marched out to the cell. The glare he gave Laura as she took one step out of the door was enough to make her retreat inside again. Very little time elapsed before he returned, more tight-lipped than ever.

"Why are you so cross?" asked Laura.

"Cross? I'm worried. Traditionally, no one can refuse the First Poet the tools of his trade, but if he vilifies Alendis again...." Tralvar's voice trailed into silence, and in fact he remained silent for so long that Laura asked:

"Are you talking to Idenion?"

"No. It's not allowed. Prisoners mustn't use their perception."

"How can it be prevented?"

"What you don't seem to realise," Tralvar said wearily, "is that with telepathy there's rarely such a thing as a private conversation. If a detainee tries to communicate, Alendis will eventually get to hear of it. And for every breach of the rules he lengthens the imprisonment by one day. Simple, but it works." He subsided onto an ancient settee, retrieving the wine jar; and because he'd been so distracted since Alendis' visit, Laura didn't try to take it from him.

"What's on your mind?" she prompted.

"Alendis wants me to explain what will happen tomorrow," Tralvar said reluctantly. "Just in case you decide to throw a tantrum."

"What's he going to do?" Laura's voice held a tinge of fear.

"It's nothing painful," Tralvar assured her hastily, "but you might find the concept intimidating." He took a swig of wine. "He wants to make a recording of your memory. There's a machine called the retracer - "

"Another of your inventions?"

Tralvar managed a wry smile. "No, not this time. It was invented by a botanist called Tyvian."

He's got the wrong word, Laura thought. He can't mean botanist.

"Discords, girl, I'm not drunk!" he roared. "Not as drunk as I'm accustomed to being, anyway. Tyvian uses plants in the retracer - plants with perception of a kind. They're called prill. He found them on some hothouse world, quite by accident."

"I'm to have my mind read by a *plant*?"

"By several." Tralvar finished the wine and shoved the pitcher aside. "It's quite restful, apparently."

"*You* haven't tried it, then."

He scowled. "I didn't feel like sharing my

232

memories with all and sundry. But Idenion's made a retrace, and so's Lydion, if that reassures you."

"It isn't the process that worries me," Laura said. "I had my memory read by a whole roomful of students this afternoon, so I think I can handle a few plants!"

"That's all right, then," said Tralvar, closing his eyes.

"No, Tralvar, it *isn't* all right. I thought Alendis was simply going to ask me questions. Whatever came into my head would have been momentary, difficult for him to make sense of. But if I understand correctly, this retracer can make a transcript - something to be studied over and over. And that's what he'll do, along with Strephin and Asterion. They'll soon know everything I know about Earth's wars and weapons. How can you sit there and doze off? You should be thinking of a way out of this."

"There's nothing I can do," Tralvar muttered.

"Yes there is!" Laura sat down beside him, pulling at his arm until he turned to face her.

"Don't say it, Laura. Please don't say it."

"You could release us," she went on relentlessly. "Idenion and me. We could go to the spaceport and take the sphere that's been waiting since this morning."

"Idenion suggested that too," Tralvar said sadly. "I can only tell you what I told him: one, the flitters will all be at their re-charging stations; two, you'd be caught in the blackout if you tried to walk; three, if you managed to get to the spaceport you'd find it deserted, as it should

233

have been Halon's tour of duty tonight. Could you tell one sphere from another, in the dark? I'm sure Idenion couldn't."

"You could help us," ventured Laura.

"No." Tralvar was adamant.

"Oh, please!" Laura entreated. "You've *got* to."

"I can't. Alendis is testing me - don't you see that? I daren't disobey him."

"You've let him dictate to you long enough," Laura declared. "Do what's right for once."

He grew angry. "Don't try to control me! You come here and disrupt everything, wear Tristell's clothes, drive me mad with your questions - I've had enough, Laura!"

"Then let me go."

He said nothing; and mistaking his silence for indecision, she repeated her plea, trying to read some sign of acquiescence in his stern, sombre face.

"I think I should lock you in the other cell," he stated at last.

"Oh no - please don't do that!" cried Laura frantically, seeing her only chance of escape slipping away from her. She had to talk him round. "I'm scared of being alone," she continued, knowing it was futile to lie, but not knowing what else to say. "Let me stay and talk to you a bit longer. I won't be a nuisance." There, that was better. He wasn't looking so angry now.

"Laura," he said quietly, "this is so unwise of you....."

Pain, unheralded, zig-zagged through her skull. The subdued glow of the light-tubes stabbed at her vision like needles. "My head," she wailed, covering her eyes. "Tralvar, I've this terrible headache - " A sudden suspicion made her pause. Peering blurrily through her fingers, she saw him watching her calculatingly.

"Did *you* do this?" she asked piteously.

"Forgive me." His voice was a mere whisper.

"Oh, *why* did you? I thought you were on my side!" She wept then, from helplessness and dejection, dabbing her eyes with a cloth from the trolley.

If she'd expected comfort, she was in error. Dimly aware that Tralvar was no longer beside her, she looked up in time to see the apartment door closing. The lock clicked with finality. Forsaken, Laura curled into a tight ball on the settee, burying her face in a cushion to shut out the light. And despite the crescendo in her head and her cramped surroundings, she was soon asleep - perhaps because some outside agency willed it so.

***

"Tralvar, I'm surprised at you," said Rietta.

"She provoked me," he snapped. "Now would you please defer the lecture and tell me if she's taken any lasting hurt."

Rietta gazed intently at the sleeping girl. "None that I can detect," she said at last. "She's simply tired out, and very unhappy. What's been going on?"

"Don't interrogate me," he said evasively. "I've had enough questions for one day. Just do as I ask, please, and take care of Laura. Put her to bed, stay

235

with her for a while." He went into the wardrobe area, removed his scolia robe and hung it up, and put on a tattered grey overall.

"Where are you going?"

"I've work to do." Tralvar made a rapid circuit of the apartment, picking up the therite jar, the guns and the key to Idenion's cell. "I'll be away for the rest of the night. If Laura revives enough to be curious, let her see that I've removed this key. That should put paid to any notions of escape. She wouldn't go anywhere without Idenion." He placed the weapons carefully in a satchel and prepared to leave.

"I'll stay till daybreak if you like," Rietta offered.

"She's not a child," Tralvar said emphatically. "You need your rest too. But by all means look in on her tomorrow."

"About this retrace, Tralvar," Rietta ventured. "It might reveal something about Vitorr. I have to be present."

"I understand," Tralvar said quietly. "All right, we'll go together. Don't say anything to Alendis beforehand - he can't do much about it once you're there." He paused in the doorway. "Now remember: when you leave, lock this door and take the key with you. Don't let anyone know you have it. No-one is to enter before morning - not even me. Is that clear?"

"Perfectly," said Rietta impassively.

Tralvar went toward the basement exit, risking a glance at Idenion's mind as he passed the cell. Scribble, he thought to himself. So it *was* Zenzie he

236

wanted to write about. Now she'll catch it!

The squat, silent outlines of his workshop were just visible in the light from the akron's windows. The workshop itself had no windows, which for once would be in his favour. He let himself in and barred the door, then transferred the therite to a sink and the guns to a tabletop. He'd brought one more item: a twist of cloth containing the bullets he'd retrieved from the wall in Tivenne. They would suffice a second time. Then, selecting the more accurate of the two guns, he began preparing the percussion device which fired it.

It was a slow, intricate process involving a series of tiny instruments. Even with an extra lamp and a magnifying screen, Tralvar could scarcely focus his eyes on the work, and his hands weren't as steady as they needed to be.

"Discord take all winemakers and their stinking brew," he muttered, wishing he could remember some of the interesting curses in Laura's vocabulary. She hadn't used them, but she certainly *knew* them. Without the stimulus of her mind, however, his memory of English had faded as if it never been. One solitary phrase, Laura's edict, remained with him: "Do what's right for once." He hoped he was. That phrase had driven him out here, coupled with the belated realisation that Laura would be in need of help once the retrace was over. Whether he was capable of providing it, he wasn't sure; but at least he'd make ready. He reached into the therite jar with a pair of tongs, and holding the volatile pellet firmly, scraped three tiny particles off it. Three grains would provide enough firepower; a greater quantity could ignite prematurely.

At last the gun was primed and loaded. Tralvar replaced it in the satchel, bundling some rags on top of it. Then, hugging the bag to him, he stepped thankfully out of the stifling little building into the cool night. Most of the akron's lights had been extinguished, and the plaza was in darkness too; but moving with the ease of familiarity, he soon located the basement stairs. He went straight to the unoccupied cell, where he intended to remain until morning. Idenion was asleep now, he noted. He didn't dare check on Laura. He hid the gun in a laundry chest and went immediately to bed, confident that for tonight at least, Alendis wouldn't be dispensing any bad dreams.

***

Kyrin, the akron's relayist-in-residence, quietly made preparations to deal with the night's messages. Kyrin was young, and took his work very seriously. During the latter part of the evening he meditated to increase his concentration. He ate no supper, wishing to keep his mind as alert as possible. Tonight, as usual, he would be dealing with ancillary matters, with one or two exceptions: Alendis was preparing to shower Zenzie with gifts and wanted a selection of jewellery, perfumes and gowns. And Tralvar had requested a fresh consignment of resnay.

At the designated time, one ild past nadir, Kyrin seated himself comfortably and prepared to link his thoughts with the other relayists. Alcis, to the east, was ready and waiting: Tylo, to the west, was late as usual. Kyrin reprimanded him gently before commencing.

About half an ild later, the easeful ebb and flow of their communication was interrupted by staccato bursts of anger from somewhere inside the akron. Kyrin tried to ignore it, but in vain. Aggrieved, he informed his colleagues of the disturbance and told them to stand by. Then, after hasty deliberation, he left his rooms and went downstairs.

***

Strephin and Asterion sat facing one another in one of the akron's conference rooms. The room contained a large table and eight chairs, and was carpeted in deep crimson. On the walls were ancient tapestries depicting pastoral scenes and legends. On the table was a full pitcher of red wine and the remains of another.

It seemed typical of Asterion to have chosen such a formal location for a meeting, as he was making little attempt to socialise. Strephin found him secretive, evasive and generally unforthcoming. After nearly two ilden, he still knew very little about this newly-discovered ally except that he'd been a spy for Alendis, moving in the artistic and musical circles where sedition was usually to be found. Why he'd chosen to shed his anonymity in such a startling way was still a mystery. Strephin was growing bored and irritated - a dangerous combination. Why in the name of discord had Asterion asked to see him? He'd made it sound so

239

important.

"I wonder how Alendis and Zenzie are getting on?" Asterion said unexpectedly.

"Badly, I daresay," Strephin replied promptly. "He won't be able to handle her any more than Idenion could. And when she gets tired of gazing into mirrors, I'll be waiting."

"You have such confidence in yourself," Asterion smiled. "That's what I like about you."

"If you've a point to make," said Strephin, still thinking about Zenzie, "I wish you'd spit it out. It's late and I have to be up early if I'm to see anything of the retrace."

Asterion sighed. "You still haven't guessed why I wanted to see you?"

"Surprise me," said Strephin disinterestedly.

There was an odd silence, then Asterion moved quietly into the chair next to his. "As you wish," he murmured.

Strephin's mind was unshielded. Shielding took energy and, since virtually no-one ever tried to read him, he had no need to guard himself against unwelcome contact. Not usually. Someone's mental touch flitted across his neglected senses: cool, tranquil, with a hint of seduction in it. Despite what Asterion had just said, Strephin simply didn't associate him with the thought-impulse. He half-turned, quite expecting to find that Zenzie had arrived in search of a real man. Then, suddenly, the truth dawned.

"That was *you*!" he exclaimed in outrage.

"I desire you, Strephin." Asterion's voice was quiet and assured, far removed from the pleading tone he'd adopted in Tivenne.

Strephin hit him across the mouth.

"You didn't have to do that," Asterion protested.

"Oh, didn't I? You appear out of nowhere, all secrets and lies. You belittle Tralvar's work and alienate most of Tivenne in a single afternoon. And now you're trying to screw up my working relationship with Alendis - or did all his rants against same-sex bonding escape your notice in whatever misbegotten place you've been hiding?"

"Please - I don't want to quarrel - "

"Then listen very carefully, because I'm only going to say this once. I don't like men, I don't like your presumption, and I don't like *you*. You're a waste of space, Asterion."

The other man sighed, visibly disappointed. "So be it. You're trapped by convention of course, and the belief that our civilisation will fall if some of us don't conform. Have you forgotten that sciesha celebrates *all* forms of love? Observe our ancestors!" He pointed at one of the tapestries, which depicted a rustic celebration. There were dancers, musicians, garlanded women ... and two half-clothed men embracing passionately. "They look happy, don't they?"

"Pah!" exclaimed Strephin in contempt; and seizing the full pitcher of wine, he hurled its contents at the offending scene. The ancient material absorbed the moisture greedily.

"You moron!" breathed Asterion. "You stupid, provincial fool!"

Strephin snarled something inarticulate and

punched him. Asterion hit out defensively and they both fell backwards, splintering a chair.

"Strephin, stop!" Asterion cried. "I don't want to fight you!"

"You started this," Strephin retorted, "and now I'll finish it!"

They rolled across the floor, kicking and flailing, Strephin's unshielded anger racketing into the far recesses of the building. Asterion, who fought with much indignation but no skill, soon found himself in trouble. He curled up, trying to ward off the worst of the blows and wishing himself elsewhere. Then the door to the stateroom suddenly swung open and Strephin scrambled guiltily to his feet.

A young man entered and stood regarding them with an air of censure. Asterion gingerly picked himself up and treated the newcomer to an appreciative stare. He was almost as tall as Strephin, with the same unconscious grace. But his manner was gentle and unwary, and he had dreamer's eyes. Strephin won't waste time on him, Asterion thought; but, impudently reading his adversary, was startled to witness pure hatred for their visitor.

"I am principal relayist here," the young man was saying, and Strephin's reaction was swiftly explained. It was no secret that many people shunned his mind, and therefore he often needed the help of relayists. He found that type of dependence galling, and resented the entire profession.

"I must ask you to moderate your quarrel," the relayist continued. "Your thoughts are disrupting my work. Please try to exercise some self-control."

242

"I don't appear to have much choice," Asterion said wryly.

"I'm glad to hear it. Now, with your leave, I'll return to my duties."

"We don't grant you leave," Strephin said. "Do we, Teri?"

"Indeed not," said Asterion softly, thankful for the diversion.

Strephin's ire was now exclusively centred on the young relayist, who was waiting with only a trace of anxiety. "What's your name, lad?"

"Kyrin," the youth answered.

"And do you know who I am?"

"Yes," Kyrin replied uneasily.

"I detest relayists," Strephin said casually. He issued a silent directive to Asterion, who discreetly took up a position between Kyrin and the door. Too late, Kyrin realised that he'd made a serious error of judgement. He should never have come into the room, but relayed his complaint instead. And he would have done, except -

"Except it would have meant sharing thoughts with me," Strephin concluded, his voice suddenly harsh. "And you weren't about to do that, were you, my delicate one? Someone should teach you not to be so picky."

Unnerved, finding his retreat cut off, Kyrin rashly decided to inform the relayist chain. Surely they'd be able to do something. +Attend, Alcis. Priority alert. I need - + Something exploded against his skull. Pain fragmented his concentration and sent him stumbling backwards. Suffused with incredulity, he realised that he'd been struck extremely hard.

"Hang onto him, Teri," he heard Strephin say. His arms were pinioned behind him as Asterion complied.

"Well now," Strephin smirked, only a hair's breadth away. "First you spy on us, then you try to involve your pals. You really do need a lesson in manners, my lad." So saying, he began delivering vicious but measured punches to Kyrin's ribs and diaphragm.

Asterion, repelled yet fascinated, realised that Strephin was quite calm. He'd made an art form out of such beatings, hesitating just long enough between blows to make his victim think he'd finished. With every punch Kyrin's body convulsed afresh, and Asterion supported him with difficulty. He'd released his arms; Kyrin, it was now obvious, would neither flee nor defend himself. At last, Strephin paused to study the results. The young man was mute and limp, too fearful even to cry out, totally unresisting.

"We'd better leave off," Asterion suggested. Strephin ignored him.

"Apologise," he ordered, seizing Kyrin's hair and forcing his head up.

Kyrin's eyes were dark with pain. He tried to speak, but bitter fluid rose in his throat, silencing him.

"Insolence," hissed Strephin. His knee jabbed upwards; Asterion winced in sympathy, and a moment later was obliged to let go of Kyrin, who had suddenly become a dead weight.

"I told you to hold onto him," Strephin said

irritably.

"He's had enough," Asterion insisted.

Strephin thought otherwise. He kicked the prone figure twice, aiming for the kidneys. Kyrin, barely conscious, made a pitiful and unsuccessful attempt to crawl under the table. Strephin drew back his foot for another kick.

"For harmony's sake, Strephin, have done!" Asterion said sharply.

"Are you going to stop me?" Strephin responded, eyes glinting dangerously.

"If I must," Asterion said. "Now show some sense, will you? He only came down here because you were making a row."

"Whose fault's that?"

"Never mind whose fault it is. When Alendis discovers what you've done to his pet relayist, we're both going to be in serious trouble."

Strephin laughed. "The only trouble will be over that spoilt tapestry. This one - " he glanced down at Kyrin - "won't say anything. His sort never do. However, since you're so concerned, I won't discipline him further. If he's ready to apologise, that is." He rolled Kyrin over, grasped a fistful of tunic and raised him up slightly, "How about it, relayist?"

From the depths of Kyrin's tortured throat came the faintest of whispers. "I'm.... sorry...."

"Again," ordered Strephin.

"I'm sorry," Kyrin repeated, then started to cough. "A drink, for pity's sake....."

"Hear that?" Strephin asked Asterion. "He wants a drink." He let Kyrin fall back onto the floor, then picked up the remaining wine decanter and slowly poured its contents over Kyrin's shirt. "Oh dear, there doesn't seem to be any left."

Asterion looked exasperated. "You don't know when to stop, do you?"

"Look who's talking!" Strephin remarked, giving him a good-natured shove. "Come on, let's leave this drunkard to sleep it off. If he dares to annoy me again, he knows what he'll get."

They wandered away - Strephin genial, his anger sated; Asterion regretful, glancing back several times. The heavy door slammed shut and Kyrin was alone. Crushed and feverish, he raised his wine-sodden sleeve to his lips and tried to moisten his parched tongue. He couldn't allow himself to be found in this state. But in spite of his desperation, the darkness which hovered at the edge of his senses began to close in. From a seemingly infinite distance he heard Alcis trying to communicate with him, and managed to send a brief reassurance, taking care that none of his pain showed in the sending.

+Very well, Kyrin. We'll resume tomorrow+ said the other relayist, sensing nothing amiss. Kyrin, his tiny strength exhausted, closed his eyes. Time moved inexorably past. Much later, someone shook him awake.

"It occurred to me," said Asterion, "that your discretion would be to no avail if I left you lying here in this uncivilised fashion. Can you sit up? That's right, lean on me. Now I want you to drink some of this. It's spiced liman - my own recipe."

Kyrin trembled a little, but accepted the flask

and drank.

"Poor lad," Asterion said, genuinely contrite. "I agree you've little reason to trust me. But I shall try to earn that trust, if I can." A speculative finger traced the young man's cheekbone. "Which way to your apartment?"

Kyrin said nothing. His mind yielded only blankness.

"Don't be tedious, little hero," drawled his rescuer. "I'm not like Strephin. I spoke up for you, remember."

Haltingly, Kyrin whispered a reply.

Asterion sighed gustily. "The top floor, and no elevators. I do give myself some problems, don't I?" Forthwith, he hoisted the youth across his shoulders. "Just keep still," he advised as he slowly trudged upstairs with his burden. "I won't hurt you. I'm sorry I let *him* hurt you."

The laborious footfalls echoed softly through the deserted main hall, then receded. Silence returned to the dimly lit galleries, the shadows growing ever deeper as the solar units lost their charge. The akron, its disparate occupants at last in slumber, awaited the dawn.

Chapter Nine

Laura was awake, with no recollection of having woken. She simply realised that she was staring at a pattern of light on the ceiling. Daylight, filtering through a window high above. She was lying in a narrow but comfortable bed, the covers securely tucked in - and she had no idea how she'd got there. Sitting up, she discovered she was wearing an ill-fitting white shift with voluminous sleeves. Her day clothes, watch and pendant were piled neatly on a nearby chair. Then she saw Tralvar's scolia robe hanging on a rail, and memory returned in a rush. Her pleas to be released - that blinding headache -

She froze in sudden embarrassment. She'd spent the entire night in Tralvar's apartment! Had *he* put her to bed? Looking again at her clothes, she thought not. Neatness wasn't a word she associated with the First Scientist. Someone else had been here. She faintly recalled a soothing, gentle presence amid the turmoil of pain and disappointment. She slid out of bed, noting that her headache was gone. In fact, she felt refreshed and alert. The prospect of the retracer failed to daunt her, although she still wished it could be avoided for the Celestrians' sake.

Tralvar's washroom had no bath, just a shower unit with a few meagre accessories: one flask of soap, a sponge, a comb, a small mirror. There was something forlorn about this little collection after the opulence of Tristell's domain.

The hot air system didn't work. Laura uttered a few choice words about engineers who didn't keep their own property in order, and went in search of something to dry herself on. She found a coarse robe in one of the bedroom closets, still damp from the previous day. It was only when she went back to borrow Tralvar's comb that she realised what was missing

from his few basic possessions. There was no shaving kit, nor anything remotely like one. Perhaps, she mused, Celestrians didn't need to shave. She hadn't noticed any beards or moustaches. And Tralvar was surely a candidate for stubble, if it were possible for him to have any.

She approached the apartment door and gave it a desultory tug. It was, of course, still locked. Wondering how long it would take for anyone to turn up, she retreated to the bedroom. At least it wasn't as untidy as the main area, probably because there was so little to be untidy with. The natural light had increased, and for the first time she noticed a discoloured patch on the wall, as if a picture had been removed. Tristell! she thought instantly, and began to hunt for the portrait she was sure had been there. It briefly crossed her mind that she'd seen no portraits of any description, anywhere, but she kept on looking - and finally found it jammed behind a cupboard, facing the wall, its frame smashed. She tugged it out carefully, and turned it around to find that it wasn't a portrait, but a photograph. And it wasn't Tristell, but Alendis as a younger man. He was breathtakingly beautiful, his expression grave and wise. Laura felt an

249

unreasoning stab of anger toward Tralvar for having damaged the picture. Then her sanity returned. She knew how manipulative Alendis could be, and it was just like him to capitalise on his looks - especially if no one else was in the habit of posing for the camera. No wonder everyone had adored him. No wonder some people still did.

At that moment she heard the door being unlocked. Hastily she returned the photograph to its hiding place and pulled the borrowed robe tightly about her. When Tralvar appeared, a little shamefaced, she greeted him cheerfully.

"I'm surprised you're still speaking to me," he remarked.

"Why should I be angry?" she countered. "I was pushing my luck and you gave me a slap. A mental slap, because that's the way you do things here. I probably deserved - " She fell silent as she realised Tralvar was not alone. A middle-aged woman had followed him into

the apartment. Like Floren, she was tall and graceful, but with greying hair and an aura of melancholy.

"This is Rietta, Alendis's sister," said Tralvar. "Don't be alarmed; she's a friend."

Laura looked more closely at the newcomer, seeing a vestige of Alendis's beauty in her weary face. "Were you here last night?"

Rietta inclined her head, but did not speak.

"Yes, I sent her to look after you," Tralvar said brusquely. "Now will you please get dressed? Alendis doesn't like to be kept waiting."

Laura didn't move.

"Discords, Laura, do as you're told!"

"Not until you leave the room," she replied hotly, folding her arms.

Tralvar, thinking she was stalling for time, stood his ground. But Rietta, who had a better grasp of the situation, took his arm and ushered him out.

"Why do you rage at her?" she asked mildly.

"Guilt. What else?" Tralvar said. "She begged me to prevent the retrace and I've let her down." To divert his attention from the bedroom, he fixed his gaze on the congealed remains of last night's meal. The girl's inhibition - and presumably that of her society - disconcerted him. It was so much at variance with the beguiling nature of her mind.

Before too long Laura emerged, fastening her belt.

"Ready?" Tralvar asked in as pleasant a tone as he could muster. "Then let's be on our way."

"But I haven't had breakfast," she protested.

"No breakfast. Nothing to drink, either. Being retraced is like being sedated, and Alendis is very fussy about people being sick in his presence. I can vouch for that." A brief smile touched his lips.

Laura raised no more objections. There was little point. "Where are we going, exactly?" she asked.

"To Tyvian's lab; it's quite close. Rietta will stay with you if she's permitted."

"I want *you* to stay as well," Laura said. Tralvar looked taken aback.

"Why?"

"Because I'd feel safer," Laura answered quietly. "I believe you care what happens to me."

251

Tralvar, looking even more troubled, turned and led the way out.

They walked in single file past Idenion's cell. "He's still asleep," Tralvar volunteered.

"I hope somebody gives *him* some breakfast," Laura muttered.

"Our prisoners are deprived of nothing save company," Tralvar reminded her.

They left the shadow of the akron and stepped into the bright morning sun. High above, Alendis' flags had unfurled in the persistent breeze, but Laura, preoccupied, didn't look up.

Tralvar led the way across the plaza, heading for one of the numerous paths which descended to the next lateral. Several people turned to gaze at Laura, and one or two even looked as though they might challenge Tralvar. But he glared at them, and they moved away.

"You've quite a following, First Singer," he observed as they began the descent.

"A lot of good it'll do me," she returned sulkily.

"I've one encouraging piece of news," Tralvar continued. "Strephin and Asterion won't be in attendance. They got into a fight last night and Alendis is disgusted with them both. So Rietta says."

Laura stole a sidelong glance at Rietta as she paced silently in Tralvar's wake. She seemed lost in a reverie - and by her expression, not a very happy one. Laura decided not to ask what was wrong. If it concerned the retrace, she'd find out soon enough. Instead, she attempted to clarify an earlier matter.

"I have a question, Tralvar."

"That makes a change," he commented.

"About my headache," she went on.

He was instantly defensive. "I've apologised, haven't I? What more do you want? It won't happen again."

"I'm not cross with you," Laura assured him gently. "But there's still one thing that puzzles me."

"What?" asked Tralvar as discouragingly as he could.

"Alendis laid Idenion out cold after the concert, just by thinking at him."

"I heard about it," Tralvar said.

"Well, when I was talking to Alendis afterwards, he said he couldn't use my mind in that way. So how did *you* manage it?"

"Alendis' - technique - wouldn't work on your species," Tralvar replied after a lengthy pause. "He targets his victim's perception. It's his speciality."

"And he's tried it on you, hasn't he?" Laura said with a rare moment of insight. "That's why you wouldn't let me go."

Tralvar didn't try to deny it, though he resented her sympathy. He wondered if she'd be as sympathetic once she'd learnt the truth about her headache. But fortuitously Laura's attention left him, and the explanation was never completed.

Beside the walkway, workers in one-piece overalls had lifted some squares of turf to reveal a metal plate. They removed this also - with some difficulty, as it had rusted - and disappeared down a manhole.

"Is that a sewer?" asked Laura.

"Of course. What else would it be?" said

Tralvar disinterestedly.

"That cover was rusted solid," Laura said. "Why isn't anyone using that alloy that seals itself? It's better than metal, surely?"

"Theridolyte is only used for spacecraft," Tralvar said. "It takes years to process even a small amount."

"There was some in Tristell's - in *my* - bathroom. At the Lyricon."

"Only because I put it there," Tralvar answered. "To please Tristell." Always Tristell!

One of the overalled figures - a girl - reappeared and ran past them. Even the sewage workers are like dancers, Laura thought. I wish I were slimmer. Everyone's so ethereal - they must think I'm such a lump.

"Nonsense, Laura!" Tralvar declared. "We're not all the same size. *I'm* not ethereal, am I?"

"Yes you are," she averred. "A bit."

Rietta made an amused comment.

"She doesn't quite see me as a creature of light and air," Tralvar said drily.

They had reached the adjoining lateral - a broad avenue of white one-storey dwellings. Laura saw some evidence of cottage industry; a stack of pots outside one house, some partly assembled furniture near another. "Where are the craftsmen?" she inquired.

"Having breakfast," Tralvar replied succinctly.

Laura wished she hadn't asked, even though apprehension was keeping her hunger at bay.

"We're here," Tralvar announced, heading for a modest structure of glass and steel.

254

"It looks more like a greenhouse than a laboratory," Laura remarked.

"Tyvian's a botanist, as I told you. He has a lot of rare species here. The retracer was only a by-product of his research, although it seems to have taken over his life."

"Does he resent that?" asked Laura, sensing a potential ally.

"It's possible," Tralvar said guardedly.

Noiselessly the door swung back. Laura, head obstinately held high, stepped inside. Rietta followed, looking more nervous than Laura had. Tralvar, suddenly on edge, brought up the rear. Once the door had closed, Laura could see very little. The glass panels in the roof and walls were tinted and let only a dim light through. Then Alendis, in an outfit of simple black, detached himself from the shadows and strolled forward. The uncertain light turned his hair to burnished bronze.

"Welcome, Laura," he said. "And thank you, Tralvar, for delivering her safely. It must have been such an effort for you." He spoke in English, ignoring Rietta. "This way, Laura."

Tralvar spoke briefly in his own language, drawing Rietta forward.

"If it makes Laura happy, of course you may stay," Alendis replied with mock graciousness. "But keep your distance, both of you, and on no account use perception. I shall personally eject anyone who does." With this pronouncement, he guided Laura past some indoor trees toward a large glass tank with pipes and cables leading to it. Next to the tank was a couch, and further on, a desk bathed in a pool of angled light. A figure, presumably Tyvian, was poring over a computer terminal. He stood up as Laura approached. He was in late middle age, tall and stooped, with long hair like Idenion's.

"I attended your concert, Laura," he said, his eyes gentle and troubled. "I want you to know that I - I regret having to do this."

Alendis looked vaguely irritated. "We can do without the apologies, Tyvian. Begin."

The other man turned hastily back to the keyboard.

Begin what? thought Laura, bewildered. She couldn't see anything that looked like her notion of the retracer. She had expected some kind of headgear with lots of wires attached. Alendis chuckled.

"Since when did telepathy, as you so quaintly call it, need wires?" he inquired. "We have a computer, we have you, and we have the prill. That's all we need."

Laura cautiously approached the large tank. "And these are the prill? The telepathic plants?"

"In all their glory." Alendis moved aside to let her peer at the heated interior. "Not very pretty, are they?"

Laura had to agree. The plants, eight of them, were dull yellow, with large pustules on every flaccid leaf. "How did you discover them?"

"Tyvian found them about ten years ago, on a planet we still haven't named. Much of the flora emitted a constant wave-form, an identity pattern, which our minds could detect. The interesting thing

256

about *this* species was that it assumed the wave-form of whatever happened to be growing near it, and we soon discovered it could mimic people too. The name 'prill' means 'mimic'. We also found the aldacite crystals in our computers had an affinity with these plants." He raised his voice. "Isn't that right, Tyvian?"

Tyvian seemed to shrink into his chair.

"So, Laura," Alendis continued, "all you have to do is relax and let the prill take over. These four pairs of crystals - " he indicated each corner of the tank - "will resonate in sympathy with the prill, and the output will be transferred to our database. And then, as memory is seldom linear, Tyvian can have fun sorting it out."

The eight tiny crystals had begun to emit a subtle sound, faint and fragile, like the tinkle of distant laughter.

"I've heard something like that before," Laura said. "In transposal."

"No more talking," Alendis ordered. "Get on that couch. Now."

Laura obeyed with bad grace, giving a yell of protest as he fastened two restraining straps around her.

"Calm down," he admonished. "Sometimes retracees can get quite energetic. We don't want you falling off, do we?"

Laura eyed him mistrustfully. "My uncle says I've a head full of useless information," she stated. "I hope all the completely useless stuff rises to the top!"

"We'll see," said Alendis, gliding away from

257

her.

The computer screen lit in readiness. Tyvian's hands moved deftly over the keys.

"What's going on?" Laura asked, her words beginning to slur. Beyond Alendis' tense figure she caught a glimpse of Tralvar, his face expectant in spite of himself. For a moment she thought of rebuking him; then she no longer cared. Eight crystals, she thought vaguely. Eight, like the lattice. She was surrounded by it, just like before, only she could sense it this time. She was pleased about that. No, not just pleased. Happy. So very happy...

"I think she's ready," Alendis said.

"How did he know the prill would accept her?" Rietta whispered to Tralvar.

"*We* can read her. Why shouldn't they?" Tralvar hissed back.

"What's Tyvian putting on his forehead?"

"It's a diagnostic sensor, modified. He can supervise everything that way - the crystal balance, the prill, and the subject. Pretty brave of him if you ask me - I wouldn't like to work with that much aldacite."

"Tralvar, stop that running commentary!" Alendis snapped. Then, to Tyvian, "Aren't you getting anything yet?"

"Nothing coherent."

"Then I'll prompt her. The prill won't sense me straight away. Warn me if they react."

"Very well. Start with something simple." Tyvian's gaze remained fixed on the monitor screen and its shimmering display of static. The jewel-like sensor at his temple took up the faint resonance of the crystals.

+Laura+ Alendis' thought was pure loving concern, a tribute to the healers who had taught him in his youth. +Laura, show us your mother+

"Don't want to," she mumbled.

+Now, now, Laura. You're not trying. You can remember your mother, surely?+

"Yes..." Her eyes unexpectedly filled with tears.

Tyvian shivered suddenly. "Alendis, something isn't right," he began.

The monitor blazed into life. On it appeared a slim, attractive woman with elaborately coiffed hair. Her dress, skin-tight and ankle-length, glittered as she moved. Her wide, mobile mouth framed words; her outflung arms denoted a hidden audience.

"Discord's dreams, *another* singer!" Alendis groaned.

"Interesting dress," Tralvar commented. "Is that some sort of metallic fibre? And how does it stay up?"

Alendis spared him a withering look.

There was no sound, of course. Only Tyvian was a party to that, along with taste, scent, touch and every stray thought and emotion that made up the memory. Tralvar continued to watch pensively. He'd once thought that the retracer held the key to sound recording, but it had proved impossible to segregate the sounds or to retain sufficient continuity. As if to emphasise his thoughts, the image of the woman dissolved and vanished. The screen went ominously dark.

"Tyvian, you're not focused," Alendis

259

remonstrated.

"I am," he answered distantly. "That darkness *is* a memory. Look closely. There are trees - and rain. She's in a ground-based vehicle. I hear music..."

"You seem to have quite a rapport," Alendis remarked. "What else can you detect?"

"The sequence is repeating," Tyvian said after a moment. "She won't let it go on."

"Then divert her to something else," Alendis said impatiently.

"I can't. There's some kind of obstacle - a suppressed event. The prill don't like it. They won't leave it alone." Tyvian bowed his head over his clenched hands, wincing. The crystals whined. "Alendis...I can't control them..."

"Alendis, help him!" Rietta cried.

"I told you to be quiet," her brother said coldly. "This hidden sequence could be important. If you want to make yourself useful, watch *her*." He jerked his head toward Laura, who was stirring restlessly.

"I am not to approach her?" Rietta queried.

"You do not approach her, nor do you read her," reiterated Alendis as if to a dull-witted child. "Just use your eyes." Then he switched his attention back to Tyvian, reaching out with his deft, assured mental touch to reinforce the other man's faltering perception against the insidious drone of the crystals and the brainless dinning of the prill. He was quite confident that the troublesome memory would soon emerge. Tyvian, calmer now, knew it too. Having restored the balance, Alendis maintained only a nebulous contact with him – just enough to share the main details of the retrace. Smugly, he observed Tyvian's reluctance vanish, swept aside by curiosity and eagerness. It was always that way with Tyvian.

The breakthrough, when it came, was so sudden that they both cried out. Something exploded, and the straight line of ghostly trees slewed crazily round as the car spun out of control and plunged down an embankment. There was a sickening smash, and silence.

"What happened, Tyvian?" queried Alendis, who had flinched away at the crucial moment.

"We...they...hit a tree," he replied shakily. Alendis was disquieted by the mixture of pronouns. Why was Tyvian so involved, so soon after accessing the girl's memories? But of course, his rapport was not with Laura but with those disgusting prill. Wasn't that how he'd discovered them in the first place?

"I still have continuity," Tyvian ventured.

"Are you sure? I can't see a thing," Alendis responded, not offering to re-engage. Tralvar, who could see nothing either, edged nearer to the screen.

Tyvian let himself drift back into Laura's past. He no longer needed Alendis's presence; everything was unfolding smoothly now. Nothing in Laura's world seemed strange to him. Perhaps it would, later, when he was no longer the channel for the information. But for now, he felt omniscient.

She had been thrown to the floor of the car behind the driver's seat, striking her head on something metallic. For a short time she lay semi-conscious, aware of the minutiae of her surroundings, but not the events which had put her there. She smelt the leather upholstery, tasted blood in her mouth from a bitten tongue, heard the steady patter of rain on the roof. There was worn carpet beneath her fingers. She could see nothing except a faint glow from the radio dial. At last she sat up, moving her limbs one by one, afraid they wouldn't respond. But apart from her bruised head, she was unhurt.

"Mum? Dad?"

Her voice sounded childlike in her own ears. At that moment the headlights of a passing car afforded her a brief glimpse of the thicket outside, the massive tree they had hit, and the still forms of her parents slumped in the front seats.

At this point, she began to panic. She tried the door nearest to her; it opened, but only fractionally, blocked by a tangle of roots. The other door had jammed. She screamed, yelled and pounded on it, while the entity that was Tyvian could only endure helplessly.

Then, quite suddenly, Laura's stubborn common-sense asserted itself. "This is stupid," she said aloud. "Think it through. There's no smell of petrol, so there isn't going to be a fire. Take your time." And she lay down again, drew up her knees and kicked the door squarely with both feet. At the third kick it flew open and she tumbled out, grabbing her plastic mac and buttoning it hastily. Rain trickled down her neck. Briefly she touched the handle of the front passenger door, then backed away. *I can't look at them.* The guilty thought

262

pursued her as she struggled up the muddy embankment, sliding backwards in the tyre tracks, clutching at handfuls of grass.

Finally she reached the roadside, and once there, realised her ordeal wasn't over. It was late, and the traffic was sparse on this stretch of dual carriageway. Each time a car appeared she tried to flag it down, only to see it sweep past.

"They can't see there's been an accident," she said to herself. "They think I'm hitching. How can I make them stop? Someone *has* to stop!" Another set of headlights approached, and in desperation she took off her mac and waved it above her head. The car did not slacken speed.

"Bastard!" she shrieked after it.

Another set of lights, and another. The repetition was beginning to seem hypnotic. As Laura grew ever more frantic, her efforts to signal her distress became more and more feeble, until finally she was simply standing motionless at the side of the road. By now she was soaking wet, her clothes plastered to her, her mac lying crumpled on the ground.

"Please," she whispered intermittently. "Please..."

Tralvar had gravitated closer and closer to the screen, and now stood next to Alendis.

"Do you still envy her?" the latter asked without turning round. "*This* is what it means to be nonconversant. She cannot communicate her trouble. Of what use is a singing voice at such a time?"

Tralvar said nothing. He wasn't in the mood for

263

an argument. In the retrace another set of lights flew by, casting sinister shadows in their wake.

"Frankly, I'm bored with this," Alendis said. "But Tyvian says it has to run its course. Discords, how much longer? She could have been there all night."

Tralvar turned from the predicament of Laura-the-child and gazed across at the captive Laura. She had ceased her struggles and now lay with her face turned toward the prill, as if resigned to their intrusion. Rietta was still keeping vigil.

"She is well, but her responses could change at any time," she said. "I don't trust that machine after what it did to Eptal."

Eptal, a colleague of Tyvian's, was the retracer's one fatality. He had apparently tried to make a retrace alone, without an operator, and had set the aldacite resonance too high.

"Eptal was a fool," Alendis said dismissively. "Nothing will happen to Laura while she's under our supervision. No retracee has ever been so well attended!"

"Look," said Tralvar, pointing to the monitor. A car had stopped. The surge of relief emanating from Laura was so intense that Tyvian almost forgot it was in the past. The car's occupants, a mature couple, were speaking to her through the window; her small pale hand came into view, pointing, pointing. Now that rescue had come, she was unable to speak. The couple alighted. The woman put a coat about Laura's shoulders and made her sit in the passenger seat, while the man took a powerful torch and scrambled down the bank toward the dark, forlorn wreck. He came back shaking his head.

"I'm sorry," he said, inadequately. "I'm so very sorry."

For a moment, Laura looked up at him uncomprehendingly. Then a terrible guilt began to seep slowly through her mind. "If they're dead..." she said haltingly, testing the words. Then, with measured calm: "It's my fault they're dead. I've been here for such a long time. No one would stop."

"It's *not* your fault," the woman said gently.

"Yes! Yes it is!" Laura's voice suddenly became shrill. "I wouldn't stand in the road. I was too scared. I let them die..." She flung off the borrowed coat and the hands that sought to restrain her, took a few faltering steps, and collapsed. The monitor went black.

Alendis grasped Tyvian's shoulders and shook him unceremoniously back to reality. "Pull yourself together, you idiot. There's no need for *you* to pass out! That's better. So, having wasted half the morning on this emotive nonsense, are we now ready to retrieve something useful?"

Tyvian moistened his thin lips. "If you insist."

"Surely you're not going on?" Tralvar objected. "She's already given more than most people do at a single session."

"Rietta, is she in any distress?" Alendis inquired.

"No," admitted his sister reluctantly.

"Then we go on. I had an interesting talk with Idenion over supper last night; he was telling me about Symerid Three and its telecasts. Apparently

265

there are a great many, as one would expect with nonconversants. So Laura should have a good visual record of her world's capacity for war."

"What, specifically?" asked Tralvar.

"Watch," Alendis replied.

He turned to Laura and, in the short interval before the prill could notice him, swiftly and surely cajoled another memory into view. Tralvar was grudgingly impressed by his skill.

The screen showed a verdant landscape dominated by magnificent trees. In the foreground was a stream with a footbridge over it. Laura was sitting by the stream, trailing one hand in the clear water.

"I love this place," she said to her companion, a red-haired boy. "But just think - some idiot could push the button and it would all be gone!"

Alendis translated this remark for the benefit of the two spectators, leaving Tyvian to admire the trees. "That was the first thing I read in the girl's mind," he said to Tralvar, "and the first thing *you* should have read, if you weren't always so obsessed with music. Something has the potential to destroy her environment - some fearsome weapon. And now, if I'm not mistaken, we're about to see what."

A massive monochrome explosion rolled and boiled its way up the screen. Just *how* massive, Tralvar wasn't sure, as there was nothing to give it scale.

"Tyvian, report," Alendis said impatiently.

"She's remembering a telecast, as you predicted," Tyvian said, a little dazed. "No personal involvement."

"But what are we looking at, you dolt?"

"There's reference to a bomb - no, *the* bomb," said Tyvian, trying to make sense of the fragmented commentary. "Some sort of test, I think they said. Sorry, I'm losing the track..."

"A little different to *your* demonstrations, Tralvar," Alendis commented. "Would you now agree that I was justified in taking this retrace?"

Tralvar didn't reply; he was considering the dispersal pattern of the explosion. He had his own ideas about the cause.

"It seems you're still undecided. Perhaps you need more evidence." Alendis darted a peremptory command at the semi-conscious girl, all pretence of solicitude forgotten. +That was excellent, Laura. Now show me *war*!+

She obeyed. She had no choice.

"Impressive," Alendis remarked after a time. "How are you coping with this carnage, Tyvian?"

"She has no personal involvement," he repeated.

"Why would anyone commit all this to film?" Tralvar asked helplessly.

"To study their methods of war and improve on them," Alendis said sagely. "Now what do you suppose *that* is?"

A small aircraft sputtered across the screen, exhaust flaring.

"It's a flying bomb," Tralvar said morosely.

Alendis glanced at him sharply. "She spoke of this?"

"Not exactly. She said you'd soon know everything *she* knew about weapons, and promptly thought of this one. She was taught about it, I think."

"They teach war to their children?" Alendis was startled.

"Apparently," said Tralvar.

"You've done well - " Alendis began, but just then Rietta gave a loud cry and rushed forward, elbowing Tralvar out of the way.

"Alendis, that place - that army - that's where Vitorr took you! Look at the flags, Alendis!"

He rounded on her in a fury. "You had to say it, didn't you? The moment you saw anything remotely like my brother's delusions!"

"For pity's sake, Alendis, look at them! Tell me you remember!"

He slapped her face, hard. "Get out, Rietta."

She stood her ground. He raised his hand to hit her again, but Tralvar seized his arm. Alendis screeched at him; Tyvian turned to view the commotion and lost his link with the prill. The retrace, left to find its own level, settled back into the pastoral scene with the flame-headed youth.

Tralvar loosened his grip and stepped back irresolutely. He'd never dared lay a hand on Alendis before, and couldn't imagine what would follow. Nothing did.

"You chose your moment sensibly," Alendis remarked, abruptly and dangerously calm. "To strike at your perception here and now would distress the prill. But later...." He paused significantly. "Now take my sister and go. You weary me."

They reluctantly withdrew from his presence,

268

pausing outside. The cottage industries were doing a brisk trade, and the sheer normality of the scene was comforting.

"Are you sure that was the right army?" Tralvar asked.

"As sure as I *can* be," said Rietta.

"So he still doesn't remember," mused Tralvar. "A pity we can't have *him* retraced."

"He's not likely to agree to that, is he? And even if he did, he'd probably find some way of thwarting the prill." Rietta sighed. "I must go. I'm expected at the hospital."

"I'll stay," Tralvar said. "I can't abandon Laura."

"Don't go back in there. If he attacks you, you won't be in any fit state to help her." Rietta started to walk away, then turned back briefly. "And make sure you *do* help her, Tralvar."

Left alone, Tralvar found a bench encircling a tree trunk and sat down to wait, ignoring a few glares from the tradespeople opposite, who obviously thought his brooding presence would be bad for business.

Alendis was well aware that he hadn't gone far. "I won't chase him off," he declared. "He pretends he's only here out of concern for the girl, but you didn't see how fascinated he was by those scenes of war and that flying device. He's more like me than he cares to admit. Now, shall we resume our work?"

"We've already gone on too long," Tyvian said. "The stimulus is losing its effect. We can only retrieve her most recent memories."

"Good! Then let's see what happened at Tivenne," said Alendis cheerfully. "And I *don't* mean the singing. Commence after it's over, if you please. I'll assist you."

Together they wrested Laura's dreaming mind away from the riverside idyll. The scene focused a little unsteadily on Melor's roof garden and the final stages of a meal. Essi, looking flushed and pretty, was handing out second helpings.

"I hear you had dinner with Alendis last night," she said to Laura. "That must have been nerve-wracking for you. What did you think of him?"

Tyvian drew a sharp breath and tried to change the setting, but Alendis had other ideas. His mind closed over Tyvian's like a vice. "Let us see what she thinks of me," he suggested.

"Well," Laura answered, "he's impressive, no doubt about that. He almost had me convinced that he could restore an age of glory singlehanded. Then I realised the past was only an excuse - he just fancies himself as a conqueror."

Her audience was silent and attentive.

"I've only been here a little while," she continued, "but one thing's already clear: you people could never be soldiers. He's got that all wrong. I feel a bit sorry for him actually. He's never going to get what he wants."

Alendis relaxed his concentration as suddenly as he had imposed it, and the trace was lost. But, contrary to Tyvian's expectations, he was not enraged. He simply appeared very determined.

"Laura represents the worst setback I've ever encountered," he confided. "Her chance remarks,

270

and her thoughts in general, have seriously undermined my authority. Idenion has turned against me. So have Floren, Melor, Halon - even Dena."

"You can't blame Laura for Idenion's disaffection," objected Tyvian. "Did he have your interests at heart when he went looking for a singer?"

"An ineffectual scheme, soon forgotten - or it would have been, if Laura had not colluded with him," Alendis pronounced. "She refused to give up her role when she was asked, and now it will no longer be enough to send her away. If I'm to put a stop to this insurrection, if I'm to ensure that no more singers are brought here, I must make an example of her." He stared thoughtfully at the idling screen. "And Eptal has shown us the way. Increase the resonance!"

Tyvian snatched the diagnostic sensor from his forehead and stood up, overturning the chair. "I refuse!" he declared. "I developed this machine to educate - to record space travellers' experiences. I was proud of my achievement. But you, as usual, came along and spoilt it - had me retracing your real and imagined enemies. I let you coerce me into that. But I will not help you harm this girl!"

"Be careful, Tyvian." Alendis' tone was lightly contemptuous. "Otherwise I might confiscate your precious retracer."

"I could build another."

"Not if I removed the prill cultures and forbade you to go offworld," reasoned Alendis. "Or I could simply tell everyone your little secret - that the retracer feeds your habit."

Tyvian swallowed hard. He'd never confessed to anyone how the prill waveforms, amplified, had become like a drug to him; but somehow Alendis had found out. And had taunted him about it ever since. "Doubtless I'd suffer without the prill," he said, forcing himself to meet Alendis' gaze, "but I'd suffer even more if I abetted your murderous scheme."

"Then I'll do it myself," Alendis said calmly, setting the chair straight and picking up the discarded sensor. Tyvian stared as he made practised adjustments to the circuitry controlling the crystals. Then he turned and fled, colliding with Laura's couch in his haste.

Tralvar was still seated outside, minutely examining a leaf. Tyvian dashed it from his hand.

"Tralvar, *do* something - he's going to kill her! He knows how to misalign the crystals. Harmony help us, I think he killed Eptal!"

Now that the long-awaited crisis had come, Tralvar felt amazingly clearheaded. "How long before the emissions reach a critical level?"

"Only two or three astallen. He's using the prill to enhance... Tralvar, where are you *going*?"

"I'm trying to save Laura, you cretin." Tralvar was already halfway across the street, and Tyvian had to run to keep up. "If Alendis stays linked with the prill, we might just succeed."

"But what - "

"The less you know, the better our chances." Tralvar approached a flitter laden with materials which had just alighted in front of the framemaker's

272

house. He hauled the startled occupant out of the cabin and took his place with no word of apology. Moments later he was at the akron and running down the basement stairs. A few large drops of rain pursued him, a prelude to one of the sudden squalls common to the Alda Mexa region.

"Good," Tralvar said to himself. "Perfect."

He entered the empty cell, took the gun from its hiding place and checked it rapidly. He'd risked Laura's safety by not pocketing the gun that morning, but he wouldn't have had a hope of keeping it concealed. Alendis knew him far too well, and would have disarmed him at the first guilty twitch. In any case, he'd never believed himself capable of acting alone. Idenion had got Laura into this mess; now he could help get her out. Unlocking the door to the other cell, he unceremoniously bundled the poet up the stairs and out into the rain.

Idenion seemed unsurprised. "I knew you wouldn't let Laura down!"

"We've very little time," Tralvar replied, then paused - much to Idenion's outrage - to reconnect the flitter's power pack. "I had to disable it," he apologised. "Someone could have made off with it."

Idenion eyed the cargo of timber and made no comment.

"When we get to Tyvian's," continued Tralvar, "I want you to do exactly as I tell you, without question. Laura's in danger. Just keep that in mind." The flitter took off with a lurch and Idenion nearly fell off his seat. Tralvar's natural impatience

273

didn't interact well with city transport.

Tyvian had taken refuge with Chale, the framemaker. The flitter thudded onto the pavement nearby and Tralvar disembarked, ready to parry any attack on his bad citizenship. Chale, however, had more sense.

"Tyvian has explained," he said respectfully. "Do what you have to do, First Scientist. I will guard the flitter for you."

Tralvar thanked him perfunctorily and drew Idenion and Tyvian away. They paused under the tree while Tralvar gave rapid orders.

"Tyvian, go to the back of the lab and open the sliding panels. I want a howling gale blowing through there. I'll go in the front way and get Laura clear of the retracer field. Idenion, you come with me. I want you to take this and shoot the tank when I tell you."

He held out the gun. Idenion took it as if it were red hot.

"Me? Why can't *you* do it?"

"Because that's what Alendis would expect," Tralvar snarled. "I'm *trying* to outwit him. Well, are you both ready? Tyvian?"

"You'll destroy the prill," the botanist said mournfully.

"Get into position," Tralvar said, furious. Then, after Tyvian had scurried off: "Discords, Idenion, hold the gun properly! *Grip* it, that's right. This is the trigger: squeeze it firmly and watch out for the recoil."

"Supposing I miss?" Idenion asked through bloodless lips.

"Don't," said Tralvar meaningfully.

They charged through the front entrance, leaving it open to the elements. At the same time Tyvian rolled the other doors back. Fragile blossoms tumbled and fallen leaves whirled in the sudden draught. Tralvar bounded to Laura's side, wrenched the straps undone and hauled her off the couch. She was heavier than he'd anticipated and he only just managed to lift her. Alendis leapt up from the console, pure venom in his eyes, the sensor gleaming on his brow.

"Now, Idenion!" yelled Tralvar.

Idenion raised the gun in both hands, aimed wildly and too high, and fired. The bullet grazed a corner of the tank. The recoil almost made him drop the weapon.

"Idenion!" Alendis cried disbelievingly.

The poet took better aim and fired again, this time hitting the tank squarely. The glass shattered into fragments and the precious heat was instantly lost. The prill, exposed to the inimical climate, furled their leaves in a pitiful attempt to keep the cold at bay. The aldacite crystals, undamaged, resounded with the plants' agony. Alendis slowly doubled up and fell to the floor, his body arched and rigid. One flailing hand dislodged the sensor, but too late: the resonance had reached danger level and he was caught in the field.

"Leave him, Idenion!" Tralvar sounded quite calm. "Come and help with Laura." He'd placed her on a pile of sacking and was attempting to sit her up. Together they tried to revive her, shaking her and slapping her face lightly. Finally her eyes focused and she smiled in recognition.

"Idenion...? Why did you wake me up? I was having such a lovely dream about Jimmy."

"We have to go," Idenion told her. "Can you stand?"

"I think so..." Laura did her best, but her knees buckled. "I feel so woozy..."

"Laura, we can't stay here. Put your arm round my shoulders - that's right - and your other arm round Tralvar. Now off we go. Mind the broken glass."

Laura's sleepy gaze fell on the prill, already shrunken and withered. "Oh, the poor little things! They're dead!"

"Keep walking," Idenion told her, but she'd already noticed Alendis. He lay where he'd fallen, his face a rictus of pain.

"What's the matter with *him*?"

"Never mind. Come on!"

Laura began to be aware of her peril and made an effort to walk faster. They reached the street without incident and were soon airborne, accompanied by the pragmatic Chale, who was determined not to lose his goods a second time. They flew east, heading for the comparative safety of the spaceport.

Left behind, Tyvian crept out of the shadows. He approached the terminal, extending his hand toward the switch that would cut the power to the aldacite. Then he hesitated.

"Tyvian..." Alendis moaned. "Help me. The cold...the cold..."

Tyvian backed away in a torment of indecision.

"No!" he cried at last, shrilly. "You turned my machine into an instrument of murder. Now save yourself, if you can." And then he wept. But he did not turn off the retracer.

At this point, a lesser man might have given up the struggle - but not Alendis. The prill had almost ceased to radiate their death-throes, making his task fractionally easier. Then one of the crystals failed, and the resonance became impure. It was enough to sway the balance. Slowly, laboriously, he reached into his own mind, temporarily dampening his perception so that he no longer sensed the crystal emanations. Once this was done, he was able to block the residual pain and restore his body temperature to normal.

Suddenly his eyes snapped open; Tyvian jumped as though he'd been stung. With studied nonchalance Alendis stood up, shook some dust and glass particles from his tunic and smoothed his hair. The look he gave Tyvian was a mixture of triumph and malice. Then, without speaking, he turned and walked quietly from the laboratory into the bright aftermath of the rain.

***

"Oh, Idenion, I wish I'd seen you with the gun!"

Laura, much recovered, was sitting with the poet in what used to be a spectators' lounge near the top of the spaceport tower. As well as affording scenic views of the landing field and its environs, it was also a good vantage point to watch for pursuers.

"I'm glad you *didn't* see me," he replied. "I was

277

petrified. I kept thinking, why the gun? I'd have been happier with a brick."

Laura was hastily devouring Jarras' lunch, which he'd generously handed over. "A brick might not have smashed the tank," she opined, pausing for a moment between mouthfuls of cake. "It wasn't made of ordinary glass. The broken bits were like little stars!"

"I didn't notice," Idenion admitted. "Which only proves I'm not the hero of the piece. It was Tralvar who saved your life."

Laura repressed a shiver. "Two attempts on my life in two days," she remarked. "You didn't warn me to expect that!"

"Be as angry with me as you want - it *is* my fault," Idenion said instantly. "I thought *I'd* be the one at risk. I couldn't see Alendis for what he truly is."

"But you're learning."

"Oh yes. Rapidly."

Laura put down her plate and stared pensively out of the window. "I hate running away like this. Nothing's been resolved."

"Not yet," Idenion conceded. "But you've made a lot of people very disobedient. They've realised they don't have to put up with Alendis anymore. He'll find his influence much diminished."

"We shouldn't have left him in so much pain," Laura reflected.

"That doesn't sound like an Earth sentiment," remarked Idenion. "He'd have done the same to you or me. He still might, if he catches up with us. I hope that sphere will be ready soon."

Laura scrutinised the maintenance block, looking for some sign of Tralvar or Jarras. "I thought they'd have it standing by. What happened?"

"I suppose someone else has been using it. We don't have that many."

"So I've noticed." Laura cast a critical eye over the shabby furnishings. "Why's everything in such a decline, Idenion?"

"It's a complex story," he replied. "I couldn't begin to tell it here and now." And as if to confirm his statement, a flitter appeared on the horizon.

They watched its approach apprehensively, squinting into the afternoon sunlight. The flitter circled the tower rather inexpertly, and Laura was surprised to see three girls on board. The craft finally skittered to a halt near the maintenance buildings, and Tralvar hurried out to meet it. One of the girls disembarked and a conversation ensued.

"Who are they? What do they want?" asked Laura.

"They're shielding," Idenion said with a frown.

Laura watched the flitter depart, saw Tralvar turn and glance up at the tower. "Is it time to go? Can I have a last look round?"

"Afraid not. Tralvar wants us this instant." Idenion sounded a little puzzled. "He says there's been a change of plan."

***

Tralvar had just discovered why the sphere's systems were off-line. "Why didn't you tell me that

Strephin had taken a copy of the Hellas programme?" he demanded.

"What could you have done?" returned Jarras. "Anyway, the programme won't lead him or anyone else to Laura. It's incomplete."

"It'll tell him where Laura's planet is, won't it?"

"That's never been a secret."

"It should be, from now on," Tralvar muttered.

"I did manage to keep the flight log hidden," Jarras added. "He thinks it's still at Treva, but I never sent it."

"Then where is it, may I ask?"

"Here." Jarras fished a small pouch out of a nearby toolbox. "I haven't had a chance to study it yet."

"Never mind: the details can wait. As soon as the system checks are complete, enter the landing coordinates for Idenion. He probably doesn't remember where he went."

Jarras began to make an irreverent quip; then, suddenly, both he and Tralvar turned as one toward the bay entrance.

"This could be trouble," Tralvar observed.

"Who's out there?"

"I don't know, but it seems they're looking for me. I'd better go and deal with them. Keep working on the sphere." Tralvar disappeared in the direction of the landing field. Jarras reapplied himself to the familiar routine, hoping it would settle his nerves.

Tralvar was back almost at once. "Minx!" he muttered.

"Pardon?"

"One of Tyvian's botany students, enjoying her little brush with danger while her friends giggled in the background. These people have no idea what danger *is*." He cleared his throat, wishing he had some resnay at hand. "Tyvian was supposed to be giving lectures this afternoon," he continued. "When he didn't turn up, they went looking for him. They arrived at the lab just in time to see Alendis depart on foot. He looked like a sleepwalker, according to the girl."

"I suppose Tyvian had turned the retracer off?"

"No, it was still running. Now, of course, he's terrified. He told the girl to find me and report what she'd seen."

"At least he kept the relayists out of it," Jarras commented.

"That's a temporary advantage at best. Chaos take Alendis! How could he just stroll away from an aldacite backlash? I thought he'd be out of action for days." Tralvar ran his fingers through his unruly hair, as Jarras had often seen him do when confronted with an engineering problem. "This changes everything," he said at last. "Alendis will summon Strephin, *he'll* tell him about the duplicate programme and they'll be straight down here. Laura and Idenion are on their way from the tower; ready or not, this sphere has to leave immediately. And I'd like *you* to be on board, Jarras."

"Why?"

"Because if Laura's agreeable - and I'm sure she will be - I want Idenion to remain on Symerid Three for a while. There's going to be a reckoning and he'll be one less person for me to worry about."

"What about you? You're in just as much trouble as he is."

"I'll survive," Tralvar answered steadily.

"Very well, I'll do as you say," Jarras agreed reluctantly. "I'll finish loading those planetary coordinates while we're in transposal."

"When you get back, report to me and only me," Tralvar instructed. "No one else is to see any detail of the flight log. I'll be in touch with you during the journey if there's any risk of pursuit. Alendis might attempt to track you."

Just then Laura and Idenion appeared, holding hands.

"You're looking much better, Laura," Tralvar said approvingly. "And now, I've a little treat to compensate you for all you've suffered. How would you like Idenion to spend some time on Earth?"

Her eyes widened in astonishment. "Are you serious?"

"Absolutely."

"Idenion, did you know about this?"

"Not until Tralvar sent for us."

"Well, Laura? Are you in favour?" Tralvar inquired.

"You bet! Thank you, Tralvar, thank you!" She hugged him, nearly throwing him off balance.

"You'd better leave at once," he said, extricating himself. "Jarras will pilot you and explain my decision."

She hesitated, not knowing whether she should say goodbye with any finality.

"Go on, all of you!" Tralvar said tersely. "Oh, one more thing, Laura."

282

"Yes?"

"You saw those girls in the flitter? As they were leaving, one of them shouted: 'We'll save the Lyricon for you, First Scientist. Laura's told us how'. Can you explain what that meant?"

"They're going to hold the sit-in!" Laura was even more elated than before. "Floren will tell you all about it. Come on, Idenion - you don't have to protect the Lyricon anymore. It's out of your hands now."

Chapter Ten

Alendis walked toward the akron with only slightly less than his normal dignity, never omitting to return the gaze of anyone who dared stare. His mind was a tangle of pain, his perception temporarily useless. Nausea smote at him with every step. But he did not falter. He had an appearance to keep up. He reached the akron and looked for an unoccupied conference suite, knowing that even his iron will would not carry him to the top floor. At least, not yet. As he opened doors haphazardly, one of his administrators appeared with a sheaf of papers and a string of questions. Alendis spoke courteously to the man, instructing him to take the documents to his audience room. At length he reached an empty suite and hastened thankfully into the utility area. Unlike Laura and Tyvian, he hadn't deprived himself of breakfast that morning. He'd seen no reason to. Bitterly regretting his lack of foresight, he leant over a sink and vomited with an energy that seemed at odds with his fragile state. A significant time passed. Finally, exhausted and lightheaded, he decided it was safe to move on. He sipped some water, washed his face and cleaned the sink meticulously. Then he inspected himself critically in the nearest mirror, pinching his cheeks to bring a little colour back into them. Only then did he emerge from the empty, echoing stateroom and ascend to his quarters.

He could hear Zenzie shouting before he'd

reached the top of the stairs.

"What does it take to get through to you? I'm not interested! Now keep your hands to yourself, you zarf!"

Despite his misfortune, Alendis had to smile. The zarf was a mythical creature renowned for its voracious sexual appetite. He opened the inner door just as Zenzie hurled a small footstool at Strephin.

"Thank harmony you're back!" she exclaimed without turning around. "Can you please keep this oversexed moron under control? I've been fighting him off all morning!"

"If he'd been in earnest, he wouldn't have let you fight him off," Alendis said wearily. "Strephin, stop your nonsense."

Zenzie turned to look at him then, and her eyes widened. "Discord's dreams! What happened?"

"It looks as if the Hellas songbird's ruffled his feathers," Strephin laughed, unrepentant.

Alendis couldn't even summon a glare. "Your concern is noted," he replied with just a trace of his acerbic wit. Then, waving the anxious Zenzie aside, he slumped into his favourite chair and rested his head in his hands. Zenzie knelt at his feet.

"Who has caused you this hurt?" she asked.

"Your ex-partner," said Alendis, seldom without a sense of the dramatic. His ravaged throat was affecting his voice, and he tried to moderate it. "Yes, Idenion," he repeated. "He destroyed the prill's biosphere while I was attuned to them. Then, as I lay helpless, he and Tralvar fled with Laura. Tyvian stood by and didn't lift a finger to save me."

Zenzie, taken aback, made no reply. Strephin

285

raised an eyebrow.

"Laura's to blame," Alendis went on. "She's turned them all against me. Do you know, she had the nerve to say she was sorry for me? That brat of a nonconversant, sorry for *me*!" He discovered it was painful to shout, and went on more calmly. "She's gone, of course. She'll have left for Symerid Three by now. There's no way to catch up with her."

"Maybe there is," Strephin said slyly.

"Oh?"

"I had Idenion's flight programme copied. I thought it would come in useful."

"So you've been following your own agenda, have you?" Alendis demanded ungratefully.

"I acted in your interests, as always," Strephin said, aggrieved. "I anticipated something like this. And incidentally, I don't think Laura *will* have left - not yet. The sphere will have to be re-initialised."

Alendis sat bolt upright. "Then we'd better go after her. Well, don't just stand there, you oaf - get me a flitter! Bring it to the side entrance."

"With pleasure," Strephin replied with an anticipatory smile, and swaggered off.

Zenzie voiced an objection, but Alendis ignored her and hurried into the bedroom. From his supply of medicines he took a tiny phial of green liquid and sprinkled half the contents onto a cloth. A pungent vapour arose, which he inhaled deeply.

Zenzie watched him from the doorway. "What *is* that?" she asked suspiciously.

"Just some pain relief," he replied airily. "I may have defeated death by aldacite, but I've never

286

been able to cure my own headaches."

Zenzie pursed her lips. Whatever the liquid was, it was certainly no headache potion. Some dubious concoction mixed by the Corayn herbalists, perhaps, or something of Alendis' own devising. He was already looking more like his old self. To compliment the effect, he selected a russet tunic which would improve his colour and disappeared into his dressing room with it.

The apartment door clicked open again, to admit Asterion. "Hello," he said, his keen nostrils detecting the faint odour of the drug. "Who's been using starfire?"

Starfire. Zenzie didn't question how he knew. She gave a brief, worried explanation, adding: "I thought starfire had been abolished?"

"Oh, it has," Asterion assured her. "But our estimable First Citizen has doubtless found a way round that. I hope he knows what he's doing. It revitalises, yes, but at a price."

Zenzie remembered. Starfire boosted the user's perception, but at the risk of damage. In the past, relayists had used it to increase their range in an emergency, only to suffer burn-out. And she knew, chillingly, why Alendis had chosen this drug above other safer ones which could have restored him. With Tralvar against him, he only had one weapon left - his mind. She was suddenly very afraid for Idenion.

Alendis emerged from the bedroom. "Where have you been?" he asked Asterion irritably.

"At the Lyricon," the other replied amiably. "There's some kind of disturbance going on. Some students - quite a lot of students actually - have occupied the auditorium. They say they'll occupy it day and night, in relays, to deter you from moving in. Judging by the noise they're making, they're likely to succeed."

"Who's the instigator? Floren?"

"She might well be, since she wasn't there to ask. Neither was Dena."

"Zenzie, do you know anything about this?" demanded Alendis.

"No," she began, innocently enough; then she remembered what Laura had proposed the previous morning. She'd talked about a mass protest. Was this it?

Alendis sighed in exasperation. "I should have known. I'll deal with this foolishness when I get back."

"You're not going without *me*," Zenzie said promptly.

"I wouldn't dream of it. Idenion has embarked on a perilous course of action, and you might - just might - be able to sway him. I hope for his sake you can. You'd better accompany us, Asterion, as you were always so adamant that Laura was dangerous. I may need your assistance."

Zenzie looked from one to the other in growing helplessness.

Asterion shifted his balance uneasily. "Did you....complete the retrace?"

"Oh, please," said Alendis with a return to irritability. "No more warnings about contamination. The retrace will convince my people of the need to arm themselves. And now, if you're

288

quite ready, we have some miscreants to catch."

***

Tralvar, alone in the control tower, saw the flitter arrive. The scanner, its giant screen covering most of one wall, displayed the track of the newly-departed sphere. It was already halfway across the Alda system, accelerating smoothly. In just under two ilden, it would achieve transposal.

He had left the maintenance bay wide open to show that it was empty. There was just a hope that Alendis would call off the pursuit, as there were no other spheres in the landing area. But as he watched, the dictator wheeled angrily about and headed in his direction, closely followed by his two henchmen and a reluctant Zenzie. Moments later the elevator door opened.

"You're too late," Tralvar announced.

Strephin was the first to emerge. "All alone? That's uncommonly brave of you!"

Tralvar shrugged. He didn't feel very brave. It had simply been expedient to get everyone else out of harm's way.

Strephin halted uncertainly. He'd always been quick enough to insult Tralvar, but had never yet been able to offer him violence. There was something forbidding about the First Scientist - something best left undisturbed.

Alendis was studying the screen. "I understand the flight programme does not include landfall," he said quietly. "Where is the log of Idenion's voyage?"

289

"Jarras has it," Tralvar replied as calmly as he could. "And Jarras is on board that sphere, by my order."

"Do *you* know the landfall coordinates?" asked Alendis gently.

Tralvar knew that tone, and inwardly braced himself. "No," he said. The wrench that followed, as Alendis acquainted himself with the truth, wasn't as severe as he'd expected. He noted the artificially enhanced perception, backed by underlying weakness, and instantly felt more confident. Alendis wouldn't be handing out any punishments today - he'd have to conserve his strength for whatever lay ahead.

"He doesn't know," Alendis told his disciples.

"Is that a problem?" asked Asterion. "All you have to do is wait for the sphere to return, and you'll have your information."

"Alendis, don't take this any further," pleaded Zenzie. "Laura won't come back. You're rid of her now."

"But I'm not rid of her legacy," he said stubbornly. "I shall obtain those coordinates and track her down."

"Oh, I don't think that's a good idea," Tralvar declared hurriedly. "Laura's people will defend her. They all have guns - *big* guns!" He extended his arms to demonstrate.

"We both saw the retrace, Tralvar," Alendis said indifferently.

"You didn't see this," Tralvar persisted. "In Laura's village they eat their meals and clean their guns at the same table. Her guardian has an array of weapons in a cabinet. Obviously he hands them out in times of trouble, since he can't wield them all himself."

"And yet," Alendis said thoughtfully, "you've sent Idenion to take refuge with these people, knowing he risks injury or death at their hands."

Zenzie rounded on Tralvar. "Is this true?"

"He can't deny it," Alendis continued smugly. "He sent him off without the benefit of this knowledge."

"Does Zenzie know what happened at Tyvian's?" Tralvar retaliated. "Did you tell her why Idenion attacked you?"

"It's true, dearest," Alendis said in his most beguiling tones, "that when I saw the atrocities on that retrace, all I could think about was shielding my people from the mind which produced them. You know what an emotional experience taking a retrace is. You must have seen how it affects Tyvian. I simply wasn't myself. Admittedly the countermeasures could have been less drastic, but Idenion must have panicked. We were all on edge."

Asterion looked on admiringly at this inspired piece of acting. Tralvar turned away, remembering all too well how that seductive voice had once worked its spell on *him*. Zenzie would believe what Alendis wanted her to believe.

"I've had a chance to view the problem rationally," Alendis continued, "and I've decided that Laura should apologise, via the radio, for meddling in our society. She should ask the citizens to accept their voiceless state and request the students to call off their protest. Idenion can translate for her."

Zenzie, by now terrified for Idenion's safety, clutched at this straw. "Let me speak to him!" she cried. "Tralvar, call them!"

"Put it on visual," Alendis suggested. "After all, it may be the last time we'll see him."

Zenzie choked back a sob as Tralvar reluctantly set up the connections.

"What do you want, Zenzie?" Idenion's face gazed stonily from a corner of the screen.

She told him, stumbling over the words. He listened impassively until she'd finished.

"How inventive," he said at length. "I'm still trying to decide whether you're being duplicitous or just plain stupid. The latter, I suspect. Tell Alendis I'm not turning back."

She started to plead with him, brushing her fingers against the image of his face.

"Don't say another word," Idenion cut in. "Don't ever speak to me again. Goodbye, Zenzie."

The image blinked out. Zenzie remained where she was, gazing miserably at the screen.

"We have one other option," said Alendis, unruffled. "If we pursue them immediately and emerge from transposal before they land, we'll be able to track their course and follow them down. If we're quick enough, Laura won't have time to rally her tribe."

"And what will you use for a sphere?" inquired Tralvar.

Alendis glared. "Display all orbital flights in progress," he ordered.

With a glance at Strephin, who was

292

experimentally punching the air, Tralvar obeyed. He fervently hoped there wouldn't be anything aloft. But as luck would have it, the scanner revealed a lone sphere in transit. "It's heading for Treva," he said.

"Not anymore," said Alendis. "Divert it."

Tralvar re-aligned the transmitter as slowly as he dared. "Alda Mexa tower to orbiting craft," he said at last. "Please alter course for the capital. We need your transport."

"Nothing doing, Tralvar!" came a good-natured reply. It was Rillan. "I've been up here all day working on that faulty satellite. If I don't get back to Treva at once, I'll miss a very important assignation with a very important girl."

Alendis shoved Tralvar aside and took over. "Pilot, this is your First Citizen. You will divert to Alda Mexa at once. On landing, you will disengage your programme crystal and leave all systems on standby."

"Very well," came the reply, after an uncertain silence. "Changing course now."

Alendis gave a satisfied smile and turned his attention back to Zenzie. "Don't worry, my little flame. Idenion still cares for you, and we may yet persuade him away from those barbarians. You *will* journey with me, I trust?"

"Do I have to?" she asked tremulously. "I fear space travel."

"Please, Zenzie. I need you."

"As a hostage, perhaps," commented Tralvar, surprised at his own audacity. Alendis was unperturbed. A bright point of light sped across the

293

sky, denoting Rillan's imminent arrival.

"Strephin," said Alendis briskly, "go down and wait for him. As soon as he vacates his craft, begin to load the new programme."

Strephin grinned and departed with the precious crystal.

"I'll come with you," Zenzie said suddenly, "but only if you leave Strephin behind. I'm not sharing a confined space with *him*."

"Very well; I'll meet that condition," replied Alendis, a little surprised at her abrupt change of stance. "Asterion, you'd better join us instead."

Asterion looked distinctly upset at the prospect. "Oh, thanks very much. Just what I've always wanted to do - get shot at by a horde of rampaging Hellenes."

"Let *me* worry about them," Alendis said loftily. "All I want is someone to look after the sphere; Idenion has the only working remote. Zenzie, I hope you don't have any foolish notions about protecting Idenion from the natives."

She looked at him sorrowfully. "No, only from you," she replied, and went to summon the elevator.

Asterion gave a resigned sigh. "Well, let's get this over with."

"Take Zenzie to the sphere. I'll follow in a moment," said Alendis. He waited until the elevator door had closed, then turned swiftly to face Tralvar. "Don't think I've forgotten your part in all this. Once I've dealt with Laura I'll be able to give you the attention you deserve - and I promise you it won't be pleasant."

"For once, my conscience is clear," Tralvar

returned calmly.

"That nonconversant has addled your wits," Alendis said in disgust. "And now, I suppose, you're going to warn her I'm in pursuit. Go on, send your message. It will take more than that to save your precious singer."

"You're very sure of yourself," Tralvar commented, still unhappily aware of Alendis' magnetic presence.

"It's a question of superiority," Alendis responded. "Mine!"

"How do you know her people will fear you?"

The elevator door whispered open. Zenzie had obviously sent it back. Alendis moved toward it with unhurried grace, seemingly ignoring Tralvar's question. Then, as he stood framed in the open cage, he smiled devastatingly and said:

"Oh, they won't fear me, Tralvar. They will *love* me."

On his way to the sphere he encountered a disgruntled Rillan, who was giving Strephin a wide berth. "Is the satellite functional?" he inquired of the young man.

"Yes, First Citizen."

"Good. I shall soon have a use for it," said Alendis approvingly. "I regret the disruption to your schedule. When I return I shall make a personal apology to your girl."

"There's really no need," stammered Rillan.

"There's *every* need. Your children are the planet's best hope for the future: bright, scientific minds like your own."

"But I don't have any children," said Rillan,

295

bewildered.

"Not yet," smiled Alendis. "I see that your relationship is at a delicate stage. Therefore I insist you allow me to speak on your behalf. I owe it to you." Then he went on his dignified way, leaving Rillan puzzled but impressed. He'd never met Alendis before, and instantly began to doubt some of the stories he'd heard about him. He seemed fair and generous.

Tralvar, shamelessly eavesdropping on Rillan's musings, looked defeated. Many times he'd been on the verge of telling all he knew, in the hope of discrediting Alendis once and for all; and just as many times he'd refrained. Not simply because of his own involvement, but because he'd undoubtedly have ended up taking every scrap of the blame. Alendis could still command a following. Rillan's reaction was typical. Pensively he watched the youth head toward the technicians' lodgings, then turned back to the transmitter, thankful that Jarras at least had the true measure of Alendis.

Strephin, at Zenzie's insistence, was waiting outside the sphere. Contrary to Alendis' expectations, he didn't seem too worried about being left behind. "I'll pay a visit to the Lyricon while you're away," he said. "Asterion's news was intriguing."

"Very well. Report to me on the extent of the problem," Alendis replied.

"Are you giving me a free hand?"

"With the demonstrators, yes. But you are not to harass Tralvar, and you're to stay away from Tyvian. They're mine to punish. Is that clear?"

"Absolutely," Strephin assured him.

Alendis walked swiftly up the ramp, turning momentarily when he reached the top. He gazed toward the tower with an expression so chill that even the robust Strephin flinched.

"Tralvar, I'm glad I'm not you," he murmured.

***

"It's as I feared," Idenion told Laura. "Alendis is coming after us. But Jarras thinks we're far enough ahead to outrun him."

"I believe I can land and take off again while he's still in transposal mode," said Jarras in slow, careful English. "He'll then have no idea where I set you down."

"You'll have to stay out of his way when you get back," advised Laura.

"Tralvar will take care of that," said Jarras, unworried. Laura hoped his confidence wasn't misplaced.

Less than one astal later they entered transposal, and the usual communications blackout began.

Jarras immediately set to work on Idenion's flight log, hoping to extract all the relevant information before transposal was complete. Laura began to talk, a little too rapidly, about the best way to explain Idenion's presence in Cheveney.

"Uncle Nat will have to know who you really are, but we mustn't tell anyone else. We'll say you're an exchange student. No, you don't need to know what that is, only that you *are* one. And we

297

can say the airline lost your luggage - yes, that does happen! But which country do we pretend you're from? Finland maybe, or Iceland...."

Idenion let her talk, knowing she was trying not to dwell on recent events. He recalled the incident when Melor's students had uncovered a memory which disturbed her: obviously something similar had happened during the retrace, and this time she hadn't been able to interrupt it. The prill, especially with Alendis in charge, were always quite adept at revealing the obscure. Sooner or later she'd have to face whatever it was.

A sudden exclamation from Jarras interrupted his reflections.

"Discords, Idenion, what happened here? Did you lose control?"

Laura didn't understand the words, but the concern in the technician's voice halted her monologue. Idenion excused himself and joined Jarras at the computer.

"Sorry, I should've mentioned I'd had some trouble. There's a cloud of debris near the Symerid system, and I almost ran into it. If you look at my return journey, you'll find a safe alternative route."

"This programme put you on a collision course?" Jarras inquired sharply.

"Yes. Yes, it did. That area was supposed to be clear."

"Then why didn't you *tell* us?"

"I meant to," Idenion said defensively, "but there was such a lot going on! Someone always checks for these things, don't they?"

"Not this time."

"I'd have remembered before we got there," Idenion added, none too convincingly.

"You still don't realise, do you?" said Jarras ominously. "Strephin made me copy the programme. Alendis is using that copy." He studied the contents of the log more closely. "You only avoided the cloud because you'd begun to reduce speed. Alendis isn't likely to do that." He paused again. "So what should we do? Alert him? If we send a signal he'll know exactly where we are."

"What's wrong, you two?" asked Laura plaintively.

They told her.

"We'll have to warn him," she said immediately.

"But will he believe us?" countered Idenion.

"If we continue toward Earth," Jarras elaborated, "he'll think the message is just a ruse to slow him down. We'll have to remain near the hazard, so he can see it for himself."

"But that would mean losing our advantage," said Laura.

There was a moment of silence as all three struggled with their consciences. It would be so easy to let events take their course. There was ample time to decide. Until both spacecraft were clear of transposal, no contact between them was possible.

"If we do nothing, we're as bad as he is," Idenion said at last.

"I agree," said Laura resignedly.

"Me too," said Jarras. "We'll lose transposal

very soon: I'll locate the cloud, and then we'd better disengage the Drive and get into position."

They carried out these manoeuvres and prepared to wait. Laura and Idenion tried to resume their planning, but with little enthusiasm. Jarras, always forensic, began a careful study of the cloud's composition and origin.

"The debris was probably formed by asteroid collisions," he observed. "Recently too, as it's still settling into the plane of the ecliptic. I suspect it wasn't on this heading a year ago, and in another year it will have moved away."

"That doesn't help us now, does it?" Idenion said irritably. "Keep scanning for Alendis - we'll have to get his attention promptly."

"I *know* that," said Jarras, equally tense.

At last a scattering of symbols appeared on the monitor, denoting Alendis' arrival. As Jarras had predicted, the sphere was making no attempt to reduce velocity.

"We have two astallen, no longer, to get our message across," he said.

Idenion reached up to the communications panel, swiftly keyed in a sequence, and waited. When nothing happened, he repeated the code more carefully. There was still no response.

"Move over," said Jarras. He tried the command again, making some minor adjustments.

"Is he ignoring us?" asked Laura.

"No," said Idenion. "Our signal isn't getting through."

"He's receiving another transmission," said Jarras, "or making one. I'll try Alda Mexa."

300

Another pause, another silence.

"The transposer at the spaceport is in use. They're obviously speaking to one another."

"Can't you break into the conversation?" asked Laura.

"Transposed communications aren't the same as radio," Jarras reminded her. "There are no waveforms. There is a shift - a change - " He gave up trying to find the words. "Due to its nature, only one transposed message can be dealt with at a time. Our attempts are simply being deflected."

"But you do *have* a radio, don't you?"

"We never use it in deep space," said Idenion. "Even if Alendis put his receiver on, he'd never hear us through all the racket coming from Earth."

"That's true," said Jarras, "but I could configure our radio to emit a pulse - something that should get us noticed by his scanners. Although they don't seem to have detected that cloud."

"Neither did mine, till I was nearly on top of it," remarked Idenion as Jarras went to work on the circuitry.

Laura didn't understand the computer display, but she did remember that two astallen equalled twelve minutes. They had first seen Alendis' sphere eight minutes ago. "We *have* to get through to him!" she cried.

"How can we? He's still talking to Alda Mexa," said Idenion helplessly.

"I'll try calling Treva," said Jarras. "If there's anyone on duty they could radio the tower."

"If," repeated Idenion without much hope.

"Once I've re-aligned our beam, we won't know

if the other transmission ceases," Jarras added.

"*Do* it!" Laura shrieked.

To Idenion's surprise the Treva ground station answered immediately, and Jarras issued rapid instructions. "I'll call Alda Mexa at once," said the unseen operator. "Please stand by."

Jarras stepped back from the panel and flexed his cramped fingers. "That's our last option," he said to Laura. "We're out of time."

***

Strephin's visit to the Lyricon was short-lived. Any notion he might have had about picking on a few misguided students soon faded when he saw the extent of the gathering. His methods simply didn't work in crowds. And the sheer ebullience of this crowd was something he'd never experienced before.

Some junior scolia players had occupied the stage, but any attempt at a disciplined performance had long since degenerated into twangs and giggles. Their youthful audience applauded, stamped, embraced, chased one another round the walkways or just sat quietly. Some had even brought their books with them. A hastily constructed banner, suspended between two apartment windows, proclaimed: "The Lyricon is Ours." Every now and then a fragmented chant rippled through the ranks: "Music, harmony, love!"

Five apprentice builders approached Strephin. They were smiling, but they were also barring his way.

302

"Have you come to join us?" asked one. "If you've only come to spy, we'd like you to leave."

"Maybe he's looking for sciesha," said another. "He usually is."

"He'll find no sciesha here," said a third. "This is a serious protest." And indeed, the prevailing mood was one of determination, not euphoria.

Strephin decided to make a strategic exit. Baiting Tralvar suddenly appeared to offer more in the way of entertainment. And on further consideration, it seemed good policy to be on hand when Alendis returned.

**

Shortly after Alendis' sphere had achieved transposal and vanished from the tower's screen, another craft arrived at the spaceport. It had come from Scapirion, near the south pole, and carried - among other things - the crate of resnay which Tralvar had urgently requested. He promptly seized one bottle and took it back to the control room. After a few swigs his confidence began to return, and he decided to make one more attempt to disrupt Alendis' plans. He would speak with the dictator but aim his remarks at Zenzie and Asterion, neither of whom wanted to be on the trip. If he could alarm them sufficiently, they might force a retreat. He hadn't Alendis' subtlety, but he hoped he wouldn't need it. Carefully he worked out the precise moment that the sphere would emerge from transposal; then, fortified by the strong alcohol, he sat down to rehearse his message. When the time came to activate the transmitter he opted for visual, placing the half-empty bottle where Alendis wouldn't see it and trying to appear calm and authoritative.

"Ah, Tralvar!" Alendis greeted him nonchalantly. "Predictable as ever."

Tralvar immediately began to feel foolish. "I've a duty to make you see sense," he began, nonetheless. "I can't believe you're willing to expose your wife and your friend to Earth's dangers."

"They're under my protection," Alendis replied airily. "I'm more than ready to cope with any risk." And in blatant disregard of onboard protocols he unfolded a square of firi, produced the phial of starfire and shook it vigorously over the material.

"Discords, Alendis!" came Asterion's voice. "You've no business using that in here. I'm turning up the filtration unit."

"Don't you ever stop complaining?" This was Zenzie.

"If it weren't for *your* complaints I wouldn't even *be* here!" retorted Asterion. A squabble followed.

Alendis made no move to intervene. "My happy crew!" he remarked to Tralvar, who hastily modified what he'd been about to say.

"What happens when that drug wears off? You'll be helpless. I think you should come home."

"He's right, you know," said Asterion. "What in chaos' name is wrong with these filters?"

" If they won't perform at maximum you're running systems you don't need," Tralvar said.

"We won't need the long-range scanners till we reach Symerid Three," Asterion decided. "I'm diverting power."

"Do that, if it'll keep you quiet," Alendis said irritably, applying the firi delicately to his nose.

"For harmony's sake, Alendis, stay away from Earth!" Tralvar persisted.

Alendis appeared to consider the plea. His image gazed thoughtfully out of the viewscreen. He was not looking at Tralvar, however, but into the middle distance. "I always knew there would come a time," he said, "when I alone would be loyal to the cause."

"*What* cause?"

"I always knew," Alendis continued in the same dreamlike manner, "that I'd have to carry on singlehanded. But I won't flinch from that responsibility. I made a promise to my father."

"You've never met your father!" Tralvar exclaimed. Rietta had often lamented that fact.

"He was so proud of me," Alendis went on, not seeming to hear him. "He wanted me to be strong - to help make a strong society - and I've laboured ceaselessly to do that. It hasn't been easy, surrounded as I am by fools and weaklings."

Off to Tralvar's left, the shortwave radio began to emit Treva's call-sign. Intent on what Alendis was saying, he ignored it. It was bound to be someone for Rillan.

"You've always courted failure, my poor friend," Alendis was continuing. "You failed in your musical aspirations and you failed to sustain the dream we once shared. You've never amounted

305

to anything in my service and you never will. Perhaps if you'd paid me half the attention you paid Tristell - "

"I don't have to listen to this," Tralvar declared, and moved to cut off the transmission.

"Wait, Tralvar." Alendis' mellifluous voice, slightly marred by the intervening light years, stayed him. He paused with his hand on the switch. The radio beeped again; again he took no notice.

"In happier times," Alendis said with measured deliberation, "I appointed you my successor. I believed you were the best person to implement my policies. Obviously this is no longer true, and I therefore intend - "

A klaxon shrieked out, drowning his words. The cabin lights turned crimson, outlining him in their baleful glare.

"Alendis, what do I do?" cried Asterion.

Tralvar saw Alendis fling the other man aside and take the controls. He heard someone shout "meteors" and heard Zenzie scream. There followed one brief glimpse of blue-white flame as the Drive imploded: and suddenly there was no longer a receptor for the transposal beam. Only the merest trace of static, soft as drifting snowflakes, showed that the beam was still active. Tralvar, in stunned disbelief, continued to stare at the emptiness.

"Oh, well done!" said a sardonic voice from across the room. Strephin.

Tralvar whirled to face him. "Do you think that was deliberate?"

"Well, wasn't it? You and your little pal Jarras

must have cooked it up between you. There was something in that flight log, wasn't there - and you knew about it!"

The Treva callsign shrilled for a third time. Strephin ambled forward and tuned in the receiver.

"Alda Mexa tower," said an agitated voice from the other spaceport, "you must tell Alendis he's in danger. The Hellas programme has a flaw."

"We know," said Strephin laconically, and flipped the power off. "Seriously, Tralvar - why don't you own up? You thought *I'd* be on that sphere, didn't you? And I would've been, if Zenzie hadn't been playing hard to get."

"I didn't plan this!" Tralvar insisted.

"Have it your own way." Strephin smiled sourly. "Now, I suppose, you'll become acting First Citizen - even though we both know it isn't what Alendis wanted."

"Isn't it?" Tralvar countered.

"He was going to dismiss you. I heard him."

"Did you?"

"If you nominate yourself First Citizen," Strephin snarled, "I'll do everything I can to bring you down. The position should have been mine, and you'll never hold onto it, you drunkard!"

"Listen to me, Strephin." Tralvar's voice was low and cold. "I never wanted to be First Scientist and I'm not looking forward to being First Citizen. But I'll do it, if only to keep you out. I may not be the best person for the job but you're the undisputed worst. Now get out of this facility. I've some important matters to attend to."

"Finding leadership a burden so soon?"

307

Strephin queried insolently. "All right, I'll do as I'm told - for the moment."

Tralvar watched him leave, picked up the resnay bottle and put it down again. He couldn't risk getting drunk - not now, nor in the foreseeable future. He wished he didn't feel so weak. He'd lived too long on a knife-edge, and although his chief tormentor had perished, he'd still be denied the peace he so desperately craved.

He wondered why Jarras and Idenion hadn't called in, then belatedly realised he hadn't disengaged the transposer. Hastily he corrected the error and was soon conferring with Jarras, gratefully noting that his trainee was calm, alert and on top of the situation. Reluctantly he asked to speak with Idenion, knowing as soon as he saw the poet's expression that he'd guessed what was to follow.

"Idenion," he began, "Zenzie was..." He couldn't complete the sentence. His voice faltered, his eyes grew moist, and to cover his confusion he took another swig of resnay. "I apologise," he continued after a moment. "That was unseemly."

"Why did she follow Alendis into space?" Idenion asked quietly. "What inducement did he offer?"

"She was worried about *you*," Tralvar said lamely.

"I told her Alendis would destroy her," Idenion went on. "But not so soon. Not like this. Would you do something for me, Tralvar?"

"What?"

"That poetry I was writing in my cell - it's about my break-up with Zenzie, and it isn't very

308

kind. I'd like you to burn it."

"Are you sure?" asked Tralvar dubiously.

"I'm sure. She doesn't deserve that kind of epitaph. And besides -" Idenion forced a faint smile - "haven't you always wanted to incinerate some of my work? Here's your chance!"

Laura, across the cabin, silently witnessed this exchange. She didn't understand much of it, but she saw Tralvar fighting back tears, and silently blessed him for his display of grief. It was reassuring, and something she could identify with. Idenion, typically, had his emotions well under control.

"He's dealing with his loss," Jarras said quietly. "It's the way of our people."

Idenion finished speaking to Tralvar and came over. "We should move on."

Laura gazed down at the little monitor screen where Jarras had tracked the sphere to its destruction, and which still showed a lazy swirl of debris. She felt embarrassed. At the instant the explosion had registered she'd thought, piercingly: "No, oh no! That beautiful man!" The others must have been all too aware of her sentiments.

"Many people loved his beauty, despite his evil deeds," Idenion said understandingly.

"I.... suppose there's no reason for you to stay on Earth now," Laura ventured.

"There *is* still a reason," he assured her. "Tralvar says there'll be questions asked about this accident, and the last thing he needs at present is a brush with the administrators. And frankly, I couldn't face them either."

"There's bound to be an enquiry," Jarras

confirmed. "Our space safety record was impeccable."

"With me absent, the hearing will be deferred," Idenion continued. "I've agreed to study Earth, as best I can; it'll give me an excuse for being away, and give Tralvar some breathing space to sort out his problems."

"Strephin, for instance," said Jarras. "He'll be twice as bad without Alendis to restrain him."

"A loose cannon," Laura remarked.

"That's an accurate description," Jarras agreed after pausing to divine what a cannon was. "Although Asterion was a greater threat to *you*, Laura."

"That child-killer!" Laura said contemptuously. "Good riddance. I don't think anyone will be shedding tears over *him*."

***

Kyrin had slept until noon, then awoken hardly able to move. His mirror had revealed an array of colourful bruises, the legacy of Strephin's beating. Once he was dressed, however, not a single mark was visible. Strephin had been very careful about that.

Relayists, as a rule, had little to do in the afternoon. Kyrin fulfilled his duties adequately but mechanically, wondering how he'd manage the more demanding late session. He'd just embarked on some mind-clearing exercises when a junior administrator brought the details of Alendis' death.

Kyrin's reaction was immediate and startling.

Shocked, immobilised, he didn't even acknowledge the messenger. A sense of deprivation, more intense than anything he'd ever experienced, swept over him. His training was forgotten. Numb and desolate, he sat motionless in his room, oblivious to the passing of time. The thoughts of the other relayists fluttered ineffectually against his consciousness.

Presently the door opened and light footfalls hastened toward him. Someone called his name breathlessly, and a gentle touch on his shoulder made him look up. A young woman with a thin, serious face stood in front of him.

"Kyrin? Kyrin, it's Alcis. Relayist, eastern zone."

"What...?" He blinked dazedly.

"I know I shouldn't have left my post," she continued, "but I was so worried about you. Can you carry on? Should I call a substitute?"

He focused on her then. "Are you really Alcis? I didn't know you were a girl."

In answer she gave him the brief self-concept which preceded all her sendings.

"Ah. I know you now." Kyrin looked relieved. "Forgive me, I'm not being professional. This news... this news has - "

"It's stressful for all of us," Alcis said earnestly, "but more so for you, I imagine, since you worked with Alendis so closely."

"Yes." He nodded slowly. "Yes, that's the reason."

"I hate to pressure you," Alcis said, "but we have to inform the city as soon as possible. Can you cope?"

"I'll be all right," Kyrin replied. "Give me a moment or two."

"Is there anything I can get you? A drop of wine, perhaps?"

"Just water." Kyrin's voice became a little stronger.

She fetched it, suddenly shy. "I'd better go now, Kyrin."

"Thank you for your concern," he said formally.

"May I - " she hesitated. "May I visit you again?"

"If you like." His tone was neutral, but she sensed a lack of interest and her face fell.

"I'm pleased to have met you at last," she said with forced brightness. "I'll set up the chain when I'm back in my zone. Be sure to tell me if it gets too much for you."

"I will," he replied, his face softened by sadness.

The news travelled the city, the relayists' thoughts spreading like ripples to encompass every lateral. Soon all of Alda Mexa knew that Alendis was dead. From the akron, radio messages went to the other city states, and their relayists swiftly took up the story. Too much confusion remained in the air for routine commerce; thankfully, Kyrin closed off his perception and allowed the strictures of his training to slip away once more.

Instantly his sorrow returned, more strongly than ever. He fought it. It was unacceptable, a potentially disastrous mindset for a relayist. This he

312

knew, yet was powerless to help himself. Weeping, he threw himself onto his bed and hid his face in the pillow. And then, for the first and only time, he cried out the name of the man who'd inspired such grief.

"Asterion...Asterion...Asterion!"

***

"I'm ready to make landfall," said Jarras.

Laura scrutinised the viewscreen. "But we're still in a high orbit, aren't we? Don't you want to look at anything?"

"I don't want anyone looking at *us*," Jarras stated. "Did you realise how many different sources were tracking you, Idenion? Oh yes, they're still logged - even though you turned off the panel display!"

Idenion looked guilty.

"So from here, I go straight down," Jarras informed Laura. "Just as soon as Idenion tells me which of the two landing sites is the correct one. We'll be heading into darkness, so I don't want any mistakes!"

"Darkness?" repeated Laura, startled.

"Yes, it's night in your country," Jarras pointed out.

"But it can't be..." Laura began, then stopped. It *could* be, and was. Celestra's extended day had confused her reckoning. "Er...do you know how long it's been since sunset?"

"Not exactly. Several ilden, I'd say."

"Hell's teeth!" said Laura.

313

Two quizzical pairs of eyes regarded her.

"I'm sorry," she continued, flustered. "You probably think I'm being silly, but I've been dreading facing my uncle. And now you tell me it's the middle of the night. We'll have to wake him up."

"Is he really that bad?" asked Idenion.

"Worse."

"Worse than Alendis?" queried Jarras, alarmed.

"Well, no," Laura admitted. "He doesn't go around killing people."

"Then there's no reason to fear him," Idenion declared. "Don't forget I shall be with you, Laura. I'll take the blame for your absence."

This is going to be interesting, thought Laura.

"As for those landing sites, Jarras," Idenion continued, "we must opt for the first one. The second was in the middle of a wood, and we'd never find our way out in the dark."

"It won't be easy finding our way through the village," said Laura. "There aren't any street lights."

"I'm used to that!" Idenion reminded her.

Jarras took the sphere down swiftly and expertly, ignoring the viewscreen. In any case, it showed very little of the descent. Laura had no sensation of vertigo, and in fact remained standing throughout the final lap of the journey. She only knew they'd touched down when Jarras announced it.

"It's a pity you have to turn straight round and go back," she said.

"I'm a technician, not an explorer," he

314

confessed. "Besides, I promised Tralvar I'd hurry back. He needs my support, for what it's worth."

"Because of Strephin?"

"Not just Strephin. Tralvar won't find it easy being the acting First Citizen. He isn't well-liked."

"Surely," said Laura, "all he needs to do is get rid of his guns and give the Lyricon back to the people?"

"That may not be enough," said Jarras gravely. "Now you must go. Idenion, are you ready?"

Idenion seemed intent on finishing a long drink of liman. Jarras, reverting to his own language, uttered some kind of warning, and Idenion reluctantly put down his drink and stood up. The hatch unsealed, and curled outward to form the exit ramp. Outside, the night was black as pitch.

"Haven't you got any lights on this thing?" asked Laura in a stage whisper.

"Of course," said Jarras. "But I'm not using them!"

"Are you sure this is Cheveney?"

"This is where Idenion landed," Jarras replied. "Please leave now. I detect no thoughts in the immediate locality, but that could change at any moment."

Laura stepped outside, wondering why her shoes seemed to have lead in them. Idenion followed, equally disoriented by the increased gravity. But unlike the last time he kept his footing, and turned to have one final word with Jarras. Then the hatch closed, a sudden breeze whipped the long grass, and the sphere was no longer there.

Laura breathed the air of an August night,

warm with just a hint of dampness. Overhead, familiar constellations twinkled reassuringly, and a full moon was just visible above the trees. An owl hooted in the distance. Idenion sneezed in her ear.

"Are you okay?" she asked him.

"I'll soon adjust," he replied, taking a couple of steps into the darkness. "Your house is this way, I believe."

Laura, impressed by his good orientation, confirmed that it was. They began to walk, acclimatising themselves to the moonlight.

"What did you say to Jarras before he took off?" she asked. "You sounded a bit worried."

"I told him not to lose track of the days," Idenion said. "In sixteen Celestrian days, he must return for me."

"Why's that?" asked Laura, grabbing him as he stumbled in a rabbit hole.

Idenion didn't answer. He turned briefly to gaze in the direction of Cheveney's main street. "I thought I heard..." he began. "No. No, that's not possible. I must have been mistaken."

Laura would have asked him to explain, but as they neared Windbourne she saw a light in Nathaniel's study. "He's still up," she said apprehensively.

"I've been aware of that since we landed," Idenion said.

"So that's how you knew which way to go!" remarked Laura. "Is he cross?"

"Not at the moment. He isn't even thinking of you."

"Well, *that* doesn't surprise me," Laura said,

annoyed. "Come on, let's remind him he has a niece." She marched up to the window, rapped on it to attract Nathaniel's attention, then went to the back door. Idenion followed silently. In a moment, he would have to convince Nathaniel of his integrity; and after only a brief inspection of the other man's mind, he knew exactly how to do that.

The door was on the latch. Laura led the way to the study, where Nathaniel had just risen from his desk. Idenion, entering in Laura's wake, had his first good look at Nathaniel Gilcoyne, and was not unimpressed. Straight iron-grey hair, alert blue eyes and a strong jawline. But, as Idenion had already seen, a caustic, embittered temperament.

"I suppose you realise," Nathaniel said coldly to Laura, "that the entire village thinks you ran off with Jimmy Stretton?"

Laura wasn't expecting this opening gambit and didn't reply.

"The only reason I didn't call the police," her uncle went on, "was that Margaret said - insisted - that your visitors were good people."

"That's right," Laura began eagerly.

"*I'll* be the judge of that, when it becomes appropriate." Nathaniel's cool gaze remained fixed on his niece. "Your behaviour is the subject under discussion, in case you hadn't noticed. Do you think it's acceptable to disappear for three days, then arrive back here at two a.m. with some anaemic boy? And what the deuce are you wearing? Pyjamas?"

Laura stared at the floor. "I can explain..."

"You can apologise!" thundered Nathaniel.

317

"And then you can get out of my sight. We'll conclude this matter in the morning. As for you - " he rounded on Idenion - "I want you out of my house. Now."

"Nathaniel," said Idenion softly. Their eyes locked, and Laura held her breath.

A moment later all the colour drained from Nathaniel's face. He clutched at the desk, sending a paperweight clattering to the floor. "Dear God," he breathed.

"Are you ready to listen, or do you need more proof?" Idenion asked after a pause.

"You have no right - " began Nathaniel. Then he sighed and sat down, averting his eyes. "Perhaps you *do* have a right. I don't know how to contend with this. I simply don't."

Laura was having problems of her own. She'd experienced another brief flashback to the night her parents died. Not the familiar avenue of trees, but a struggle with a door which wouldn't open. It seemed symbolic, but she was suddenly too tired to think about it. The influence of the retracer had not entirely left her.

"Idenion," she ventured.

He turned to her momentarily. +Yes, go and rest+ his thoughts said. +Leave Nathaniel to me+

Despite an uncharitable wish to see her uncle shamed, Laura was glad to slip away to her own room. Somehow, it appeared smaller. She took off her yellow tunic and the filmy undergarment which went with it, and stowed them at the back of the wardrobe. Her nightdress felt rough and heavy in comparison. Hanging her pendant round the

318

bedpost, she lay down and let herself drift into the dream she knew awaited her.

When she woke about three hours later, the gap in her memory had vanished - and so had the guilt feelings which had been so much a part of it. Her parents had died at the moment of impact; her inability to summon assistance had made no difference at all. She'd been told this by an ambulanceman who'd seen death too often to be circumspect about it. She'd then blacked out a second time and forgotten every detail of that night. Idenion, of course, would tell her she could now put the past behind her. For the first time, that didn't seem so impossible.

Hearing some activity outside, she sat up and looked blearily out of the window. What she saw was so surreal that she thought it must be another dream. There, in the dawn light, was Idenion, surrounded by garden birds of all varieties. They darted in his wake as he wandered along, fluttered boldly round his feet and, one by one, alighted on his outstretched hands to accept bread. Tib, Mrs. Moffat's cat, watched with interest from the garden path. Further off was Nathaniel, holding a camera and - to Laura's disbelief - smiling broadly.

"Now I *know* it's a dream," Laura murmured, and in a few minutes was asleep again. But she too had a smile on her face. The adventure wasn't over.

Chapter Eleven

Laura was eating toast and marmalade at eleven a.m. when Nathaniel strolled into the kitchen.

"Good morning!" he said brightly.

Laura again marvelled at his good humour. "You can't have had much sleep, Uncle Nat."

"Oh, I can make do with four hours once in a while. I've had a very interesting chat with our guest. I hope we didn't disturb you."

"No, I didn't hear anything. But I woke up and saw him in the garden, with the birds."

"Quite the little St. Francis, isn't he?" Nathaniel remarked. "I had to ask him not to repeat that trick in front of anyone else, if he wanted to avoid awkward questions. Tib's taken a fancy to him as well, but I told him it was all right to befriend a cat."

"Is he still asleep?"

"I imagine so, but perhaps we'd better check. I wouldn't put it past him to go wandering about on his own."

Nathaniel went quietly upstairs to the spare room with Laura tiptoeing behind him. They opened the door and peeped in, swiftly realising their fears were groundless. Idenion lay peacefully asleep in the huge Victorian bed, with Tib curled in a tortoiseshell ball at his feet. Laura glanced sideways at Nathaniel. He looked almost paternal. Idenion, it seemed, had worked some miracle on him.

"Was that one of my nighties he was wearing?"

she inquired when they were back in the kitchen.

"You're nearer his size than I am." Nathaniel busied himself with the kettle. "We'll have to find him some clothes from somewhere, and quickly."

"What were you talking about last night?" Laura asked a little hesitantly.

"About his world, and how he came to be on this one," Nathaniel replied. "His English kept falling apart, which flummoxed him a bit. Apparently I'm not an easy person to read." He looked vaguely pleased with himself.

"And what was it he said to you initially?" Laura pursued. "You looked as though you'd seen a ghost!"

Nathaniel poured a little warm water into the teapot and swirled it absently. "I had, in a way," he said. "Just before you arrived, I was thinking of a dear friend I lost in the Blitz. Idenion threw that thought, that image, back at me. It stopped me in my tracks, as it was meant to do."

For one brief instant, Laura thought she saw pain in his eyes. But before she could be certain, he turned away and rummaged in the pantry. When he emerged with some biscuits he wore his usual business-like expression.

"There's something rather odd about this inability to sing," he commented. "Don't you agree? Everything in Nature sings, or gives voice. So why has an entire species suddenly lost touch with something so basic?"

"Idenion blamed it on telepathy," Laura replied. "Uncle, now that you know him a little...do you think I was right to go with him?"

Nathaniel finished making his pot of tea. "I think you were monumentally foolish, Laura," he said at length. "I also believe you had no alternative. He's so damned trusting! He's agreed not to reveal his identity to anyone else, but we'd better keep a close eye on him to make sure he doesn't."

"We? What about your work?"

"I'll take some leave. You don't think I'm letting you two stay here alone, do you? By his own account, his people are a bit..."

"Free-spirited," offered Laura.

"Quite. And teenage boys will be teenage boys, wherever they're from. I assume you've not been intimate with him?"

"Oh, uncle!" Laura blushed scarlet. "It never crossed my mind!"

"Maybe not, but I'm sure it's crossed his. I want you to promise - "

Laura was saved from further embarrassment by the arrival of Mrs. Moffat.

"Laura!" she cried delightedly. "You're back! What did I tell you, Nathaniel? I knew those youngsters were reliable. Where did they take you, Laura?"

"Er...Salisbury," said Laura. "Actually, we've got Idenion staying here. He liked Cheveney and asked if we could put him up for a while. He's an exchange student."

"Oh, that'll be nice for you. And what about his sister? Is she here too?"

"No. She...er...got homesick."

"What a shame!" Mrs. Moffat elbowed

Nathaniel out of the way and took her pinafore from a peg inside the pantry door. "You'd have loved her, Nathaniel. Such a sweet little thing. But she didn't seem too happy, right enough. Where does Denny come from?"

"Iceland," said Laura.

"Finland," said Nathaniel in the same breath.

"Oh dear," said Mrs. Moffat. "Whichever it is, he might not care for my cooking. What does he eat, Laura?"

"I...think he's a vegetarian," she faltered.

"Cheese," stated Nathaniel. "I've already found that out. And very strong tea."

"I'll do a cheese and potato pie, then," decided Mrs. Moffat.

"Please keep in mind, Aunt Margaret," said Laura seriously, "that Idenion's here to practice his English. He's already very good, but he might sound a bit strange at times."

"More importantly," added Nathaniel, "there's a problem with his luggage. Apparently, it was sent home with his sister's. We need a change of clothes for him. Any ideas?"

"As a matter of fact I have," the housekeeper beamed. "I was talking to Mrs. Stretton earlier, and she was threatening to give all Jimmy's clothes to a jumble sale. I'm sure I'll be able to borrow some. Denny's about Jimmy's size, isn't he?"

"Thinner," said Laura.

"Mm, yes, I remember now," Mrs. Moffat reflected. "He looked as if he could do with a good feed. Where *is* he, anyway?"

"Asleep."

"Well, that proves it - he's got no energy. Steak and kidney pudding's what he needs, not vegetables. Oh by the way, have you seen Tib? She didn't turn up for her breakfast."

"She's taken a shine to Idenion," explained Nathaniel. "She won't leave him."

"Isn't that strange!" exclaimed Mrs. Moffat. "She's normally so stand-offish."

"Cats can be very discriminating," Nathaniel said quietly. "I think we'll find, in the days to come, that Idenion is quite an exceptional young man."

***

The day after Alendis' death, Tralvar called an informal meeting of all the administrators. Some, of course, he already knew, but the solitary nature of his work had meant exclusion from much of the akron's daily life. He wanted to acquaint himself with every member of staff, in the faint hope that one of them would be fit to shoulder the burden of First Citizen in his place. He soon realised the impossibility of that. These people were efficient, ceaselessly maintaining the city's myriad functions, but not one of them was a leader.

Of necessity Tralvar appointed a secretary from their ranks to deal with the routine aspects of First Citizenship. Already, a batch of aggravating questions had been levelled at him - everything from the condition of the city sewers to the colour of the gallery walls. He wondered how Alendis had managed to deal singlehandedly with such trivia.

The secretary's name was Kevis, an elderly

good-humoured man who was not afraid to speak his mind when asked. His first assignment was to upgrade Tralvar's public profile, and they met in Kevis' quarters to discuss the details.

"First of all, we'll have to do something about your apartment," the administrator said.

"I'll get it cleaned up," Tralvar promised.

"I don't mean that. People will wish to see you, and unless you want to spend half your day trudging from the basement to the audience rooms, I suggest you move to somewhere more convenient."

"I'm not having Alendis' suite," said Tralvar emphatically.

"Then what do you suggest we do with it?"

"Nothing, for the moment." Tralvar didn't even want to think about making an inventory, which he supposed would have to be done sometime. "Isn't there anything less ostentatious that I could use?"

"I'll organise something," said Kevis. "And next, you really must get some new clothes."

Tralvar sighed. He was beginning to hate this job already.

"It's customary for a new First Citizen to speak on the radio," Kevis went on. "The people will wish to hear your plans."

"I'm not looking forward to it," Tralvar confessed. "I'm no good at making speeches - or writing them. Perhaps, if I drafted out the main points, you could knock them into shape?"

"Of course."

"Even if you don't like what I intend to say?"

"I'll do what you've employed me to do," stated Kevis. "If the people dislike your manifesto, they'll

325

doubtless make their opinions known."

"Doubtless," said Tralvar.

"Before we start work on it, there's one issue I need to raise," Kevis said, suddenly uneasy.

"What?"

"Strephin. What are you going to do about him?"

I might have known it would be down to me, Tralvar thought privately. "What *can* I do?" he said aloud. "I've tried ordering him back to Tivenne. He won't go. And even if he decided to, that's no solution. At least I can keep an eye on him if he stays here."

"You could give him the basement apartment, perhaps," suggested Kevis.

"To show him who's in control?"

"Something like that."

Tralvar smiled sourly. "The notion does have a certain appeal," he commented. "Very well, I'll try it. But if he fancies himself as jailer, he'll be in for a disappointment."

"You'll remain in charge of the cells?"

"There won't *be* any cells," Tralvar said heatedly. "They weren't my idea - doesn't anyone realise that? So, I'm getting rid of them. Find someone to remove the locks. No, on second thoughts, *I'll* do it."

"May I suggest," said Kevis, "that you mention this in your speech?"

"I certainly will," said Tralvar, warming to the idea of publicising his new regime.

"And who will be appointed to First Scientist? Jarras?"

"Discords, no. Let him enjoy his youth," Tralvar replied. "He may well be First Scientist one day, but for now I'll reserve that position for myself. I may not last as First Citizen."

"Will Idenion continue as First Poet?"

"Naturally. Why shouldn't he?"

"You don't like his work," Kevis said.

"Maybe not, but everyone else does. It's the wishes of the majority we're concerned with, isn't it?"

"Absolutely. And bearing that in mind, will you reinstate our new First Singer?"

Tralvar gave him a stony stare. "I have no plans to do so," he answered.

Kevis looked startled. "But we thought - "

"Then you can think again," Tralvar snapped. "And now, if there's nothing more to discuss, I'll make a start on those locks."

"Tralvar," Kevis said seriously, "I'm aware of the regard you still have for Tristell. Perhaps you don't wish Laura to supplant her. But denying the Hellas girl's popularity would be a bad start to your term of office."

"This has nothing to do with Tristell!" Tralvar declared angrily. "Don't you understand, Kevis, that Laura's society is no longer that of Hellas? If you want reasons for my decision, go and see Laura's retrace. Her people are emergent, and I will *not* have our technology compromised."

"You let Idenion stay there."

"Only on condition that he makes a full report, possibly a retrace, on his return. Once you've studied the evidence, I think you'll concede that

Symerid Three should be off limits to all travellers."

"That has to be an administrative decision," Kevis said stubbornly.

Would you have said that to Alendis? Tralvar wondered, but again kept his thoughts to himself. He didn't want to clash with anyone this early. How typical that his first disagreement should have been over Laura! That girl was trouble, even when she was light years away.

He'd almost finished dismantling the locks when he was confronted by an irate Strephin. But not, he realised apprehensively, Strephin in one of his extrovert rages. This anger was controlled, and altogether more menacing.

"What in chaos are you doing?"

"I should think that was obvious." Tralvar kept his eyes on his work.

"I see. Alendis is dead and all his plans go to waste," Strephin remarked. "How typical of you. I knew you didn't have the backbone for leadership."

"I don't see any need to take prisoners," Tralvar answered steadily.

"That's because you're weak." Strephin's insolence, at least, hadn't changed. "Is this meant to appease your public? It won't work, and we both know it."

"Go away, Strephin," Tralvar said wearily.

"Not a chance. I'm going to be your shadow, Tralvar, because I want you to fail. You will, you know. You've already begun. I'll watch you make wrong move after wrong move until you're forced to resign. In the end, you'll beg me to take over."

His complacency was unnerving. Tralvar left

him lounging against the wall and slammed into his own apartment, letting the cluttered interior soothe him with its familiarity. But something was different. An open bottle of resnay stood on the table, in the middle of a space that had not been there earlier. Angrily he went forward, stoppered the bottle and pushed it aside. Then he sat down and attempted to write his speech.

From the outset, he had problems. Alendis had always begun with "My people!" so he couldn't repeat that. Citizens sounded too formal. People of Celestra? No, he wouldn't say Celestra. Everyone would think of Idenion and Laura, and not pay attention to what followed. Eventually he dispensed with any form of greeting.

Presently Kevis looked in. He'd found some transcripts of Alendis's propaganda, and thought they might help - if only by showing Tralvar what he shouldn't say. Tralvar read them dutifully. Surprisingly, he felt encouraged. The words, without that superlative voice to deliver them, were hollow and empty. Surely he could do as well as this?

"You can't hope to match his skill as an orator," said Kevis, "but you have one quality he never possessed."

"Which is?"

"Humility. Make it work for you, Tralvar. At the moment, it's your best asset."

Tralvar doubted it. Humility was too much like subservience, and he wanted to play down the craven way in which he'd served Alendis. He struggled with his task for several ilden, mulling

329

over various issues, growing ever more frustrated when the words would not behave. Finally, when he found himself reaching for the resnay bottle, he threw down his pen, snatched up his random jottings and shamefacedly delivered them to Kevis.

At length, having been assured that a serviceable speech would be ready for him the following morning, he went to see Jarras at the spaceport.

"Can you have the satellite array online at noon?" he asked. "I'll need the morning to find my way around the script."

"Don't forget to notify the relayist chain tonight," Jarras advised. "Otherwise, you'll be talking to yourself."

"I wouldn't mind that in the least," Tralvar admitted. "But I'll see that Kyrin puts the word out."

"Getting stage fright?"

"Let's just say I'll be glad when it's over. It wouldn't be so bad if I didn't have to do it again in the evening."

"You can't expect people on the other side of the world to stay up all night," Jar⌐   ⌐aid reasonably.

"It wouldn't be necessary if I'd found a way to record sound," Tralvar grumbled. "It's ridiculous that we still can't do it. There's something I've been missing all this time, something basic." He ran his fingers through his hair.

"Didn't Laura give you any clues?"

"She thought of a spinning disc. I asked her what kept it from vibrating to pieces, and she didn't seem to know what I meant. But I don't need her input, Jarras. I'll work it out for myself."

"You're really determined not to have her back, aren't you? Did something happen between you two?"

Tralvar didn't quite know how to reply, but was saved by the arrival of a sphere from Atris. He waited until Jarras had finished with the routine responses, then said: "I'd like to stay and keep you company, but I'm having to change apartments tomorrow afternoon. I need to sort out a few things. I don't want anything vital thrown out with the rubbish."

"Don't lose the Hellas crystals, for harmony's sake. I still think you could have trusted me with them."

"Strephin might decide they're safer with *him*," Tralvar opined. "For your own protection, it's best you don't know where they are - although after tomorrow, everyone will know that I've given the two flight logs to the administrators for further study. Strephin won't dare take them back. He wants everyone in authority to think he's a reformed character."

"Do you genuinely believe he'll try for the leadership?"

"Oh yes. I only wish I knew when, and how."

"Do the administrators have the flight programme too?" Jarras asked anxiously.

"No, I still have that," Tralvar assured him. "Strephin will never find it. When it's time to fetch Idenion, I'll return it to you. Jarras....?"

"Yes?"

331

"I've never thanked you for believing in me. Your friendship means a great deal, especially now."

"I know my faith in you will be justified," Jarras said quietly. "Do you want me to provide technical support during your broadcast?"

"It's your afternoon off."

"If it will help, I'll be there."

"Yes, I believe it *would* help." Tralvar treated the young man to one of his rare smiles.

"Then I'll meet you in the akron radio room at mid-day tomorrow," promised Jarras.

In fact, it was only mid-morning when the young trainee hurried into the basement apartment. "Tralvar? So you *are* here! I've been trying to reach you."

"Sorry, I was closed off. I had a few things to amend in this text. Why are you so early?"

"I came to check the satellite uplinks," Jarras said. "But I couldn't, because the transmitter isn't working. I think it may have been sabotaged."

Tralvar stood up with a sigh. "You'd better show me."

They ascended to the first floor, where the radio room was located. On the way they passed Tralvar's new residence - comfortable, unpretentious, with a balconied window overlooking the plaza.

"Was someone moved out to make way for you?" asked Jarras.

"No; it was reserved for delegates from other cities," said Tralvar. "It was only used three times last year. I'll have something to say about that in my speech."

332

Superficially there seemed to be nothing wrong with the transmitter, but a thorough inspection revealed a badly damaged piece of circuitry.

"There's your sabotage," Tralvar commented. "It looks like he removed it, stamped on it and replaced it."

"Strephin?"

"Who else? Though I fail to see why. This isn't going to prevent me from speaking."

"Can it be repaired before noon?"

"Unlikely. We'll have to broadcast from the spaceport." Tralvar straightened his shoulders and looked quite cheerful. "Now that Strephin's tried to stop me, I feel much better about it!"

"Should we leave immediately?"

"*You* go; I'll be down later. I want a word with the removal team about the zirid. I don't want to spend forever re-tuning it!"

"You don't play it," Jarras pointed out.

"Then maybe it's time I started again. Don't worry, Jarras. I won't be late, much as I detest this rigid structuring of my day."

At noon, calm and resolved, he sat down to deliver his message to the world. Jarras had run an extension cable into the spaceport lounge, away from the control room and its background noise. The microphone was positioned in a corner alcove. Two days ago, Idenion and Laura had been sitting in that very spot.

"At times like this," Tralvar began, "it's customary for a new First Citizen to describe himself and his background. But since a great many of you know me already, I don't propose to do that.

I will, however, speak of my plans for the near future. I would ask you, for the duration of this broadcast, to set aside any preconceptions you may have about me and judge my intentions on their own merits.

"I'm concerned about the increasing lack of interdependence displayed by our city states. We've already lost Scapirion in terms of ready communication and population exchange. Only an impersonal form of trade remains, and there are signs that this type of isolation is spreading. A fragmented society ultimately leads to a divided society, which is the last thing anyone wants. So, to combat this trend, I propose a schedule of repair work on all defective monorails, plus an increase in the number of seafaring vessels. The existing programme of sphere renewal will continue.

"Students from around the world are already encouraged to spend at least one year in Alda Mexa. There will now be similar opportunities for study in other cities. Administrators will be invited to make working visits to other regions, to study differing methods of organisation and, it is hoped, appreciate each area's problems more fully."

Tralvar paused to sip the water Jarras had provided for him, then continued to read, all too aware of how stilted and awkward he sounded. The next part of the address would be even worse: it had been composed entirely by Kevis, and while the language was workmanlike, it simply wasn't the way he, Tralvar, would have said things. Kevis had outlined Alendis' last proposals, still being debated by the administration. There was one in particular which Tralvar wanted to keep; namely, a shift in education toward science and engineering. This, he announced, was essential in order to provide workers for the repair and redevelopment programmes. But this did *not* mean the arts would suffer. No one with a vocation would be forced into a career they didn't want.

The other proposals were for improved maternity care and minor calendar reform. After detailing these, Tralvar listed the appointments which would not be changed, concluding with the First Poet.

"And now," he continued, "to a more sensitive topic: my work as First Scientist, and my work for Alendis, which were often one and the same. Did I create weapons because I was ordered to, or because I believed in what he was doing? It would be easy to say that I simply followed orders, but it would not be the truth. When he first came to power, I shared his dream of a revitalised society venturing again to the stars. I *still* wish for that. But I never shared his desire to conquer and subjugate, and I never willingly held anyone prisoner. My first act as First Citizen was to abolish the detention suite.

"Doubtless you're expecting me to cease my weapon-making and promise never to do it again. I'm not prepared to make such a promise at this time. The universe does not stand still, unlike our society. Other civilisations have evolved, becoming emergent - and as I have lately seen, continuing to make war even as they take their first tentative steps into space. If you do not understand the nature of this threat, I urge you to see the retrace Laura gave

335

while she was here. Copies of the relevant images will be made available on request. Her planet, Symerid Three, has wars and weapons undreamt of by any of us. Of course, many light years separate us from that world - but how can we be sure its inhabitants aren't about to discover transposal?

"Where there is one such planet, there will be more. Are we to wait in apathy until our peace is threatened, or do we begin to construct a worthwhile defence? Alendis believed in the power of the lattice, and indeed, it's reassuring to have proved the lattice can function as a weapon. But it takes too long to generate, and it requires eight highly trained people to wield it. We need something better than that.

"I have no new inventions at the ready, nothing tangible to put before you. I'm simply expressing my beliefs in the hope that you'll allow me to act on them. You'll soon have a chance to put this matter to the vote. Please, think of your future and give me leave to protect it in the way I know best.

"Lastly, it goes without saying that the Lyricon will remain the property of the people. There's no need to enlist the help of nonconversants over that issue."

The last line had been unscripted.

+Power off+ Tralvar told Jarras, then stood up and stretched.

"That ending was a bit uncalled for," Jarras remarked from the doorway.

Tralvar agreed. He hadn't meant to sound quite so sarcastic. "Well, at least I've made my point about the Lyricon," he said. "That should put an end to the student occupation. Now, shall we go and eat? I want to discuss the repair programme with you."

"With *me*?"

"Why not? I always value your opinions. Besides, I'd like you to take charge of the work on our monorail terminal. The sphere replacements can be put on hold for a time."

"It's a bit out of my field," Jarras said dubiously.

"But it will keep you in Alda Mexa until I'm more certain of my way ahead. Until Idenion gets back and Floren returns from wherever she's hiding, you're the only one I can count on."

"What about Kevis?"

"He has no loyalty to me, only to the office of First Citizen. At least say you'll consider my request."

"I'll think it over," said Jarras.

Only when their flitter had touched down near the akron did they realise why Strephin had damaged the on-site transmitter. The door of Tralvar's workshop stood wide open, some broken glass lay just outside, and something blue had been spilt on the flagstones. With a despairful epithet, Tralvar vanished into the little building. After a moment or two, Jarras followed.

"He's taken the guns, the launchers and every particle of therite," Tralvar said dejectedly. "There aren't any stray pieces lying about, so he must have re-neutralised whatever was in the broken jar. I've been an idiot, Jarras. I should have guessed why he wanted me out of the akron."

337

"Can he make use of these things?"

"Not the handguns - he wouldn't be able to prime them. But he knows how to fire the launchers. He took a great interest in their development."

"Then - are we in danger?" asked Jarras apprehensively.

"No. No, I don't think so. He's trying to control me, and since he can't do what Alendis did, he's testing other methods. He'll probably threaten to use the weapons if I don't do as he wants."

"And what he wants is to be First Citizen," Jarras concluded. "Ludicrous!"

"Not as ludicrous as it first appears. The administrators would find it difficult to deny him his chance if I nominated him."

"So he thinks all he has to do is wear you down?"

"Precisely - but he isn't going to. He certainly knows how to be a nuisance, though. I was going to close this workshop, destroy the contents and try to develop something safer to handle. Now I'll have to make more launchers, just to keep ahead of him. And that won't go down well with the people, not when I've virtually promised to suspend my work."

"Maybe that's the only reason he's done this," Jarras suggested. "To create some bad publicity."

"Then he's succeeded." Tralvar set about restoring order to the ransacked premises, making much more noise than was necessary. At length Jarras put a hand on his shoulder and gently but firmly brought him to a halt.

"This can wait," he said. "We were going to

eat, remember? We can both sit down to a meal in your new apartment, in comfort, and decide what to do next."

Tralvar allowed himself to be led out of the workshop, pausing only to turn the key which Strephin had insouciantly left in the lock. He was wretchedly grateful to Jarras for his level-headed response to the problem.

"If it weren't for you I'd have been on my second bottle of resnay by now," he said after they'd finished their lunch. "I hate to ask any more favours, but do you think - if we both worked on it - that there's a chance of fixing the akron transmitter before it's time to re-broadcast? I want to stay put for the rest of the day."

"I'm sure we can manage that," Jarras said.

And they did, with scarcely an astal to spare. Tralvar delivered his speech surrounded by discarded wiring and pieces of panelling. He spoke well, not having had time to grow nervous. And, sensibly, omitted the impromptu last line.

Afterwards, Jarras finished replacing the panels and Tralvar went to see if any reactions to his noon broadcast had come in. There weren't many, apart from an aggrieved message from the power station, relayed to Kyrin and transcribed by Kevis.

"We can't generate enough current to electrify the monorail *and* run the Lyricon weathershield. Are we supposed to stop the trains every time there's a concert?"

"It was possible once. Tell them to find out how our ancestors coped," Tralvar said irritably when Kevis asked if there was any reply. "And tell

339

them there's no need to run the weathershield for those students. They'll disperse more quickly if they're cold and wet!"

The rest of the evening passed quietly. Jarras returned to his rooms at the spaceport and Tralvar relaxed in his new quarters. He ate a leisurely supper, checked the tuning on the zirid and was just growing pleasantly sleepy when there was a commotion in the plaza. For a moment he thought it was an outbreak of sciesha, and was about to resign himself to another sleepless night, but then he realised the voices were calling his name.

+What do you want+ he asked, trying not to convey any apprehension.

+Come out+ they responded collectively. They were young, of course - their raw energy made him feel ancient. Wearily he unlatched the window and stepped onto the balcony. There were about a dozen students below, of both sexes, jostling one another and laughing. They looked up expectantly.

+What do you think you're playing at?+ Tralvar demanded. +If you want to take issue with my broadcast, come and see me tomorrow+

+What we want+ said one young man, +is Laura+

+The Lyricon needs its First Singer+ said a girl.

Then they all began to chant "Lau-ra! Lau-ra!" until Tralvar retreated inside. Eventually they dispersed, noisily.

+We'll prolong the sit-in until you change your mind+ the girl vowed as she and her companions departed.

340

Tralvar was exasperated, then angry. No objections to his proposals for expansion and education, not even any protests about armaments. All they wanted was Laura. They could see no further than the beauty of her voice and the creation of a perfect lattice. How he envied them.

"Interesting," said Strephin, almost in his ear.

"If you keep sneaking up on me like that," Tralvar snapped, "I shall hit you with the nearest solid object."

"Nerves getting to be a problem?" asked Strephin lightly. "Have a drink."

Tralvar glared. "I'm surprised you had the cheek to come back here today."

"I live here, remember? And as for your weapons cache, well, you'll thank me later. I've stopped you from doing anything stupid like throwing them all away." He gazed thoughtfully out of the window. The students had gone. "Don't you think you're being a bit highhanded, telling everyone they'll have to do without Laura?"

"I have my reasons," Tralvar said succinctly. "You're one of them."

"Are you inferring I might harm the girl?" Strephin looked the picture of injured innocence. "That hurts me, Tralvar. It really does. *I* never made any attempts on her life. Alendis had this idea that she was polluting the lattice, and Asterion thought she was dangerous. I kept out of it as much as I could."

"A pity you can't keep out of my apartment," Tralvar retorted. "You wouldn't have barged in on Alendis without an invitation."

341

"I wanted to see you," Strephin said mildly.

"Do I have to put a lock on the door?" inquired Tralvar.

"Don't be so antisocial." Strephin was in no hurry to leave. "I say give the people what they want. They're so easily pleased."

"Will you *go*?"

"Maybe I should make my position public," Strephin deliberated. "I'd like it to be common knowledge that I favour Laura's return." He picked up a vase, shook it and replaced it, then peered inside the zirid.

"Goodnight, Strephin," Tralvar said meaningfully, holding the door open for him.

Strephin made a show of irritation. "That's the last time I offer you advice. If you want to set everyone against you, you're going the right way about it. I'll just let you get on with it, shall I?"

"I wish you would," said Tralvar, resisting the urge to slam the door after him. Then, his resolve at a low ebb, he poured himself some resnay. He intended only to have one measure, or at the most two; but when he finally crawled into bed he'd consumed most of the bottle. His dreams, unsurprisingly, were vivid and disturbing, although nothing like the tortures inflicted on him by Alendis. This time he was only a bystander, watching as the images of war from Laura's retrace translated themselves into his native surroundings.

Soldiers marched triumphantly through the streets of every city, while invading aircraft roared overhead. Amid the fleeing population, the students came and stood beneath his window. "Save us,

342

Tralvar!" they cried. He tried to tell them he couldn't, that he was unprepared, but they continued to plead. And then a brilliant sunburst lit the sky over the Lyricon, and the graceful building was instantly pulverised. A vast shockwave spread its circle of devastation through all the laterals, carrying everything before it.

Tralvar woke to find himself enmeshed in a tangle of bedclothes. To calm himself, he opened the casement and stared out at Alda Mexa, solidly real beneath a canopy of stars. When he finally drifted back to sleep it was only to become locked into a dream-argument with Laura, rekindling his fascination with the music in her mind. This unsettled him more than his earlier nightmare. Awaking at dawn, as he usually did, he pondered on the dichotomy that was Symerid Three. Beauty and cruelty: creation and destruction. So vital, yet so deadly. He was still lost in thought when Rietta arrived with his breakfast.

"You don't have to wait on me anymore," he chided her.

"I want to," she replied simply.

He drank deeply of the liman and to his surprise, felt better. "*You* agree with my policy on Symerid Three, don't you?"

"Need you ask, after what that planet did to Alendis?" she replied.

"The trouble is, we've never had any proof that it was Earth," Tralvar mused. "Everyone else, even Jarras, thinks I'm being too extreme. Will you do me a favour, Rietta?"

"If I can."

343

"Things can only get more difficult, and I can't trust myself to stay off the resnay. I want you to take charge of it and give me only two measures at a time."

"If you were desperate enough you'd send to Scapirion for more," she observed.

"The delay would make me think twice," Tralvar said. "Please, Rietta."

"Oh, very well," she said good-naturedly. "And what do I say when you demand it back and start calling me names?"

"Remind me of this conversation," he answered steadily. "I'll have the crate delivered to you later."

She turned to go, leaving the tray. "Is there anything else I can do to help?"

Tralvar hesitated. "Just be there, as you've always been," he said after a moment. Rietta was kindness personified, but while he trusted her with his welfare, he couldn't treat her as an ally. She'd give way too easily if trouble threatened. And besides, she still had a little too much affection for Strephin, her former fosterling.

Rietta accepted this guarded response without rancour. "Are you sure Idenion will come to no harm on Symerid Three?" she inquired as she reached the door. "He's such an impetuous young man."

"He won't absorb anything detrimental, if that's what you mean," said Tralvar. "He's too strong-willed for that. And besides, he has Laura to look after him."

"I don't envy her," commented Rietta, and disappeared.

Tralvar permitted himself a whimsical smile. He couldn't begin to imagine Idenion's precise circumstances, but he suspected - as did Rietta - that Laura and her guardian were already finding it difficult to keep him out of mischief.

***

During the next few days, Idenion settled cheerfully into life at Windbourne. The speed with which he adapted to his surroundings made Laura wonder just how many times her mind was being read, but when she saw what simple pleasure he derived from each new experience, she hadn't the heart to object.

Initially, he made a thorough exploration of the half-acre garden and the woods beyond, barely listening to Laura's warnings about wasps and nettles. He marvelled at the lush greenery, the majestic trees, the countless varieties of flora and fauna.

"What a beautiful planet!" he kept exclaiming, despite Laura's attempts to keep him quiet. But the few people who heard him smiled indulgently at his flawed vocabulary, and agreed that England was indeed a beautiful country.

At mealtimes, he happily ate everything that was placed in front of him, once he'd negotiated a reduction in the salt content. At most other times he could be found in or near Nathaniel's library. Once he'd read all the Greek texts - or rather, the ones he hadn't already seen - he turned to English poetry, which he identified by the length of the printed line.

He then trailed after whoever was nearby and asked to be read to. It was like having a three-year-old about the place, as Nathaniel remarked. They tried to divert him to other entertainments, without much success. He paid scant attention to the radio, and none at all to recorded music. He made a few attempts to watch television, but the rapid changes of viewpoint confused him. His companions were no help in this instance. Laura seldom concentrated, and Nathaniel only wanted to watch the news.

One radio programme did succeed in capturing his interest, but only because it featured another Laura. It was "Brief Encounter," broadcast two evenings after his arrival.

"Do try this play," Laura urged. "It's a favourite of mine. Very romantic!"

Idenion listened obediently, odd though it was to see Laura growing rapt and emotional over a work of fiction. As she was familiar with it he followed the story well enough, but that didn't stop him being perplexed by its ending. He couldn't understand why the couple hadn't run off together. Neither could he understand Laura's belief that they'd acted nobly in not doing so.

"You people seem to revel in making life difficult for yourselves," he remarked.

"That's quite an old play, Idenion," said Nathaniel, who had just entered the room. "Things are a bit freer these days. Although - " he paused significantly - "not as free as all that!"

After he'd forsaken radio and television, Idenion tried asking various people to sing to him.

Nathaniel declined. Mrs. Moffat obliged with a raucous version of "What's New, Pussycat?" ending in a shriek of laughter. Mr. Moffat rose to the occasion admirably with "The Eddystone Light," rendered with gusto in his hearty baritone. Idenion thanked him and retired, baffled. More myths! This culture seemed riddled with them, just as Ancient Hellas had been. He considered asking Laura to explain the song more fully, particularly with regard to mermaids, then thought better of it. The underlying theme of seduction, reproduction and betrayal wouldn't go down well with Nathaniel, who seemed to have an aversion to such matters.

On occasions, his English could still let him down. Mrs. Moffat bustled in one evening to start dinner, commenting:

"What a lovely day it's been!"

"Yes," he replied. "And behold! Yonder moon hath raised her lamp on high."

Mrs. Moffat gave him a searching look. "You *what*?"

Idenion's face fell. "Was that incorrect?"

"Not exactly, love, but you don't want to go quoting from those old poetry books. People just don't talk like that!"

Idenion accepted the reproof with some disappointment. It was the same with "Pirates of the Nine Moons" - all those fine long words and ringing phrases, obsolete. How could anyone hope to write decent poetry without them?

Despite his eagerness to live each day to the full, he tired easily, and resorted to dozing in an armchair. Tib had become his constant companion, and Laura was the first to notice that the cat always slept when he did. She was sure this had some significance, but didn't think it worth mentioning. She was outraged, however, when she discovered Tib slaughtering a mouse while Idenion calmly looked on.

"Why didn't you stop her?" she demanded.

"Was I supposed to?" Idenion asked.

"Of course you were! We feed her, don't we? There's no need for her to kill mice."

Idenion shrugged. "Tib doesn't think she did anything wrong."

"And what did the mouse think?" inquired Laura sarcastically.

"I cannot read the minds of rodents," Idenion said, taking the question seriously. "Tib herself is only just within my range."

But that didn't explain why he hadn't stopped her. It had been instructive to observe the way such a docile, peaceful creature had suddenly turned into a killing machine. Instructive, and just a shade alarming. Tib's bloodlust broadcast itself remarkably strongly, and it had been difficult to avoid being unsettled by it.

Eight days had now passed. Idenion reluctantly began to think of the duty he had to perform for Tralvar - to make as thorough a study of this society as his situation allowed, in order to help the administrators decide whether or not to ban further visits. Such a study could not be conducted exclusively in a country village. He would have to go to London.

He was in the front garden, kneeling by an ant

hill to watch the purposeful scurryings, when he realised he had company. Turning his head, he found himself gazing at a pair of impractical, high-heeled sandals and two shapely legs. He stood up slowly.

"Hi," said the owner of the legs. "You must be Laura's exchange student. I'm Tracey."

"I am Idenion," he responded.

The girl grinned impishly. "Sounds like a vegetable."

"Mrs. Moffat calls me Denny," he volunteered.

"Then so will I," said Tracey demurely. But her thoughts said: "I *want* this boy! And I'll get him, sooner or later."

"I haven't seen you in the village," Idenion said, puzzled at the vehement way she'd just laid claim to him. It wasn't desire as *he* understood it; it seemed more like avarice.

"I've been to Ibiza for a week," Tracey explained. "Do you like my tan? *You* don't look as though you've been in the sun much."

He made a noncommittal reply which hardly registered with her. She looked him up and down, making no secret of her interest.

"Hey!" she exclaimed after a fractional pause. "Are those Jimmy's jeans?"

"I was given them when my luggage was lost," said Idenion, reciting a prepared speech.

"You look good in them. Shall I tell you how I knew they were his?" Tracey lowered her voice conspiratorially and pointed to a small hole on the upper left thigh. "See that? I did that. Cigarette ash."

349

"You should be more careful," Idenion remarked.

Was that an innuendo? thought Tracey. Idenion's bland expression gave her no clue. She continued to study him while making banal comments about life in Cheveney, still trying to establish why she found him so intriguing. It wasn't his appearance particularly; he was slight, and her preference was for well-toned muscles. Then, suddenly, she had the answer. She'd known shy boys, forward boys, modest boys and brash boys - but she'd never encountered anyone so at ease with his own sexuality. She simply had to find out what kind of lover that made him. But just then she spotted Nathaniel on his way down the garden, and decided to renew her campaign later on.

Nathaniel reached Idenion's side and they both watched Tracey retreat along the footpath, ostentatiously smoothing her mini-skirt as she went.

"Laura was dreading this meeting," said Nathaniel. "I suppose you knew that."

"How could I not?" Idenion answered reflectively. "She believed - *still* believes - that Tracey will beguile me into revealing my origin."

"Tracey is a force to be reckoned with," observed Nathaniel.

"She doesn't interest me," Idenion stated. "She's calculating and selfish. I shall reassure Laura at once." He turned towards the house, but Nathaniel detained him.

"I've been meaning to have a little talk with you," he said. "This may not be the best place to do it, but at least Laura's out of earshot. You realise, of course, that she's very fond of you?"

"I do realise. And I know what you intend to say."

Nathaniel shuffled his feet awkwardly. "Promise me," he said at last, "that you will not make love to her."

Idenion turned his burning gaze upon him. "She's not ready. I won't try and persuade her otherwise."

"And supposing she decides she *is* ready?" Nathaniel persisted.

"I will respect your wishes," Idenion assured him.

"Thank you," Nathaniel said gruffly. "Perhaps I should explain why I thought this discussion was necessary. In our society, there's a stigma attached to unmarried mothers - "

"Then your worries are needless," Idenion declared. "I cannot impregnate Laura."

"And how did you reach that conclusion?"

"When my ancestors came to Hellas, they soon formed relationships with local women, who had never before been treated as equals. None of the women became pregnant. I've read many accounts from that time, and they all say the same thing."

"I'd prefer not to place my faith in two thousand year old documents, if you don't mind," Nathaniel remarked drily.

"I understand your scepticism, and will abide by my promise," Idenion said solemnly.

Nathaniel looked satisfied.

"May I ask a favour?" Idenion continued.

"Name it."

"I want to go to London. Can you help me get there?"

Nathaniel exhaled slowly. Idenion certainly knew how to keep him off-balance. "I'll have to confer with Laura about this," he said. "Let's go inside."

Laura was less than pleased. "Oh, uncle, how could you agree to anything like that?" she protested while Idenion was having his evening nap. "Tralvar had no right to ask him. Supposing he gets hurt and someone discovers he isn't human? Or at the very least, he might start acting strangely and get into trouble."

"Nonsense, Laura. London's full of weird young men with long hair. Idenion couldn't be conspicuous if he tried. And if you're worried that he won't cope with the traffic, then you'd better go with him, hadn't you?"

Laura began to voice another objection.

"No buts," Nathaniel said in a tone which brooked no argument. "This Tralvar sounds an eminently sensible fellow. He's realised that the attraction of our music might lead to a lot of indiscriminate tourism - unless he convinces his ministers that it's a bad idea. I happen to think it is, and I know you agree with me."

Laura nodded reluctantly.

"So what's Idenion going to tell everyone if he spends all his time in Cheveney? That he was welcomed, waited on hand and foot and had a damned good rest? No, Laura, that won't do at all. He has to feel completely out of his depth for once - and London's the best place to bring that about.

Size, noise, bustle - "

"Dirt," Laura suggested.

"You're getting the idea." Nathaniel stood up and squared his shoulders. "I suggest you take him on a shopping trip - you know the West End well enough. I'll drive you to Newbury and you can go by train. That way, he'll see more of the countryside."

Laura admitted defeat. "When?" she asked.

"The day after tomorrow. That'll give you time to plan what you want to do. Talk it over with him."

"I'm still not very happy about it," said Laura. "Couldn't you come with us?"

"Out of the question. I've too much work to catch up on. You're more than capable of looking after Idenion."

***

It was becoming more and more obvious that the mantle of leadership didn't sit well on Tralvar's troubled shoulders. In the space of a few days he'd had confrontations with several administrators, with engineers from the monorail, with a representative from the power station, and with Kevis. He swore at Rietta, as she herself had predicted, for rationing his resnay; and he even directed a few sharp words at Jarras, invaluable as the young scientist was proving to be.

Under less fraught circumstances, Tralvar would probably have coped with these difficulties. But every day, the students came to the akron and

353

clamoured for Laura. And every day, petitions were handed in by ordinary citizens, requesting her return. The demonstration at the Lyricon continued, and Strephin regaled him with snide comments. And there was something else - one single aspect of his work for Alendis that hadn't yet come to light. To reveal that secret would, Tralvar was sure, end his tenure of the First Citizenship and bequeath the title to Strephin. By keeping silence, he nurtured his guilt when he longed to confess it, and his conscience began to torment him.

Jarras was the only person who could revive his spirits. By day, the hardworking trainee had been dividing his time between the spaceport and the monorail, but had made a point of returning each night to have supper with Tralvar. It gave them both an opportunity to unwind. Tralvar wished he could leave the akron's stultifying confines and help the monorail repair crew, get his hands dirty again and not have time to sit and brood.

"You mustn't let Strephin get to you," Jarras declared. "Is that all you're going to eat? Well, give it here. I'm starving."

"It isn't just Strephin," Tralvar replied, fidgeting with his wine glass. "Things just won't settle down. I can't control the people - "

"You can't control the students. That isn't quite the same."

"They detest me."

"Nonsense! It's just high spirits. Aside from the Laura question, most of the citizens think your policies make sense."

"I don't believe that."

354

"It's true!" Jarras insisted. "Why do you think no-one's disputed them?"

"There's no need to be kind to me, Jarras. I know I'm barely tolerated."

"You *don't* know, because you haven't been out and about," Jarras said. "Believe me, a lot of people respect what you're trying to do. Maybe they can't meet your ideas head-on, but given time they will."

"If you say so." Tralvar gazed moodily out of the window. The street lights flickered into life, driving back the encroaching dusk. "Perhaps I'm giving in too soon. Strephin actually left me alone today."

"But you still have to sort out this Laura business," Jarras went on, undeterred by an exasperated sigh from his companion. "Maybe there's some way to reach a compromise - "

"Never mind Laura. How's the repair work coming on?"

"Slow but sure. We re-electrified several silmi of track as of lunchtime today. The local farmers will be pleased."

"Good! In that case, I'd like you to visit the Tivenne depot tomorrow and - "

The wall-mounted lamps and Tralvar's desktop light were suddenly extinguished, leaving only the solar tubes, their radiance ineffectual in such a large room. Outside, the street lighting was gone. Further off, a wide swathe of darkness bisected the lower laterals. A clamour of many minds erupted within the akron, mainly from the kitchens and from the entrance hall, where a departing group of people were trapped by the automatic doors.

"Discords, it's started already," muttered Jarras.

Tralvar rounded on him, eyes pale and wide in the uncertain light. "What's started? What have you been keeping from me?"

"I thought it was just rumours," protested Jarras. "The men pick things up. Half the stories don't amount to anything."

"This one does, apparently. And I dared to think I was winning! Who's behind this?"

"The electricians are siding with the students. When the reserves run low, they're going to cut the power to the akron instead of closing down the weathershield."

Tralvar set his jaw stubbornly. "Chaos to the lot of them. The reserves are never depleted in the rainy season - the Lisir's almost a torrent. They're doing this on purpose."

"I told you the Laura problem wouldn't go away," Jarras declared. "Why don't you let me bring her back when I fetch Idenion? It would put an end to all this unrest."

"No, Jarras." Tralvar was firm. "I can't prolong our contact with Symerid Three."

If Tralvar believed things couldn't get any worse, he was wrong. The following day he overslept, as a result of drinking several glasses of wine, and woke to find Rietta shaking him insistently.

"Leave the tray. I'll eat later," he mumbled.

"I already left it and you haven't touched it," said Rietta reproachfully. "Do wake up! They want you in the radio room."

"What...?"

356

"Something's happened at Treva. They need to speak to you."

Her words finally penetrated. Tralvar sat up in haste, took the tiny glass of resnay she was offering and downed it gratefully.

"Get Jarras!" he ordered, heading for the washroom. "This sounds serious."

The call was from Wemm, the engineer currently in charge of the theridolyte processing plant. "There's a problem with one of the vats," he said in his strong regional accent. "The environment's been compromised. If the pollution reaches the culture beds we'll lose a whole year's harvest."

"Can't you seal the vat off?"

"The seals are damaged."

"Surely it wasn't Strephin?" breathed Jarras.

"He was absent yesterday," Tralvar reminded him.

"But how would he know what to do?"

"He wouldn't. He'd simply find someone who did, and persuade them to help him."

"None of us is familiar with emergency shut-downs," Wemm was continuing. "We've never had to do one. We need Jarras back."

"And that, of course, is precisely what Strephin wants," Tralvar said after assuring Wemm of his co-operation.

"To prevent me working with *you*," Jarras said unhappily.

"That's right. Divide and conquer," Tralvar said with a flippancy that belied his real mood. "We'll have to assess the damage in person. It's no

357

use asking Wemm for technical details over the radio - neither of us can cope with that Atrisian dialect. Firstly, we'll need to know exactly what this pollutant is; then, hopefully, we'll know how to stop it spreading."

"We? Are you coming as well?"

"For the time being," Tralvar said. Kevis, who had been hovering in the background, advanced determinedly.

"With respect, Tralvar, you're not free to do that. A First Citizen's primary duty is to his public."

"I am also First Scientist," Tralvar reminded him.

"You can't just disappear!" Kevis objected.

"Don't tell me what I can and can't do!" Tralvar snapped. "And I'm *not* disappearing - I'll be on the other end of that radio if you need to consult me."

Kevis continued to look piqued.

"I'll leave you in charge," Tralvar added.

Kevis instantly looked mollified, although he tried not to.

"And," Tralvar concluded, "if you *do* call me, make sure you've something important to say. I don't want to hear about the akron's leaking roof or the peeling paintwork in the kitchens. If anything in the city needs repair, authorise it. Use your initiative."

"Very well," said Kevis solemnly.

"Good man. Now, Jarras, let's be on our way. We'll need a sphere, so I'd better pull rank to secure one."

"I think you'll enjoy doing that," Jarras remarked lightly.

358

"Possibly," Tralvar admitted. "Being First Citizen has to have *some* advantages. Let's just hope we're not too late to save that theridolyte."

Treva was the least aesthetic city on the planet, but despite its heavy industry there had been many attempts to keep the landscaping pleasant. The theridolyte plant was largely open to the skies, and many of its walkways were lined with small trees. Water was essential to the laborious chemical process which transformed dangerous therite into dependable theridolyte, and a tributary of the Lisir had been diverted into numerous tiny channels, some of them purely ornamental.

Tralvar had radioed ahead and asked Wemm to collect a sample of the contaminated product for analysis. The sphere touched down near the on-site laboratory where the cultures were continually checked and re-checked, and the two scientists were immediately shown to a restricted area where the transparent capsule containing the suspect material had been placed. The damage could be seen at a glance. Theridolyte, in its half-formed state, should have resembled a grey viscous soup. Instead, it was lumpy and semi-transparent, with a layer of bubbles on the surface.

Tralvar put on a protective mask and gloves and, despite Jarras' plea for caution, scooped out some of the foam. He studied it minutely, then, grimly amused, rubbed his hands together to form a lather.

"You can relax," he announced, pulling off his mask. "There's nothing dangerous here, apart from the usual risk of the gel bonding with your fingers.

I'll have the team analyse this, but I already know what they'll find. Soap."

"Soap?" echoed Jarras.

"Yes, quite ingenious really. A nuisance rather than a hazard, but messy enough to need our expertise. Wemm reckons it will be a couple of days before the vats discharge into the system, so there should be enough time to replace the seals on the faulty one. Once that's done, I'd better get back to Alda Mexa."

"Do you want me to stay here?"

"Of course not, but it looks as if you'll have to. A controlled shut-down might still be needed. That vat will have to be scoured - more than once, probably - and you'll have to make absolutely sure there's no soap in the pipelines."

Jarras grimaced. "That sounds like fun!"

"But whatever happens," Tralvar continued, "we mustn't forget about Idenion. His protections will only last another eight days."

"Seven," said Jarras.

"Discords, is that right? Well, I'll deliver the programme to you before that. Speaking of spacecraft, don't destroy the tainted theridolyte if you can help it. It won't be any use for spheres, but it might have other applications."

They located Wemm and told him of their findings.

"Do you still think Strephin had an accomplice?" asked the engineer.

"Oh, quite likely. Strephin isn't very bright," opined Jarras.

"Then we must find the culprit and dismiss

360

him," Wemm declared.

"You'll find him easily enough," Tralvar returned. "He'll be young, good-natured, serious about his work and currently absent for no good reason. But you're not to punish him - is that understood?"

"Why not?"

"Because he'll have acted under duress. I don't want him dismissed or reprimanded - I don't even want to know his name. Just let the incident be forgotten."

Jarras threw him an admiring glance.

"As you wish," said Wemm uncertainly.

"And now, I'd like to investigate those damaged seals," said Tralvar. "I'm looking forward to doing something useful!"

But honest labour proved not to be the diversion he sought. He was so distracted during the repair work that even Jarras grew annoyed. And at night he dreamt of angry confrontations and insoluble dilemmas, with derisive student voices adding a counterpoint. And sometimes there was another voice, low and bitter:

"Dwell in discord, murderer!"

"I wish you'd tell me what's on your mind," said Jarras the following afternoon. Tralvar ignored him, and Jarras unwisely tried to read his troubled colleague. The rebuff made his eyes water.

"I'm sorry," Tralvar said at once, "but you can't help me this time. I have to deal with this in my own way."

"Then you might as well go back to Alda Mexa," Jarras declared. "I can manage better

361

without you."

"Maybe the whole world can," Tralvar said morosely. Gathering up his few belongings, he departed without another word.

Arriving back at the akron, he discovered that a few student protestors had actually entered the building and were ensconced in the middle of the main hall. Unobserved, he retreated to the side door and let himself in via the kitchens. The caterers watched him impassively. When he reached his apartment he wasn't entirely surprised to find another full bottle of resnay on the table. This time, he drank it.

***

"Why have you come here again?" asked Tyvian querulously.

"Now is that any way to greet a benefactor?" asked Strephin with a broad insincere smile. "I helped put your workshop to rights and installed a new tank for your prill - the least you could do is make me welcome."

Tyvian didn't reply. He hated Strephin's mock pleasantries even more that his threats.

"Alendis always said you were tiresome," Strephin remarked. "Since you're not in the mood to be polite, I'll come straight to the point. I want to study Laura's retrace."

"You've seen it."

"I've seen the sanitised version Tralvar commissioned," Strephin corrected him. "Now I want to examine the original. In full, not just on a screen!"

"I don't think Laura's childhood memories hold the type of experience *you'd* enjoy," said Tyvian disparagingly.

"Don't try to spar with me, you old fool," Strephin said irritably. "Just run the retrace, and be quick about it. Oh, and just in case you've got any ideas about re-configuring the crystals, *you* can channel the playback."

"The full crystal array isn't used for re-runs," Tyvian pointed out. "One crystal and one prill are enough to interpret the data."

Strephin scowled. "I don't trust you, plant man. Will you monitor the datastream willingly, or do I have to rearrange this place a little? Some of this greenery's quite rare, I understand. It would be a pity if anything happened to it."

Belatedly, Tyvian realised why Strephin was so intent on deputising him. Either he believed himself incapable of linking with the prill, or he was too nervous to try. Whichever it was, further opposition would undoubtedly result in the loss of that infamous temper. Sighing, Tyvian set up the link, seated himself and placed the sensor on his forehead. Strephin eagerly drew up a chair and sat next to him. The replay commenced, Tyvian doing his best to ignore the uncouth mind that hovered on the fringes of his perception. But Strephin wasn't easy to ignore.

+Never mind all this stuff+ he interrupted peremptorily as Laura struggled up the rain-sodden embankment. +Find the section with the big bomb, and start again from there+

363

Tyvian reluctantly obeyed, telling himself that Strephin would derive nothing fresh from a further look at the war. After all, Laura had no first-hand knowledge of it. But as the sequence progressed, Strephin's robust presence became less and less intrusive, subsumed – with complete willingness on his part - into the core of the retrace. Tyvian was alarmed, but didn't dare intervene until the scenes of conflict had come to an abrupt halt. Strephin sagged in his chair as the replay ceased, and Tyvian hastily propped him up.

"You stopped it," Strephin accused groggily.

"No, that was the end. Alendis picked a fight with Rietta and I lost the trace."

"Stupid of you," Strephin mumbled. "Did you see them, Tyvian? Those warriors, those weapons? Discords, what am I doing on this boring planet?"

Tyvian forced himself to inspect the muddied depths of the other man's mind, hoping for a brief moment that Strephin might recall the events which had blighted his infant character. But there was no such recognition. What he had derived from the retrace was simply Laura's sense of her own humanity. For the duration of the programme, he'd felt he belonged somewhere.

"Hey, plant man!" Strephin's voice was still euphoric, but stronger. "Why are you digging around in my head? I don't usually like that, you know. But since you've been so very accommodating, I'll forgive you this once." He stood up and stretched. "I'll be back soon for a repeat performance. And next time, let's have a peek at Alendis getting tangled with the aldacite.

364

That ought to be a laugh."

"I deleted it," Tyvian said. "It wasn't very pleasant."

Strephin grinned. "But you sampled it first, didn't you? Sometimes I almost like you, old man. Maybe we can work together after all. Well, I must go. I must draw up some plans while the retrace is still fresh in my mind."

"What plans?" asked Tyvian faintly.

"To visit Hellas - Symerid - whatever it's called," said Strephin airily. "Just for study initially, but later I might co-opt a few natives. Of course, I've still got to persuade Tralvar to part with that flight programme, but that shouldn't be too difficult. In another few days he'll beg me to take charge of Celestra!"

Chapter Twelve

Idenion gazed intently out of the train window. Laura sat opposite him, alternately fidgeting with her handbag and the hem of her pink polka-dot skirt. She didn't like minis, but refused to visit the West End looking like a country cousin. Everything seemed remarkably mundane: England on a warm August morning. So infinitely familiar to her, yet so strange to her companion. She tried, and failed, to imagine how it would appear to him.

Idenion was outwardly relaxed, but beginning to grow a little nervous. At first he'd enjoyed the motion of the carriage and the sight of fields, trees, roads and homesteads fleeing by. But then the train had jolted to a halt at a large, dirty, crowded station, and a horde of people - mostly women with children in tow - had piled on board with much shouting and slamming of doors. No one entered their compartment, which, according to Laura, was "first class" and cost more "money" to ride in. Laura was still surprised that Nathaniel had paid for this privilege. Idenion derived little benefit from it. He might not be able to see the new arrivals, but their thoughts were growing intrusive.

The train was travelling more slowly now, and the fields had given way to urban sprawl. He remembered his initial reaction to the multitude of Earth radio stations as he and Dena had searched for Hellas: "So much of it! So many of them!" He had similar thoughts now.

To divert himself, he scrutinised the passengers

in his compartment. Men in plain, uncomfortable-looking clothing, reading copies of the same newspaper that Nathaniel read. Their thoughts centred around their work, their colleagues, and "money". And once or twice, him. Slight resentment at his mode of attire, his hair, his general demeanour. Out of place. Feckless. Shiftless. And not one, not a single one, was going to meet a woman in secret. He was surprised at that. According to Brief Encounter, that was what the English did at railway stations.

The train crawled ever slower, then stopped with a final lurch. The men folded their newspapers and prepared to disembark.

"Come on, Idenion!" said Laura, interrupting his reverie.

He stepped out onto a vast expanse of concrete. Doors began slamming again as the train disgorged its passengers, the noise echoing from the distant walls and the high translucent roof. He paused to look up and two people immediately collided with him.

"Idenion, don't just stop like that!" Laura said anxiously. "Commuters are always in a hurry. Now, we've a bit further to go. We could use the Underground, but Uncle gave me enough money for a taxi. You'll see more of the city if we take a cab."

"Whatever you think is best," said Idenion meekly.

"You were very quiet on the train," Laura remarked as they began to walk.

"Our conversation would not have been private," Idenion returned. "You told me to mind

367

what I - " He began to cough, and left the sentence unfinished. "Apologies," he said at length. "The air seems impure."

"It is a bit," Laura admitted. "It'll be fresher once we're outside."

But it wasn't. The grimy odour of the station gave way to a fume of car exhausts and hot asphalt. Not that Idenion knew precisely what he was inhaling; he only knew it was unpleasant. But he made no complaint. The sun was shining, Laura was by his side - looking very pretty in her little pink skirt - and he was about to be shown a fascinating city. He was determined to enjoy himself as much as he could. Just as he reached that decision, Laura said: "I know I wasn't very keen on doing this, Idenion - but let's make the most of it now we're here!"

Idenion was inwardly delighted. It wasn't the first time he and Laura had been in such accord, and he was beginning to think they were destined to be a bonded couple - despite the restriction placed on him by Nathaniel.

Laura approached the taxi rank, opened the door of the leading cab and motioned Idenion to get inside. He did so, then all but slid off the seat as he made room for her.

"There's nothing to hold on to," he objected.

The driver's weather-beaten face creased into a smile. "Where's your friend been, miss, that 'e ain't ridden in a London cab before?"

"He's led a very sheltered life," Laura said laughingly.

"Well, let's give 'im a treat," the cabbie said.

"Where to?"

"Carnaby Street," she replied. Almost before she'd finished speaking, the cab performed a U-turn and hurtled forward. Idenion turned a shade paler than usual and gripped Laura's arm tightly. It was only her lack of concern which stopped him from pleading to be let out. The cabbie negotiated road junctions and phalanxes of oncoming traffic with practised ease, taking the scenic route past Hyde Park and Marble Arch. Idenion, preoccupied with the frantic nature of the journey, hardly noticed these details, but as they approached Oxford Circus the traffic slowed, and he recovered enough to make a hasty survey of his surroundings. They were travelling down a broad, busy avenue with rows of glass-fronted buildings on either side. These, then, were the shops: massive and forbidding. And the people...! He'd never seen so many people, and there were many more he *couldn't* see. He sensed a multitude of minds, a nonconversant background roar which threatened to clog his faculties every time he used his perception. He was thankful that no-one was actually sending thoughts. The cacophony would have been unbearable....

Laura saw him raise his head suddenly, as if startled. "Are you all right?" she asked.

"It's nothing," Idenion assured her.

The cab turned off the main road, traversed some smaller streets and came to a halt. Idenion still hadn't released Laura's arm, and she had to prise him off. Then she paid the driver, handed over a generous tip, and alighted. Idenion followed in haste. Moments later he was standing rather shakily under the notice which read: "City of Westminster: Carnaby St. W1". Laura wished she had a camera.

"Does this sign have some significance?" Idenion asked.

"You bet!" Laura replied. "This is *the* place to buy clothes. Wouldn't you like your friends to know you've been here?"

"They'll see my retrace," Idenion reminded her.

"Oh, don't let's talk about retraces," Laura said, fleetingly uneasy. "We've got all day in front of us, and thirty pounds crying out to be spent. I'm still amazed at Uncle Nat - he's usually so tight-fisted. You've worked wonders on him."

"It was about time he learnt to appreciate you more," Idenion remarked. He took Laura's hand and together they strolled down Carnaby Street, looking like any other teenage couple. Idenion's spirits rose as he gazed about him. The narrow thoroughfare was teeming with young people who frequently spilled into the road and reduced the traffic to a crawl. In their minds, as they glanced at him, Idenion read instant acceptance and a brash optimism which was quite exhilarating.

The shops were reassuringly small. Some displayed their wares outside. Others, as he understood from Laura, were staffed by skilled workers who made garments on request. There were many similarities to the textile quarter of Alda Mexa, Idenion decided. The main exception was the blare of recorded music issuing from every open door. His English was now fluent enough for him to understand the stylised presentation of the songs. Love anticipated; love gained; love requited.

Which was just the way it should be. A pity there were no live singers to put the message across properly.

"I like this place," he said. "I thought the shops would be huge, like the ones I saw from the taxi."

"They were department stores; these are boutiques," said Laura obscurely. "Come on - I'll help you choose some gear. Then you can pay for it the way I showed you."

"With pieces of paper?" Idenion queried.

Laura didn't comment. She'd already tried to explain, but it seemed the more she elaborated, the less he understood. She led him to a shop selling his-and-her fashions: they browsed through the assorted racks, and after lengthy deliberation Idenion chose some mauve jeans, an orange shirt and a multi-coloured kaftan. Not to be outdone, Laura selected a mini-dress with green and mauve stripes.

"Are you sure you want that?" she then asked, eyeing the kaftan critically.

"I like it," Idenion said stubbornly. "Give me the money notes, and I will pay."

"You'd better try the other things on first," Laura said, pointing to the men's' fitting room.

"Aren't *you* coming?" asked Idenion.

"It's not allowed," explained Laura. "If you want me to check on the fit, you'll have to come out and show me."

Idenion obligingly disappeared into a cubicle.

"And don't come out unless you're dressed!" Laura yelled after him, just as the music reached a temporary pause. A couple of girls who'd been examining mini-skirts looked up curiously.

"He can if he likes," said one, and they both giggled.

Idenion managed to put on the clothes and take them off again without committing any misdemeanours. Laura then went to try on her dress. She returned to find Idenion deep in conversation with the two girls, who had stopped giggling and were beginning to look enraptured. Laura retrieved him and pointedly steered him toward the till. She gave him several pounds too much, hoping he would count it out correctly; but rather to her disappointment, he handed it all to the assistant.

"I wish to pay for this gear," he said seriously. The cashier disinterestedly handed him his change and packed his gaudy purchases into a large carrier bag. The girls watched wistfully.

"He's fab," one of them whispered to Laura. "You're so lucky."

Idenion gathered up the remaining cash. "That was easy," he said cheerfully as he and Laura left the shop.

"I assume you're talking about the money?" she replied with a hint of sarcasm. "I didn't see you counting it. How much is left?"

Idenion checked carefully. "Fourteen pounds, six shillings, eleven pence," he announced.

"Right. I'll take the coins, but would you hang onto the notes? Put them in your side pocket."

"Why?"

"Because where there are tourists, there are thieves," Laura stated. "I've just broken the zip on my bag, and my jacket pockets are a bit too accessible. No-one could possibly get their hand in *your* pocket. And even if they tried, you'd read their intention."

"Not necessarily," said Idenion. "You've no idea of the racket I'm trying to shut out." But to please her, he kept the money.

"I'd like to buy some shoes now, to replace the ones I lost," Laura said. "The shop's some distance away - you're not feeling tired yet, are you?"

"No, but I'm getting hungry," Idenion confessed.

"We'll eat as soon as I've bought the shoes," Laura promised.

They set off for Oxford Street, Idenion glancing back regretfully at the little enclave they'd just left. They were heading back toward the department stores, he realised, and sighed inwardly. As they walked, the pair were approached on three separate occasions by foreign tourists wanting directions. Idenion, having gleaned the relevant information from Laura, answered the first enquirer in fluent French and the second in Japanese. The third time it happened, Laura was baffled.

"What language was that?" she asked when the passer-by had gone.

"If *you* don't know, how do you expect *me* to?" Idenion replied succinctly.

Laura supposed that was logical.

As they neared Oxford Circus, she saw two students selling metal jewellery from a makeshift stall. Some of the necklaces were quite beautiful - interlinked circles adorned with rows of dainty steel petals. "Shall we buy one of these for Dena?" she asked.

Idenion felt a pang of remorse. He hadn't thought about Dena for several days, although she was bound to be worrying about him. He bought two necklaces.

It seemed that lunchtime was never going to arrive, though he was glad to sit down while Laura dithered over several pairs of shoes. He was beginning to feel slightly breathless, and wondered if he'd ever get the reek of the city out of his nostrils.

Almost as soon as they were back on the street, Laura gravitated to a shop window display. She'd spotted a dress that she loved at first sight. Idenion was not so impressed: its dramatic swirls of red and black seemed more suited to Tracey. Not that he was tactless enough to say so. Again he waited; again he handed Laura a five pound note from their dwindling supply. Finally, just as he was about to remind her that he needed to keep his strength up, she announced that it was time to eat.

They had lunch at Torino's. The midday rush was almost over, and Laura was able to procure a table by the window. Idenion attacked his meal with enthusiasm, twirling spaghetti with an expertise which Laura was unable to match. His alert, inquisitive eyes missed no detail of his busy surroundings. Then, halfway through dessert, he suddenly paused as if listening.

"What is it, Idenion?" Laura asked. "You keep doing that. What's the matter?"

He finished his apple pie before answering.

"There are latent telepaths on your world," he stated at last. "I've noticed several. Two are nearby at this moment."

"Who? Where?" asked Laura, looking round at the other diners.

"I can't tell - not with so many people around me," Idenion replied. "I'm not talking about perception in any real sense. But every so often, I detect random impulses without form or structure. Those responsible won't have any idea they're doing it, and they certainly wouldn't be able to receive anything in return. Young children of my species, when they first try to communicate, produce something like this."

"If you were very close to one of these senders, would you then know who it was?"

"You're not one of them, Laura," said Idenion softly. "I'm sorry, but that *is* what you wanted to know. And yes, I could identify a sender if I were close enough. It may still happen. I hope it does."

"But you'll lose your chance after today, won't you?"

"Not entirely." Idenion sipped his tea with slow deliberation. "These minds aren't only to be found in London. There's one in Cheveney. I've known since the night we arrived."

Laura, somewhat lost for words, stared into her teacup.

"Don't let it disturb you," Idenion added. "It's of little significance really - you people aren't going to turn into conversants overnight. But the potential is there."

Laura, wishing she didn't feel patronised,

375

signalled for the bill. "Well, after that intriguing revelation, you'd better tell me how you want to spend the afternoon."

"I'd like to see live singers," Idenion said promptly. His eager smile quickly dispelled her truculent mood.

"That could be a bit difficult," she said apologetically.

"Why? Surely there must be some?"

"Yes, in theatres and concert halls. We can't afford those. Anyway, most of the performances are at night."

"Then *you* choose something," Idenion suggested. "Only - not more shopping! I'd like to sit down from now on."

Laura cogitated. "I know - we'll go to the Planetarium," she announced after a moment. "That should be interesting for you, and for Tralvar. It'll show you how we view the universe."

"An observatory?"

"No, more of an entertainment. They project the constellations onto the ceiling and talk about them. And," she added mischievously, "no one will notice if you fall asleep."

"Lead me to it," Idenion grinned, then watched curiously as she picked up her change and left a tip on the plate. "You've left extra money. You paid the taxi driver extra as well."

"That's right."

"But not the shop assistants. Why is that?"

"I...well...it just *is*," Laura said, gathering up the various bags. It didn't seem right to ask him to carry any.

376

The petrol fumes seemed stronger than ever as Idenion left the restaurant. His breathlessness grew worse, and he began to long for some fresh country air. He was glad when Laura left the street and led the way down a flight of stone steps, but his relief was short-lived. They had entered an artificially lit concourse filled with hurrying people, whose paths crossed and re-crossed in diagonal lines like some strange dance. A faint mechanical rumbling sounded from afar. Laura approached a row of free-standing machines and fed coins into one. It produced two tickets.

"We are to travel underground?" Idenion queried unhappily.

"Yes, to Baker Street station," Laura replied. "Don't look so worried - it's only a couple of stops. You won't find it as scary as the taxi ride."

Idenion was all set to complain about the air quality when, incredibly in these grim surroundings, he heard singing. Not a pre-recorded, amplified voice: this one was indisputably real. Without waiting to see if Laura was following, he darted off in search of the source.

A shabby young man with an unkempt beard was singing in raw but passionate tones about the fate of the world, accompanying himself on a stringed instrument. Despite his poor ear for music, Idenion realised that there was more enthusiasm than accuracy in the performance. But what audacity to confront these unfriendly crowds and try to divert them from their errands! He drew closer and noticed that the singer's instrument case lay open on the ground, coins glinting in its depths. As he watched, some passers-by threw more money into the case. To Idenion, this made perfect sense. The singer was being rewarded! Impulsively he took all the remaining money from his pocket and threw it down. Then, realising that Laura was not beside him, he hastily retraced his steps. She had put down the shopping and was standing with her arms folded, tapping her foot impatiently.

"Sorry," Idenion apologised. "There was a singer - "

"If you can call it that," Laura grimaced. "Well, you got your wish - after a fashion. Shall we go?"

They passed through a turnstile, which Idenion negotiated with difficulty. He then found himself at the top of an extremely long moving staircase, its machinery producing the rumble he'd noticed earlier. A gritty breeze rushed up at him, constricting his throat. Every instinct told him to stay where he was. But Laura had already stepped onto the escalator, and he had to follow.

They moved inexorably down, past a long row of framed photographs which Laura called "ads". Idenion vaguely wondered why there were so many pictures of undergarments, but he was having such trouble breathing he didn't want to talk. He'd ask Laura about it later. Perhaps.

At the foot of the escalator was a network of corridors, and more meaningless pictures which everyone seemed to ignore. As they walked, Idenion became aware of a sinister sound. It started as a kind of snarl, and he had visions of some wild animal being on the loose. Then it changed to an

378

all-pervading roar, and finally to a thunderous hammering. He froze, and put his hands over his ears. A stream of commuters overtook him at a run, and Laura hastily drew him to the side of the corridor. The hammering started again, but receded rapidly.

"What...what was that?" he quavered.

"Only a train," Laura said reassuringly.

"But it wasn't like the other train," Idenion said feebly.

"Sorry - I should've warned you about the noise," Laura apologised perfunctorily. "The tunnels amplify everything."

She led the way onto a drab, draughty platform. The tunnel was a black maw at either end, and a vague thrumming in the distance indicated that another train wasn't far away. Behind them, the platform began to fill with people - and Idenion, not normally given to claustrophobia, felt a stab of panic.

"...have left?" Laura was inquiring.

"What?" he asked, trying to stay focused on her.

"I said, how much money do you have left?" Laura repeated. "I'm down to my last sixpence."

"But I don't *have* any money," he replied. "I gave it to the musician."

Laura's face registered incredulity, then outrage. "You gave that busker all our money? Oh, Idenion, you blockhead!" And before he knew what was happening she'd run off, heading back along the corridor.

Idenion tried to run after her, terrified of losing

her in the crowd. Even with the shopping to slow her down, she was moving a lot faster than *he* could. The exertion strained his lungs, but he forged on, trying to ignore the pain in his chest. Finally, when each new breath had become agony, he stumbled to a halt. Impatient commuters jostled him. Laura had disappeared. Frantically summoning his last reserve of strength he reached out to her mind, scarcely able to perceive her amid the blanketing background din.

+Laura! Help me!+

Desperation gave him the necessary edge. He sensed her startled reaction. Then, exhausted, he leant on a wall and waited to be rescued.

Laura turned back in search of him, aggrieved by the eerie summons. How had he managed to get into trouble in those few moments? There'd be no hope of waylaying that busker now. But when she caught sight of Idenion, her impulse to harangue him was forgotten. "Whatever's wrong?" she gasped.

He raised his head with an effort. "No....air."

"Oh, hell's teeth. I'd better get you up to the surface."

"I...can't...walk," he moaned as she tugged at him.

"You'll *have* to," she insisted. "You can't stay here. Lean on me and try a few steps."

He tried, and nearly overbalanced. Laura realised she needed both arms to support him.

"This isn't working," she announced. "Tell you what: hang onto the shopping - that's right - and I'll hang onto you. Good job you don't weigh very much. Now, one foot; other foot..." Laboriously she led him the short distance to the escalator. Idenion clung to the rail like a drowning man as they drifted upward.

At the top they resumed their slow progress, only to find their way suddenly blocked by a uniformed arm.

"Tickets please."

"We haven't *been* anywhere," Laura said angrily. "My friend's ill."

"Tickets please."

Exasperated, Laura fumbled in her pocket and found them. "Here, take the damn tickets. They're no use to us now in any case." Then she coaxed Idenion back across the concourse, speaking brightly to him, although his dragging footsteps and harsh breathing were beginning to alarm her. They passed the spot where the busker had stood. There was no sign of him.

At last, after what seemed an age, they reached the stone stairs leading to the street. Laura paused in dismay. How on earth was she to get Idenion up those?

"Come on," she urged. "We're nearly there. You can do it."

"I...can't." His whisper was scarcely audible. Laura managed to haul him up the first few steps, not helped by an assortment of people rushing down them. By now she was out of breath herself, and his bony arm was beginning to hurt her shoulders. When they reached the half landing, she halted to shift his weight. Outside, three double-decker buses trundled past, their exhausts belching blue smoke.

381

The fumes wafted down the stairs. Idenion made a choking sound and collapsed, scattering carrier bags in all directions.

"Oh, please get up!" cried Laura, shaking and pummelling him. He gave a tiny squeak of protest and tried to curl into a ball.

Laura snatched up the bags before they were trampled on and attempted to turn the softest one into a makeshift pillow. He promptly rolled off it. She stood up then, irresolute, hoping for some sign of sympathy or concern in the faces that passed her. She found none. Everyone made a wide detour round her stricken companion, save those who stepped over him or tripped over him. Their expressions ranged from indifference to contempt.

"Drunk?" she heard one woman say to her friend.

"Drugged, I expect," the other replied.

Laura almost panicked. But she wasn't a child any more, trying to flag down cars on a stormy night. This time, she'd make people listen. "Would someone please help? He's got asthma!" she yelled as loudly as she could.

For a moment she thought she'd have to try again. After the last influx the stairs were virtually empty. Then a smartly dressed woman in her thirties elbowed her aside and peered closely at Idenion.

"Well, don't just stand there," she said to Laura. "Help me sit him up." Together they propped Idenion against the wall. He slid down it a little, wheezing painfully.

"Ben, love, let's have your inhaler," said the

382

woman; and for the first time Laura noticed a thin pale youngster on the stairs above. He obediently dug the inhaler out of his blazer pocket, removing a piece of fluff before handing it over.

"I know you don't like carrying it," continued his mother, "but see what happens when you don't." She turned back to Idenion. "Can you hear me? Good. Just pop this in your mouth for a moment. Now, when I say breathe, I want you to take a deep breath and hold it as long as you can - "

Laura watched dumbly. She hadn't anticipated this. What if the medication did something dreadful to him? But to her relief, he appeared to respond quite normally. His face lost its haggard look and his breathing quietened.

"That should do the trick," said his benefactress, and was gone in a swirl of Chanel and a clatter of high heels, dragging the ever-silent Ben in her wake. Idenion stood up nonchalantly, dusted himself off with only moderate success, and picked up the bags.

"Come along, Laura," he said, smiling.

"Are you all right?" inquired Laura suspiciously.

"Never better," he replied. "Shall we go and see the stars you told me of?"

"We can't, because we've got no money," Laura said with exaggerated patience. "We'll have to go home. I've got return tickets, thank goodness. But I'm afraid it means a long walk to Paddington."

"I would prefer to catch a train," Idenion said airily, setting off down the stairs.

"Where do you think you're going?" demanded

383

Laura, planting herself in front of him. "I told you I'd no money."

"I saw you buy tickets here."

"Only to Baker Street," Laura said. "And I had to hand them in. So, unless you can rustle up one-and-fourpence, we're stuck."

A trio of youths rushed past, vaulted the barrier and sprinted for the escalator.

"We could do that," Idenion suggested.

"Oh no we couldn't. We can't risk trouble with the authorities. If they caught us they'd want our names and addresses."

"So?"

"Have some sense, Idenion! You've a false identity and no passport!"

"Well then," said Idenion brightly, "you could sing. People would give you money, and then we'd have our fare."

"No we wouldn't, because I'm not doing it."

"Try."

"If you think I'm going to stand here and make a fool of myself - " began Laura heatedly.

"Then *I'll* give them a song!" Idenion declared. "Oh, my father was the keeper of the Eddystone Light, and he married a mermaid one fine night - "

Laura had often wondered what happened when Celestrians tried to sing. For some reason she'd assumed they were mute, like laryngitis sufferers. But that obviously wasn't so. Cracked, hideous sounds issued from Idenion's throat, prompting a few startled looks.

"Pack it in!" Laura shouted wrathfully.

"My apologies," he said, suddenly serious.

384

"That was remiss of me. We made a vow - all of us - that we wouldn't attempt to sing. It's vexatious to the laws of harmony."

"You can say that again," Laura remarked. "Are you *sure* you're all right? You're not usually so boisterous."

"I'm simply glad to be well again," Idenion assured her, then paused to eye two policemen who had strolled in via another entrance.

"They're looking for buskers, I expect," Laura said pointedly.

Idenion stared. "Why?"

"Because it's illegal to busk."

"Your planet has the oddest laws," Idenion said disapprovingly. "Well, it seems we *must* walk; so we'd best get it over with. Race you to the top!" And he bounded up the stairs, leaving the shopping in a heap at Laura's feet. She picked it up resignedly and followed. When she reached the exit, he was gazing around at Oxford Street as if seeing it for the first time.

"Why did I ever think London was drab?" he exclaimed. "Look at all the colours!" And he stared mesmerised at traffic lights, neon signs, awnings, even the people, with their pleasing variety of skin tones.

"I thought you were in a hurry?" inquired Laura, after he'd spent several minutes contemplating a flower stall.

"Oh....yes. Yes, of course," said Idenion abstractedly, and set off at a meandering pace.

At this rate, thought Laura, it'll take all afternoon just to reach Marble Arch. She was about to ask him to get a move on when he suddenly turned aside, favouring a young woman with his most dazzling smile.

"Thank you for your appreciative thoughts, Carol. Unfortunately there are no more at home like me, but I would be happy to make love with you, as that is your wish. Laura, what's my telephone number?"

Laura hastily dragged him away, leaving the girl open-mouthed in the middle of the pavement. "What's got into you, Idenion? You can't go around saying things like that!"

Idenion merely laughed. Moments later, to Laura's horror, he said something very similar to a tall, distinguished man in a pinstripe suit. The man turned pale and quickened his pace, then turned briefly and gave Idenion an infinitely sad stare.

"Oh, Idenion, how *could* you?" Laura lamented, blushing.

"I distressed him," Idenion mused.

"I'm not surprised," said Laura. "His lifestyle's illegal, and you knew his secret."

Idenion paused to digest that piece of information. "Is anything *not* illegal here? Things have certainly changed since Ancient Hellas!"

"Listen, Idenion." Laura spoke as firmly as she could. "That medication the woman gave you: I think it's made you drunk or stoned or - "

"Exhilarated!" Idenion declared, spreading out his arms.

"But," pursued Laura, "if you carry on saying outrageous things you'll end up in real trouble. The next time anyone, um, fancies you, I want you to

386

ignore them. Do you understand?"

"Even if it's you?" asked Idenion wickedly.

Laura, acutely embarrassed, said nothing, but walked stolidly on. Idenion fell silent too, and Laura began to hope that he'd taken her instructions to heart. Then, abruptly, he spun round and accosted a scrawny youth who'd been walking just behind him.

"May I have a word with you, sir?" he asked politely. "It's no use trying to take my money - I've given it all away. If you wish to avail yourself of some, why not try that man over there? He's carrying two hundred pounds."

"What's your game?" The pickpocket eyed him warily, unsure whether to hit out or run.

"Get lost!" Laura said peremptorily, and to her relief the boy sloped off with nothing more threatening than a v-sign.

"That wasn't very civil of you, Laura," Idenion said reprovingly.

She looked exasperated. "Fine. Next time I'll stand aside and let you get thumped. Only there isn't going to *be* a next time, because you're going to keep quiet until that damn stuff wears off!"

He ventured a protest.

"Not another word, Idenion - not one word. Is that clear?"

"Yes, Laura," he said mildly.

"Good. Now come on - we've a train to catch. Eventually!"

Idenion seemed contrite, and Laura took the opportunity to foist the shopping on him. He carried it for a hundred yards or so, then spied a man performing card tricks at a little table and went to join the small knot of spectators. The man displayed three cards, then placed them face down and switched them about at lightning speed.

"Try your luck, sir, madam: who'll find the lady? Only sixpence. Thank you, sir. Watch the cards, keep your eye on the cards - where's the little lady hiding? *That* one? Oh, bad luck, sir. Who's next?"

"Laura," said Idenion urgently, "give me your sixpence."

"What?"

"You said you had sixpence. I want it."

"Idenion, you can't!" Laura hissed, realising what he was about to do. "You'd be cheating!"

"I lost your money. Now I shall win it back," he replied staunchly.

Laura, thinking of the long walk ahead, didn't protest too much. She handed over the sixpence, took charge of the shopping once again, and watched as Idenion proceeded to fleece the unsuspecting man. Three times he placed a bet, three times the dealer performed his sleight-of-hand. And three times Idenion, without hesitation, pointed a forefinger and said:

"This is the lady."

"Nah," said one of the watchers to his crony, "he's not really winning. It's a put-up job. They do it to bring in the punters."

"You in the Magic Circle, mate?" the cardsharp asked Idenion after he'd won a fourth time.

"Nah," said Idenion. "I am a telepath."

388

There were one or two sniggers from the little group.

"You're a comedian, anyway," said the disgruntled man. "Well - nice doing business with you." And he packed up his props and went in search of another, more lucrative, pitch.

Laura, grudgingly pleased, helped Idenion count his winnings. "Three and six," she announced. "Not a fortune, but it'll get us to Paddington. And we'll have enough over for a cup of tea."

"Am I forgiven?" Idenion asked.

"I suppose so," Laura conceded. "But I'm not taking you down the Underground again. This time, we're catching a bus!"

During the bus journey, and later in the station cafeteria, Idenion became very quiet.

"You're not feeling poorly again, are you?" Laura asked anxiously.

"I think the inhalation's wearing off," Idenion said, chasing tea leaves round his cup. "But now, I feel unhappy. I shouldn't have spoken to the man who desired me."

"Oh, him," said Laura awkwardly.

"He didn't interest me," Idenion went on earnestly. "But he thought me beautiful, and I was flattered. I didn't mean to cause him anguish."

"Don't worry," Laura said lamely. "You weren't to know there was a law against it."

"There shouldn't be," he said morosely. "Not here. *Your* population isn't in decline. *You* don't have to forbid or discourage such relationships."

She looked up in sudden realisation. "Is

Celestra's population in decline?"

"You must have noticed," he returned wearily.

"But these trends do reverse themselves, don't they?" asked Laura, much concerned.

"Do they?" he countered, and said nothing more for at least five minutes.

"Our train's in," Laura said eventually. "You must be exhausted, Idenion, but it's an easy journey from now on. Uncle Nat will pick us up at Newbury."

On the train Idenion's introspective mood persisted. Laura, increasingly tired herself, closed her eyes for a few minutes. When she again looked at Idenion she was dismayed to see that he'd been crying.

"What is it? What's wrong?" she asked.

"This is a terrible place," he responded brokenly. "How did I ever contend with it? Everywhere there's duplicity and deceit. So much unhappiness, so many lies. And the others, the latent ones - calling out, calling out. And no one will answer. Oh, Laura, it's unbearable..." He began to weep afresh. Tentatively, she put her arm round him: he leant his head on her shoulder and sobbed loudly. The commuters rustled their newspapers and looked the other way. His tears began to form a damp patch on Laura's jacket, but she continued to hold him, and presently he appeared to fall asleep. He revived just before the train reached Newbury, and with touching reticence, apologised to Laura for the outburst.

"I believe I'm myself again," he added with a wan smile.

"It's good to have you back," she replied, and gave him a swift kiss.

Arm-in-arm, they trailed along the platform. Once outside, Laura found a phone box and dialled Windbourne.

"It's me, Uncle Nat," she announced. "Could you come and fetch us? It's been quite a day!"

Nathaniel wisely refrained from questioning the pair on the way home. Idenion in particular seemed the worse for wear; he couldn't even summon the energy to be nervous in the car. As soon as they were indoors, he made for the stairs.

"Forgive me, Laura, Nathaniel," he murmured. "I must rest."

Laura hastened to find hangers for the new clothes, and tried to smooth out the worst of the creases. Then she made a reviving cup of coffee and sat down to apprise Nathaniel of the day's events.

She was just describing the debacle in the Underground when there was a soft thud from Idenion's room. She went to investigate, but it was only Tib, who had entered the open window via the conservatory roof. Idenion was fast asleep on top of the quilt, still wearing his shirt and jeans. Laura draped an old coat over him and went back to Nathaniel.

"Hmm," said her uncle when she had explained. "I rather overestimated his stamina. Still, he'll bounce back. A good night's sleep is all he needs."

"But uncle," said Laura, "supposing he gets ill. I mean, *really* ill. What would we do? Even a cold could kill him!"

391

"Have you only just thought of that?" Nathaniel chided. "I quizzed him about it the first night he was here. Apparently, Celestra has some sort of built-in protection against viruses. Anyone leaving the planet takes this immunity with them, for a time."

Laura recalled Alendis raising that very subject on his arrival at the Lyricon. She hadn't understood the significance then.

"Idenion claims he'll be safe for two and a half weeks," continued Nathaniel. "After that, he'll be increasingly at risk until he returns home."

"That's why he warned Jarras not to be late," Laura reflected.

"He doesn't know how this immunity works," Nathaniel went on.

"Why am I not surprised?"

"Hear me out, Laura. *No-one* knows how it works, and therein lies a tragedy."

"What do you mean?"

"Whatever grants the Celestrians freedom from disease is also a form of population control. The ancients, as Idenion calls them, engineered it to suit their needs. But of course, they hadn't bargained on a meteor strike. Ever since, the survivors have tried vainly to repopulate their planet, struggling against artificial limits they don't understand and couldn't get rid of even if they did. Idenion freely admits they know little about medicine."

"Why did he tell you all this?" asked Laura faintly.

"I - ah - criticised his lax attitude toward marriage," confessed Nathaniel. "But since his

392

society's obliged to produce as many children as possible, you couldn't expect him to behave any other way."

Laura was silent and troubled.

"Now then!" said Nathaniel gruffly. "No need to look like that. You can't shoulder *all* their burdens."

"But it's so unfair!" she protested.

"Life is seldom fair," Nathaniel stated. "Well, aren't you going to finish telling me what happened today? If you'd lost all your money, how did you get back to Paddington?"

Laura recommenced her tale, but decided not to mention the girl nor the gay man. Instead she concentrated on the incident with the pickpocket, and Idenion's very individual approach to Find the Lady.

"Quite an adventure," Nathaniel commented.

"Adventure? I thought he was going to die on the Underground steps. The whole trip was a mistake, and if I ever see Tralvar again I'll tell him so."

"I'm sure Idenion will put it all down to experience," pronounced Nathaniel. "We can help by making what's left of his stay as pleasant as possible."

"Yes, all right," said Laura glumly. She didn't want any more reminders that Idenion's visit was finite.

"And do stop worrying about him. He won't get into any more scrapes. Nothing untoward ever happens in Cheveney."

393

Chapter Thirteen

At Kevis' insistence, Tralvar had made himself available to the public for two ilden every day. And the public, dissatisfied and contrary, stayed away. The demonstrators still chanted outside his window at dawn and dusk, but their one attempt to infiltrate the akron had ceased abruptly on his return from Treva. The power workers continued to stage their daily strikes, refusing to negotiate with him, and the Lyricon was still under occupation. A steady stream of written petitions was delivered to the akron, each one asking for Laura, but very few citizens lingered to plead their cause in person. Kevis believed this was due to nervousness. Tralvar himself believed it was a sign of contempt.

For the fifth day running, he sat by himself in the audience room. He had never felt so lonely nor so isolated. Jarras was still busy in Treva; Floren and Dena remained absent too. Even Strephin was keeping his distance. When Tyvian appeared, then, he should have been grateful for the company. Instead, he gave the botanist a surly glare.

"What are *you* doing here?"

Tyvian hated to see him so despondent. Normally, Tralvar's anger was sharp and positive. Today he had lost all his fire.

"I asked why you were here," he repeated.

"I.... wondered how you were..." began Tyvian indecisively.

"Don't prevaricate: you're no good at it. You didn't come here to pass the time of day. Tell me the

394

bad news."

"I've had several visits from Strephin," said Tyvian reluctantly. "I didn't want to bother you with this, Tralvar, but he's been acting so strangely I thought you should know."

"Has he been threatening you?"

"I said, he was acting *strangely*," Tyvian repeated with a grim little smile. "No, he doesn't threaten. Quite the opposite. He seems to want me as an ally."

Tralvar's morose expression didn't change. "Go on."

"He's viewed Laura's original retrace - or should I say absorbed it? Six times he's been back, insisting that I run it again. I have to direct the proceedings, because he's incapable of doing so, and each time he comes out of it ranting about warriors and heroes. He's obsessed, Tralvar. He says he's going to Earth to recruit allies, as Alendis was about to do."

Tralvar said nothing.

"Haven't you been listening?" asked Tyvian peevishly.

"What am I supposed to say?" Tralvar returned. "Yes, he's obsessed. Maybe I should just hand him the programme crystal and let him go. His potential recruits would make short work of him."

"But then they'd own one of our spacecraft."

"Which ruins an otherwise attractive solution. The trouble is, he knows Idenion's time's nearly up. He might try making his move when I take the crystal to Jarras."

"Send someone else with it," suggested Tyvian. "Or fetch Idenion yourself."

"Haven't you any sensible suggestions?" Tralvar asked wearily.

Tyvian accepted the rebuke without protest. "I wish I had."

"Why don't you spare me the pitying stares and say it?" Tralvar's voice was quietly self-disparaging. "I'm falling apart. Strephin watches and waits; the whole city watches and waits, except the ones who stand and yell. They want me out of office, Tyvian. Perhaps I should give them what they want."

"Tralvar, I *know* most of these students," Tyvian said earnestly. "They don't want you to resign. They only want Laura back."

"That's just an excuse," Tralvar declared. "If I brought her back, they'd still call for my resignation."

"There's no reason why they should," persisted Tyvian. "Unless something's happened that I don't know about."

"What's that supposed to mean?" Tralvar inquired sharply.

Tyvian blinked. "Nothing," he replied with obvious sincerity. "I only meant that I'm not up to date with akron politics."

Tralvar subsided. "Don't think I haven't considered sending for Laura," he said. "It might give me some peace - for a time. But you of all people should know how dangerous it is to prolong our contact with Symerid Three." He stared reflectively into the distance. "They've already taken their first step towards transposal, though they

396

don't know it. The theory's been with them since the time of Ancient Hellas. Possibly one of our explorers said more than he should."

"Laura told you this?"

"She called it the music of the spheres - celestial bodies resonating in harmony."

Tyvian looked aghast.

"Close, aren't they?" Tralvar commented. "And they think it's just an exercise in aesthetics!" He gave a hollow laugh. "Now, as for your problem: I imagine your supply of prill is running low?"

"Indeed yes - the last batch was weak and sickly. I believe they absorbed the death-throes of the ones that perished. I can only run the retracer once more, and then I must collect new specimens or wait until my seedlings have matured."

"Strephin, of course, will insist you visit the prill world," said Tralvar.

"He isn't likely to wait for the seeds to grow."

"Quite. In that case, I forbid you to make the trip. If he doesn't like it, refer him to me."

Tyvian murmured grateful thanks.

"I only wish *my* problems were so easily solved," Tralvar sighed. "And now, you'd better make yourself scarce before he discovers you've been here. I don't know quite where he is at the moment, but I'm sure he won't be far away."

After Tyvian had left, Tralvar lapsed into another unhappy reverie. Long after his tour of duty had ended he sat and ruminated, not seeing the shadows growing longer across the tiled floor and ornate high-backed chairs.

"First Citizen?" said a child's voice; and, turning abruptly, he beheld Tioni standing at his elbow. Tioni, who had lain dead at his feet, her breastbone shattered by one of his bullets. She wore a plain yellow tunic, but one of her characteristic crimson ribbons adorned her curls. With a shy smile, she held out a petitioner's scroll.

Her shyness dispelled the momentary illusion. Tralvar, recovering, realised the girl was much younger than Tioni. A man, presumably her father, hovered just beyond the open door at the far end of the room.

This is your doing, Strephin, thought Tralvar coldly. He made no move toward the girl, who, having failed to hand him her scroll, placed it on the table and turned to leave.

"Wait," Tralvar said, trying not to sound peremptory. He unsealed the petition and read it. Unsurprisingly, it asked for Laura's return. "Why have you brought this to me?" he continued quietly. "Petitions go to my secretary's office."

"We were going there," said the girl, glancing round to make sure her father was still present. "But a man saw us and said it would be best if I brought it to you instead. He made me wait while he fetched this ribbon. He said you'd like it."

Did he now? thought Tralvar.

"But he tied it too tight," said the girl, fidgeting. "It pulls."

Tralvar carefully undid the knot and laid the ribbon aside. "What's your name, little one?"

"Lirini."

"And why do you want Laura to come back,

398

Lirini?"

"Because she could sing," answered the girl, surprised. "What a silly question! That's why *everyone* wants her back."

"Of course," said Tralvar, half to himself. What would this child know about the intrigue that had surrounded Laura? How she had turned the entire administration on its head and disrupted the lives of everyone she'd come into contact with? He wasn't aware that his own dark thoughts had reclaimed him until he felt a tentative touch on his hand. Resisting an urge to snatch it away, he switched his attention back to his young visitor.

The child had laid her small hand over his. "Please don't be sad," she said earnestly. "Father says I'm not to absorb from you, so I don't know what the matter is. But it must be very difficult being First Citizen."

"It's quite difficult," Tralvar said gently.

"I thought so," said Lirini. "Maybe if Laura was here, she could cheer you up. She makes people happy."

Then she tripped away, prompted by the shadowy figure beyond the door. Silence returned. Almost an ild later, Kevis found Tralvar still at the table, his head pillowed on his folded arms, the crumpled ribbon lying nearby. But contrary to the secretary's suspicions he was not drunk, merely exhausted.

"Death and destruction," he muttered. "Melor was right - I chose my path years ago. How long must I continue this charade?"

"Come away from here," urged Kevis.

Tralvar obeyed without riposte or argument, which in itself gave Kevis cause for concern. But he asked no questions. He knew there would be no point.

***

"Did you hear what I said, Strephin?" asked Tyvian edgily. "This is the only prill I have left."

"Then let's use it," said Strephin, seemingly unconcerned.

"Tralvar has forbidden me to fetch more," Tyvian reiterated.

"Why are you saying everything twice, plant man?" Strephin inquired. "Not getting senile, I hope? That would be a shade inconvenient."

"You don't seem to understand the situation," Tyvian said, increasingly nervous.

"I understand only too well." Strephin positively oozed complacency. "Did you enjoy your visit to Tralvar? It must have been quite an eye-opener. Now you've seen the state he's in, I think you'll agree that I'm more than capable of deposing him."

Tyvian was beginning to believe it. Sick at heart, he activated Laura's retrace once again. Strephin sat down eagerly and relaxed into its now-familiar patterns, closing his eyes and stretching his long legs. Symerid Three's war machines began their enticing parade through his thoughts.

Then, suddenly, the trace dissolved and the monitor went black. Strephin roared his disbelief.

The solitary prill, deprived of its symbiosis with the aldacite, set up a persistent keening which scratched at Tyvian's perception like fingernails on slate.

"Get it back on!" Strephin bellowed.

"I can't - there's been a power cut," Tyvian said, afraid to state the obvious.

"You've got standby generators, haven't you? Get them started!"

"They only run the artificial environments," Tyvian answered timidly. "There's nowhere near enough current for the retracer."

Strephin cast his chair aside, grabbed Tyvian and shook him furiously. "If I find out you planned this, old fool..."

"I had nothing to do with it," Tyvian whimpered. "Take it up with the electricians."

Strephin released him abruptly. "Chaos rot them all," he spat. "I'll take it up with them all right. It's about time someone put a stop to this nonsense." And he stormed out, quite forgetting about his tacit endorsement of the Laura campaign.

Tyvian was worried enough to call the nearest relayist and issue a warning to the power station, not realising that Strephin had a different objective in mind.

***

"Oh, *please*, Lydion. Come and run the shield." The girl with her dainty foot in the technician's door was exquisitely pretty and extremely persistent.

"I'm not on duty," Lydion objected. "Ask

401

Tonor."

"We don't want Tonor, we want *you*," she declared. "Every time Tonor's in charge of the shield, it goes wrong. You're the best, Lydion."

"Of course," he said immodestly. "But it's still my day off."

"Please," said the girl beseechingly. "It's cold in there."

"Then put some more clothes on," Lydion said, trying to sound disapproving and not quite succeeding. His visitor wore only firi, and not very much of that. "I suppose you're a dancer," he added.

She drew herself up haughtily. "I'm a student of philosophy," she informed him.

"And what's your name, student philosopher?"

"Irivel," she replied, hugging herself to keep warm in the stiff breeze.

Lydion's good nature, not to mention his fondness for pretty girls, was beginning to get the better of him. He had no plans for the day; he could spare a couple of ilden. He offered Irivel a cloak, which she accepted gratefully, then said: "It'll take me about three astallen to get the field set up."

"You're a treasure!" she declared, and embraced him briefly before darting back inside the Lyricon.

Lydion's house was quite close to the stage entrance, so he required only a few moments to reach the generator room. He removed the safety bar from the heavy door and attempted to push it open, but as usual it jammed on the uneven

402

flagstones. Cyphos and his team had been about to repair the floor when Alendis had used the pediment for target practice - which, naturally enough, had diverted the team's efforts. Using the bar as a lever, Lydion finally managed to open the door wide enough to slip through, although at least two astallen had now passed. Better hurry up, Lydion, he told himself with a wry smile. Irivel will be getting impatient. Depositing the metal bar in a corner, he began to flip switches methodically; and while he waited for the power to build, idly wondered if the girl would seek him out later. He was fairly sure she would. Under his expert touch the shield flared into life, and he gave a satisfied sigh.

"Turn that off!" said a harsh voice.

Lydion whirled, then blanched. "You!"

"Surprised to see me?" queried Strephin. "I've left you alone too long as it is. While you're busy abetting this demonstration and taking your pick of the women, the city's being crippled by power cuts. Or hadn't you noticed?"

"I don't want to argue with you," began Lydion.

"Then turn off the shield. Or shall I do it for you?"

"Don't touch that!" exclaimed Lydion, attempting to push him aside. "It's dangerous, you idiot. Can't you read the warnings?"

Strephin's tenuous self-control deserted him. The metal bar gleamed invitingly from its corner; he snatched it up and brandished it in an arc. "I'll show you what dangerous is!" he snarled. "Get out of my way. I'm turning this thing off - permanently!"

"No!" shrieked Lydion. He hit out at Strephin - a defensive, openhanded slap which Strephin walked straight into. Blood spurted from his nose. In a blind rage, he hefted the bar and swung it down. Lydion tried to dodge aside, failed, and took the full force of the blow on the side of his head. He fell like a stone.

A stifled scream brought Strephin to his senses. Irivel, wide-eyed, hands to her mouth, stood just inside the door. She seemed rooted to the spot.

Strephin had a habit of fleeing from the scene of his misdemeanours, but this time he fought down the impulse. He'd have to stay and brazen it out, or forever lose all hope of becoming First Citizen. The incriminating bar lay at his feet, where he'd dropped it; he surreptitiously nudged it aside and took a couple of steps toward the girl.

"He picked a fight with me," he said with as much earnestness as he could muster. "He hit me first. You saw him." He wasn't at all sure that she had, but to his relief her answer confirmed it.

"Yes...but why?"

"Never mind that now," Strephin said coolly. "He needs our help." Staunching his nosebleed on his sleeve, he knelt by Lydion's inert form and touched his neck. A weak, shallow pulse beat beneath his fingers. "We have to call the medics," he continued. "Can you quieten your friends and get a message through?"

She pulled herself together. "Tylo's in the Lyricon," she said. "Tylo, the relayist. I'll speak to him."

In less than an astal, a team from the hospital

arrived and bore Lydion away. Irivel went with them. Strephin, still in the process of whitewashing his misdeed, then did something which on the face of it seemed incomprehensible. He sent for Tralvar.

When Tralvar arrived, in even less time than it had taken the medical team, he was already acquainted with the facts of Strephin's latest crime. But if he'd expected the culprit to throw himself on the mercy of the city, he was sadly mistaken. Strephin had already prepared his defence. The electricity had been cut while he was in the middle of absorbing a retrace - which had left him in a disoriented and disturbed state, as Tyvian would have to attest. And the girl Irivel had arrived just in time to see Lydion strike the first blow of the fight which had landed him in hospital with a fractured skull. There would be a hearing, of course, but with these two vital witnesses the administration would doubtless rule in Strephin's favour.

"So you see," Strephin concluded gleefully, "no one's going to expel me from Alda Mexa. I just didn't want you to get your hopes up."

Tralvar glowered. "One day, Strephin, you'll make one mistake too many."

Strephin laughed. "Not me! I'm fireproof."

"I should have *you* retraced. Someone still has to answer for Relto's murder."

"Retrace me, then, if you want to look a fool. I didn't do it. I thought Alendis did."

"Zenzie didn't seem to think so."

"Then it must have been Asterion. Either way, Tralvar, you're stuck with me." He was still laughing.

"Is that the reason you dragged me over here?" asked Tralvar icily. "To taunt me?"

"As if I would," said Strephin blandly. "I sent for you because everyone ran off and left me minding this valuable machine." He gestured toward the shield controls. "I wouldn't have a clue what to do if it malfunctioned. And I do believe it's just starting to."

Projector four had begun to oscillate. Tralvar trimmed it with swift impatience.

"What an idiotic situation to be in," Strephin commented lightly. "Helping to maintain a demonstration against yourself!"

Tralvar ignored him and waited for the field to stabilise. It didn't take kindly to being shut down whilst still cold, otherwise he'd have extinguished it and left. "There's only one reason why Lydion would have hit you," he said at length. "To prevent you from damaging this equipment."

"How astute of you."

"He was trying to save your worthless life," Tralvar said grimly. "Not to mention his own. If you'd managed to destroy one of the projectors, there wouldn't have been much left of this room."

"Really?" Strephin was intrigued.

"The projectors each generate a section of the field, but they also draw energy from the parabola and redistribute it," Tralvar explained briefly. "If the flow were disrupted, that energy would have to go somewhere. In fact, it - " he bit off his words abruptly, ashamed at his train of thought.

"Go on. It might make a good weapon - that was what you were going to say, wasn't it?"

"Differently configured, it might," said Tralvar reluctantly. There had been no perception involved, but Strephin had read him unerringly. Was he really so transparent?

Strephin regarded him intently. "If I were First Citizen, I'd give you all the time and resources you needed for weapons development," he confided. "It's what you really want to do. Why pretend it isn't?"

"May I remind you, Strephin," said Tralvar after a slight pause, "that you're hardly in a position to offer me anything?"

"Not yet," said Strephin complacently. Tralvar had hesitated. That meant he'd been tempted. Strephin didn't pursue his advantage; he was rapidly learning when to keep silent. But privately he was exultant. Success, in the form of the First Citizenship, had never been closer.

***

"Hi, Laura!" Tracey skipped into Windbourne's kitchen just after lunchtime the following day. She was wearing a skinny-rib top and a skirt that was decent by about half an inch. "I've come to see your new outfits. Fancy old Scrooge paying for a trip to Carnaby Street!"

"Shhh," said Laura. "He'll hear you."

"I'll soon fix that!" Tracey grabbed the transistor radio from its shelf, wrinkled her nose in disgust at finding it tuned to the Home Service, and twirled the dial expertly.

"Caroline!" shrilled the radio.

"Caroli-yi-yi-yine!"

"That's better," Tracey declared as the pirate station launched into Good Vibrations. "I wanted to ask you something."

"What?"

"Have you, er, you know. With Denny?"

Laura pretended not to understand.

"Have you *still* not done it?" Tracey was genuinely astonished. "What are you waiting for?"

The door opened to admit Nathaniel. "What's all the row? Oh, I might have guessed it was you, Tracey."

"Afternoon, Nathaniel."

"It's Mr. Gilcoyne to you," he informed her. "Do turn that radio down. Idenion's asleep."

Tracey lowered the volume fractionally.

"Tracey came to see my new dresses," Laura explained.

"Then show her quietly," ordered Nathaniel. "I'll be in my study. And if I can still hear that din, I'll be out again!"

Tracey stuck out her tongue at his retreating back.

Not wishing to allow Tracey upstairs, Laura brought down her two new minis and hung them on the back of the kitchen door. "Idenion bought a kaftan and some other stuff, but you'll have to see that some other time," she said. "I don't want to disturb him."

"He sleeps a lot, that boy," Tracey began, then stopped short as she beheld the red and black dress. "Oh, wow! Can I try that on?"

"If you like," said Laura indifferently. "It was

an impulse buy. I'll probably never wear it."

"Can I buy it off you?" asked Tracey eagerly. "If it fits, that is." Unselfconsciously she stripped down to her bra and tights, and stepped carefully into the coveted dress. "Zip me up," she instructed, then dashed out to inspect herself in the hall mirror. On the way back she almost fell over Tib, who had wandered downstairs. That meant, of course, that Idenion was awake and would soon follow.

"Blast!" said Laura under her breath.

"Well, what do you think?" asked Tracey impatiently.

"It's a bit tight on you," Laura commented.

"It is *not*!" Tracey contradicted with a flash of hostility. She was sensitive about her weight. But just then, the radio twanged out the introduction to "Stop Stop Stop" by the Hollies; she immediately brightened and performed an impromptu belly dance around the table.

At that moment Idenion walked in, looking sleepy and dishevelled. He said nothing, but regarded Tracey's gyrations with some interest. She promptly redoubled her efforts, until a sharp "miaow!" announced that she'd trodden on Tib.

"Watch out!" said Laura, irritated.

"Well, tell the silly cat to stop getting underfoot!" Tracey retorted. "Look at her - she's all over the place. Haven't you fed her?"

"Of course I have!" Laura replied testily.

"Please could I have a cup of tea?" Idenion asked plaintively.

"That goes for me too," said Tracey, sitting down next to him.

Fuming, Laura made tea for them both, then watched Tracey pose and preen and gaze calculatingly at Idenion over her teacup. Idenion should have been able to outstare her, but instead seemed ill at ease. The radio played "Pretty Flamingo" and "Lovers of the World Unite." And all the time, Tib weaved in and out of the table legs and would not settle.

Then Mrs. Moffat arrived. "Oh, Tracey, you *are* here. Your mum's looking for you."

"What for?" asked Tracey disinterestedly.

"She's probably got some last-minute instructions," Mrs. Moffat replied briskly. "Your dad's just finished loading the car."

"He's *not* my dad," said Tracey vehemently. "And the sooner they clear off to Minehead and leave me in peace, the better I'll like it." She stubbed out her cigarette in her saucer. "Well, I suppose I'd better go and see what the old bag wants."

"Aren't you forgetting something?" asked Laura acidly.

"Oh, your dress!" said Tracey sweetly. Laura tensed, expecting her to strip it off in front of Idenion; but instead she picked up her jumper and skirt and disappeared modestly into the hall. Laura clicked the radio off in the middle of "Witches' Brew". Tracey reappeared, dumped the dress in Idenion's lap, grabbed her cigarettes and departed.

"See you, Denny!" she called just before the door slammed.

"That girl gets worse," tutted Mrs. Moffat.

"She really hates her stepfather," Laura mused.

410

"Tib is preparing to mate," Idenion announced suddenly.

Mrs. Moffat looked startled, then regarded Tib with a critical eye. "I do believe he's right. Look at her, rubbing her little head round everything. That's a sure sign."

"It's the wrong time of year," objected Laura.

Idenion carefully laid the discarded dress aside, catching a whiff of Tracey's perfume as he did so. "I'm not mistaken," he insisted.

"We'll soon know," said Mrs. Moffat. "By tonight she could be yowling for a tomcat. Make sure you keep her locked up, Laura."

Idenion was scandalised. "You cannot deprive her of a mate!" he exclaimed.

"She's already had one litter this year," Laura told him gently.

"It's high time we had her neutered," declared Mrs. Moffat, and busied herself with the duster.

Idenion escaped to the drawing room, leaving Laura and the housekeeper to discuss the problem of Tib. There was such an abundance of fertility on this world. It amazed him, and saddened him too. He wondered why he felt so out of sorts, particularly after a long and satisfying sleep. Could his protections be failing already? He'd calculated that he had three more days at least. Of course, Tracey's presence hadn't helped. Her aggressive sexuality and reptilian stare had disturbed him more than he cared to admit. He went across to the piano and fingered its keys idly. Maybe he should ask Laura to sing for him - that ought to calm his spirits.

In fact, it did the opposite. During her brief

411

recital he became acutely aware of the rise and fall of her firm young breasts, and was quite glad that no one could perceive what he was thinking - provided he didn't stare. In Earthly terms, as Nathaniel had once pointed out, he was still in his late teens, and well accustomed to sudden erotic promptings. He'd experienced many during his stay at Windbourne, and had handled them – and Nathaniel's ban - with his customary ease and good humour. But now, he realised he wasn't altogether in control.

By late evening, Tib was uttering mournful wails and presenting her hindquarters to the empty air. Laura locked her in an outhouse with some bedding and a saucer of milk. Idenion was now in no doubt that Tib was responsible for his own escalating desires. He'd thought her killing instinct alarming, but her desire to mate was infinitely more powerful. It communicated itself on a subliminal level, and from there seeped into every aspect of his consciousness. Closing off his perception made no difference. Like a blaze of light through closed eyelids, the sheer intensity of Tib's need could not be ignored.

Soon he'd no longer be able to hide his distress from his hosts. Pleading tiredness, he went to his room, knowing that sleep was impossible. His head ached, his groin ached, and he was alternately sweating and shivering. In desperation he went into the bathroom and splashed his face and neck with cold water. It helped, but not for long. He could hear Laura in the next room, innocently getting ready for bed. He leant his forehead against the cool surface of the mirror and told himself that he would not, dared not, go to her.

Part of his mind, coldly analytical, realised he had the answer to a puzzle. It had long been accepted that Celestra's neo-primitives were the first psi-conversants, and that they'd slaughtered whatever animals had survived the meteor strike. Hitherto no one had known why; Idenion now believed he did. His ancestors, struggling to control their newly evolved powers, had acted out of self-preservation. Tib was only a domestic pet. The mating instinct of wild creatures must have been unendurable - maybe even a threat to sanity. And perhaps something of what the primitives had absorbed remained in the form of sciesha...no, it wasn't a good idea to think about sciesha.

It was now 11.30. The night had hardly begun. He waited until Laura was asleep, then went downstairs to find Nathaniel.

"Sir," he said formally, "I have a problem." And proceeded, in simple but graphic terms, to explain what it was.

"That's...awkward," Nathaniel said, nonplussed.

"What am I to do?" Idenion went on. "I don't trust myself to keep my promise." He dragged a hand across his clammy brow, looking more woebegone by the minute.

"I see you've tried the cold shower," Nathaniel commented, noting his damp hair. "What about going for a walk? It might clear your head."

Idenion agreed, without much conviction. It would at least put some distance between him and Laura.

413

Nathaniel handed him a torch. "You'll need this - there's no moon. Idenion - "

"What?" asked the Celestrian miserably.

"Thank you for being so honest."

Idenion stammered out some kind of reply and stumbled away. Nathaniel watched the torchlight bobbing down the lane, then went slowly toward the outhouse. Tib, hearing him, scratched frantically at the door.

"Margaret's not going to thank me for this," he muttered to himself, "but there's really no choice. I just wonder how I'm going to explain it." He unlocked the door, and immediately a small furry body hurtled past him and vanished into the darkness. Above, the constellations shone gloriously, unrivalled by moonlight. He stared thoughtfully up at them for several minutes before returning to his study.

Idenion trailed along the footpath toward the centre of the village, paying no heed to the direction he took. The first dampness of autumn was already in the air, and he wished he'd worn a jacket. He sensed Tib's escape from her prison; Nathaniel had at least taken his plight seriously. Now all he had to do was stay out for a while. He leant on a tree, let the torch droop and tried to breathe normally.

"Hi," said a familiar voice.

He started; the beam of light jerked upwards.

"Hey!" protested Tracey, shielding her eyes. "It's only me." Her blonde hair looked white in the torchlight, and for a moment, in his dazed state, he confused her with Zenzie.

"Why are you out here, my little love?" he

414

murmured.

"Why are *you*?" she countered. "Don't answer, let me guess. Not that I *need* to guess. I know frustration when I see it." She leant provocatively against him, and gently but firmly took the torch away. "There," she continued, switching it off. "We don't want nosey parkers spying on us, do we? Now why don't you relax and let Tracey take care of you?"

Idenion had one brief moment of sobriety. "Don't, Tracey. This isn't right!"

"It's what we both want," she returned. "Poor Denny! She's really got you in a state, hasn't she?"

"She...?"

"Laura. I bet she led you on and changed her mind at the last minute. She did that with Jimmy, you know. What *you* want is someone who..." Her voice faded into the middle distance. Elsewhere, Tib had rejected the advances of one tom and was now encouraging another. The keen edge of her desire modulated into something more settled - the mental embodiment of a purr. The ritual of mating was almost complete. Idenion, too, succumbed to the inevitable, and allowed Tracey to lure him into her house. He had been only yards from her front door; whether by accident or instinct, he couldn't say. She led him upstairs, noting the hazy look in his grey eyes and wondering if he'd been smoking pot.

"Aren't you going to kiss me?" she asked. He did, very carefully, as if he wasn't used to it. Nor did his lovemaking have the expertise she was sure he was capable of. His efforts were hasty, almost

415

clumsy, ending in a cry which sounded suspiciously like despair.

"You've been too long without it," she commented, tilting the table lamp to get a better view of his face. He still looked as though he didn't know where he was.

"Apologies," he said hoarsely. "I'm not being much use. Let me rest a moment."

"Yeah. Right," she replied cynically.

Idenion was soon able to continue, although he was far from happy. At first, his need for release had been so great that he hadn't sensed anything amiss. But now, as he strove to bring a degree of pleasure to the girl, he realised he was making little impression. Sex with a nonconversant was nothing new to him - he'd experienced that on Myrma. But his Myrmian lady had been warm and delightful. There was something innately cold about Tracey, although she made all the correct responses. One tiny kernel of her mind held a searing contempt for him and for all men - and he was probably the only man on Earth capable of seeing it.

Elsewhere, the brief mating over, Tib rounded on the tomcat with a snarl, claws extended. He fled. Tib, back to normal, began to wash herself vigorously.

Sated yet discontented, Idenion rolled onto his back and surveyed his surroundings for the first time. Tracey's bedroom was full of dolls. Their blank, inane little faces stared at him from display cabinets, the chest of drawers, and the bedside table. Tracey's expression was equally unreadable. She sat up, put on a dressing-gown and reached for her

416

cigarettes.

"Want one?"

"No. Thank you."

Tracey drew her legs under her, dragging deep on the cigarette and staring straight ahead. All calculated to make me feel inadequate, Idenion thought. She doesn't enjoy sex, only the control it gives her. But why? Why is she like this?

Moments later, he had his answer in the form of a plaintive mental cry - the same cry that had disturbed his sleep more than once since he'd been in Cheveney. Tracey was the latent telepath. And at close range, he'd detected a faint image in the projection - a footfall on a creaking stair, a hated male presence.

"What're you staring at?" she asked irritably.

Idenion focused his perception and replied as strongly as he could. There was no recognition. Disappointed and still not quite his rational self, he blurted out:

"Who is the man on the stair?"

She froze, and the half-revealed memory crystallised. She was ten, and her stepfather was speaking the words she dreaded...

"It's time for our secret game." Idenion vocalised the phrase unwittingly, realising as soon as the words were out of his mouth that he'd committed a dangerous blunder. He instantly sobered up, but too late. Tracey backed away from him, wide-eyed.

"How did you know that?" she cried. "I never told *anybody* that!"

Idenion, not wishing to add to the damage, said

nothing. Tracey grabbed his clothes and threw them at him.

"Just get out," she ordered. "And don't ever come back. You're weird. I don't want to see you or speak to you again."

"You won't have to. I'm leaving England," Idenion said gravely. He dressed with dignity, taking his time.

"Get a move on," Tracey snapped. "You know where the front door is. Use it."

"In a moment." Idenion came to a sudden decision. Without another word he went up to Tracey and hugged her fiercely. She didn't struggle. Presently some of the anger went out of her, and she drooped sadly in his arms.

"Does your stepfather still molest you?" Idenion asked, though he knew the answer to that too.

"Not since I grew up," she replied in a small voice. "You frighten me, Denny. How did you *know*?"

"Maybe I'm psychic," he said. "Or maybe we both are. What matters is that you've wanted to tell someone for a long time. And now, I want you to make some changes. For years you've been manipulating people to prove you're no longer helpless, but that has to stop. Take charge of your own life, Tracey. Don't let him ruin it."

Then he released her and went downstairs. Picking up his torch from the hall table, he opened the front door and sought refuge in the clear, cold night. He was shaking with tiredness. As he neared Windbourne, an equally weary Tib appeared and

418

trotted alongside him.

"This is a wicked world, Tib," he said softly.

It was 2 a.m. Nathaniel had gone to bed, but the back door was on the latch. Idenion reached the sanctuary of his room without disturbing anyone, and was soon deeply asleep.

The following morning his arms and legs were covered in midge bites. He gazed at them in dismay. So his protections *were* failing, although his time wasn't up for another day and a half. Fortunately Jarras was a most conscientious individual, and could be relied on not to be late.

***

Under Tralvar's shaky guidance the akron administration had grown erratic, and Kyrin became accustomed to receiving work from many different individuals. When someone placed yet another instruction on his desk he took it absently, and only looked up after he'd read it.

"I trust I've made myself clear?" inquired Strephin.

A sick dread came over Kyrin. The dull pain in his right side, which had remained with him since he was attacked, suddenly seemed to grow worse. "I...can't send this. It's a lie."

"Nevertheless, you will send it," Strephin said evenly.

"I know what you're trying to do," Kyrin went on. "This could undermine the goodwill between Tralvar and the scolia. He'll deny it, but stories like this aren't easily suppressed."

419

"Especially when they carry your mental autograph, Kyrin," said Strephin complacently. "Send it. That's an order."

"I have a responsibility to the First Citizen elect," said Kyrin stubbornly. "This pronouncement would damage him."

"I'll damage *you* if I have any more refusals," Strephin said ominously. "Don't you know what happened to Lydion?"

"What use would I be to you, unconscious?" Kyrin ventured, although he was trembling.

"But you wouldn't *be* unconscious," Strephin replied in thoroughly reasonable tones. "You'd be awake and in a great deal of pain. Be very careful what you say next. Asterion's dead: there's no one to protect you now."

Kyrin stared silently at the desk top, his colour rising.

"By harmony," Strephin murmured softly. "He *said* he was going back to you; I never believed he would. You should be punished for exploiting his weakness."

"No!" Kyrin protested.

"Then send the message," Strephin intoned patiently.

"No," repeated Kyrin.

Strephin suddenly grasped the relayist's chair and swivelled it, toppling the young man onto the floor. Kyrin saw Strephin's foot descending and tried to roll aside, to no avail. The blow smashed into his ribs and he lay agonised.

"Get up," Strephin ordered, and Kyrin struggled to obey. Strephin took careful note of the way he

420

moved. Then, with his usual studied viciousness, he propped Kyrin against the nearest wall and began punching him with his left fist, again aiming for the ribcage. When he let go, Kyrin slid untidily down the wall and lay sobbing.

"Tomorrow, you might think better of your decision," Strephin commented. "I shall visit you again at noon-plus-one. And stop that snivelling. I've let you off lightly and you know it."

Then he was gone, but his laughter echoed in the distance. Kyrin, despairful, managed to crawl back to his desk. He knew, as did Strephin, that he couldn't endure another beating. Tomorrow he would obey his tormentor, and in the meantime Tralvar would know nothing. Strephin hadn't even bothered to warn him against reporting the matter. Kyrin dried his tears and tried to put aside his shame. He'd done all he could. Tralvar was on his own from now on.

***

Tralvar was at a loose end. He'd gone to see how Lydion was, only to be chased away by the healer in charge.

"With respect, First Citizen, my task is difficult enough already without you emoting all over the place. Lydion needs peace and quiet, as do I. His condition is serious but not life-threatening. Be assured, he will recover - in time."

So Tralvar had gone back to the akron, only to be confronted by Strephin in another of his strange ranting moods, extolling the dubious virtues of

Symerid Three. He could think of no argument to silence him.

Once back in his apartment, he simply sat watching the light fade. The students didn't come to his window, which vaguely surprised him. There were, his reason suggested, things to be done. He should be contacting Jarras to arrange the transfer of the Hellas programme. And then there was the matter of the therite launchers. Despite his resolutions he hadn't assembled any fresh ones - which meant all the armaments were still in Strephin's hands. But he couldn't face handling therite at the moment. He was too tired, too disoriented.

Once more he toyed with the idea of resigning, but he put it off in the knowledge that he'd always have that option. And, though he was scarcely aware of it, because he still possessed a grain of stubbornness.

On an impulse he donned his scolia robe and sat down at the zirid. He played until his hands ached, played everything he could bring to mind - from tunes he'd written long ago to the wonderful music he'd seen in Laura's memory. And as he played, he admitted to himself for the first time how much he wanted her back.

It was late when he finally closed the keyboard and stood up. As he did so, Kevis entered discreetly.

"You have a fine talent there, First Citizen," he remarked.

Tralvar made a dismissive gesture.

"Jarras has just radioed from Treva," Kevis continued. "He was expecting to hear from you today. He says Idenion's time is up."

"Yes, he's right," Tralvar said guiltily. "Tell him to come to the Alda Mexa spacefield at - " He hesitated briefly. He'd been about to say dawn, but decided it would be better to have more people present.

" - at noon tomorrow," he finished. "I'll meet him there."

"I will inform him," said Kevis. "Also, I've taken the liberty of bringing you some supper. Shall I serve it?"

Tralvar realised he was hungry, thanked him, and settled down to eat the salad and fruit. He hadn't been near his supply of resnay all evening - and even more remarkably, hadn't felt the need to. Music, it seemed, was at least as intoxicating as liquor.

He took his time over the meal, gazing thoughtfully across the plaza. He'd just pushed aside his plate when the street lights went out, signifying midnight. He yawned, and was just considering having a very small glass of resnay - purely as a nightcap - when a soft, surreptitious call nudged at his perception.

+Tralvar+

He was on his feet in an instant. +Floren? Floren, where are you?+

+At the basement door+ she replied.

+Then go round to the kitchen entrance. I've given Strephin my old apartment+ Tralvar was already halfway down the main stairs. He dashed through the deserted kitchens and opened the outer door with clumsy impatience. When Floren appeared, he hustled her straight up to his rooms.

"Where have you *been*?" he exclaimed as soon as he'd secured the apartment door.

"In hiding. I needed to think," she replied.

"Have you any idea what's been going on here?" he demanded. "Strephin's gone crazy - he's threatening to visit Symerid Three and disclose our science. I've confiscated the flight programme but that won't stop him much longer. He's stolen all my guns, and he's trying to take over the leadership. And those students, the ones from the Lyricon - " He heard himself babbling, but couldn't seem to slow down. "Every day they're under my window, screaming for Laura. Oh, Floren, thank harmony you're back. You started the sit-in, didn't you? You can reason with them, get them to stop - " He paused, suddenly aware of her eyes upon him.

"We need to talk," she said calmly.

"What about?"

Floren sat down and folded her hands in her lap, still maintaining her cool accusing gaze. "I know what you did, Tralvar. I know you killed Tristell."

Chapter Fourteen

Tralvar stared at her in a mixture of shock and relief, all his long-suppressed memories laid bare. He again felt the slight chill in his palm as Alendis handed him two glass capsules, each containing a fine white powder. At the same time a far greater chill had smitten him as he realised what he was expected to do.

"I'm rather proud of this poison," Alendis was saying. "There's no odour, no taste, and no pain. Empty these into Tristell's drinking water. She will simply fall asleep and die peacefully."

Tralvar had stood rooted to the spot, wanting to crush the capsules to fragments but unable even to close his hand.

"I devised this method because I've nothing personal against Tristell," Alendis continued. "She can't help being the way she is. But there are other less merciful ways to remove her. Would you rather I employed one of them? If you destroy those capsules you'll leave me

with no alternative."

With a sob Tralvar wrenched his mind back into the present. Worse, far worse, had followed, and he lacked the strength to confront it.

"It *was* a peaceful death," Floren told him quietly. "Everyone save Zenzie thought it was from natural causes."

"How you must despise me," Tralvar said dully.

"It was Alendis I despised."

"It's only fitting that *you* should be the one to

expose my crime," Tralvar went on as though she hadn't spoken. "Tomorrow I'll make a public confession and accept banishment."

Floren's gaze softened. "Before you rush off to confess, I've a few things to tell you," she said. "Alendis had a healthy respect for you, although he kept it well hidden. When you began to question his authority he considered you a potential threat. He confided his fears to Zenzie."

"Alendis? Afraid of *me*?"

"Very much so," Floren affirmed. "He realised he'd pushed you too far."

Tralvar remained sceptical.

"Once Alendis had started to unburden himself, he told Zenzie some terrible things," Floren continued. "Remember the strange red flowers that Eptal kept bringing from off-world?"

"I remember. Tristell liked them but they wouldn't grow here."

"They were the source of the poison. Alendis kept demanding more of them. Eptal finally realised why, and decided to challenge him."

"Oh, the fool," Tralvar murmured. "So that's why he was killed. Why didn't he tell someone else what he'd discovered?"

"He underestimated Alendis - like many before him," Floren said. "But the story doesn't end there. Because his supply of the drug was gone, Alendis only had enough for what he called his special cases. One was Tristell: the other was you." She paused to assess his reaction. "Why so shocked? You were fast becoming his worst enemy. What else did you expect from him?"

Tralvar shuddered. "Idenion once told me I was walking the edge of eternity. It seems he was right." He groped for the resnay bottle: now he really did need a drink.

"On the morning of the retrace - the day after she and Alendis were pairbonded - Zenzie woke to find him preparing two more capsules," Floren went on. "She didn't know what to do; she only knew she couldn't stand by and see you killed. So she turned to her mother, as she always did when she was worried. I promised I'd warn you, but before I could make a move, Alendis had gone chasing after Laura. And afterwards..." She spread out her hands eloquently. "Afterwards, it didn't seem to matter."

Tralvar digested these revelations, sipping slowly at a double measure of resnay. Zenzie had wanted to save his life, even though she'd have been justified in leaving him to his fate. He remembered the tears he'd shed after the headstrong girl had perished alongside Alendis, and how embarrassed he'd been at his lack of self-control. Now, he was glad he'd wept. He'd misjudged her so badly.

"Since the danger's past, why are you telling me this?" he asked eventually.

Floren studied him compassionately. He looked so forlorn, so tired. She fervently wished there was some way to avoid what she was about to say. "I told you I'd been in hiding," she began. "But I haven't been out of touch. I know what's been going on, particularly with regard to Strephin. I've had meetings with the scolia, with the student leaders, and various responsible citizens. I speak for them all. You might say I'm here to petition

427

you.

"Strephin is now a deadly danger to us, individually and collectively, and there's only one way to stop him. You must administer the poison as you did before. You must execute him."

"Floren, no!" Tralvar's cry of protest was not so much in disagreement as in amazement that she could have said such a thing.

"Others believe," she pressed on, "that it's your social conscience preventing you from acknowledging what has to be done. But I know you're being stifled by your own guilt over Tristell."

Tralvar backed away, subsided onto a nearby couch and buried his face in his hands. "Leave me alone!" he muttered weakly. "You've no idea what you're asking."

"I'm asking you to be realistic," she returned. "If we locked Strephin up he'd simply break out. And he'd never submit to exile. Who's going to be his next victim, Tralvar? You? Me? Idenion? Maybe even Laura; you don't *really* think he wants her back, do you? Or he might waylay Jarras, after you've handed over the Hellas programme. Jarras, who's been like a son to you. He'd doubtless put up a fight, and he might not be as lucky as Lydion. And what then, after Strephin's introduced himself to the warmongers of Symerid Three? I hope you're preparing to welcome them, because that will be your duty as a First Citizen who failed to protect his people!"

Tralvar refused to look at her, and shrank back when she touched his shoulder.

"However this may appear, I'm not trying to use

428

you," she continued more quietly. "If there were time, we could pass a new law to deal with Strephin. That would be the correct way, the civilised way. But there *isn't* time. And you're the only one who can get close to him."

Tralvar, cornered, found a reserve of anger. "And you consider me expedient, do you?" he demanded. "You and your fellow aesthetes? Yes, let's get Tralvar to do the dirty work. He's killed before, so he won't mind. And afterwards we can swiftly send him packing and get on with our lives."

"Nobody else knows you killed Tristell," said Floren calmly.

"Then let's talk about Tristell, shall we?" Tralvar carried on wildly. "Make yourself comfortable, Floren, and let me tell you what it took to make me poison her. I suppose you think I obediently did as I was told as soon as Alendis asked me? No, not I. I'd rather swallow these myself, I said, than harm her. He just laughed. He knew I was too fond of my own wretched life to do anything like that.

"And then the nightmares began: Alendis' favourite method of keeping me in line. He could get into my mind when I was asleep - some twisted variant of his healer training. Every night for the next twenty nights, he demonstrated all the ways that Tristell *could* die. I saw her thrown from the top of the Lyricon, strangled with one of her own scarves, drowned, electrocuted, pushed from a sphere.... Squeamish, Floren? Then imagine how I felt. I believed every one of those dreams. He could do that - convince me it was really happening.

Eventually, when I was half demented through lack of sleep, I went to see Tristell after a performance. We all knew her health was failing because she drove herself too hard. I thought if I could persuade her to retire from the Lyricon, Alendis would leave her alone. I took the poison with me, thinking I might even warn her of the danger. But as soon as I suggested retiring she tried to pick a quarrel. Previously I'd asked her to come away with me, and she thought I was trying a different approach. She said some unkind things - very unkind things - and I grew angry. And while I was angry I tipped the powder into the carafe of water, just as Alendis had instructed. Then I panicked and tried to get rid of it. 'This water's stagnant,' I said. 'I'll get you a refill.' 'Oh, stop fussing, Tralvar,' she replied, and downed a glassful before I could stop her. I threw the rest away. And then I came back here and got very drunk."

He'd been staring into the distance as he spoke: now, still defiant, he turned back to Floren.

"Not exactly what you were expecting to hear, was it? Not quite the fearless assassin? Because I couldn't stand up to Alendis I destroyed the woman I reverenced - and the irony is, he didn't stop the nightmares. He never intended to. And no matter how I try, I can't see her as she was - only as he made me see her." His body shook with dry sobs. "Tristell .... Tristell!"

Floren was alarmed, and quietly furious with herself at having misread his state of mind. She'd had no idea that Alendis had come so close to breaking him. Strephin had continued the process, with low cunning in place of subtle guile; and the students' campaign, which she herself had overseen, had worn him down even further. She was still intent on her way forward, but she now knew it would be far less easy than she'd imagined.

"I should never have disappeared for so long," she declared. "But I'm here now, and I'll stay if you'll have me." And she gently indicated her wish for unity.

He held her off, surprised and defensive. "What's this, Floren? Trying to emulate your daughter by bringing comfort to a poor beleaguered First Citizen?"

"I've always cared for you, Tralvar," she answered simply. "If you hadn't been so enamoured of Tristell, perhaps you'd have noticed that."

Much to his astonishment, she was sincere. But he still resisted her in something akin to panic. "Don't, Floren! I'm not worthy!"

"Yes, you are," she said firmly. And gradually, as she'd hoped, his resolve crumbled. But it was not a response in any true sense. He passively allowed her to read him in the belief she'd then give up.

Only a swift intake of breath betrayed Floren's horror at the way Alendis had savaged Tralvar's sleeping mind. The key images - Tristell's many deaths - were still present in all their malign intensity. And even now, when she sought to love him, he was behaving like a victim.

"They're only dreams," she intoned quietly. "Forget them. Forget them."

"I can't!"

"You can. I'm going to show you Tristell as she

really was when she died. See her once more, Tralvar, and free yourself from these false memories." She pictured Tristell as she'd found her that day, lying carelessly on the couch in her dressing room, her glorious golden hair spread across its draperies. Her eyes were peacefully closed, there was a slight smile on her face, and only a bluish tinge around her lips hinted at something other than natural sleep.

Desperate to experience the truth, Tralvar drank in the image of his lost love - and in so doing allowed Floren to achieve the unity she desired. Only for an instant, but long enough to break down the rest of the barriers he'd raised against the world. Wretchedly grateful and blushing like an inexperienced boy, he stammered: "Should we - go to bed, do you think?"

"I think that would be appropriate," she said gravely. He escorted her there, leading her by both hands as if afraid to relinquish what he'd so newly attained.

They made love in a state of wonderment, amazed that it had taken them so long to discover one another. After their shared perception had faded and their separate identities had ebbed back to them, they lay entwined and silent, unwilling to let reality intrude on their momentary peace.

Floren spoke first. "Tralvar, there's no wickedness in you."

"You're biased." He smiled wryly into the near-darkness. "You're a wonderful woman, Floren. Such strength, despite your losses. I wish the same were true of me."

"I had the support of my friends. You had no-one."

"And now I have *you*." He still seemed only half convinced. "Now, about this.... errand you mentioned. You were right. I have to do it."

Floren regarded him with a trace of sadness. "Don't even think about tomorrow," she murmured. "Think about us."

Her own need had surprised her. It had been nearly a year since Relto's death, but she hadn't realised how much she'd begun to miss unity and its unique closeness. Nor had she imagined Tralvar would bring such tenderness to the love-act.

"I thought you weren't trying to use me?" he said softly, teasingly. She was gratified to see him so comforted. But as was often the case with him, his words had a dark side. She'd now seen how his eager pursuit of science had been perverted to Alendis' cause: had seen how the wide-eyed optimism of his youth had been shattered, replaced by disillusionment and guilt. Here was a man whose life had been manipulated until other lives were forfeit - a man who would kill to make restitution. Yes, she would utilise that ability. And she would cherish him now, because she knew he'd never be free of his unhappy past. Slowly she traced the length of his lean body with her fingertips.

"We have till dawn to become better acquainted," she said.

***

On what he assumed would be his last day on

433

Earth, Idenion accompanied Laura and Nathaniel on a Sunday afternoon stroll. They took a footpath which led them past the church at the far end of the village. Throughout his stay Idenion had scrupulously avoided having anything to do with religion, saying it was the surest way he knew of putting his foot in it and offending his alien hosts. Apparently he'd done precisely that on Myrma, though he didn't go into details. Resolutions, however, were made to be broken. Through the church's open door came the sound of children singing. Sunday School was in progress. Idenion, captivated, tiptoed into the nave and listened.

Nathaniel sat down on a bench and waited for him to come out, and after a moment Laura followed suit. It was a beautiful day. Blackbirds carolled, rooks cawed, and late summer flowers scented the air.

"I'm surprised we didn't get Tracey tagging along," said Laura. "I haven't seen her all week."

"Just be thankful for small mercies," replied Nathaniel, although he had a shrewd idea why Tracey was keeping her distance.

When Idenion reappeared he glanced once at his companions, then wandered off by himself. He paused by the stream which bordered the churchyard and stood with his head bowed, gazing into the water. Laura started to follow him, but Nathaniel held her back.

"Leave him be," he said quietly. "Don't you understand, Laura? He's saying goodbye to her."

"Who?" asked Laura blankly.

"Zenzie. His little wife." Nathaniel's tone was

434

the gentlest she'd ever heard him use.

"I thought he'd just written her off," Laura said a little awkwardly.

"So did I. When he first told me his story I believed his people were silly and frivolous, incapable of grief. But I was wrong. What I mistook for indifference was the most incredible display of self-discipline." He regarded Idenion's distant, forlorn figure with a degree of benevolence. "He's been through quite a lot in his young life - fame, disenchantment, bereavement - and coped exceedingly well, in my opinion. So we mustn't intrude on his feelings now."

It wasn't very long before Idenion came back, his face sombre but composed. "I've made my peace with her," he said, looking straight at Nathaniel. "And now, isn't there someone *you* should say goodbye to?"

"Yes, I suppose I must," Nathaniel replied. "For the first time in all these years, I feel I can let her go."

Laura looked from one to the other in growing bewilderment. "Who are you talking about?"

"The girl Nathaniel loved," Idenion explained. "She was killed when the bombs fell on London."

"We'd been engaged just one week," said Nathaniel, taking up the story. "One of those wartime romances you still hear so much about. Her name was Ida. I met her at a lunchtime concert in 1941."

"But - Dad never mentioned this," Laura stammered.

"He never knew," Nathaniel stated. "We hardly

435

saw one another during the war. And afterwards, I saw no point in telling him."

"Then - it was *her* you were thinking about when Idenion first met you?" asked Laura.

"Yes - and there's rarely been a day I *haven't* thought of her," Nathaniel admitted. Then, wordlessly prompted by Idenion: "I should apologise, Laura, for my indifference to you and your ambitions. Ida was studying classical music. Didn't you ever wonder why I had a piano? It was hers. And the old gramophone you found in the attic - that was hers, too. I believed you'd take up the piano seriously - I'd have found some consolation in that, I think - but you preferred to be a singer like your mother, and I'm afraid I never really forgave you. Perhaps, one day, you'll be able to forgive *me*."

Laura, unsure of what to say, squeezed his arm and gave him a tiny kiss on the cheek. Then she turned to Idenion and hugged him. Sunday School came to an end, and the churchyard was suddenly full of laughing, chattering children.

"Life goes on," Nathaniel added. "That's a lesson we all have to learn, sooner or later."

For the rest of the evening, Laura remained so intrigued by Nathaniel's confessions that she failed to notice Idenion's increasingly worried mood. He'd now been on Earth for eighteen days. On Celestra, sixteen days had passed. And there was still no sign of Jarras.

***

436

"We have until dawn," Floren had said, but in fact she stayed past daybreak. She lay wakeful and introspective, watching the sky brighten. Tralvar lay beside her in an exhausted doze. Floren, observing the marbled pallor of his face and the violet shadows beneath his eyes, reflected that it had been less than kind to deprive him of much-needed sleep. Quite selfish, in fact. But she simply hadn't been able to leave him alone.

This was due in part to his forensic approach to sex; he couldn't resist studying his partner and trying to increase her pleasure. But his own enjoyment was left to chance. And as for unity - Floren sighed aloud in exasperation. It was that above all which had kept her there, trying ceaselessly to improve it. But, she concluded, there was something built into him which made perfect unity impossible. He'd entered her mind readily, almost *too* readily, wishing to see and know everything. But when she tried to reciprocate, his response was incomplete. She'd probably seen everything that mattered, but not in its entirety. Always there had to be a safe area, a place he could retreat to. He couldn't give all of himself. Was that why he'd been thrown out of the scolia?

"I wasn't thrown out," he muttered. "I was never allowed in."

Floren gave a guilty start. She hadn't realised he'd woken. "It's not your fault," she said lamely. "Tralvar, I have to go."

He slid a languid arm round her waist. "Not yet..."

It was tempting, thought Floren, to stay a while

437

longer - to try and forget there was a madman downstairs with a cache of guns, a man who, if Tralvar failed to destroy him, would doubtless learn of her complicity and dispose of her.

Tralvar, if he perceived her sombre thoughts, disregarded them. His body was weary but his mind still wanted her, and almost before she knew it they were again in unity. This time she remained quiescent, allowing him to rove freely and draw strength from her unsatiated need. Why did she find him so fascinating? What was so intriguing about him, compared with the tranquil aimlessness of Relto and the equally placid lovers of her youth? Of course, the answer was self-evident: purpose, longing, the drive to achieve something positive.

Abruptly she was herself again. Tralvar hadn't been able to sustain the bond once her attention started to wander.

"I've never known anyone quite like you," Floren said aloud. "I wish...."

"What is it?" Tralvar asked anxiously as her eyes filled with tears.

"I wish I could still conceive. I want a child – *your* child," Floren replied in an odd monotone.

Tralvar, taken aback, held her wordlessly. "Isn't that just Nature's imperative at work?" he ventured at last. Floren, with an effort, regained her composure.

"Now, see what you've done by delaying me?" she said, sitting up and stretching. "Too much unity always makes me depressed. But seriously, you should get yourself a child or two if you can. Celestra needs a few more original thinkers."

438

"Breed a race of scientists?" inquired Tralvar, stumbling into the washroom and dabbing ineffectually at his tired eyes. "That's what Alendis suggested...oh, discords, look at me. Anyone can see what kind of a night I've had."

Floren gave a feminine chuckle and went in search of her dress. She's thrived on this, thought Tralvar privately. But then most people did. He'd never heard of anyone else with his particular problem - craving unity yet avoiding it for years at a time. Suddenly pensive, he stepped into the sunken bath and turned every lever on full. Warm scented water swirled from the inlets, and a cloud of fragrant steam enveloped him. Floren, returning, hesitated in the doorway. Common-sense told her she should leave as soon as possible, first having made sure he was equipped for his "errand", as he'd called it. But she ignored her inner voice in favour of one last indulgence. Picking up a flask of soap, she eased herself into the water next to him.

"And when did Alendis order you to procreate?" she asked, soaping his back with a light appreciative touch.

"He didn't say it to *me*," Tralvar replied. "It was to Elanir, while we were married."

"Elanir?" exclaimed Floren. She remembered the girl: tall, studious and intense, she had once worked with the Lyricon scolia. "You partnered Elanir? I didn't see her in your thoughts, not once."

"Probably because I didn't really love her," said Tralvar rather sadly, contemplating the bubbles which eddied around his limbs. "It seems so long ago. She knew I'd been rejected by the Guild, and

439

she was kind to me. But she disliked my experiments, and detested Alendis. I worshipped him then, of course. Far more than Idenion ever did."

"I know that," Floren said softly. "Tell me the rest."

Tralvar hesitated, then continued. "About the same time as I was commissioned to make weapons, Elanir discovered she was pregnant. Unfortunately she mentioned it in front of Alendis, who delivered his little speech and told her she was very privileged to be in the vanguard of the new world order. And that, as far as Elanir was concerned, was the end. She left me that same night."

"But Tralvar, what about your child?" Floren gripped his shoulders, eyes shining. "Didn't you ever check the archives?"

"I saw no reason to. Elanir was quite explicit: she'd have the baby and raise it, and if it dared show an aptitude for science she'd personally steer it in some other direction. I was never to go near it, or her. Can you blame her? I'd have made a disastrous father."

After that statement, which Floren didn't feel she could contradict, they both lapsed into silence - Tralvar believing he'd forfeited all hope of any peace, and Floren again beginning to feel cheated out of motherhood. They stepped into the drying area, where the omnidirectional airflow winnowed their hair and caressed their skin; but although they stood naked and unselfconscious before one another, their intimacy had all but vanished.

"Shall we enter our pairbond in the records?"

440

Tralvar asked formally as they were dressing.

"What for?" re-joined Floren irritably. "There'll be no offspring." Then, when she saw him looking rather hurt: "All right, we'll register if it pleases you. But *not* today."

The emphasis wasn't lost on him. "Then let's get today over with," he said grimly. "May I ask just one more favour?"

"What?"

"Please stay close so I can contact you if anything goes wrong."

"As you wish," said Floren quietly.

"And if I succeed, what then? How do you suppose the people will react when they hear about Tristell?"

"They'll stand by you," Floren assured him.

"I doubt that very much."

"Take my word for it, Tralvar, they *will* forgive you. Yes, you were besotted with Alendis - but then you came to your senses. You opposed him in numerous small ways. And you ended up saving Laura's life not once, but twice. That earned you a lot of respect."

"I don't see why anyone should respect me."

"Because," Floren said patiently, "you've embraced evil, yet ultimately rejected it. That places you above the average citizen who's never had to make a choice at all."

Tralvar sighed. "I don't feel very superior at the moment. Well, you'd better show me where this poison is, so I can wreak my evil will for the last time."

In silence they ascended to Alendis' rooms.

441

Tralvar again wondered at the dictator's complacent attitude toward his subjects. There was no lock on the apartment door, and never had been. Floren picked her way through the reception area with its ornate trappings, resolutely pushed open the door leading to the bedchamber, then halted in dismay. Zenzie had warned her about the contents, but she hadn't expected to see quite so many mirror images of herself.

"Chaos!" breathed Tralvar as he followed her over the threshold. He'd seen the room before, but such blatant vanity had always been offensive to him. And it angered him that he hadn't yet felt capable of having the apartment stripped.

Swallowing hard, Floren edged past the bed and approached one of the wall-mounted mirrors. Beneath it was a wooden shelf supported by three sturdy columns. "The top of this opens somehow," she said, tugging ineffectually at the central fixture.

"Let me try it," said Tralvar. His slim sensitive fingers moved carefully over the seemingly unbroken surface; presently there was a subdued click and a small section of the pillar slid aside. "Hmm, just as I thought. This type of seal is normally used on stardrive casings. It keeps out meddlesome amateurs."

Floren reached into the tiny compartment and drew out a transparent box. Two capsules nestled inside.

For a moment Tralvar stood motionless, gripping the shelf. "Tristell," he whispered. Not with remorse or regret, but as a kind of salutation. Then he took the box from Floren with a hand that

442

trembled only slightly.

Just then, a faint cry of "Laura!" wafted up from the plaza far below. Floren blushed.

"I told them to stop," she cried. "They think it's just a game. I'll tell them again - "

"No!" exclaimed Tralvar, seizing her arm. The cry had galvanised him: he had kept Floren with him too long, unwilling to face the day alone. "If they want to demonstrate, let them. I don't want Strephin to be forewarned in any way." He propelled her to the exit. "Leave now. Use the side stair. Give me until noon-plus-two. Hurry!" And Floren ran blindly into the hazy morning sun, feeling as isolated as he.

***

"Hello, what's this?" asked Strephin from the depths of a huge armchair. Tralvar had just entered the apartment, carrying a tray which he set down carefully. Strephin sat up. "Nice of you to wait on me, Tralvar. All part of your subservient nature, I suppose."

"I expect so," Tralvar replied noncommittally. "Actually, I thought I'd take some refreshment with you. We've things to discuss." Strephin scrutinised the tray's contents; a pitcher of wine, with two glasses already filled.

"Wine? At midday?"

"Why not?" said Tralvar. "I think you'll want to celebrate when you hear what I've decided."

"You're going to resign?" asked Strephin eagerly.

443

"Yes. You were right all along, Strephin - I can't control the people. You seem to have the spirit of leadership in you, so I'll nominate you my successor."

"When?"

"Later today. I'll make a broadcast." Tralvar picked up one of the brimming glasses and held it out. Strephin accepted the drink with a mocking smile.

"I might need you as a second-in-command," he said carelessly. "Might. And I shall certainly commission more weapons. I hope you're prepared to work hard."

"Naturally I'll do whatever you wish," said Tralvar, raising his own glass. "I drink to your future success."

"I drink to your past failure," Strephin replied insolently.

And that, thought Tralvar, is that. All so simple, so orderly. All I have to do now is wait.

Despite the warmness of the room, he shivered.

Strephin replaced his empty glass on the tray and regarded him suspiciously. "Something wrong?"

"N - no, nothing."

"This is no time to daydream, is it? There are plans to be made. The deed of abdication must be drawn up immediately, with close attention to the wording. Standard procedure will have to be scrapped. Obviously the people can't be allowed to vote this time."

"Obviously," said Tralvar.

"I want," continued Strephin, "absolute

444

authority in all matters of state, no matter how trivial. Find some paper, would you, and take this down. We'll prepare the final version later, but I'd like to outline some new policies while they're fresh in my mind."

Numbly, Tralvar began to write, with frequent recourse to the wine jar. He didn't dare look Strephin in the eye. How long before the drug took effect? How long had it taken to kill Tristell? He didn't know. And in the meantime he had to stay calm, indulge the whims of his doomed rival, draft out abhorrent laws which would never be enforced...

"Read the last item back, would you?"

"Wh - what?"

"I said, read it back. After that, we'd better leave it a while. I can't seem to concentrate. I told you it was a silly idea to drink wine this early."

"Sorry," said Tralvar. "The last section reads as follows. The Lyricon and all goods and materials therein shall become the property of the First Citizen. A labour force shall be assembled to convert the building into a detention centre."

"All right, that's enough," Strephin interrupted. "We'll resume later."

Thankfully Tralvar laid the paper aside.

"Of course," Strephin said airily, "I know why your mind's not on the proceedings. You're missing him, aren't you?"

"What do you mean?"

"You miss that delicate torment in your dreams. Nothing quite like it, was there?"

"True," admitted Tralvar.

"I hope the woman made up for it a little," Strephin went on. "I was aware of someone having an exuberant night, but I never imagined it was you. But now that I look at you ..... by harmony, I do believe you're embarrassed! Who was it, Tralvar? She couldn't get enough of you, could she? If you can't manage her, perhaps you should invite me along next time....."

Tralvar closed his eyes and gradually ceased listening, or maybe Strephin had stopped talking - he wasn't sure which. He felt immeasurably tired. The heady drink, the tension of the past few days, the excesses of the previous night - it was all catching up with him now. Unless - and this would be the ultimate irony - he'd muddled the wine glasses? He tried to stand up in a room which was suddenly full of wrong angles, and found he'd struck his shoulder on the floor. In the distance, he heard an object fall and shatter. He ought, he supposed, to find out what that was. Or at the very least, he ought to get back in his chair. But in the end he did neither.

***

Floren had taken refuge in a quiet corner of the central registry, adjacent to the city archive. The contrast between the two buildings was marked. Here there was no dust, no disorder: the interior was air -conditioned, a row of computer terminals gleamed beneath the cheerful lighting, and - most unusual of all - there was a chronometer on the wall. In this room, and its counterparts in other cities, was a complete and systematic record of births, deaths, marriages and family trees. The Celestrians took genealogy very seriously.

The registry was close enough to the akron for Tralvar to contact her, but that wasn't the only reason she'd chosen it. Earlier, she'd run a trace on Elanir, and found she was living in the town of Kassi at the southernmost tip of the continent. Four years ago she had given birth to a girl, Nefyrra. The father was Tralvar. No current partner was listed. But Floren's hopes - and she'd hardly dared formulate any - were dashed on cross-referencing Nefyrra. There were no adoptive parents. The girl was still with her mother, and Elanir was obviously carrying out her vow.

Alone, Floren alternately brooded over her findings and watched the chronometer. It was now noon-plus-three, and there had been no word from Tralvar. Finally, ignoring the risk, she cast her perception back toward the akron, questing, framing his name. There was no response, nor any hint of his thought patterns.

She was already beginning to sense curiosity and apprehension from people on whose minds she'd impinged. Dismissing them, shutting them out, she vacated the registry, forcing herself to walk unhurriedly. The way to the akron had never seemed so endless. Alda blazed down from the afternoon sky, the paving stones were warm beneath her sandals, but she felt only a twilit foreboding.

Inside the building, her fragile calm evaporated. Her mind screamed out for Tralvar and, when there was still no reply, she collapsed sobbing on the stairs leading to his quarters. Then Rietta was before her, quizzical, slightly accusatory.

"Please," whispered Floren, unable to meet her eyes. "See if he's all right. I can't - I daren't."

"It's no use looking in there," Rietta said. "He went to Strephin's rooms about noon and told us he wasn't to be disturbed." She seized Floren's elbow and raised her up, none too gently. "Just what is going on?"

Haltingly, Floren explained. Rietta displayed no shock, only disapproval.

"You had no right to impose that task on him," she declared. Then, after a pause: "I can't reach either of them. You'd better come with me."

Mute and tearful, Floren obeyed. Whatever's waiting for us down there, I'll be responsible, she thought bleakly. So this is what guilt is. So this is what I've chosen for myself.

Rietta flung open the apartment door and they took in the scene at a glance. Strephin was slumped in a chair, his lips blue. Tralvar lay face down on the floor, a broken wine jar at his elbow. Floren froze; Rietta went quickly to Tralvar and turned him over, placing a hand on his forehead.

"It's all right," she announced, to Floren's immeasurable relief. "He's alive. He's not even hurt. He's sleeping very deeply, and that's why you couldn't reach his mind." She inspected the pitcher, which had been nearly empty when it fell. "I'd say he was one-third exhausted, two-thirds intoxicated. He can virtually live on that disgusting resnay, but a little wine always goes straight to his head."

Floren's eyes grew wide with outrage. "You

mean he put me through all this just because he decided to get drunk?"

"You shouldn't be angry," Rietta said remotely. "He did as you wanted, Floren. Strephin's dead." Her voice was infinitely sad, and she suddenly looked older. Her sorrow was not for Strephin but for herself. The last of her three "children" was gone. Her life was her own again. And she had absolutely no idea what to do with it.

"Shouldn't we take Tralvar out of here?" asked Floren after a barely respectful pause.

"Yes. Yes, of course," said Rietta, abandoning her brief introspection for the practicalities which still faced them. "I would have spared him this, had you confided in me," she added.

"No, Rietta," said Floren softly. "You couldn't have done it. Your place is to heal, not destroy."

Rietta bowed her head in acquiescence. "He'll need us when he wakes," she said. "Or perhaps he'll only need *you*."

Just then, a light footfall sounded on the stairs. It was Kyrin. He surveyed the tableau with commendable calm, and Floren found herself blushing as he confronted her. She had no doubt that this quiet youth with the steady grey eyes already knew more than she'd intended anyone to know. She wondered how her seduction of Tralvar might be construed by Kyrin or by the city in general.

"Your unanswered cries to Tralvar alarmed your friends," Kyrin said, "and they in turn spread alarm to others. There's a crowd gathering. Shall I tell them what has happened?"

449

"Not yet," Floren said. "Tell them to disperse, that Tralvar is safe, and that another announcement will follow."

Kyrin did his best to settle the uneasy populace with his clear, unhurried thoughts. While he tried to disentangle the various responses, Floren took the sheets of paper from the table and examined them. Her lips compressed angrily; these were Strephin's insane plans for Celestra, yet the handwriting was Tralvar's. Strephin had studied Alendis' methods well. Swiftly she folded the documents and thrust them into her pocket.

"I can't persuade anyone to leave," Kyrin reported. "They know there's been another shift in power. They want to see Tralvar for themselves."

Floren glanced at Rietta. "Can you get him on his feet long enough to speak to them?"

"I expect so," Rietta said reluctantly. "There are medicines in his quarters. Kyrin, would you help us carry him there?"

The relayist hesitated, then came forward. Rietta thought he winced a little as he stooped.

They negotiated the door with difficulty, and Rietta paused a moment to lock it and remove the key. Tralvar, although insensible, seemed to do everything he could to make the ascent awkward. His head lolled, his arms refused to stay around the shoulders of his rescuers, and his weight seemed to have doubled. Kevis appeared, and was fobbed off by Rietta; the few other staff they encountered looked intrigued, but said nothing. They'd heeded Kyrin's message. In any case, the sight of Tralvar in his cups was becoming quite familiar.

450

Whilst edging past a window, Floren caught sight of the crowd she'd inadvertently summoned. To her guilty eyes, it seemed as if half the city was out there.

At last, thankfully, the trio deposited Tralvar on his bed. This time Kyrin's gasp of pain was unmistakable, and his hand went briefly to his side.

"What ails you?" Rietta inquired.

Kyrin, suddenly embarrassed, avoided her gaze. "Don't waste time on me. It doesn't matter now."

Something about his behaviour seemed very familiar to Floren. "Kyrin," she said gently, 'we've all been hurt in one way or another. Don't be afraid to share your trouble."

Slowly, unwillingly, Kyrin unlaced his shirt to reveal a mass of purple bruises around his ribcage.

"Strephin?" Rietta asked, very quietly.

Kyrin hung his head.

"Why? Why you?"

"Yesterday I refused to act as relayist for him," Kyrin explained. "He wanted me to say that every musician who attacked Tralvar in Tivenne would be banned from the scolia for life."

Floren gave a cry of anger.

"Those bruises are more than a day old," Rietta observed.

Floren saw Kyrin blush crimson. "Don't interrogate him, Rietta," she said hastily. "It's over: we don't need the details." Kyrin threw her a look of pure gratitude and shakily refastened his tunic.

"I couldn't fight him," he said, almost to himself. "I felt so ashamed, so weak..."

"You protected Tralvar," Floren said. "Be

451

proud of that, and plead his case before the citizens."

"Gladly," Kyrin declared.

Just then, an extremely agitated Jarras burst in. "I've been waiting for Tralvar at the spaceport," he explained. "I came here as fast as I could once I realised what was happening, but there were no flitters to be had. And then I found all the akron entrances were barred!" He paused to catch his breath, then went on: "I have to fetch Idenion immediately - I'm a day late already. And *he* - " He pointed a finger at the unconscious First Citizen - "is the only one who knows where the Hellas programme is!"

"Wait. You'll have your answer," Floren promised. Then everyone stood back and watched Rietta as she began to revive their stricken leader. She took up a flask, sprinkled a cloth with a few drops of aromatic oil and held it under Tralvar's nose. Then, when he stirred and protested, she sat him up and bade him drink from a beaker of pink liquid. He choked and spat, but she persevered, and finally he swallowed enough of the draught for it to take effect. Pallid but rational, he extended a hand to Floren. She took it silently.

"So it's done," he murmured with a sad smile.

Rietta frowned. It wasn't calm she sensed in him, but the tired neutrality of a mind which could revile itself no further.

"Tralvar," Floren was saying softly, "Jarras is here. Where did you hide the Hellas programme?" She had to ask the question twice.

"What? Oh...yes," Tralvar replied at last,

452

infuriatingly vague. "I sewed it into the belt of my scolia robe."

"This robe? The one you're wearing?"

"The same," said Tralvar, grinning foolishly. "Clever, wasn't I? It was right in front of Strephin the whole time!"

He laughed, then started to cough. Jarras divested him of the belt and wrenched the stitching apart, looking vastly relieved when the crystal rolled out.

"Don't try to leave yet," Kyrin advised. "You'll only hinder yourself. Wait here with Tralvar. This matter will soon be settled."

"I hope you're right," said Jarras unhappily.

"Listen carefully, Tralvar," Floren was continuing. "You aren't fit to make any prolonged speeches, so Kyrin's going to address the people first. You'll have to go outside when he's finished."

"People?"

"Quite a crowd. They're waiting to pledge their allegiance."

"Or throw me out of the city," Tralvar remarked wearily.

Floren, ignoring this, turned to Kyrin and rapidly outlined what she wanted him to say. "Make this your best relay ever," she added.

"It will be heartfelt. That should be enough," said Kyrin. Then, opening his mind to its full sonorous capacity, he began his vital announcement. +Attend, citizens. Strephin is dead, despatched by Tralvar at Floren's behest. Floren knew, via her daughter, where Alendis kept a supply of poison. She placed the box in Tralvar's

453

hand. So, if you condemn him for this act, you must condemn her also+ He paused to ensure that he had the crowd's attention, then continued. +Strephin was irrational and irresponsible. He intended to approach Symerid Three with our science, imperilling our way of life and perhaps our very existence. Those of you with contacts in Tivenne will know of Strephin's amoral nature. He lived only to appease his brutality, and we should not regret his passing.

+You are all well acquainted with the work Tralvar performed in Alendis' service. What you do *not* know is that for years he worked under duress. If he failed to comply, Alendis would persecute him, using a cruel reversal of our sleep-healing techniques. Tralvar suffered this torment in secret, convinced that no-one would care if he tried to explain. *Do* you care, citizens? If so, prepare to show him you do. But try not to inundate him with your thoughts; he's too exhausted to cope with such pressures. Lastly, consider this. If it were not for his loyalty to music and his old friends of the scolia, Laura would not have given her concert. Alendis ordered it stopped. As always, Tralvar's defiance cost him much pain. Attend, citizens+

Kyrin finished sending and turned back to the little group at Tralvar's bedside. "It's time," he announced.

Tralvar stood up obediently. His expression was one of dread, but his steps didn't falter. Floren gasped as she followed him onto the balcony. Since she'd last looked out the crowd had trebled in size, and more people were still arriving.

The late afternoon sun dazzled Tralvar, and he didn't immediately see the extent of the gathering. But he knew that many minds throughout the city were waiting expectantly - waiting, so he believed, to depose him. He projected his thoughts with difficulty into that receptive emptiness.

+People of Alda Mexa, I am not fit to govern you. You know my crimes, and I appoint you my judges. What penance would you ask of me?+

A susurration of warmth, sympathy and reassurance enveloped him, and for a long time he stood dumbfounded, clutching at the balcony wall. He wanted to laugh or cry, but was too stunned to do either. +I ... I do not deserve this+ he managed at last.

+You have destroyed the enemies of Celestra+ declared one individual. +Lead us, protect us+

+But I've killed!+ he protested helplessly. +I killed Tristell!+ He let them read the truth of that, though it caused him anguish to do so. The wash of reassurance ebbed momentarily, then resumed.

+You loved Tristell+ came a different response, indubitably female, one of the scolia. +You could not let her suffer at Alendis' hands+

+You gave us Laura, you gave us song+ a third citizen added. +You defended harmony. Defend us+

+He has not been properly inaugurated+ said the scolia woman again. +He should speak the words+

"Elanir?" Tralvar said incredulously against the rising tumult. +Elanir!+ But the woman, whoever she was, had withdrawn.

"Speak the words," demanded the crowd in

455

many voices; and at last, although they heard only his thoughts, Tralvar uttered the traditional vow of a newly-elected First Citizen.

"I promise through my service to dispel discord and uphold harmony," he proclaimed, then added: +And I will defend you always, while I live+

+And what of Laura?+ inquired someone.

+I shall entreat her to return - + Tralvar began. Instantly there was pandemonium. Tralvar's perception, sensitised by the drug, cringed from the onslaught. White walls and long shadows suddenly blurred into one as his vision darkened. Rietta and Floren dragged him half-fainting from the balcony, leaving Kyrin to upbraid the demonstrators.

+Is this how you thank your First Citizen?+ his thoughts blazed. +He has made it safe for Laura to come back to us. Now be silent and let him rest+ And the people, sensing the relayist's own concern for Tralvar, slowly regained a measure of sobriety and began to drift away.

In the quiet aftermath of their departure, Tralvar lay in a stupor while Floren anxiously watched over him. Rietta, in the knowledge that she was the only person to have cared for Strephin, had gone to tend the body. Kyrin, his duty done, had simply disappeared. Jarras remained, but had discreetly stepped out of the bedroom. Eventually Tralvar rallied enough to realise he was alone with Floren, but his words were not the endearments she felt she deserved.

"Was that Elanir in the crowd?" he whispered. "Was it her?"

"You should know," Floren retorted, her voice

456

sounding thoroughly unreasonable in her own ears. And if it was, she thought, did she have Tralvar's daughter with her? And would the little girl remember this day, with the sun so bright and the people so animated? Would she remember Tralvar's dignified humility and respect him from afar?

"Jarras mustn't go to Symerid Three alone," he was saying. "Where's Dena?"

"Staying with some of her dancer friends," said Floren. "And fond though she is of Idenion, I don't think anything would induce her to make the trip again."

"Then find Halon - or Rillan, even." Tralvar was growing flustered. "Someone has to go with Jarras."

"Then send me," Floren said patiently.

"Have you been offworld before?"

"Relto took me to Myrma once. I can cope with space, Tralvar."

"I believe you can." He looked at her admiringly. "Well, once again my fate is in your hands. I hope Laura can be persuaded to return. Transmit her decision to Communications and I'll have it relayed here."

She resisted the urge to tell him about his child. Now was not the time.

"One more thing," Tralvar said as she stood up to leave.

She turned back expectantly. "Yes?"

"Laura's people can record sound. Can you possibly find out how it's done?"

Floren laughed ruefully. "I begin to see why

457

Elanir was so anti-science," she said.

Tralvar looked blank. "I don't understand."

"Of course you don't. Go to sleep, dread scientist. I'll bring Laura back."

***

By the next day, it was obvious that Idenion was unwell. He spent the morning in bed; when he finally woke he was lethargic and subdued, and complained of a sore throat. His normally silken hair looked lank and greasy. He had no appetite, and refused lunch. Laura sat with him in the drawing room, holding his hand and trying to be cheerful.

Mrs. Moffat had gone shopping, which meant Idenion was spared any well-intentioned fuss. Nathaniel left him and Laura saying their protracted farewells and went to catch up on his neglected paperwork. He had no enthusiasm for the task. Eventually he abandoned it, made himself some tea and sandwiches and took a deckchair onto the front lawn.

He wasn't aware of having dozed off until some low-flying jets woke him. The sun had disappeared behind the trees and there was an autumnal nip in the air. He had the feeling that something was about to happen. Shortly afterward, Laura appeared in a state of suppressed elation.

"They've arrived," she said. "Jarras had to land in the woods to avoid being seen, and Floren - that's Zenzie's mother - is on her way here. Idenion's guiding her." She paused, then added in a rush:

458

"They want me to go back. Can I, Uncle Nat?"

Before Nathaniel could reply, the garden gate clicked open. A fair, slender woman in a white dress was leaning on the gatepost and shaking pebbles out of her sandals. She performed this action with an elegance that Nathaniel found quite breath-taking. She looked slightly less than immaculate, having left the forest by the most direct route rather than the easiest: he found that delightful, too. He stood up hastily as she approached, and nearly became entangled in the deckchair. Laura suppressed a giggle.

"I am Floren," the newcomer said. "You, I perceive, are Nathaniel."

"Enchanted to meet you, dear lady," he replied, and kissed her hand. She looked slightly puzzled, then lifted his hand and returned the kiss. Laura tried even harder to look serious.

"Forgive my haste," said Floren, "but would you please take me straight to Idenion? Then I will explain what has happened since Laura left us, and why I was delayed."

Nathaniel escorted her indoors. Despite her dignity, she was very nervous. Her eyes were never still, and she flinched when a blackbird swooped across the path. Nevertheless, she had ventured onto a strange planet alone, and Laura was suitably impressed. Obviously there was more to Floren than met the eye. Idenion didn't seem surprised to find her in the role of emissary. He offered her a barley water and eagerly requested news of his homeworld.

After inspecting the piano and staring

459

suspiciously at Tib, Floren began her story. To avoid repetition she attempted to converse in English, only to meet the twin barriers of Nathaniel's intractability and Laura's mounting excitement. So she reverted to her own language, leaving Idenion to translate.

"Oh, poor Tralvar!" Laura exclaimed when she'd heard the tidings. "I knew Alendis had some kind of hold over him, but I never imagined anything so cruel. I'm glad the people forgave him."

"Let's hope he can forgive himself," Idenion commented.

"And are you sure Lydion will be all right? I'd like to see him as soon as he's allowed visitors," Laura continued, then broke off guiltily. Nathaniel still hadn't said she could go. She asked him again, terrified that he'd suddenly revert to his authoritarian ways.

"I don't see how I can possibly refuse," Nathaniel answered, though he looked less than overjoyed.

"Come with us!" Idenion said impulsively.

"And what effect do you think *that* would have on your children?" replied Nathaniel caustically. "No, Idenion. I'm too old and too cynical. And now, you'd better be off. Unless, of course, you're waiting till it's dark?"

"No, we must leave now," said Floren. "Jarras will only use the forest location. He says everywhere else is too public."

"I hope the sphere hasn't been on the ground all this time," said Laura.

460

"Jarras has more sense than that," replied Floren. "When we're in position, I can signal him." She drew a small prismatic object from her pocket.

"A short-range communicator," Idenion explained, then was seized with a fit of coughing.

Nathaniel frowned. "The sooner you get home, young man, the better."

"There's just one more thing," said Floren. "Tralvar wishes to study your methods of recording sound. I promised to bring him that knowledge, but I'm not sure how to go about it."

"He said he'd recorded things but couldn't make them play," Laura put in.

"Then what he needs," declared Nathaniel, "is a working model. And we have the very thing - don't we, Laura? I'll fetch it from the attic."

Laura stared. "Ida's gramophone? But isn't that kind of - special?"

"My memories were never dependent on souvenirs," he replied. "Take it, with my blessing."

Just then the back door opened and slammed. Floren nearly jumped out of her skin.

"Only me!" called Mrs. Moffat. "Sorry I'm so late, Nathaniel - awful traffic jam. Is Denny still here?" She bustled into the drawing room, stopping short when she saw Floren. "Hello! You must be Denny's mum."

"I'm here to take him home," said Floren.

"Well, I'm glad I caught you, Mrs. - ?"

"Floren."

"I just want to say, Mrs. Floren, that it's been lovely having Denny here, and we'll be happy to have him back any time." She turned to Nathaniel.

"I'll just go and change my togs, and then I'll see to dinner."

"Don't worry, Margaret," Nathaniel said. "I'll be dining alone tonight, so I'll cook for myself."

"Dining alone? Where's Laura going to be?"

"With Idenion and Floren," Laura confessed.

"Oooh! You never said," exclaimed Mrs. Moffat.

"It was a bit last-minute," Laura extemporised.

"She needs to broaden her horizons," Nathaniel added. "It's always difficult when children grow up, but I daresay we'll get used to it."

"We will look after her," said Floren.

"I'm sure you will," beamed Mrs. Moffat. "Well, goodbye, Denny love." She gave Idenion a hug and a kiss, which he endured stoically.

"Time we were off to the station," Nathaniel said briskly. "I'll put the - er - luggage in the car. Give me a hand, please, Laura."

She took the hint and followed him out of the room.

"You three can't go traipsing off to the woods," he declared when it was safe to talk. "Not with Margaret hovering about. And that record case weighs a ton. I'll drive you to your pick-up point, or as near as I can get to it, and stooge about for a while."

"Thanks for being so helpful, Uncle Nat," Laura said warmly. "I - um - don't know how long I'll be gone this time...."

"Long enough to start their record industry, I suppose," Nathaniel said with a wry chuckle. "I hope they know what they're letting themselves in

462

for! Anyway, I suggest you worry about your new vocation and let *me* worry about your cover story. Now, run along and get organised. Oh, and if you're going to wear that pyjama suit, put a coat over it."

Somehow, they managed to keep up the pretence. But then, Nathaniel reflected, I've always been complimented on my efficiency. I'm glad I can still rise to the occasion - even when delivering my niece to an alien spacecraft.

Although the daylight was fading, he drove very slowly. Floren was even more frightened of the car than Idenion had been. After making a detour round the lanes, he pulled off the road at the place Laura indicated. He then carried the heavy box of 78 rpm records to the little clearing which Jimmy Stretton had christened the Cradle of the World. Laura led the way, carrying the gramophone, which in its era was deemed portable and had the appearance of a small suitcase.

"We'd better say our goodbyes now," said Floren. "Jarras won't want to linger here."

Nathaniel shook Idenion's hand formally. "Well, good luck, son. And - " he paused meaningfully - "don't go putting your trust in two thousand year old documents!"

Idenion gave a wan smile. "I won't, sir."

Laura wrongly assumed they were talking about literature, and asked no questions.

About ten minutes later, as twilight deepened into dusk, a bemused Nathaniel wandered back to his car. He lit a cigar and smoked it without enjoyment, still astounded at the nature of the craft

463

that had borne Laura away. He'd been told the spheres looked delicate, but he simply hadn't expected to see something akin to a meringue, with an entrance that had seeped open as if it were about to melt all over the forest floor. It wasn't the ephemeral look of the sphere that bothered him the most, however, but Laura's growing dependence on Idenion. There was no telling how that might end.

Windbourne was deserted and depressing. Nathaniel put the Home Service on and began peeling potatoes for his dinner. After a moment or two, Tib sidled into the kitchen.

"It's just you and me now, Tib," Nathaniel remarked.

Tib ignored him and went to the back door. Once outside, she turned and gave him a disdainful stare before strolling off in the direction of Mrs. Moffat's house.

464

Chapter Fifteen

The journey seemed to take less time than before, possibly because Laura was less nervous about it. During the early stages, she pressed Floren for more details of the sit-in, amazed to hear how it had escalated. She was rueful, however, about its effect on Tralvar.

"I really must apologise to him," she said.

"Doubtless he'd appreciate that," replied Floren, "although if it weren't for the sit-in you might not be here now. He wouldn't agree to your return until today."

"I don't think he likes me," Laura said mournfully.

"Oh, he does," Floren contradicted with a slight smile. "But yours is an emergent world, and he must keep the risks in mind."

Jarras was very quiet throughout the flight, speaking only when spoken to. Idenion, in his kaftan, reclined on the pink bunk, sipping liman and complaining that it wasn't chilled.

"The refrigeration unit isn't working," Jarras told him irritably.

"It was working on the outward trip," Floren pointed out.

"Things do malfunction sometimes," said Jarras defensively. "It's hardly an emergency, is it? Have some wine instead."

Laura had said very little to Idenion since they'd boarded the sphere. Once her initial high spirits had worn off, she'd begun to feel awkward.

Earlier that day, before she knew she'd be returning to Celestra, she'd told Idenion she loved him. Well, not quite. She'd said "I think I love you" - which was bad enough.

"I want to keep you in my life," he'd replied. "I have to go home now, but only because I'm getting sick. I'll come back, I promise."

Laura was left wondering if he really cared for her that much. Had he been saying what she wanted to hear, in the belief that he'd never have to see her again? She waited for some sign of encouragement from him, but none came. Perhaps he was too out of sorts to notice her state of mind. To pass the time, she asked Floren to teach her a few Celestrian phrases, beginning with "What is your name?" and "What shall I sing?"

Once the sphere had completed its eerie sojourn in transposal, Jarras received a succession of calls from Alda Mexa.

"It's still fairly chaotic in the city, and there are no flitters at the landing field," he told Laura. "I've already been stuck there once today, and I'd rather not repeat the experience. The duty operator has been liaising with Kevis: they suggest I should land outside the akron, where you'll be given rooms for the night. I'm afraid the Lyricon is still uninhabitable."

"Who's Kevis?" asked Laura.

"Tralvar's secretary," explained Jarras. "He's loyal and sensible. You'll like him. He warns that there's still a hard core of demonstrators in the plaza, refusing to go home until they've seen you. Fortunately they haven't made much noise, so

466

Tralvar has been able to rest."

"But not for much longer," said Floren. "He's insisted on being awakened as soon as we arrive."

When it was time to make landfall, Laura asked for the viewscreen to be activated. As the sun had set on Alda Mexa there was little detail until they were almost on the ground, but Laura then saw that the plaza was dotted with little coloured lights. The stark facade of the akron was dancing with rainbow reflections.

"Peisistrata lanterns," said Idenion. "At the end of the festival there's a midnight procession to the Lyricon."

"The students have chosen this way to signify their presence," Jarras said approvingly. "But I imagine they'll be a little less quiet when we land."

He made the final approach with extra care. The onlookers scattered, then surged forward again as the sphere came to rest.

"Brace yourself," Idenion said to Laura, and unsealed the hatch. She smiled at him and stepped forward resolutely.

A delighted yell went up: but after that, the youthful crowd behaved extremely well. They chanted her name and clustered round, but were careful to leave her a breathing space. They were justifiably pleased with themselves. Their campaign had come to a successful end - possibly the first time in their history that organised protest had overturned an unpopular ruling. Dena appeared, looking anxiously for Idenion; when he emerged a little shakily from the sphere, she ran to him with a glad cry. Then Laura felt a tug at her

467

tunic and, looking down, saw a diminutive boy holding a bunch of flowers.

"For me?" she asked.

He thrust the slightly bedraggled blooms toward her.

Laura accepted them politely, though she suspected they'd been picked from one of the communal gardens at the edge of the plaza.

The boy remained where he was. "Is your name Elika, Armilla or Pelline?" he piped.

Laura understood him, although she was none the wiser. "No, I'm Laura," she replied.

"Then I may marry you!" exclaimed the child, to the amusement of those nearby. Floren gently shooed him back to his mother.

"What was that last bit?" Laura asked Floren. The answer left her even more mystified. "Why did he say that? And why did he recite those girls' names?"

"Later," said Floren.

Tralvar had left the akron and was making his way toward them. The spectators parted to let him through, and didn't close ranks again. Their hubbub diminished steadily, and some even began to drift away. They're still nervous of him, thought Laura. And why not? He's a killer. But he's also the best ruler they could possibly have - someone who'll fight to protect them.

When Tralvar reached Laura's side he gazed at her long and searchingly; then, without a word, fell to his knees before her. The erstwhile protestors looked on curiously.

"Tralvar!" cried Laura in dismay. "Get up!"

Unapologetic, he did so. "Now I don't have to make a speech," he said.

"Come and see what we've brought you," Laura said, hustling him onto the ramp before he could think of any more ways to embarrass her.

Jarras was still in the sphere, running some kind of systems check. He looked tense, as he'd done throughout the voyage. He and Tralvar had a short, serious conversation, and Laura was convinced they were discussing *her*. Not because they used her name or glanced at her, but because they didn't.

Then Tralvar turned his attention to the gramophone, which Laura had just removed from a storage compartment. He raised the lid and gazed intently at the mechanism - the turntable with its worn felt covering, the arm, the winding handle. Then he picked up the tin of needles and shook it.

"This is fascinating, Laura," he said with boyish enthusiasm. "But it will have to wait just a little longer. First, we have to get this sphere down to the maintenance bay. I'll accompany Jarras in a flitter, and bring him straight back. The refectory has stayed open for us - and for once, I'm famished."

"It's good to hear you say that," Laura commented.

"Perhaps you'd take the machine to my apartment," Tralvar continued. "My *new* apartment, that is."

"I hope it's an improvement on the old one," said Laura with a grin.

"I haven't wrecked it yet, if that's what you mean," Tralvar replied; and for once, his smile had some humour in it. "I think you'll approve. Floren will show you where it is."

Floren, in fact, had just come back into the cabin to see what the delay was. "Come along, you three. No experiments until tomorrow!" she chided.

"I'll need some help with these records," said Laura, but a moment later found she could now lift the case. She set off toward the akron's main entrance. Floren followed with the gramophone, carrying it in both arms and looking like a priestess in some pagan rite. The doors whisked apart. Rietta was there to greet them, together with a cheerful elderly man who identified himself as Kevis.

Idenion and Dena came in next, Dena laughing merrily at something Tralvar had just said. Seeing Laura's quizzical look, she explained:

"There's been some talk of casting a new bell for the Lyricon, but Tralvar says Idenion's saved us the trouble. We'll stand *him* in the bell tower, wearing that horrible coat. It's loud enough to attract the entire city!"

"It's a kaftan, not a coat," Idenion corrected her. "And it isn't loud. It's...er...vivid."

"That's one way of putting it," said Laura. "I hope you don't think I chose it for him, Dena. It was entirely his doing."

"I always knew he was tone-deaf, but I think he must be colour-blind as well," Dena remarked with mock seriousness.

They made for the refectory. Laura and Floren left the others briefly and delivered the gramophone and records to Tralvar's rooms.

"I do hope he isn't wasting his time over this

470

sound-recording," Floren said, depositing her burden thankfully. "It's always been one of his pet obsessions. No one else seems very interested."

"They *will* be, when he succeeds!" declared Laura. Then, more quietly, "I'm glad he's in better spirits. It must have taken a lot of courage to confess everything in front of a huge crowd."

"Kyrin made it easier for him," began Floren, then paused. "That reminds me - where *is* Kyrin? He should have been here, or at the very least, been relaying news of your arrival." She concentrated a while, then gave up. "He isn't answering. I think I'd better go and check on him. Tell the others I won't be long."

She hastened up the long staircase. Kyrin's apartment was in darkness, but she went in anyway and turned up the lights. Kyrin was lying on his bed, his eyes closed, his body rigid. Floren touched him gingerly.

"Kyrin?"

He recoiled from her unseeingly. "Don't hurt me!" he cried. "Don't hurt me!"

Very gently, Floren took him by the shoulders and settled him back on the pillow. "No one will ever hurt you again," she promised.

Finally Kyrin recognised her. "Is everything going to be all right now?" he asked waveringly.

"Yes, Kyrin," Floren assured him. "Everything will be all right."

"Then - would you please contact the hospital? I think I have a broken rib."

Floren tried, with no success; there was too much local excitement. It was typical of Kyrin that

471

he eventually found the strength to send the message himself. He also notified the relayist chain of his indisposition. Floren offered to stay with him until the medical team arrived, but in his usual self-effacing manner he declined further help and sent her back to the others. She went, wondering how many of Strephin's other victims had yet to come forward.

The meal occupied the rest of the evening. The refectory had pale green walls and a wooden floor, with several alcoves for secluded dining and a long trestle table down the centre of the room for those who didn't require privacy. Rietta and Kevis had seated their guests at the long table.

Everyone ate heartily save Idenion, who opted for a jug of liman. But he was in good spirits. "This will help me get well," he insisted.

The room was warm, and Laura was becoming sleepy. She'd asked everyone to restrict their use of English so she might learn Celestrian more quickly, but the endless concentration taxed her.

Gradually she became aware that something odd was happening. Floren was giving Tralvar some intense looks, and the jocular Kevis was being very attentive to Rietta. Dena suddenly burst into tears, and was comforted by Jarras. Idenion spoke sharply to him. From outside in the square came a sudden shriek and a burst of laughter, and from inside the akron came the sound of running feet.

"Sciesha," said Idenion softly.

Laura was wide awake in an instant. Was she at last going to find out what sciesha was?

"Laura, go to your bed," Tralvar ordered.

"Before things get any worse."

Idenion ventured a remonstrance.

"We can't expose her to this!" Tralvar told him angrily. "Any young citizen would think he was complimenting her by offering sciesha, and wouldn't realise she'd be affronted or scared. We have to keep her out of it."

"I'm quite capable of seeing off any celebrants," Idenion objected.

"And who's going to see *you* off?"

"Discords, Tralvar, I don't want to take sciesha. I'm not well!"

Laura looked from one to the other, trying to make sense of the dispute.

"We cannot trust ourselves to take care of her," Tralvar went on more quietly. "Rietta, which room did you prepare for Laura?"

No reply.

"Rietta!"

She dragged her attention away from Kevis. "The second civic exchange suite," she replied.

"Next to mine. Oh, well done," Tralvar said witheringly. "Why in chaos did I take the locks off the cell doors? I should have anticipated this." Then, to Laura: "During sciesha, people have little inhibition and even less sense. Please do as I say. Shut yourself in your room and bar the door with something."

"I could stay with her," Dena said hesitantly. "The sciesha hasn't touched me."

A crash sounded from upstairs.

"Agreed, Dena. Now take her away, quickly."

The gathering broke up. Kevis and Rietta

disappeared arm in arm. Jarras found the nearest exit and, fleet of foot, hastened downhill toward the student quarter. Idenion went to his allocated room, climbed into bed and pulled the covers over his head. He was soon fast asleep. Floren, tacitly silent, went with Tralvar to his apartment.

"Shall we?" she asked succinctly.

"I've not taken sciesha for years," he said doubtfully.

"Then it would be silly to miss this opportunity," Floren pronounced.

Joining hands, they opened their minds to the city.

At an adjacent window, Laura gazed across the plaza. She could see little out of the ordinary except an occasional running figure, although several lanterns had been dropped and now lay sputtering on the ground. Dena, beside her, looked sad and wistful.

"Why did you cry?" Laura asked her.

"Every time there's sciesha I try to give myself to it," she said. "And every time, I can't. I'm still not ready."

"What *is* sciesha?" asked Laura. "I know the word doesn't translate, but surely you can tell me more."

"Idenion calls it a delirium of the spirit," Dena replied. "It's spread via our perception, but we don't really know why it happens or what triggers it off. It's an overwhelming desire to mate, sometimes with your current partner but more typically with a stranger. We don't discourage it because it ensures a good genetic mix." She paused a moment. "This

474

sciesha is concentrated in the student quarter. That's good. There should be several children conceived tonight."

"But doesn't that play havoc with your public records?"

"Indeed it does not!" said Dena robustly. "Everyone's taught to remember their duty to society at such times. An exchange of names usually suffices, but if a boy believes his chosen won't remember him, he can give her a scieshanar - an identity tag with his name and lineage."

Laura sat down on the edge of her bed and stared pensively at the floor. "I'm so confused," she said plaintively. "A few hours ago I was preparing to say goodbye to Idenion, and in time he'd have become just a memory. A very precious one, but no longer part of my life. I'd have gone back to school or got a job, and the three days I spent here would've begun to seem like a dream. Now, instead, I'm back here indefinitely, and you're trying to explain sciesha to me and it's all so *strange*..."

Someone tried the door, but Laura had wedged a heavy table across it. "...and am I right in thinking," she continued, "that if Idenion was his normal self he'd either be attempting sciesha with me, or be out there having sex with a girl he didn't know?"

"You're tired," said Dena diplomatically. "Idenion said it was mid-evening when you left Earth, just as it was when you arrived here. But, you were in space more than three ilden. It's nearly midnight now, and so - "

"So I've been up till the equivalent of the small

475

hours," Laura concluded. "No wonder I feel shattered!"

"Then let's go to sleep," prompted Dena. "In the morning, things will be back to normal."

Laura, for all her misgivings, slept soundly. As usual she woke before anyone else, although this time it was broad daylight. She inched the table away from the door and peered out. The gallery was silent. The plaza was equally deserted. She washed and dressed, and was in the middle of brushing her hair when, to her surprise, Idenion appeared in the doorway. She was wretchedly pleased to see him.

"You probably think I'm being silly, but I was a bit scared," she confessed. "I'm glad it's over. How are you today, anyway?"

"A little better, but it will take days for the protections to build up again," he replied. "And as soon as they have, I've a date with the retracer and the space safety committee. I think I'll stay ill a bit longer!"

To avoid waking Dena, they went back to the refectory.

"I've an absolute craving for liman," Idenion confided, hunting about in the kitchens. "This happened once before, after I'd been on Myrma."

"I think you finished all the liman last night," Laura said.

Idenion emerged from the cold store emptyhanded. "It looks as if I did," he said ruefully. "And the delivery flitters will probably be late, so - how about a walk down to the bakeries on Lateral Three? We can get breakfast there, and it's a part of the city you haven't seen yet. And," he added, "we'll probably have the streets to ourselves."

"Ready when you are!" responded Laura, and accompanied him up the steps to the plaza.

It was a cloudy but warm morning, with a light breeze. Here and there, Laura saw traces of the previous night's revelry: torn paper lanterns strewn across the flagstones, a broken window, a flitter parked drunkenly on a steep slope. And one of the large circular flowerbeds on the third lateral showed every sign of having been trampled on. Laura went to lift up some of the flattened blossoms, but stopped short at the sight of a small pale hand amid the crushed greenery. Idenion carefully lifted some of the foliage aside to reveal the hand's owner - a young girl, hardly more than a child, clad only in a thin white shift such as dancers wore. She was in a deep sleep, her chest rising and falling imperceptibly. At her neck was a glint of silver: a tiny metal disc on a short chain.

"She wears the scieshanar," Idenion whispered.

Laura peered more closely at the prone figure. "What's that rash on her face?" she hissed. "You said there were no illnesses here!"

Idenion eased her away from the sleeping girl. "She isn't ill," he said reverentially. "That bloom signifies the start of a fertile phase. It means she'll probably conceive."

"But she's so young!" Laura said sorrowfully.

"It's the best time," Idenion declared. "Now let's go, before she wakes."

"We can't just leave her there!" Laura objected.

"We must. If we woke her she'd be distressed and confused. But if we leave her to revive naturally, she'll simply get up and go home."

Laura allowed herself to be led away.

"Having lived in your society, I realise how this must seem to you," Idenion added. "But that girl won't be shamed - far from it. Every birth is a cause for celebration. At her age, she won't be expected to keep her baby. There are plenty of people waiting to adopt one. Would it help if I told you that Dena and I were children of sciesha? We were adopted as soon as we were born. Our mother stayed in touch for a while, but we never met our father."

"And I suppose you're going to tell me you don't feel deprived," said Laura morosely.

"Not in the least," Idenion maintained. "Our identity is in the record of our lineage. Many of us aren't acquainted with our parents, and it doesn't worry us. So please don't let it worry *you*! After we've eaten, shall we go and watch the preparations for the Peisistrata?"

"Your street festival?"

"It begins in two days' time. The Lyricon has to look its best, and the routes of the dances have to be marked out and decorated. And later today, we'll know who will be this year's Hymorel."

"Who?"

"Our legend from the time of the meteor. The species was supposedly kept alive by one man, Hymorel, and seven women. All the young men want to play Hymorel."

"I suppose they would," Laura said wryly.

After a leisurely breakfast, they wandered up to the Lyricon. The working day had now begun, and

478

people were out and about. Laura was greeted several times, but with affection rather than adulation.

"The urgency's gone out of the situation," Idenion commented. "They know you're here to stay."

"Why aren't they taking more notice of *you*?" asked Laura. "Or am I missing something?"

"You're a celebrity," Idenion said laconically. "I'm only the First Poet, appointed by a dead dictator because he was flattered by what I wrote about him. I shall have to prove myself with other work."

"What sort of things will you write?" inquired Laura.

"I'll write about how we met," Idenion said seriously. "Maybe not immediately, but one day. And it will be the best poetry I'm capable of."

Once inside the theatre, they explored its precincts without being accosted. No one seemed surprised to see them there. A battalion of cleaners was still at work on the auditorium, removing litter, wine stains and occasional daubs of graffiti. In the adjacent halls, costumiers were cutting and measuring cloth, draping the results around their fidgeting clients. The instrument repair shop was doing a brisk trade. And a trio of shoemakers were stitching paper flowers onto green slippers.

Laura remembered the significance of the footwear, and smiled slightly. After a night of sciesha, would any girls still be seeking partners?

"Not everyone wants to take sciesha," Idenion pointed out. "Dena's one example."

"Dena *did* try to join in the sciesha," Laura objected. "It didn't work."

"Because she didn't want it to," Idenion replied. "I know my sister. She wouldn't be happy with anything so ephemeral." He paused, looking a little troubled. "Dena is that rarity, a scolia-sensitive who never joined the guild. She can hear the call and form a lattice, but she can't play music. It's a great pity - belonging to the guild would have been good for her. She'd have found partners there. As it is, she's resolutely unattached."

"But surely that's her choice," began Laura, when Idenion suddenly said:

"Oh-oh! Trouble!"

Laura waited for him to explain.

"We're summoned back to the akron," he said after a moment or two. "Tralvar's hopping mad because I didn't tell anyone where we were going. He's waiting for you to demonstrate the gramophone."

"Something tells me I'll be seeing rather a lot of Tralvar in the next few days," Laura remarked. "Oh well, I suppose it's as good a time as any for him to start his experiments. We can't move back to the Lyricon yet."

"Certainly not until after the Peisistrata," Idenion agreed. "Come on, let's look for a flitter. I've tired myself out, I'm afraid."

Tralvar was pacing about in the entrance hall when they arrived. "So you've condescended to bring her back, have you?" he inquired, glaring at Idenion. "Look at you - you're exhausted. You're supposed to be recovering your strength, not squandering it on sight-seeing!"

"I wasn't aware I needed your permission to go out with Laura," Idenion replied huffily.

"Laura's here to work," Tralvar snapped. He said it in English, to make sure she understood.

"All right, keep your hair on!" Laura retorted. "I know you wish I'd stayed on Earth, but since we *have* to work together, you could at least try to be amiable once in a while."

"I was worried about you," Tralvar said more quietly. "Sciesha can last for days sometimes."

Slightly mollified, Laura followed him up the main staircase. Idenion accompanied them as far as the first landing. "Don't work too hard!" he cautioned with a smile, and disappeared back to his room.

Tralvar, trying not to seem impatient, ushered Laura into his suite. He'd been making sketches of the gramophone, which stood on a low table near his desk.

"I perceive how this is operated," he said, "but I thought I'd better leave it to you. It's quite old, isn't it?" His mood had suddenly switched from irascibility to something approaching deference.

"Maybe I should've brought something more up to date," Laura said, with a sudden incongruous vision of her Dansette.

Tralvar glanced keenly at her. "And given me the problem of duplicating your electrical supply? I'd probably have blown it up before I could examine it. Well, don't keep me in suspense. Play me some music."

Laura obediently wound the gramophone, put

481

in a fresh needle and chose a record at random. It was "Home Sweet Home". She had a lump in her throat as the song echoed tinnily round the apartment. There was something infinitely touching about the old machine faithfully carrying out its one task, irrespective of its surroundings.

Tralvar remained absolutely motionless until the record had scratched to a halt. He hadn't taken his gaze from the rotating disc and the needle trailing toward its centre.

"How could I have been so *stupid*?" he breathed at last.

"Have you seen where you went wrong?" asked Laura.

"Yes," said Tralvar bitterly. "And for you to understand why I made the same mistake over and over, I'll have to explain about aldacite. All our information systems are based on aldacite crystals - you've seen them in the retracer and on board the spheres. And when it's in operation, aldacite resonates; that's its nature. So, when the time came to play back my recordings, I tried to resonate the very material I'd used. Sometimes nothing happened.

Usually it shattered."

"I...see," Laura said thoughtfully. It seemed a strange error to have made, but on the other hand, he'd come to the problem very late. Early recorded sound belonged to an age of steam and wheels, not an era of semi-sentient crystals.

Tralvar had begun to make diagrams on the back of his sketches. "I promised Floren I wouldn't work on this until after the Peisistrata, but I must set down my initial ideas. They're often the best. And I'll make a list of the equipment I need. We'll be working in the radio room - we can use some of its facilities."

"What do you want me to do now?" asked Laura.

"Go and see Floren. She's next door with Dena - they've had their heads together all morning. They want you to go on a tour of our other cities, and give a recital in each one. Everyone outside of Alda Mexa has heard of you, but few have *heard* you. Yet!" He tapped his sheaf of drawings significantly. "But before that, you'll perform at the Lyricon as a finale to the Peisistrata. That's what they want to discuss. And when you're choosing the songs, don't sing the one on that record. I want you to encourage people to be more venturesome, not hide in their own back yard!"

"You're getting as fussy as Idenion," Laura commented.

"Surely not!" Tralvar almost smiled.

"Can I...ask a favour?" Laura went on hesitantly.

"If you must," Tralvar said discouragingly.

"I'd like you to play for me at the Lyricon. I want everyone to see what a good musician you are."

"I'm flattered," he said with obvious sincerity. "But the zirid isn't a concert instrument."

"*Please*?"

Tralvar considered the proposal. "It's unorthodox, and I'd have to get the scolia's permission," he said. "But I suppose it's possible."

"Do please ask," said Laura, and turned to leave.

"When you've spoken with Floren, I'd like you back here for a while," Tralvar added. "I want you to tell me everything you know about the history and development of sound recording, including the manufacture of these discs."

"You're not going to attempt the work singlehanded, are you?"

"That would take too much of my time," Tralvar said with some regret. "I do have certain duties as First Citizen. I shall have to assemble a team."

When Laura had gone out he went to a wall cupboard which was already beginning to fill with junk, and after a few moments retrieved a hollowed-out globe of industrial quality crystal. "You're on here somewhere, Tristell," he murmured. "My final attempt, which I never tried to play in case I smashed it. Maybe my efforts will be vindicated at last." Then, lured by the music of Symerid Three, he returned to Laura's machine. He was well aware that it had to be used sparingly. The spring gave a protesting clunk as it was wound, and the supply of needles was finite. But he could afford to indulge himself this once.

He knew, from his previous conversations with Laura, that Earth music was divided into different strata: classical, popular, traditional, experimental, and various other categories whose names escaped him. He had no idea which of these he was listening to. But he sensed, through the persistent hiss and scratch on the records' surfaces, the vigour and vitality of the unknown performers, and wondered if he'd ever understand the complexity of styles. It would take a music student years, maybe a lifetime, to unravel it all.

Laura, hearing his selections faintly from the neighbouring apartment, wondered what he was making of "The Darktown Strutters' Ball" and "The Flies Crawled Up The Window". He was obviously taken with the Chopin nocturne he put on next, as he played it three times. A silence followed.

Tralvar had removed all the records from the case, hoping to find a visual match for the one he'd just played. He was unsuccessful. The labels and symbols didn't correspond. But as he examined them, his attention was drawn to an oddity in the collection - a disc smaller than the others, with a plain white label and a groove on one side only. It was made of steel, as opposed to the absurdly brittle substance that Laura had called shellac. Curious, he placed it on the turntable and set it in motion: then froze, assailed by the recurrent longing which had haunted him all his adult life. Poor though his knowledge of English was, he understood these recorded voices, for their message had been intended for a one-year-old. A young woman spoke first.

"Hello Laura! Are you being a good girl, and not giving Gran any trouble?"

"Laura, this is Daddy. Mummy's going to sing for you now. Listen carefully now. Listen Laura!"

There was an intolerable amount of surface noise on the record, and the song was almost inaudible. But Tralvar had heard it before, at the beginning of Laura's retrace.

"Tralvar!" Laura had crept back into the room unnoticed. "Oh, please, don't play that. I'd no idea it was in there!"

"Did you hear that, Laura?" called her father's voice. "Be good now. Be good for Mummy and Daddy."

One tear trickled down Laura's cheek. She knuckled her eyes fiercely. "I shouldn't cry," she said. "It's just that it was such a special time. You know how it is, don't you, when you're very young and everything seems so safe?"

"No," said Tralvar quietly. "I *don't* know. Your parents were cruelly taken from you, but they were with you in the years that mattered, and you've no idea how I envy you that."

Laura remembered, then, what Lydion had told her about Tralvar's mysterious origin. "Did your parents abandon you?"

"Worse," said Tralvar, and for a moment Laura thought that was all he'd say. Then he went on: "By now, you'll have learnt how important it is for us to keep track of our ancestry and prevent accidental inbreeding. Remember the child who gave you flowers? He'd already memorised the names of his female relatives, those he shouldn't marry. People often give up their children, but that doesn't matter as long as the child knows its lineage. I don't know mine. My parents never registered me."

"Then who gave you your name?"

"My first foster-parents. In your language, Tralvar means foundling. So, when I make a

486

pairbond - and yes, there have been a few occasions - I can't offer the security of my line. It's such an insult to a child, not to register it. I can't believe my parents just didn't bother. But I've given up trying to find out what happened."

"Don't you remember anything of your early life?"

"Just one thing. I fell into a snowdrift, and someone dragged me out. It's something of a clue, I suppose, but not a very helpful one."

Laura, after hearing this, thought she understood Tralvar a little better. That early betrayal must have permanently blighted his self-confidence.

"I always felt I must have disappointed someone very much," he reflected. "I've been trying to make up for it ever since. Perhaps, now, I'll be able to." He lifted the record which had prompted his confession and studied it thoughtfully. "What a superb gift for a child. If my work succeeds, I could send one to my daughter."

"You have a daughter?" Laura was intrigued, but before Tralvar could elaborate they were interrupted by Kevis, who looked half asleep. He apologised briefly to Laura, then spoke earnestly with Tralvar, who seemed surprised and pleased. As soon as the secretary had gone, Laura asked what he'd wanted.

"My weapons have been found - the ones Strephin stole," Tralvar explained. "And I hadn't even organised a search. I might have known he was too lazy to hide them properly."

"Where were they?"

"Down a storm drain. Which means they'll

probably have been ruined by damp. What an idiot! He didn't even know what happens to therite when it gets wet."

"And what *does* happen?"

"It splits apart when you ignite it, and you get dozens of tiny flares instead of one big one. Quite useless."

"It sounds pretty," Laura observed. "Couldn't you make fireworks with it?"

"Fireworks?" Tralvar repeated the word curiously. "You must tell me more. But first, I'll have to go and inspect the launchers in case anything needs to be made safe."

"And *I'd* better go back to Floren," said Laura. "She hadn't finished telling me her plans."

"She could take you to see Lydion, now that you have the time," Tralvar suggested. "She told me you were asking after him. He regained consciousness this morning."

"Oh, that *is* good news!"

"And I'm sure he'd be happy to see the First Singer. That's if he isn't being monopolised by his girlfriends."

"He's quite popular, isn't he?"

"That's an understatement," Tralvar remarked. "And he makes it seem so effortless. Anyway, if you want to see him before the Peisistrata, this will be your only chance. Tomorrow the city will start filling up and it won't be easy to travel about."

"How many people are you expecting?"

"Everyone from the outlying regions - farmers, foresters, canal workers. Plus most of Tivenne and a good proportion of Treva."

"Wow!"

"And with that in mind, Floren might forbid me to take part in your recital. It's too important to be spoilt by my playing!"

"Then we'll organise another one later," Laura declared. "We work well together - don't we?"

"I suppose so," he conceded with a grim little smile. "But you may need reminding you said that, when the *real* work starts!"

***

The Peisistrata lasted two days, the first consisting of street pageants and the second a general holiday with feasting and displays of dance. The midnight procession and concert were usually more restrained, a gentle scaling down of the festivities before the city returned to normal. The first day of the festival was the start of the new year, although seasonally it was the middle of spring.

"I shall soon be twelve years old!" Idenion revealed, and thus Laura discovered that the Celestrian year was five hundred and four days long, divided - unsurprisingly - into eight segments of sixty-four days. These were known as spans, and each sub-division of eight days was simply called an octal. The two Peisistrata days were set apart from the rest of the calendar.

By the morning of day one, Idenion was looking and feeling much better, and together with Laura joined the crowds lining the streets. The pageants were enacted on Lateral Four - the lateral whose houses had multi-coloured roofs. Laura

489

remembered thinking they resembled a coiled snake when viewed from the air; Idenion now informed her they depicted the zarf, a creature from mythology with an insatiable lust for maidens. The Zarf Dance was the highlight of the entire festival. First, however, would be the celebration of Hymorel and his wives.

Two days ago Laura had seen the processional route being marked out by rows of coloured pegs. Today, the street was garlanded with flowers. Plump ropes of grass were looped round the walls, and from nearly every window hung some kind of home-made art - tapestries, murals, and children's paintings. The lamp standards were festooned with streamers and tiny bells which tinkled in the breeze.

At regular intervals along the route, groups of eight musicians played on flutes, wooden chimes and little drums.

"There are many scolia players in Alda Mexa," Idenion said in response to Laura's question. "They can't all be in the Lyricon scolia, and some of them don't want to be. Too rarefied! There's more enjoyment to be had at this level, in my opinion."

By Laura's standards, the spectators weren't making much noise. But, she reminded herself, this was a telepathic crowd. Every so often they'd all turn in one direction like windblown reeds, or a collective sigh would go up, or the children would all squeal in unison. Beside her, Idenion reacted to the same stimuli, though he tried to moderate it for her benefit.

"Go ahead and have fun," she told him. "You don't have to restrain yourself for my sake."

490

The spectators dressed in bright colours for the occasion, livening up the basic tunic with contrasting sashes, embroidered scarves and beaded overgarments. For once, Idenion's kaftan didn't look out of place. Dena, glimpsed briefly with Floren, looked very pretty in mauve and yellow firi. She wore one of the steel necklaces Idenion had bought in Oxford Street. Floren, resplendent in silver, wore the other. Laura had opted for contrasting shades of green, but now felt it didn't suit her.

"Where's Tralvar?" she asked suddenly.

"Probably in his workshop. You know what he's like," Idenion replied.

"Couldn't we go and fetch him?"

"Not now - we'd miss everything. Here comes Hymorel."

The music increased in tempo and Hymorel duly appeared. Laura recognised him as one of Cyphos' stonemasons, a tall sturdy lad with a mischievous smile. He wore a bodysuit of thin gold net, adorned from waist to thigh with a sunburst motif. The design emphasised his genitals but at the same time gave him a degree of modesty. His wives, seven young women in diaphanous white, wove an intricate dance around him. The crowd threw handfuls of petals at the dancers as they passed.

The dance became more and more energetic, but just as the troupe was about to disappear round the curvature of the street, the music ceased abruptly with a loud thud on the drums. The performers held their final positions in a tableau.

Then a girl detached herself from the onlookers and boldly approached the motionless group.

"Hymorel!" she cried.

The young man swiftly snared the girl, looping a length of net about her waist and drawing her towards him.

"Who calls on Hymorel?" he demanded.

"I am Nyldra," said the girl, naming herself. "I would be your mate and bear your child!"

"I have seven wives already," Hymorel replied. "You must seek elsewhere." He raised his voice a little. "Attend! Here is Nyldra. Who will claim her?"

He then released the girl, who moved to one side and stood waiting. Belatedly, Laura noticed she wore the shoes with the paper flowers. Another girl hastened forward and the ritual was repeated. Over a dozen had announced themselves before the music started up again. Hymorel's wives encircled both him and the suppliants, and hustled them away. A number of young men were already leaving the crowd and following the little group.

"Well, I suppose it's better than sciesha," Laura said dubiously. "But what if someone doesn't attract any boys? That would be so embarrassing!"

"No-one's left without a partner," Idenion assured her. "Hymorel sees to that!"

"Oh, I get it," said Laura, and laughed self-consciously.

Away from the main street, tables and benches were being set under awnings to accommodate those who wanted lunch. Not everyone did. It was the custom to eat frugally on day one, in preparation

492

for the banquet to follow.

Laura and Idenion helped themselves to bread and soup. From their slightly elevated position they could see the rooftops of Lateral Five, and beyond it the Lisir, including a marina where numerous boats were tethered. Many of the visitors had travelled to Alda Mexa by river. Laura gazed keenly into the distance, eager to memorise every detail of this intriguing day.

"Hurry up!" Idenion prompted gently. "The Zarf Dance is about to begin."

"Whereabouts should we stand?" asked Laura.

"It doesn't matter too much. The zarf makes a circuit of the entire lateral. But we should be at street level to appreciate it fully."

They returned to Lateral Four, where the scolia groups were reorganising themselves. The flutes and drums were put aside, though the hanging chimes remained. Strelsis-adepts tuned their instruments meticulously. Then suddenly, as one, they began to play.

Laura shivered as the first notes reached her. This music was eerie and unsettling, far removed from Hymorel's merry pipings. The large bass strelsis set up an insidious drone. One of the chimes was struck quietly at regular intervals, and the strings shimmered like an audible heat haze. Idenion's arm tightened about her.

"Better not stand in the front," he advised. Laura obediently moved away from the crowd's edge, allowing several girls to push past her. The music made a disconcerting key change, and a single shout arose from the gathering.

493

"Zarf!"

Seven young men, their near-naked bodies glistening with oil, marched into view. They carried, on tall poles, a snake-like creature fashioned from metal rings and iridescent fabric. Its head was elongated, with deep-set eyes which gleamed in the sunlight, and a cunningly hinged jaw which swung to and fro as if seeking prey. Its tail was decked with rattling bells.

Suddenly, as if by its own volition, the zarf reared its head and lunged at one of the girls. She shrieked and darted away. The creature and its attendants gave chase, attempting to surround her, but she quickly dipped between them and vanished into the crowd. The beast paused, head rising and falling, then swept towards the largest knot of females. They scattered, giggling and screaming, some looking back as if daring the zarf to pursue them.

Now the dance began in earnest, the hypnotic drone of the music complimenting the sinuous movements of the young men and their puppet. They advanced slowly down the lateral in an undulating pattern, the zarf snapping its jaws and lashing its tail realistically. As they passed, first one girl and then another stepped forward and began to circle the dancers, imitating their swaying motion. The maddening music continued, drawing more and more young women into the dance, which was growing progressively more erotic. Laura watched uneasily. Then, when she least expected it, the music stopped. Not with a flourish, as Hymorel's had: it simply wasn't there anymore.

The girls halted, maintaining their circle.

The zarf's blank metallic gaze regarded each of them in turn before singling one out. The baleful head reared triumphantly above her. The audience waited, motionless as the intended victim. Then, with a cry, the seven men surged forward as if pulled by their beast. The girl screamed and fled. The other girls, shouting and yelling, ran in pursuit of the zarf, the boldest leaping to snatch at its tail. As they receded into the distance the nearest musicians struck up a fresh tune, contrastingly bright.

"And that's it!" Idenion said cheerfully. "The zarf-bearers will perform it all again, with different girls, until they've circled the lateral."

"Why were they plastered in grease?" asked Laura.

Idenion laughed. "Sometimes the girls forget the zarf's supposed to chase *them*. They try to grab the boys, but the oil makes them difficult to hold onto. The dance takes precedence!"

"It sounds like a recipe for sciesha," Laura said, looking suspiciously about her.

"Naturally," said Idenion, unconcerned. "I don't detect any sign of it today, though. It's probably too soon after the last outbreak. Come on - let's find out what Tralvar's up to. He's probably skulking indoors to avoid dressing up."

They walked back through the bustling city, Idenion wondering if his retrace would cause the theorists to re-write the origin of the Zarf Dance. Although it had long ago become a fertility ritual, he couldn't help thinking it derived from the time when animals had wreaked mental havoc.

Laura was glad to return to the akron, as the bright sun was beginning to make her head ache. At least, she assumed that was the reason. Tralvar's workshop was deserted, which was a good sign, but when they reached his quarters they found him poring over some papers on his desk.

"You promised Floren you'd wait until after the festival," Laura accused.

"I said I wouldn't work on the recording device," he retorted. "This is musical notation."

Laura studied it curiously. It looked like a set of fractions.

"We don't write it *all* down, as your people do," Tralvar explained. "This is in the nature of an aid to memory - a partial transcription of the piano piece you brought me. I had to re-tune the zirid to play it. Listen!"

He sat down at the keyboard and performed a recognisable version of the Chopin nocturne. Even Idenion looked impressed.

"Tralvar, you've *got* to play that at the Lyricon tomorrow," Laura declared. "Surely Floren will let you? It's only short!"

"She may," he conceded. "This music should be heard - she can't disagree with that. Now clear out, both of you. I want to practice."

Idenion had promised Laura a reading lesson, but disappointingly her eyestrain didn't abate, and she went to her room for a rest. A relentless pinging was sounding from next door as Tralvar made further adjustments to the zirid, but she fell asleep regardless. By evening she'd regained some energy and joined the others in Tralvar's apartment for a cold supper. The kitchens were off limits, as they were full of caterers preparing food for the morrow. Huge baskets of fruit were being brought in, along with sacks of vegetables and countless jars of wine.

"And anyone can just walk in here and help themselves?" asked Laura.

"Here, and various other centres throughout the city," replied Idenion. "Alda Mexa couldn't function without its regional workers. So, once a year, we honour them."

"Can Tralvar play the Chopin piece?" Laura asked Floren eagerly.

"Yes, I've given my permission," she replied. "A zirid will be placed onstage for him. But there's to be no re-tuning in front of the audience!"

The second day of the Peisistrata was as fine and cloudless as the first, though considerably quieter as everyone settled down to some serious feasting. Laura, who never ate much prior to a performance, showed little inclination to join in. She found an ally in Tralvar, who hated being idle. She spent the morning recounting the history of the gramophone and answering his questions as accurately as she could, and the afternoon studying texts in the akron's extensive library. There were several accounts of visits to Hellas, which Tralvar did his best to translate. Floren and Dena had returned to the Lyricon, having reminded Tralvar to be there by sunset. Idenion had come to see what Laura was doing, but was now embroiled in a philosophical debate with Jarras and some young

497

intellectuals from Treva.

"Are you sure you wouldn't rather be with them?" asked Tralvar, closing a connecting door on their animated voices.

"And have Idenion interrupt himself to explain things?" Laura responded. "He'd lose the argument then. Besides, he may not want me around all the time." And, suddenly in need of a confidante, she told Tralvar what she'd said to Idenion when it seemed they'd be separated.

"We all know he cares for you," said Tralvar, choosing his words carefully. "But he isn't going to rush into anything and risk offending your ideals. Give him a chance to think things through."

"Do you think I should forget about my ideals?" asked Laura.

"It's a unique situation," Tralvar replied unhelpfully, "and even if it weren't, I'm no expert on romance." He stood up, indicating that the subject was closed for the time being. "I must prepare to meet my public! Floren insists I have to look presentable, if that's possible. If you want to stay here I'll collect you when I'm ready."

The discussion in the next room was growing louder and louder.

"What are they talking about?" Laura asked.

"The ethics of spaceflight," Tralvar said. "What if we encountered a civilised but planetbound species dying from some global catastrophe? Would we stand by and watch them die, or give them the transposal drive?"

"What would *you* do?" inquired Laura.

"Nothing," he replied caustically. "When a

species doesn't have transposal, there's always a good reason. And as there's only one possible conclusion, there's no point in debating it. Students do love to waste their time!"

On arrival at the Lyricon, Laura was surprised to find it almost deserted. But as Floren reminded her, the Peisistrata belonged to the streets. At two ilden to nadir, the lantern-lit procession would begin at the sixth lateral and slowly wend its way up to the great theatre. The audience would consist entirely of visitors to the city.

Tralvar was looking very smart in a tunic of silver and scarlet. Floren voiced her approval and he went cheerfully away to tune the zirid. Laura again found herself in the First Singer's apartment, now stripped of all Tristell's possessions. All, save the yellow dress that Zenzie had so painstakingly altered. Laura wondered if she should put it on; then, out of deference to Tralvar, laid it aside. Her green costume would have to do. Her Earth clothes, washed and pressed, were hanging on an empty clothes rail. Slightly unsettled, she drew a curtain in front of them.

After dark, the other participants began to assemble: a few dancers, the scolia, and some actors who'd be performing a masque. Each section of the programme was quite short, so Laura would be required to sing two items only. She'd chosen Nuit D'Etoiles again, and to conclude, Where'er You Walk.

Because there was plenty of time in hand, two of the actresses offered to make her up, dusting her face with pink and gold powder and weaving a circlet of beads into her hair. Just as they were showing her the results, blue light flared outside the picture window. Someone was trying to start the weathershield. Three times the shape of the grid appeared overhead, then sputtered out before the next phase was reached. Laura went into Floren's apartment and asked what was wrong.

"Without Lydion to maintain it, the shield has malfunctioned," Floren said. "Tonor doesn't have much affinity with it. Tralvar's gone to see what he can do."

On the next attempt, two-thirds of the shield lit, leaving a section of the grid visible. Then, with a thunderclap, all was dark again.

"He has to get it working soon!" Floren said, frowning. "The procession's on its way."

"What will happen if he can't fix it?" asked Laura.

"The concert will still go ahead, but it will reflect poorly on the city if we can't keep our institutions in order. You'd better go down to the stage area. I'm putting you on first."

Laura took the most direct route through the terraces. The shield spat and flickered above her as she walked. When it finally lit, some lingering imperfection set tiny motes of light dancing across the empty auditorium. Peering gingerly round the door of the generator room, she found Tralvar and Tonor kneeling by some conduits.

"What are all those little sparkles?" she asked.

"Projector Four is misfiring," Tralvar said. "I can't improve it - if I use the dampers again, it probably won't re-ignite."

500

"Then why don't you leave it like that?" suggested Laura. "It's pretty. It's like a glitterball."

"A what?" he asked, dragging the back of his hand across his forehead.

"Glitterball. It's a rotating globe with bits of mirror stuck all over it. We use them in dance halls to create - " Tralvar stood up and her voice faltered to a stop.

"Create what?"

" - a romantic atmosphere," she concluded despairingly. "Oh, Tralvar, *look* at you!"

His new tunic was streaked with grime. His arms and hands were filthy, and so was his face where he'd mopped his brow.

"There goes my concert debut," he said wearily.

"You're going to play," Laura declared, and propelled him towards the enclave where the actors were gathered. "Someone must have something you can wear. Ask them."

He made his request, surprisingly reticent. Laughing, the young people surrounded him and hurried him off.

Far above, the first of the celebrants were setting down their lanterns in the entrance hall and filtering onto the terraces. Laura was still anxiously watching them arrive when Tralvar and his rescuers reappeared. They'd scrubbed most of the dirt off him and attired him in a scolia robe.

"I can't wear this," he protested to Laura. "It would offend the Guild."

"You told me you were entitled to wear it as long as you had the novice's belt," Laura argued. "And that's green, right? So's this." She removed the sash from her dress, folded it into a narrow strip and tied it round his waist. Then, pausing only to smooth his rumpled hair, she took her place in front of the waiting scolia.

At last she sang, feeling strangely remote from the gathering. The little pinwheeling lights danced hypnotically round her. Sounds of cheering, and of her name being called, reached her over a vast distance. It was as if it were happening to someone else. Dena's troupe performed their mazy dances, the actors presented their masque, and Tralvar played the Chopin Nocturne in F sharp major. He received a creditable amount of applause, but couldn't get off the stage fast enough.

"What's the matter?" asked Laura. "They liked it, didn't they?"

"Didn't you see him?" demanded Tralvar, agitated.

"Who?"

"Melor! He was in the front row, with Essi. Oh, discords, why did I make such a fool of myself?"

"You didn't," insisted Laura. "Come on - we've all got to line up and say goodnight. And not before time. I'm exhausted!"

Tralvar didn't follow her. While Floren was speaking the traditional words that brought the Peisistrata to a close, he tried to slip away. Melor, however, knew his pupil of old, and waylaid him at the stage exit.

"Greetings, Tralvar. Were you responsible for that interesting display of light particles? I found it most relaxing."

502

"It...was an accident, Guildmaster," Tralvar stammered.

"And the Hellas music was in a proscribed key," Melor continued.

"That's the key it was written in," Tralvar said defensively. "It has a poignancy, a yearning quality, which might be lost if the pitch were changed."

"The mood of the piece has to be preserved," Melor conceded. "Perhaps it's time to re-evaluate our tuning methods. As always, you've given me something to think about." He turned to leave, then paused. "Well done," he added casually, and was gone, leaving Tralvar gazing after him in amazement.

Laura couldn't understand why she was so tired. "I can't go back to the akron tonight," she told Floren. "I'm almost asleep on my feet. Can I stay the night in Tristell's - I mean *my* - apartment?"

"Of course," said the older woman, scrutinising Laura narrowly. "I shall be staying here myself, in the custodian's chambers. After all, I do live here!"

"But I thought - you and Tralvar..."

"That's something I shall have to speak to him about," Floren replied.

Laura woke very late the next morning, realising she'd fallen straight into bed without removing her make-up. The pillow was streaked with powder and there were loose beads everywhere. She vaguely remembered her hair ornament had snapped when she'd pulled her dress off. Yawning, she wandered into the washroom - and what she saw in the mirror sent her rushing headlong, still in her nightrobe, into the next-door apartment.

"Floren!" she wailed. "Floren, look at my face!"

"Ah," said Floren, seemingly relieved. "The bloom. There's no need to panic, Laura - it means our protections have adopted you."

"You could have warned me," Laura said reproachfully.

"We didn't think you'd be susceptible," Floren explained. "At least, Rietta didn't, although I never quite followed her reasoning. There was no precedent."

"So what happens next?" asked Laura, unpacified.

"The rash will fade in less than a day, if you react in the same way we do," Floren replied. "Thereafter, you'll find your reproductive cycle is dormant for long intervals. When it becomes active again, the bloom will reappear."

"Is this why I've been so tired?"

"Undoubtedly. Our space travellers always feel tired or feverish when their protections are renewed."

"Well," said Laura dubiously, "I suppose I'll just have to live with it."

"As we all do," Floren reminded her. "But look at it this way: you've responded to our biosphere like a native. It proves you truly belong here."

"Yes," said Laura, brightening. "Yes, it does. I hadn't thought of that."

***

504

A sphere made a neat touchdown on the Treva spacefield. Its lone occupant disembarked and hurried to the terminal building, where a young woman waited impatiently.

"Rillan! Did you bring it?"

"Yes, Thala, as I promised." Rillan pointed to the front pocket of his overalls. "You were right - no one was manning the Alda Mexa tower during Peisistrata. I spent all evening in the data store looking for the programme."

"Can I see it?"

"Not here. It's just a piece of aldacite, like any other. Nothing to show how precious it is."

"The longest starflight our people ever made!" Thala said reverently.

"The coordinates for Narvella, far across our galaxy near the edge of the spiral arm," Rillan elaborated. "According to the data there are *two* inhabited planets!"

"And you really think it's possible to go there," Thala breathed.

"It's a possibility, not a certainty. First, I have to make a duplicate of the crystal in case anything happens to the original. We don't want to lose our only link with Narvella. Then I'll programme a sphere for automatic return. Then, assuming we get it back, I'll analyse the flight details and make sure it's safe to make the run again."

"And then *we'll* go!" Thala's eyes were shining. "Oh, Rillan, we could start a new age of exploration. And we won't be doing it because Alendis ordered it but because we want to. Tralvar

505

will be so proud of us!"

"And I'm proud of *you*," Rillan declared. "I'm sure no other girl would be willing to risk everything for my dream."

"It's my dream too," Thala replied.

"We'll have to be patient a while yet," Rillan pointed out. "Studying the data will be a slow business. That's if the sphere comes back at all!"

"It will - I know it will," Thala said fiercely.

"And when we've made our preparations, we don't go anywhere without Controller Halon's permission," Rillan added. "We want to be history makers, not lawbreakers. Come on - let's get this programme copied. We've a lot of work to do before we can announce the dawn of a new age!"

Chapter Sixteen

Laura soon realised that a concert tour wasn't the best way to explore Celestra. At the end of sixty-four days she had visited eight city-states in the company of Idenion and Floren. She was transferred to each new location by sphere, as the cities were so far apart, and thus had acquired little knowledge of the planet's geography. She supposed there would be time for that later. She was, however, becoming an expert on the various theatres: some luxurious, some austere, but none as awe-inspiring as the Lyricon. The people were unfailingly pleasant, their reaction to her music as profound as anything she'd encountered in Alda Mexa. But few had the ability to speak English, and her knowledge of Celestrian grew exponentially.

The cities differed vastly. Atris, at the foot of a mountain range, was surrounded by endless fields of grain. Corayn, with its multicoloured gardens of herbs, was fragile and beautiful. But nowhere, save in Treva, was there any hint of space technology. Alendis had called the planet a dull pastoral backwater, and Laura could now see what he meant. But how could this civilisation turn itself around, faced with an insidious decline in its numbers?

The extent of the problem was highlighted when, on their way to Kassi, they overflew a ghost town. Jarras, who arrived every eight days to ferry them to their next venue, took the sphere down for Laura to have a closer look. The laterals were choked with weeds, the bold bright architecture laden with creepers.

"That is Ilonna," said Idenion. "It's been derelict for about seventy years."

"Why?"

"Because the population had fallen below five hundred, and was no longer viable. The people were relocated and the city abandoned. It's happened several other times in our history."

When they reached Kassi, Floren disappeared on a mysterious errand. She was away for nearly two days, and wouldn't explain why. Idenion agreed this was uncharacteristic of her, but assumed it was a personal matter.

Laura had expected to have Idenion to herself some of the time, but this hadn't happened. Two octals into the tour, he was recalled to Alda Mexa to make his retrace and speak with the administrators about Earth and the treacherous dust cloud. And once he was back, it proved difficult to be alone with him. Either her time was taken up by music students and the public in general, or Idenion was similarly monopolised by his own following - mostly girls. Laura was surprised at how many people he already knew.

"He's toured in his own right," Floren explained. "Alendis worked hard at promoting him."

"In whose interests was that?" inquired Laura.

"Alendis', of course," Floren replied. "He wanted everyone to hear the First Poet honour him in verse. It will be interesting to see how Idenion lives that down."

Jarras kept them up to date with news from Alda Mexa. "Tralvar's doing very well with the sound transcriptions," he reported while negotiating a very overgrown landing field in Kest. "He's recorded the scolia, and himself. When he played his own words back, he said: 'This still needs work. It doesn't sound anything like me.' But it *did*!"

"Everyone makes that mistake," commented Laura. "Try recording your own voice. You'll get a shock too."

"I hope he isn't using the akron for anything industrial," said Floren.

"No, not at all. He's using the radio room as a studio, but he's converted a textile factory to handle the rest of the process. He hasn't evolved a mass-production technique yet; the master discs aren't durable enough to press others in the way Laura described to him. I'm sure he'll solve it, but for now he's concentrating on improving the sound quality." He turned back to Laura. "He's going to need your help very soon. Could you take a break from your tour and work with him a while?"

"Floren, is that possible?" asked Laura.

"It's an obligation," she replied. "Technically, you're the guest of the First Citizen, and must accede to his wishes."

"Which towns haven't we visited?"

"Ninka and Virda. I'll apologise to them for the delay. You'll be free to work for Tralvar after the Kest recitals."

"I wonder if I could record some of my poems?" mused Idenion.

"You'll be lucky," Laura said in amusement. "You know what he thinks of them."

"Then I must try to change his mind," Idenion

509

declared. "While you're shut away with our First Citizen, I shall begin my new opus."

"Are you dining with us today, Jarras?" asked Floren.

"Not this time. I have to make a stopover at Corayn and pick up some hospital supplies. That stand-in relayist, Tylo, isn't very efficient - we're always running out of things lately."

"I thought Kyrin would be back at work by now," Floren said, slightly perturbed.

"So did I, but it seems he's not well enough yet," replied Jarras. "We'll just have to cope a little longer."

Kyrin, healed in body but strangely troubled in spirit, was at that moment entering Tyvian's laboratory.

"I wish to be put on retrace," he said, nervous but resolute.

Tyvian carefully set aside a tray of cultures and stood up, trying to conceal his irritation. He'd always discouraged casual callers. Surely Kyrin, of all people, might have had the courtesy to communicate with him first.

"Everyone knows my mental signature," Kyrin said, with only a trace of colour reaching his pale face. "I wanted our meeting to be private."

"I'm not sure if I can help," Tyvian said. "This batch of prill isn't fully mature, and moreover, I promised Tralvar exclusive use of them. So unless this is very important..."

"It is to me," Kyrin said. "I...I need to find out who I am. *What* I am."

Tyvian sighed. Kyrin's words came as no

surprise to him. These identity crises were quite common amongst relayists, bombarded as they were with a multitude of thoughts and experiences not their own. He also knew that such disorders were seldom easy to pinpoint, let alone correct. "Many relayists have suffered in this way," he observed, "but they don't all come running to be retraced. Doesn't your fraternity offer support in cases like yours?"

"I don't think this is typical," Kyrin said, standing his ground. "Will you at least let me explain?"

"Of course," Tyvian said, relenting. He'd never seen Kyrin look so wretched. "Tralvar owes you a favour - he'd be the first to admit that. Sit down and tell me what's bothering you. I presume Strephin's to blame?"

"In part," Kyrin answered.

"Then have you evaluated your own conduct?" inquired Tyvian. "I'm sorry, but I have to ask. You were very rash to pit yourself against someone like Strephin. Alendis had a fearsome temper too: didn't working for him teach you anything?"

"I work for the akron administration, not just the First Citizen," Kyrin said defensively. "Most of my duties are purely routine - ordering plants for the communal gardens, making sure the liman gets delivered. I never knew Alendis very well and I certainly didn't feel oppressed by him. He singled me out just once - to compliment me on my skills and to urge me to reproduce myself."

Tyvian chuckled. "He said that to you as well, did he? He used to embarrass Tralvar with remarks like that. Do continue, Kyrin."

The laughter had broken the tension somewhat. Briefly, knowing it had to be said, Kyrin outlined the circumstances of his first beating. "I suppose I should have been wary of Strephin," he added, "but I didn't stop to think. I didn't even know why he and Asterion were quarrelling." He drew a deep breath. "And that's why I'm here - because of Asterion."

Tyvian looked startled.

"I'd probably have stayed on the floor till morning," Kyrin went on, "but Asterion relented and came back. He brought some odd-tasting liman and made me drink it. Then he carried me to my apartment and bathed my bruises. I don't remember much beyond that. I think we talked. And he had his arms round me." He paused, biting his lip. "I need to know everything that was said."

"Aren't some things best forgotten, Kyrin?" Tyvian asked gently.

"Normally, I would agree," Kyrin replied. "But I can't let this rest. When the news of his death reached me I couldn't relay it. I felt bereaved. I still do, as if I've lost a lover. And to a relayist, such emotions are disastrous. I must find the cause and deal with it, or else leave the profession."

"Kyrin - " began Tyvian, then subsided. The boy was right. Obsessive love had no place in a relayist's life; obsessive love for a dead man had no place anywhere.

"I've convinced you, then," Kyrin said.

"Unfortunately yes," said Tyvian. "Well, it obviously took courage for you to approach me, and

512

I hate to send you away, but if I retraced you here and now you'd probably be sick. First, you must refrain from eating for at least seven ilden."

"I haven't touched any food this morning," Kyrin said. "I know I'm supposed to be resting, but I couldn't ignore the basic disciplines."

I might have known, thought Tyvian.

"I don't think the prill would find me very taxing," Kyrin continued eagerly. "My whole career is a form of symbiosis. I can enter a light trance, if it helps."

In fact, this proved not to be necessary. Almost before the stimulus had peaked, he slipped easily, gratefully, into rapport with the equipment. Tyvian wished there had been more time to prepare questions, but the relevant sequence wasn't difficult to locate. Wincing with pain, which was not his, he absorbed the events of that singular night, until he reached the moment when Asterion had taken the injured boy into his arms.

"*Now* I understand," he murmured; and despite being forewarned, struggled to remain aloof.

Afterwards, he heard himself uttering reassuring words which Kyrin didn't quite believe. "I'll need about four days to process the readings. I've found something germane to your problem, and when all the facts are assembled I think you'll be a lot happier. Go now. Leave everything to me."

Obediently Kyrin departed, and Tyvian set about transcribing the retrace - a task he could easily complete in half a day. He had his own reasons for deferring the playback. After the transcription was finished he went to the spaceport

513

to confer with Halon, who had just resumed his duties. Then he contacted the most reliable of his botany students and asked her to take care of his plants for a while. She thought nothing of this request, assuming he was planning another visit to the prill planet. But the sphere Tyvian boarded was bound for somewhere much closer to home.

Floren, entering the akron five days later, almost collided with Kyrin on his way out. He hung his head and slunk past her, but she was too preoccupied to give him more than a glance. She ascended the stairs reluctantly, not looking forward to what she was about to do.

Tralvar was sifting through some paperwork when she arrived. He greeted her with such pleasure that she cringed inwardly, hating herself.

"Floren! You're back! I wasn't expecting you for another two days at least."

"Laura and Idenion are still in Kest," she answered steadily. "They needed some time on their own. I came back on a cargo transport."

"And how *is* Kest?" he inquired. "Still down-at-heel?"

"Very much so."

"That's what I'd assumed," he said briskly. "So, I shall make it the manufacturing centre for disc players as soon as I've ironed out the wrinkles this end. I was going to let Treva handle it, but they've quite enough industry already." He paused and smiled at her conspiratorially. "If you haven't seen Jarras, you won't have heard my news. Come and see this!"

Floren approached the desk. Proudly, Tralvar

514

handed her a scroll. It was a certificate, endorsed by Melor, admitting Tralvar to the scolia at the most elementary level.

"This is wonderful," she enthused.

"I know I'll never reach a higher status while I'm so inept with the lattice," Tralvar said, "but that doesn't matter. The Guild has recognised my devotion to music. And more importantly, Melor has forgiven me."

Floren started to speak.

"There's more," Tralvar interrupted. "The administration has been investigating Strephin's crimes, and he's been positively linked to three murders, several disappearances and numerous serious assaults. I'm to be officially exonerated from all blame regarding his death. The record will show it was an execution."

"And so it should," Floren declared. She didn't mention Tristell. Neither did he.

"You haven't told me why you came back early," he said. "Not that I've given you much chance." Affectionately he sought to read her, and was startled by her lack of response. "You're shielding! Are you angry with me?"

"No, Tralvar." Floren's voice was infinitely sorrowful. "If I were, it might make it easier to say this."

"You want to terminate our pairbond." Tralvar's voice was expressionless.

"Yes, but that isn't all I must bring to an end." Floren spoke resolutely now that she'd begun. "I won't be returning to Alda Mexa when the tour's over. I can't live here any longer."

He stared. "You're leaving the Lyricon - your custodianship - everything?"

"Dena's perfectly capable of running the Lyricon," said Floren. "I've just been to see her and she's loving it. She'll make a good custodian."

"But *why* are you doing this?" he demanded.

"Oh, Tralvar, don't rail at me. I'd like nothing better than to settle into my old career as if nothing had happened. But I've lost too much - my lifebonded partner, my daughter, my peace of mind. You complimented me on my inner strength. Didn't it occur to you that my resilience has limits? I didn't realise what those limits were until I moved back into the Lyricon. Then I realised I couldn't continue."

"What will you do?" he asked dejectedly.

"I shall relocate to Kassi," she replied. "I know some of the scolia there."

"You will be missed," Tralvar said in the same tone of voice.

"I won't be leaving yet," she hurried on, "but I wanted you to be the first to know my plans. I owe you that. But...please don't ask me to unite with you again. If I did I'd be tempted to stay on, and in the end that would prove hurtful to me."

"You're not telling me everything," he challenged.

"No. No, I'm not," Floren admitted. "One day you'll understand why. I shall always be fond of you, Tralvar. Never forget that." She embraced him briefly, then went to the door.

"Floren - " he began helplessly, but she didn't turn back. When the door re-opened moments later he looked up expectantly, but it was only Kevis.

"Here is the latest technical report from the record factory," he said, then paused. "Is this a bad time?"

Tralvar squared his shoulders. "Not in the least," he stated. "Leave the report with me. I'll read it at once."

As he'd anticipated, there was still a high quantity of faulty pressings. Not, he was sure, due to the calibration of the equipment. Engineers accustomed to working on the stardrive wouldn't make such mistakes. No, the problem had to be with the stamper alloy. A different material was needed - something light, tough yet malleable.

"Of course," he said aloud, and hastening to the radio room, put through a call to Jarras. He was currently with the monorail team at Tivenne.

"Did you keep that defective batch of theridolyte, as I asked?" Tralvar inquired without preamble.

"Of course," Jarras replied. "Wemm thought I was being overzealous, but I finished processing it and marked it unspaceworthy. As you said at the time, it still has potential uses."

"And I believe I've just found one," Tralvar said. "Thank you for following my instructions so faithfully. I'll have Wemm bring me a consignment."

"When you called, I thought it was time for my retrace," Jarras went on, suddenly hesitant.

"Tyvian isn't quite ready yet," Tralvar said apologetically.

"I really would like to get it over with," said

517

Jarras.

"Any day now," Tralvar promised. "I'll make sure Tyvian knows of your concerns."

***

Kyrin felt lethargic and strange. The pain hadn't left him, but it seemed faraway and unimportant. He presumed he'd been drugged, but that didn't seem important either. He was lying on his own bed and Asterion was deftly removing the ruined shirt, turning him this way and that, easing the wine-soaked material from his bruised ribs. The rest of his clothes swiftly went the way of the shirt. He started to protest, then stopped, not knowing quite what he was objecting to.

"I didn't think anyone could blush all over," Asterion remarked. "Don't be so modest. You're a fine young man, Kyrin."

He disappeared for a moment or two. Kyrin, aware that he hadn't left the apartment, suddenly felt absurdly content. He closed his eyes, beginning to drift, then gasped as something cold and wet slapped his naked skin. Asterion was cleaning off the rest of the wine, first with a damp cloth and then a rough dry one. "There, that should feel more comfortable," he said when he'd finished. "Now let me make sure you're not too badly hurt. Is this painful? Or this?"

Kyrin lay quiescent while his injuries were examined. Asterion desperately wanted him to be well; this he *did* understand. So, out of gratitude, he didn't even flinch when pain flared briefly in his

518

right side.

"Nothing too serious," Asterion said at last, in the same subdued tone he'd used throughout his ministrations. "Can you tolerate some of these covers on you? It's time for you to sleep."

"Thank you for being so kind," Kyrin whispered.

"Kind?" echoed Asterion with a cynical laugh. "Oh, that's novel. I must remember that." He busied himself with the bedclothes.

"Please don't go," Kyrin said hesitantly.

Asterion paused, eyebrows arched quizzically. "Settle down and stop fighting that sedative," he advised.

"Don't go," repeated Kyrin, growing agitated. "Don't leave me on my own!"

With a weary sigh, Asterion seated himself on the edge of the bed and put an arm round Kyrin's shoulders. "Is that better?"

Kyrin relaxed thankfully, letting his head droop onto Asterion's chest. Within that protective embrace, as he deemed it, he felt happy and safe. It had been years since anyone had held him like that - not since he was an infant, living with both his parents in the town of Virda. An idyllic time, too soon and too suddenly over. How he longed to go back to it.

"What happened to your parents?" Asterion asked curiously.

"Nothing. I had to leave," Kyrin said. "I was sent to the relayists' training school in Tafret. I was only four."

"Chaos, why start so young?"

"Everyone told me I'd be the best," said Kyrin with simple candour.

Asterion, moved to sentiment, gently stroked the blond head. "Did anyone ever say you had pretty hair?"

"I don't think so," Kyrin answered after deep consideration. He was starting to drift again.

"Have you ever had a partner?" Asterion persisted.

"Sometimes, during sciesha, I find a girl," Kyrin replied drowsily. "At other times it's too distracting. A relayist is everyone and no-one, as the saying goes."

"Better than simply being no-one, like me," Asterion said morosely. "At least that was true until today. Today was special. I successfully wrecked my life twice over." He shifted a little on the hard bed. "Can I talk to you about it, Kyrin? I'd like someone to know."

"I'll listen. Please don't be sad," Kyrin murmured, briefly raising his eyes to Asterion's secretive, shuttered face.

Asterion averted his gaze, as if the look disturbed him. "Does news from Tivenne filter through this bleak little apartment?" he began. "I imagine it must do. So you'll know I tried to shoot Laura. What you won't know is why. I suppose you'll have heard all the theories - that I was trying to upstage Strephin, that I misunderstood an order, that I was actually trying to hit Tralvar. None of that is true. The fact is, I panicked. I don't want the girl put on retrace because I'm sure her planet's the one that gave Alendis his ideals. When he records

520

her thoughts he might get his own memory jogged. And if he realises his notions aren't purely Celestrian, he might turn his back on everything he's worked for. Everything that could make us strong."

Kyrin, almost asleep, listened to the low, bitter voice with dwindling comprehension.

"You see, I remember being there," Asterion continued. "The flags, the crowds, the fanaticism. Strephin being slapped because he cried. Vitorr trying frantically to get us to safety. So exciting. So much to absorb. Alendis learnt to be a leader, Strephin learnt to be a brute, and I learnt to be an outsider. It's true, Kyrin. I've never belonged anywhere. Oh, I wanted to help Alendis. I was so loyal, so quick to alert him to dissenters. I didn't realise he'd forgotten our little trip until he...he had that row with Vitorr and pushed him to his death. Chaos, I was scared. I'd forgotten *how* scared until I met Laura. And now my anonymity's gone, and I can't even tell Alendis why I did it." He paused and sighed. "And to round off a perfect day, I propositioned Strephin. Why didn't I keep my distance? I might have known it would end in a fight."

Kyrin stirred a little in his arms.

"A word of advice, little hero. Take sciesha all you want, but forget about unity. People are never what you believe them to be; move beyond the physical and they only disappoint. Strephin should have understood that. He's alone too."

"Don't let him hurt me again," Kyrin mumbled.

"He won't," Asterion said softly, his lips against

521

Kyrin's cheek. "I'll look after you. Now sleep. Sleep...."

The playback ended. Tyvian at first thought Kyrin had fallen asleep along with his retraced self, but then he saw that the young man's eyes were open and focused on the ceiling. It was the nonchalant, lofty gaze affected by most relayists. Probably, thought Tyvian, the very expression which had so infuriated Strephin. But the thoughts behind the eyes held a different story. Kyrin was engaged in a mind-clearing ritual and not having much success. Once, twice, his concentration faltered, until at last he forsook the attempt and sat up dejectedly.

"Give it time," Tyvian advised, then added: "I presume that explains a few things?"

Kyrin managed a wan smile. "Discords, yes. I'd no idea that leaving my home still carried such an emotional weight. Asterion seemed more like a father than a prospective lover."

"And when he died, you suffered your early loss all over again," Tyvian concluded.

"Poor Asterion," said Kyrin after a long silence. "He seemed so lonely."

"He wanted you to think that, Kyrin," said Tyvian dismissively. "He wasn't outside society. He'd integrated himself quite well, all things considered. His culinary skills were very popular. And no-one, absolutely no-one, associated him with Alendis and Strephin until he sided with them at Tivenne. I know, because I did some checking up."

"How?" Kyrin looked apprehensive.

"Discreetly." Tyvian assured him. "I'd been

forced to carry out retraces on some of the people he denounced. I went to them, apologised; they spoke freely about him, including his ill-considered relationships."

Kyrin waited silently.

"He caused his niece, Telsa, much distress by beguiling her first partner and discarding him the next day. That was the most quoted example of his selfishness, but there were other similar stories."

"And you think he'd have treated *me* like that."

"Given the chance, yes."

Kyrin gave a rueful sigh. The strange mental distancing came into play again as he strove to rebuild his faculties, and this time he completed the exercise. "I think you've just saved my career, Tyvian."

"I'm sincerely glad," the older man said. "Your mind's much too valuable to be trammelled by an obsession."

"It will soon pass."

"And I'm going to make sure it does. How would you like to go home for a while - home to Virda?"

"If only I could," said Kyrin wistfully. "But my family gave me up. They never invited me back nor sent any message to me."

"Because they thought you'd be ashamed of them," Tyvian said gently.

"You went there too?" asked Kyrin incredulously.

"I did indeed. Your mother has moved away, but your father's still there, working with the fishing fleet. He's very proud of you."

523

"Then...why didn't he...?"

"He's a simple man, Kyrin. When you secured such an important post, he thought you wouldn't want to be reminded of your background. It never occurred to him that you might be homesick. He said he wished he'd known sooner, and that he'd make you very welcome." Tyvian hesitated. "I hope I wasn't too presumptuous."

"No, Tyvian! You weren't." Kyrin's smile would have melted even Asterion's cynical heart. "You've gone to so much trouble on my behalf. I really don't deserve it."

"You do," Tyvian contradicted. "Your teachers were right: you *are* the best. Go to Virda and get well, and don't come back until you're ready to sort out the administrative mess Tylo's getting into."

Kyrin, radiant, stood up to leave.

"One thing more," said Tyvian. "When you first came to me, you wanted to know who you were. Did you find out?"

"Why, yes," said Kyrin with another dazzling smile. "I'm everyone - and no-one."

***

Laura, relaxed and cheerful after a long heart to heart with Idenion, wasted no time in regaling Tralvar with the outcome. "You were absolutely right about him," she confided eagerly. "He made a promise to my uncle that he wouldn't have casual sex with me. He says he knows we have a lifebond, and he doesn't mind waiting. And then, when we're both sure..."

Tralvar hadn't even looked up. "Now that you're finally back here," he interrupted, "kindly spare me the details of your love life and pay attention to the work we have to do."

Laura guessed from his manner that the rumoured split with Floren had already occurred. She followed him to the radio room, determined to give him no more grounds for complaint, but that soon proved impossible. From that day on, Tralvar became a grim-faced martinet, demanding perfection from her and everyone else at the recording sessions.

"Again!" he ordered perfunctorily each time she finished a take. "I'm still getting distortion on the high notes."

Laura began to wish she'd never heard of Nuit d'Etoiles. The scolia, too, protested at having to play the same thing over and over. Tralvar yelled at them. Laura then suggested a backing track, and he lost his temper with her for not explaining it sooner. The scolia objected, saying they couldn't accompany silence. Tralvar raved at them afresh. And when the engineers asked for time to modify their apparatus, he yelled at them too. After several days of this, Laura began to hear his voice in her sleep:

"Again! Again!"

She moved back into the akron to be near her work. Idenion came to see her every evening, but she was so weary after the day's confrontations that she found it hard to be good company. Her throat felt raw, and she simply wanted to sit quietly and rest her voice. Finally the inevitable happened and she woke one morning to find she couldn't speak.

Someone alerted Tralvar, who rushed to her side in a panic. "Oh, chaos, what have I done? This is all my fault. Laura, Laura, say something!"

She couldn't.

"How could I have been so selfish?" he went on, pacing wildly up and down. "How can I make amends? Idenion will be furious...."

Laura shook him to gain his attention. Listen to me, she thought. If you're listening, look at me.

He gave her a miserable stare.

That's better, she went on as clearly as she could. This is only temporary. Surely you know that? It happened to Tristell, didn't it?

"I suppose that's why I'm over-reacting," he confessed, making an effort to calm down. "When will your voice return?"

I'm not sure, she responded. I haven't actually lost it before. Can you find Rietta? She'll know what to do.

Much to everyone's surprise, Laura opted to stay at the akron while she recovered. Unlike Tristell, who'd made stardom a fulltime occupation, Laura had found there was little to do at the Lyricon when she wasn't actually making music. Now that Floren was busy showing Dena the custodian's duties, there would be even less company for her. The akron seemed much more at the centre of things - and if she still became bored, there was always the library.

Apart from Tralvar, everyone reacted sensibly to her plight. Rietta brought her honeyed drinks and peculiar herbal mixtures, Dena brought her trinkets left at the Lyricon by well-wishers, and Idenion brought her the opening lines of his new poem. She understood very little of it, but enjoyed hearing him read. Tralvar, true to form, remarked that she was better off *not* understanding; and Dena, surprisingly, agreed with him.

"It isn't Idenion's best work," she commented. "But he hasn't reached the part where he meets you, Laura. I'm sure it will improve."

But the poem did not progress.

When her voice was moderately restored, she set herself a programme of exercises to strengthen it. Tralvar observed these proceedings with admiration. Whatever Tristell's other attributes, she'd been a stranger to self-discipline. He delivered one last apology.

"Forgive me for ill-treating your voice. Nobody believed I'd make a success of recording sound, and I was intent on proving I could."

"Have you succeeded, then?" asked Laura.

"It was a team effort. We've cleaned up that distortion at long last, and the theridolyte has transformed our production line. I'll probably be accused of squandering a vital commodity, but I can live with that." He shuffled awkwardly. "When Tristell - " he hesitated over the name - "lost her voice, she often went to the coast to recover. She said the sea air did her good. You're singing at Virda next, aren't you? Why don't you go there early and complete your cure? I could ask the local healers to keep an eye on you."

"Can I take Idenion?"

"You might as well. Since his genius appears

to have deserted him, he's no use here," Tralvar said acidly. "Can't you have a row with him, or something? He isn't used to such a static relationship."

Laura bridled. "I'm sorry you think I don't inspire him."

"It's not your fault. It's his." Tralvar wished he sounded more convincing. "I'll contact Virda tomorrow," he went on hastily. "And there's to be no singing until the healers give you permission. I'm ordering you to do nothing!"

Virda was a thriving fishing port to the southwest. The town, an intriguing straggle of narrow streets, was built around a cove. In the bay were numerous jetties on stilts, high enough for the returning trawlers to anchor beneath them while the catch was lifted ashore. Laura expected to see the boats left stranded when the tide turned, until Idenion reminded her that there were only solar tides to contend with.

When the people were not out fishing or keeping their fleet in good repair, they practised an obscure bardic tradition. There were frequent storytelling contests, usually held in a small amphitheatre near the cliff edge. A weathershield would have been very useful, as frequent storms often drove the contestants back into the town.

The healers looked after Laura assiduously and gave her a disgusting drink made from seaweed. She wondered if Tralvar had known what they'd do. But despite the unpalatable medicine, she found Virda wonderfully relaxing. There was a timeless, elemental quality to life there. It had obviously been the same for generations. The narrative tales, at least the ones she could follow, all centred around life at sea.

One day, while Idenion was taking part in one of the story rounds, Laura went to explore the cliff top. There had been a recent squall, but the grass was already dry. The sky was purple with shafts of green-gold sunlight here and there. When she'd almost reached the tip of the headland she realised she was not alone: a blond young man was sitting on a rock near the cliff edge, gazing disconsolately across the bay. Recognising him, Laura went forward and ventured a greeting.

"It's Kyrin, isn't it? I saw you in the hospital with Lydion."

"Yes, I am Kyrin," he replied, as if he didn't quite believe it himself. Then, unexpectedly: "Do you know what it's like to want something really badly for years, then find you *don't* want it after you get it?"

"No, that's never happened to me," said Laura. "What didn't you want?"

"To come back here, to my birthplace. I thought I'd be so happy. It hasn't changed, but I have. I just didn't realise. I'll have to stay a little longer to please my father, but I can't wait to see Alda Mexa again."

"It *is* very quiet here," Laura agreed.

Kyrin ceased his study of the ocean and turned to face her. "My mistake was in thinking Virda was still my home. When I'm working in the capital I have a true sense of belonging, far more than this place ever gave me. There's always so much activity, and I need to be part of it. Even at this moment I feel I'm missing something vitally important."

"Things have calmed down a lot lately," said Laura. "Try to enjoy the rest of your holiday. I'm sure there's nothing exciting going on."

Kyrin again stared at the horizon. At the limits of his redoubtable perception, distant unreadable thoughts danced with the evanescence of a heat haze. Something had happened, or was about to happen, and he couldn't determine how he knew. "You're wrong, Laura," he said with finality. "Something's different. And I have to know what it is."

Chapter Seventeen

"I think you're quite mad," said Halon.

Rillan and Thala regarded him defiantly. All around them communications equipment idled, the greens and blues of the tracking screen casting strange lights on their determined faces.

"Are you saying we can't go?" demanded Rillan.

"It's nearly a thousand light years each way!" Halon protested. "Our spacecraft are old, Rillan. I can't believe you're willing to be so foolhardy."

"And I can't believe you're being so negative," retorted Thala angrily. "Idenion steals a programme, nearly gets himself killed, contacts a emergent species and is called a hero! Yet we, when we follow correct procedures, are treated like idiots."

"Idenion didn't steal the programme - I gave it to him," Halon reminded her.

"That's even worse! Why encourage him and not us?"

"Because I had no idea what Symerid Three had turned into," said Halon, shifting uneasily under their combined gaze and staring out at the twilit spacefield. "We have next to no information about these Narvellans, but there's one thing we can be sure of: the report that so intrigued you is just as out of date as the file on Symerid. Narvella could be at war, or looking to start one."

"Credit me with *some* sense, Halon!" Rillan said indignantly. "I wouldn't go blundering in without making sure it was safe. I've studied the data thoroughly - everything's in accordance with the original programme. There's more background radiation than previously recorded, but no suspicious energy traces from the inhabited worlds - nothing that would suggest conflict."

"And the probe wasn't scanned," Thala added. "What further proof do you need? The Narvellans won't harm us!"

"That's pure supposition!" Halon was growing flustered. "You've no business asking me to condone such a risk. I haven't the authority."

"You're in charge of all spaceflights, aren't you?" countered Rillan. "All we want is permission to study the Narvellans at close quarters. If we have any doubts at all, we won't make contact."

"I still think you should take your request to Tralvar," said Halon in a last attempt to duck the responsibility.

"He can hardly promote space exploration one moment and refuse us the next," Rillan pointed out. "But, if you like, I'll approach him. And I'll ask Jarras to put in a good word for me. He knows I won't do anything foolish."

"Oh, discords, I suppose I'll have to let you go," Halon said wearily. "But not before you've carried out quadruple checks on your sphere. In the meantime I'll have to let Tralvar know what you're doing. If he objects, you'll have to abide by his decision."

"He won't object," Rillan said confidently. "He probably won't like it, but what can he say? We can't revive our golden age by putting our feet up and dreaming about it."

Tralvar, when informed, was troubled by the proposal but knew Rillan sufficiently well to trust his judgement. Like Halon, he was more concerned with possible malfunctions in the course of the journey. Fourteen ilden in transposal would place an incalculable strain on the Drive, to say nothing of the psychological effect on the crew. But it had been achieved before, somehow. He couldn't help envying Rillan his confidence.

Laura, in the final stages of her travels, knew nothing of this. When she finally returned to Alda Mexa, Rillan had been absent for twenty days. There had been no communication from him, and people were beginning to think there never would be.

Floren quietly took her leave, still refusing to explain what she intended to do with her life. In a short ceremony she handed Dena the key to the belltower, and was gone before anyone had the chance to say a proper farewell. Dena, undaunted, set about organising the final event of Laura's tour. It was to be more than just another concert.

"Tralvar wants to broadcast it," she explained to Laura. "Our satellite array hasn't been used since his inaugural speech, and he'd like to remedy that. He wants to make a recording as well, but I think that idea may be too ambitious as yet. The broadcast alone will be difficult."

"Why?"

"Because the weathershield causes radio interference at close range. We'll have to run a land line to a portable transmitter."

"Do we *need* the shield on? It's midsummer!"

"Which means it will probably rain," declared Dena. "If I can avoid running it, I will, but I have to assume we'll need it."

"Are you going to let Tralvar play for me?" asked Laura.

"Of course, if he wants to," replied Dena. "He's part of the scolia now. Laura, may I speak my mind about something?"

"About Idenion, I suppose," said Laura resignedly.

"Yes. I can't help wondering how much longer you intend to keep him waiting."

Laura tried not to frown. "I might have known you'd take his side."

"It isn't a question of taking sides," Dena said earnestly. "A relationship has to evolve, or it becomes stale. Idenion promised he wouldn't trifle with you, but surely your uncle wouldn't object if you were married according to Celestrian law? You and Idenion both claim to have a lifebond, but you won't allow him to express his love."

"But that's just it, Dena," Laura replied unhappily. "As far as he's concerned he'll never be able to do that, not properly. I can't share total unity. And I'm so afraid he'll get tired of me once he realises what he's missing. Oh, he keeps telling me it's romantic to have some mystery between us, but that's just talk."

"He means it," said Dena. "You're his muse."

"Some muse! I stopped him writing!"

"Perhaps because his poem has no ending." Dena's expression was grave. "You have to make

534

your mind up, Laura. It isn't fair on either of you."

"I'll give him a decision soon, I promise," said Laura. "After the concert. I'll tell him after the concert." And between now and then, she reflected after Dena had left, I have some serious thinking to do.

As her performance was only a day away, she remained at the Lyricon. She put on her long yellow gown and paraded before Tristell's mirror, trying to attain the poise of a true First Singer. She only half succeeded. Then, through reciting aloud, she attempted to hone her language skills, all too aware that her accent was letting her down. Try as she would, she couldn't seem to improve it. Idenion had gone to visit his friends in the student quarter, which made it easier for her to think objectively about the future, but she was still no nearer a solution.

She'd seen Tralvar, Wemm and Jarras wandering about in the lower levels, and assumed it was to do with the outside broadcast. But, as darkness deepened on the evening of the concert, Tralvar drew her outside and made her stand at the farthest edge of the square.

"What's going on?" she asked. "I'm supposed to be getting ready."

"Wait a little longer," Tralvar instructed.

Laura then noticed there were suspiciously few people about, save one or two hurrying along with their heads down.

"What - " she began.

Something green and luminous streaked into the sky above the Lyricon, followed almost

535

instantly by a flash and an echoing crackle. An array of tiny flares drifted in a lazy parabola, fanning out as they descended until, like feathers from some mythic bird, they brushed against the colonnades and dissolved harmlessly. The second skyburst hung in the air like a beaded curtain before melting away. The third and fourth eddied down in spirals; the fifth and last was another shower of illuminated feathers.

"Fireworks," said Tralvar unnecessarily. "Sorry I could only manage green. I'll improve."

"They were beautiful!" Laura said warmly. "How do you find the time for all these projects?"

"It didn't take long. I already had the launchers, don't forget. Actually, Wemm did most of the work. He's better with chemicals than I am."

"Everyone knew what was going to happen," Laura commented as they went back inside.

"I had to ask Kyrin to put out a warning," Tralvar admitted. "I didn't want anyone to be frightened. But it was still a surprise for *you,* wasn't it?"

"Oh, yes," Laura affirmed, slightly uneasy for a moment. "Nobody said a thing."

"Good. Now, can you take me through your programme for tonight?"

Laura was suddenly all efficiency. "I'm starting with Where Corals Lie. I sang that in Virda and they liked it. Next, you and I do our version of Voi Che Sapete. Then I think I'll sing Where'er You Walk, as only the Peisistrata audience has heard it. Do you want to accompany that as well?"

"Not without a run-through," Tralvar said.

"I'll try and make time," said Laura, "but I really should rehearse what I'm to say to the radio audience. You still haven't shown me where the microphone's going to be. Oh, and I nearly forgot - is it all right if I wear Tristell's dress?"

Dena watched as they passed by, so engrossed in their conversation that they failed to notice her. Where in chaos was Idenion? How dare he go missing tonight after she'd so carefully interceded for him? But she couldn't do anything about that now. She had to call the scolia.

Shortly before the performance, as predicted, the rain arrived. Sighing, Dena gave the signal to start the shield. Tonor, who hadn't taken in a single thing Tralvar had shown him, threw the ignition switches too rapidly and caused a partial failure of the grid. His second attempt produced a disorienting strobe effect.

Tralvar and Laura had just arrived backstage.

"I'm sorry, but it looks as if you'll have to do without me," Tralvar said resignedly. "If he carries on like this, the shield will only be fit for scrap. The scolia won't mind taking my place while I sort it out."

"It can't be helped, I suppose," Laura agreed reluctantly. "Put some old clothes on first!"

"I will," Tralvar assured her. "Now remember: speak slowly and clearly, and don't worry about your accent. No-one's looking for perfection."

"If you say so," Laura said with a grimace.

Tralvar sent Tonor packing and successfully restarted the shield. As he'd anticipated, faults were constantly threatening to re-emerge, so there was no hope of leaving it to run unattended. But he'd only just commenced his vigil when someone tapped him on the shoulder and said:

"*My* job, I think!"

It was Lydion. He looked gaunt and tired, but he was smiling.

Tralvar's face lit in surprise and pleasure. "By harmony, it's good to see you! But when did you get out of hospital? Are you sure you're fit for work?"

"I'm here, aren't I?" Lydion answered laconically. "Go on, get back on that stage. That's an order, First Citizen!"

Under Lydion's skilled touch, the shield ceased its flickering and settled into a shade of blue so tranquil that it was difficult to imagine it had ever given trouble. Laura spoke a flawless greeting to her worldwide audience. The dancers radiated a sheer joy in their art. The scolia's lattice was the best they'd yet achieved, and Tralvar's playing was excellence itself. In all, it was a perfect event. Toward the end of Laura's first set, Idenion slipped apologetically onto the crowded front terrace. Dena glared at him from her place in the centre, but for the duration of the lattice had no other way to show her displeasure.

The spectators were rapt and quiet. They no longer called Laura's name at every opportunity, and she no longer needed them to. To conclude the evening Idenion came forward and recited an ode to music, and Tralvar promised the radio listeners many more broadcasts from the Lyricon. Then the scolia dispersed, the crescent-shaped microphones

538

were switched off, and Laura prepared an encore for the Lyricon audience alone. Tralvar returned to the zirid, but had scarcely begun the brief introduction to Aprés un Rêve when he was unceremoniously interrupted.

+TRALVAR!+

He turned, his unwary perception dazzled by the exuberant call. +Rillan?+

Most of the audience read this exchange, and watched in mounting curiosity as Tralvar hurried out of sight. It seemed the entertainment was about to take an entirely new direction. Laura, not knowing what had happened, hesitated a moment and then went after Tralvar. Idenion followed them both.

Rillan was hastening up the stage approach. "Sorry to be so unorthodox," he said when he and Tralvar met, "but when Halon told me there was a concert in progress I simply had to come here and surprise you."

"You certainly achieved that," Tralvar remarked. "I thought you were dead. But by the look of you, you're not even ill!"

"The Narvellans created a sterile environment for Thala and me," Rillan explained. "Is the concert over? Am I too late?"

"Too late for what?" asked Tralvar, but he already had the answer. Laura, a step or two behind him, ground to a halt and stared.

Two darkhaired girls materialised from the shadows. Their skin was pale gold, their eyes brilliant green, and they were attired in closefitting metallic red.

"I am Tarit," said one. She spoke Celestrian with an attractive lilt.

"I am Shann," said the other.

"We sing, we dance."

"We would like to entertain you."

Laura had the distinct feeling she was being marginalised. Idenion paused beside her; she turned to him for reassurance, only to see him gazing raptly at the Narvellan girls.

Tralvar's face was unreadable, and he uttered no formal greeting. "You have a keen sense of the dramatic, Rillan, but your timing's a little slack. The scolia has already disbanded and the broadcast's over."

"But the audience is still here and getting very impatient," Rillan said. "Let the girls introduce themselves, and everyone will go home happy."

"Your guests have just spent a day in transposal," Tralvar reminded him. "I doubt if they feel like singing."

Shann was staring boldly at Tralvar. "We are emissaries as well as entertainers," she said. "Why do you hide your thoughts, First Citizen? We bring a message from our government. Therefore it's vital that we're open with one another."

"Now is not the time nor the place," he replied curtly. "I'll summon the administrators tomorrow, and you may then deliver your message. In the meantime, you may sing if you wish."

They're telepathic, Laura thought in consternation. They're petite, they're beautiful, and they're going to sing. Where does that leave *me*?

Rillan put an arm around each girl and ushered

540

them toward the stage.

"Tell them to take their shoes off," Laura suggested loudly. The girls turned beatific smiles upon her and removed their dainty footwear. Then they ran lightly forward, and the restive audience was stilled. After repeating their names and occupations, the Narvellans performed an unaccompanied duet in their sweet high-pitched voices. It was competent, even elegant, but Tralvar was unmoved.

"They treat music as a social grace. They have no love for it," he said.

"Pure artifice," agreed Lydion, who'd briefly emerged from the generator room. "But interesting. I think some of our younger citizens will be impressed."

Laura, glancing sideways at Idenion's eager profile, silently endorsed that opinion.

The song over, Dena came forward and politely thanked the duo for such an unexpected finale.

"We will perform again soon!" declared Tarit. "We will learn *your* songs, *your* dances. The voices of my people will be at your disposal!"

Cries of joy greeted this announcement.

"Oh, Rillan, what *have* you done?" Tralvar muttered.

"I thought you'd be pleased," said the young explorer petulantly.

"Hasn't it occurred to you that they'll want something in return? The transposal drive, probably. And your Tarit has just made it very difficult for me to refuse - even though I must."

"Who could refuse her anything?" said Idenion

541

dreamily. Laura shot him an exasperated look.

"This might be an appropriate moment to ask where Thala is," Tralvar continued.

"On Narvella Prime," Rillan responded. "She stayed to make further studies."

"At their invitation, no doubt," Tralvar observed. "Clever. They weren't going to risk us disappearing for another two thousand years!"

On stage, Shann was fielding questions from a bevy of students. Tarit extricated herself and made straight for Idenion.

"Did you enjoy our song, First Poet?"

"Idenion, I want to talk to you," said Laura meaningfully. He aimed a look of reproach in her general direction.

"Can't it wait, Laura? These are important guests!"

"I don't wish to be any trouble," said Tarit, all contrition.

"You're not," Idenion assured her with unnecessary haste.

"You're very young to be First Poet," she continued, resting her small golden hand on his arm. "Your verse must be quite exceptional. I should like to hear some."

"Idenion!" Laura repeated.

"Not now, Laura," he said with a hint of irritation.

Laura, with great dignity, turned to Tralvar. "Would you take me back to the akron, please?" she asked.

"If you're sure that's what you want," he answered. At that moment Lydion deactivated the shield, and he could no longer see Laura's expression.

"I'm sure," she said.

***

The message from the Narvellans was stark and simple. Narvella Prime was under threat from its own sun. Over the past two hundred years there had been a relentless increase in solar flare activity, in cycles which peaked every twenty years or so. These flares had already consumed vast tracts of the uninhabited inner planets, damaged communications and destroyed spacecraft caught in transit between Narvella Prime and Narvella Four. Experts predicted that one-third of Narvella Prime's population would be wiped out at the peak of the next cycle, twelve years away. And that would be the beginning of a very swift end to life on both worlds.

"We have never progressed beyond interplanetary travel," Shann said, concluding her presentation. "There are no other stars for thirty light years in any direction. Please share your technology with us and help us to save at least some of our people."

After making this plea, the two Narvellan women faced exhaustive questioning about their society and its tenets. Thereafter, they were sent away from the akron as it was felt that their presence would hinder the ensuing debate.

"In the time I was there," Rillan said with great sincerity, "I had no idea they were living with this

543

peril. I saw no signs of panic or unrest."

"Perhaps because you weren't meant to see such things," said Tralvar cynically. "My position remains unequivocal: I will not sanction the release of our science."

"The fate of this civilisation is in our hands," argued Rillan. "We can't deny their request. Have we suddenly become the arbiters of the galaxy? What gives us the right to say who lives and who dies?"

"Save the philosophy for your student friends, Rillan!" Tralvar snapped. Then, more quietly: "Let's forget about the moral high ground for the moment, and simply try to be rational. Our ancestors, who knew far more about other species than we do, kept the transposal drive a closely guarded secret. We must do the same, or risk war."

"But the Narvellans have always been at peace," one of the administrators objected.

"They have a ruling elite which has never been overthrown. That isn't peace as we know it," Tralvar said. "I don't know why we're even discussing this. Our law is quite specific: we must never grant anyone transposal, even for humanitarian reasons. The Narvellans still have a chance to discover it for themselves. If they don't, it's not our concern."

"*We* didn't discover transposal!" Rillan almost shrieked. "We inherited it!"

"Let's not complicate the issue," advised Kevis mildly. "I move we take some refreshment and continue this discussion later. We should all reflect carefully on what has been said."

544

The meeting reconvened that afternoon. While the debate raged on, Laura sat in her room and gazed morosely down at the plaza. The whole city seemed to have paired off. Couples and more couples passed by, unhurried, serene. It was as if everyone had suddenly become very sure of their future.

She began to wish she hadn't walked out of the Lyricon. She'd done it to make a necessary point, but she'd also left Tarit and Idenion together. And now the situation could recur - the two Narvellan girls had left the akron and were doubtless on their way back to the theatre.

Intent on following suit, she found Kyrin and asked if any flitters were about to head in that direction. None were immediately forthcoming, and rather than make the long uphill climb, she waited. When she finally obtained her ride, two ilden had passed.

The market had reappeared outside the Lyricon, its wares a bright splash against their adamantine background. One of the stallholders beckoned her over as she passed.

"For our true First Singer," he said, offering her a dainty scarf. "You serve music - it does not serve you. That is how it should be. These new girls are too proud."

Laura, grateful for this one accolade, thanked him and accepted the scarf. It was firi, of course, with a delicate floral pattern, and so light she thought it would dissolve at her touch. Carefully looping it round her waist, she walked up the Lyricon steps.

Here, too, she saw couples everywhere. Lydion and Irivel; Tonor and one of the dancers; and, glimpsed fleetingly before they disappeared into the lower levels, Shann and the boy who had played Hymorel. Suddenly quite calm, Laura took the lift to the custodian's apartment, where she assumed Idenion would be.

He was there, and so was Tarit. They were sitting on the balcony that overlooked the whole auditorium - the balcony where Laura had once turned to Floren and cried: "I can't do it!" The subdued noises from below - voices, footsteps - had masked the even quieter sound of the elevator. She stood in the doorway, waiting for one or both of them to turn round. But, wholly intent on one another, they failed to perceive her presence.

"...and you're such a good lover," Tarit was saying. "So considerate."

"I'm not considerate at all," he replied unhappily.

"You're still thinking of your little non-conversant." Tarit ruffled his hair as if he were a child.

"I should have gone after her," he reflected.

Tarit said something in Narvellan.

"That's uncalled-for," Idenion said instantly. "Laura's done a lot for this planet."

"But not a lot for you, apparently," said Tarit archly.

Idenion was silent.

"In fact, she's done nothing for you at all," continued Tarit, pinching his thigh. "We're going to work so well together, you and me. Your words,

546

my music. The whole world will be jealous of our love!"

Very quietly, Laura turned and walked the length of the apartment to the opposite door. Tarit had been shopping. Dresses, cloaks and shoes were scattered everywhere. Laura picked up one of the canvas bags the clothes had been packed in, went briskly into the First Singer's apartment, seized her jeans and t-shirt and crammed them into the bag. Then she left via the outside stairs.

On her way out of the Lyricon she saw Dena, little Dena who had always preferred to be single, skipping along in the company of tall, lugubrious Wemm. Yes, everyone was paired off. Taking a deep breath she strode downhill towards the akron, taking care not to look back. If she did, she knew she would cry.

She found Tralvar alone in his suite. He'd drawn the curtains to keep out the late afternoon sun, and was sprawled in an easy chair with a bottle of resnay beside him.

"Oh, Tralvar, you're not drinking again!" she said reproachfully.

"Is it any wonder?" he replied, staring into his glass. "Don't scold - I'm not drunk. I just wanted to blunt the edges of my worries."

"How did the meeting go?"

"Badly," he said, leaning back and closing his eyes. "The best I could do was insist on a further period of study. We're sending a deputation to Narvella to find out everything we can about them. But at the end of that time, everyone will still want to give them transposal. And there won't be anything I can do about it."

"Can the administration overrule you?"

"If mine is the only dissenting voice, yes." He turned to face her for the first time. "What are you doing dressed like that?"

"I want to go home." She did cry then, but only for a moment. She was still too angry for tears. He stood up and put a sinewy arm round her, awkward as always.

"Must you give me *more* problems, you silly girl? I know how hurt you're feeling, but believe me, running away won't help. It'll all blow over in a few days."

"Why did Idenion let it happen?" asked Laura miserably.

"Because he's being stupid," Tralvar declared. "It's just his age. Tarit doesn't mean any more to him than that girl in your village - and you forgave him that, didn't you?"

"Forgave him *what*?" The blood drained from Laura's face, leaving it pinched and sickly. Tralvar realised, too late, that he'd made a bad situation worse.

"Discord's dreams," he muttered.

"Are you telling me," asked Laura, very slowly, "that Idenion had sex with Tracey?"

"I thought you knew," Tralvar said lamely. "There's so much animosity toward her in your thoughts."

Laura considered this information for a moment or two, then straightened her shoulders resolutely. "That's it, then. I'm glad you told me. Now I'm sure I'm doing the right thing. It's as my uncle said -

teenage boys will be teenage boys."

"Very well, Laura," Tralvar poured himself one more drink, then turned back to face her, glass in hand. "Since your mind's made up, I've something else to tell you. If you'd decided to make your home with us, this need never have been an issue, but now it's just become one. While you were away in Virda, another top-level meeting was held. Only this time, I was in agreement with the proposals. Symerid Three, your Earth, has been placed off limits to all space travellers. The programmes have been taken from the register, and all casual reference to its whereabouts has been deleted. If you go back, it will have to be for good."

Laura stared. It felt like another betrayal.

"On his last visit, Jarras was almost captured," Tralvar went on. "He's provided a retrace, which I think you should see. It will show you the necessity of this ban, and you might also be able to explain why your people acted as they did. Unfortunately, playback via the monitor is visual only, which won't make a lot of sense."

"Can't I view it the same way *you* would?" asked Laura.

"There's no reason why not, if Tyvian will channel for you," Tralvar said slowly. "I just assumed you wouldn't want anything more to do with the retracer."

"Since this incident made you blacklist my planet, I want to know exactly what went on," Laura declared. "And can we get it over with quickly? I don't want anyone trying to talk me out of my decision."

549

"Meaning Idenion?"

"I said anyone," Laura emphasised. She meant Idenion.

Tralvar focused his perception and contacted Tyvian on Lateral Three. +I'm bringing Laura+ was all he said.

+I'll load the programme and have it ready for you+ Tyvian responded.

"He's waiting for us," Tralvar then said to Laura, who was watching him questioningly. "I believe he was expecting this."

"Then I suppose we'd better go," she replied evenly. "Why aren't you dancing for joy, Tralvar? You'll soon be rid of me."

"I..." Whatever Tralvar had been about to say, he thought better of it. He finished his drink, set down his glass and made a nominal attempt at smoothing his hair. Moments later, they were descending the steep path to Tyvian's laboratory.

Absorbing the retrace was not the bizarre experience Laura had expected. Either because Tyvian was acting as the intermediary or because she was not telepathic, there was no illusion of being inside Jarras' head. It was more like watching a film taken by him. Laura found it difficult to believe that the sounds she heard were not emanating from somewhere in front of her.

Tyvian had seated her at the monitor and was now sitting close by, wearing the diagnostic sensor. At the nearest corner of the glass tank - a little smaller than the one Idenion had smashed - a single crystal emitted a thin whine like an insect. Inside the tank, one prill spread its ugly yellow leaves in response to the subtle prompting of the aldacite.

Laura watched Floren's white-clad form disappear into the gloom of the English woodland. As Jarras closed the hatch, she caught the distinctive odour of forest loam and gave a small cry of surprise.

"There, you see - you *can* read his senses," said Tralvar, at her elbow. "It's just a bit difficult distinguishing them from your own, isn't it?"

As on the previous occasion, Laura was glad he was there. He seemed so much more in control of things than the reclusive Tyvian, although the opposite was probably true.

Jarras was endeavouring to take his sphere into orbit and wait for Floren's signal; but when he lifted off, he knew almost instantly that something was wrong. A swift glance at the instruments assured him he wasn't going to crash, but his ascent had come to a standstill. He was still far too low. The viewscreen showed wisps of thin cloud and an indeterminate landscape. Hurriedly he found some tools and began unfastening a panel near the pilot's seat. Inside were eight tiny nodes of white light, encircled by a complex web of coils. Seven of the lights burned brightly: the eighth was barely visible.

"What's gone wrong, Tralvar?" Laura asked.

"It's a misfire in the thruster array," he replied. "The spheres can operate on as little as five energy cells, but not when a cell hasn't failed outright. The whole system's out of balance."

Laura guessed at, rather than sensed, Jarras' exasperation. Whilst travelling between cities with her, he'd often commented on the poor manoeuvrability of the spheres. "When the Drive isn't engaged, they handle so badly," he'd said. She'd wondered why he seemed so fixated.

Logically, Jarras should have landed again to make the repair. But he feared discovery, and so he worked on, drawing power from the stored back-up which would keep him aloft for an ild or more. He was angry with himself for not running proper maintenance checks before he'd left, but he'd been so late, and Idenion was relying on him...

Anger made him clumsy. The faulty cell jammed in its mounting.

On the console a warning light blinked insistently, and he took a moment to check it. The sphere was being tracked. At first he wasn't too concerned; Idenion had been spied on at some length and without incident. As an added precaution he engaged the soundsweep, although he wasn't sure what he was listening for. Then he went back to work, accompanied by shrill gusts of wind from outside. After a struggle he prised the cell loose and swiftly began realigning the remaining seven.

"Careful, Laura. This is where the real trouble starts," Tralvar warned. "Tyvian will deflect most of Jarras' reactions. We don't want you getting up and running away! Just remember, it isn't happening to *you*."

"All right," she said uncertainly.

Out of the corner of his eye, Jarras saw another shift in the panel display. At first he thought it was malfunctioning as well. There were two new readings, each a mirror image of the other. Then, with a sharp intake of breath, he realised his peril. Two identical objects were converging rapidly on his position from opposite directions, and each object had a tracking lock on him. An instant later a deafening roar filled the skies.

Laura winced and automatically put her hands over her ears. It didn't help. Two Lightnings, possibly the same ones she'd seen chasing Idenion, appeared literally out of the blue and hurtled past the sphere.

Jarras froze for a moment, then dropped to his knees and redoubled his efforts to restore power. The jets kept pace with their quarry, and the sphere's radio intercepted some brief terse exchanges between the pilots and their base. Jarras didn't understand a word, but guessed they were debating what to do with him. Frantically he slammed the panel shut, activated the thrusters and, when nothing happened, kicked the console several times.

"Pick up, you useless piece of junk. Pick up!"

The sphere rose, accelerating. The Lightnings, furiously fast, swept after it and made a close pass overhead. The sphere rocked. The two fighters banked, returned and repeated the manoeuvre, setting off the spacecraft's collision warning. Jarras scrambled for the transposer.

"Alda Mexa!" he gabbled. "I'm under attack. Patch me through to the akron - hurry!"

"What's the trouble?" asked the operator stupidly.

"They're trying to force me down!" Jarras shrieked. "Call the akron, get Tralvar!"

But there was no time to wait for advice. The jets made a third pass, the gyroscopes destabilised and the sphere began to fall. Terrified, Jarras did the only thing he could. He hit the Drive.

There was a loud pop from the newly repaired array, and the cabin filled with acrid smoke. Jarras had just enough presence of mind to take everything offline. Then he crumpled to the floor and began to weep softly.

Laura huddled down in her seat, feeling very cold. Then she sensed the reassuring pressure of Tralvar's hand on her shoulder, and returned her attention to the screen.

"Jarras!" Tralvar's voice spoke from the retrace. The transposer was still active. "Jarras, chaos take you, answer! I've just been woken from the first decent sleep I've had in octals, so this had better be an emergency!"

Jarras raised his head and looked about, amazed he was still alive. The brief fire had been automatically extinguished. The filters worked busily, clearing the last of the smoke. The viewscreen showed space and stars; numbly, he checked his position. The sphere was drifting just beyond Earth's moon.

"Tell me what happened," Tralvar said more gently. "Take your time. We're receiving telemetry - the Drive isn't damaged."

In hoarse, staccato sentences, Jarras described his narrow escape.

"I see," Tralvar said impassively. "Well, you've dealt with the major problem - now all you have to do is remember your training. You engaged the

554

Drive while the auxiliaries were still online, so they shorted out. What did I teach you to do in that situation?"

"Substitute....other circuitry," Jarras stammered.

"That's right. Most of the circuit cards are interchangeable, so choose something you don't need - the drinks cooler, for instance - and make your repair. And while you do it, turn off the transposal beam."

"No!" protested Jarras.

"You don't have the reserves," Tralvar insisted. "You've drained your back-up power, the filters have been working overtime...I can't talk you through this, Jarras. If you don't end this transmission, you really *will* be stuck, and then I'd have to come and fetch you. Don't make me have to do that!"

"Very well, I'll manage," Jarras said miserably.

"When you're ready to go back for the others, call me again," Tralvar added.

"I can't go back there!" cried Jarras, horrified.

"Do you think I *want* you to go? But you have to, for Idenion's sake. Any further delay could be fatal for him. Use the programmed landing: one unbroken vertical descent, straight to the forest. You *have* to do it!"

"I suppose I must," said Jarras, sounding a little more calm. "But I'm not going near Symerid Three again after this. Ever!"

The retrace ended. Laura rubbed her eyes, feeling dizzy and thirsty. Tyvian, seemingly unaffected, wheeled the tank away and brought her a drink of water.

"Well?" asked Tralvar meaningfully.

"I wish I'd known about this at the time," Laura said, thoroughly dismayed.

"Jarras didn't want to talk about it, and I supported his decision," Tralvar answered. "You do realise he might have killed himself with that escape manoeuvre? The Drive could just as easily have sent him earthward. He was very, very lucky. And now, perhaps, you'd tell me everything you know about these air patrols."

"It means getting into politics," said Laura reluctantly. "Before I start, Tralvar, I just want to say that none of this has changed my mind. I still want to go home."

"I know," he said expressionlessly. "And that presents me with yet another problem: who's going to take you? Not Jarras, it goes without saying. Idenion can't be trusted to get things right, Rillan's on his way back to Narvella, and Lydion's still not well enough."

"What about Halon?"

"He hasn't been offworld for years. His skills are rusty."

"Then what about *you*?"

Tralvar sighed. "I'll let you into a little secret. The very thought of space travel petrifies me."

"What? But you know more about the stardrive than anybody!"

"That's *why* it petrifies me. I couldn't do it, Laura. Not because of your jet fighters but because of space itself."

"*I'll* go," Tyvian said unexpectedly.

556

They both stared.

"I've logged as much time in space as Jarras and Rillan," the botanist pointed out, "and I've been to some very hostile worlds."

Tralvar regarded him with something akin to admiration. It was easy to forget that the older man was a seasoned traveller.

"But I think Idenion should go too," Tyvian added.

"I'm not sure I want that," Laura said quietly.

"Don't part with him in anger," Tyvian warned. "You'll always regret it if you do. See him and clear the air."

"That's excellent advice," Tralvar put in. "Now, when did you last eat? This morning? You're getting as bad as me. Well, we can at least put *that* right; and while we're at dinner, you can tell me about Earth politics. Briefly!"

She wouldn't go back to the Lyricon, so Tralvar sent Rietta to collect the few items she wanted to take with her. She'd chosen a red fringed shawl from Corayn, some costume jewellery, and a shell necklace from Virda. The firi scarf that the market trader had given her was already in her room at the akron. Rietta duly brought back the accessories: she also brought Idenion. Having delivered him into Laura's presence, she pointedly left them alone.

Wordlessly he took Laura in his arms and held her tightly. She leant her head on his shoulder and breathed in the familiar scent of his hair. "I was going to give you an answer last night," she murmured.

"To please my sister? That's the wrong

557

reason," he returned gently.

"You misunderstand," Laura said equally softly. "It's funny - I've learnt some of your language and all it's done is create barriers. Use your perception, Idenion. Learn the truth. I was going to tell you I was sorry, that I couldn't handle marriage yet. I wanted some time on Earth so I could decide where I wanted to be. What's happened in this last little while has shown me my decision was right."

"But if you leave now, the administration won't allow you back!" Idenion protested. "You didn't know about that when you decided to go. Surely it changes things?"

"It makes it much harder to leave."

"I bitterly regret what happened with Tarit," he went on. "I shouldn't have let her get away with it. Don't let my foolishness drive us apart."

"Oh, Idenion, it isn't just about you and other women. It's to do with total unity, and never being able to share it with you. It's to do with sciesha, which frightens me. And it's a lot to do with the Narvellans, or at least two of them, treating me like some kind of throwback. I love Celestra, and I love you, but I'm afraid that if I stay, everything will turn sour."

She paused, thinking she'd put her case rather well. As she finished speaking, Tralvar put his head round the door. "There won't be a sphere ready until tomorrow," he announced. "Jarras is doing the checks. It'll take him most of the night."

"I don't want to put him to any trouble," Laura began.

"He says he doesn't mind, as long as his involvement ends there," Tralvar replied. "Do you mind if I ask a favour?"

"You're *going* to ask, whether she minds or not," Idenion remarked.

"What is it?" Laura inquired, less unkindly.

"You haven't recorded anything since I perfected the process. Would you consider one last session?"

"I'll do it," Laura said, "but does it have to be this evening?"

"Tyvian wants to leave at dawn."

"Tarit and Shann wanted the scolia to play for *them* tonight," Idenion ventured.

"The scolia will play where I tell them to play," Tralvar said darkly. "Report to the studio in half an ild, Laura."

She turned back to Idenion, moderately pleased that the Narvellans' plans were about to be disrupted. "Will you sit in with us?"

"Of course," he replied unhesitatingly. "You can sing to *me*."

It was very unfair of Tralvar, she thought, to make this last demand of her when she and Idenion needed more time alone. But once the session was in progress, with the scolia playing exquisitely and Tralvar looking strangely peaceful as he monitored the sound levels, she knew there could be no better way of spending the evening than this: giving her final performance as First Singer. And later, detached and calm now that her mind was made up, she slept dreamlessly until awakened by the faithful Rietta.

559

At first light, carrying her meagre souvenirs in their canvas bag, she stole down to the refectory where a subdued Tralvar and an equally silent Idenion were waiting for her. Throughout the flitter journey she stared out of the rear window, watching Alda Mexa recede. The sun's first rays had turned the Lyricon to rosy pink.

"I won it back for you, didn't I?" she said wistfully.

"You did. And I'm going to make sure we keep it," Tralvar informed her.

A chill wind was blustering about the spacefield: the long Celestrian summer was finally at an end.

"How long have I been here?" Laura asked, half to herself.

"I guessed you'd want to know that," said Tralvar. "Almost five spans, in our terms. In Earth's, one year and a few odd days."

"Oh!" she exclaimed stupidly. "I've missed a birthday!"

"Talking of birthdays," Tralvar went on, "I meant to return your parents' record. Shall I fetch it?"

"No, I'd like you to keep it," Laura said. "It'll remind you to send that message to your daughter."

Tyvian was already on the sphere, and Tralvar went to have a few words with him. As soon as his attention was diverted, Idenion said swiftly:

"I'm not coming with you to Earth. I don't trust myself. I might do something crazy, such as running away from the sphere when we get there. I'd do anything to stay near you for a few more days!"

"Idenion..." She embraced him, the raw wind stinging her face.

"No one can ever replace you," he said, his breath warm against her neck. "A man can have many loves but only one lifemate. How can I prove it's you? When time has passed, when we're older - would you believe me then, if I came back?"

"But you can't - "

"I'll find a way round the ban. I'll wait five years - five Earth years - and then I'll look for you. Promise me you'll stay in Cheveney. I'll never find you otherwise."

Tralvar stepped out of the sphere. "Everything's in order," he said briskly. "Best not to prolong this."

"Well, I was right about the Narvellans superseding me," Laura said with an attempt at flippancy. "Where's my grateful public? You'd think *someone* would be here to see me off!"

"Did you really want them to, Laura?" inquired Tralvar. "They're not here because I gave false information to Kyrin. Everyone thinks you're leaving at noon."

"Make sure you apologise to him," Laura said reprovingly.

"Oh, I'll take full responsibility as always," Tralvar said. Laura tried to give him a farewell hug; he tensed and edged out of reach. "I've told Tyvian to vary the landing coordinates as a precaution," he added. "Will that be a problem?"

"I shouldn't think so," answered Laura. "I only have to find a telephone."

"Remember what I told you," Idenion whispered as he held her one last time.

"I'll remember," she replied softly. "But will you?" Then she went into the sphere, not looking back. Tyvian sealed the hatch, and in the next breath they were airborne.

Tyvian had left the viewscreen focused on the landing field, but Laura couldn't see Idenion. Only Tralvar remained, gazing pensively skyward. Then, as the image began to blur with distance, he turned abruptly and began to walk away.

Epilogue

Darkness, grass underfoot and the intermittent sound of traffic in the distance. A thick powdering of stars and a horizon that looked too remote.

Wherever I am, thought Laura, it's very exposed.

Tyvian had landed to the west of the given co-ordinates, near the edge of a vast open space. As soon as she'd disembarked he was gone, having had strict instructions not to delay nor look for plants.

Fortunately it was a warm night - late summer, Laura presumed. She decided to stay exactly where she was till dawn, rather than risk turning her ankles on the uneven ground. It would be easily enough done, as she felt so ungainly in Earth's gravity. She tied the firi scarf round her belt, put on her shawl and beads, and sat down on the empty bag. She remained there, reflecting solemnly on the past year, while the constellations drifted west and the sky steadily brightened. As soon as it was light enough to walk safely she stood up - and found herself gazing at something very familiar, which had been hidden from her sitting position by the lie of the land.

Stonehenge.

Couldn't be better, she thought. I'll wait for some tourists and cadge a lift, or maybe tag along with a coach party. Well done, Tyvian!

It took longer to reach the monument than she'd estimated, and when she neared it she found that someone was already there. She stared fascinated at the lone vehicle in the car park. It looked like an old Post Office van, but painted all over with bright swirls of rainbow colour. In a nearby litter bin she saw a crumpled newspaper dated 24th August 1967. Which, she supposed, was yesterday.

"Hello!" said a friendly voice. "Where did *you* spring from?"

She turned and saw a smiling, bearded young man in an embroidered shirt and patched denims. "I've been stranded here," she said. "Is this your van?"

"Yep."

"Then could you possibly give me a lift to Amesbury, or just somewhere with a phone? I've been away and I need to contact my family."

"Been travelling?"

"Er...sort of."

Two girls and another boy wandered up and regarded Laura with the same casual friendliness.

"Be glad to help," said the first young man. "I'm Steve by the way, and this is Melanie, Starshine, and Paul. And that's Corisande over there, communing with the stones."

Laura gazed at the new arrivals in a mixture of incredulity and pleasure. They seemed like a welcome echo of everything she'd just forsaken. Melanie wore a long-sleeved white smock liberally covered with ribbons and beads. The girl called Starshine was wearing an Indian print dress, a circlet of daisies, and a row of sequins under each eye. Paul wore a fringed jacket and cords, and a bright bandana round his long hair.

"We didn't catch your name," prompted Steve.

564

"Laura," she responded.

"Is it really? I've just been reading a poem about you," said Paul. "Here, I'll show you."

He opened the van, rummaged in a haversack and produced a dilapidated book. Putting on some equally battered spectacles, he read:

"Rose-cheek'd Laura, come;
Sing thou smoothly with thy beauty's
Silent music, either other
Sweetly gracing."

"Oh, shut up, Paul!" exclaimed Starshine. "You'll embarrass her!"

Paul ignored her and continued:

"These dull notes we sing
Discords need for helps to grace them;
Only beauty purely loving
Knows no discord."

"Who wrote that?" asked Laura, startled.

"Thomas Campion. Don't you like it? I think it suits you."

Corisande drifted back to the others. She had long auburn hair and looked as if she'd just stepped out of a Pre-Raphaelite painting. "Peace and love," she said to Laura. "Are you coming with us?"

"Steve hasn't said where you're going," Laura replied.

"To the Festival of Flower Children," she said gravely. "At Woburn Abbey."

"It's an open-air gig," Steve added. "Should be a good scene."

Laura blinked. Flower Children? It was an entire movement, then, not just a few individuals. And they doubtless thought she was one of them....

565

"We'd love to have you along," Steve was saying. "If you delay ringing your folks, they won't be any the wiser!"

He was right, of course. She had the freedom to do exactly as she wanted. Once she'd made that phone call, she'd never be as free again. "You've talked me into it," she said.

"Hey, doesn't anyone want breakfast?" asked Paul. "I'm ravenous!"

"We'll stop at the next greasy spoon," cooed Starshine, and kissed him.

"Right, let's split," said Steve. "Find yourself a space in the back, Laura. Mind my guitar and amps!"

"Are you playing at this festival?" Laura inquired.

"No," he admitted. "But where I go, *they* go."

"Same as Paul and his books," commented Starshine.

"I'm trying to form a group," Steve went on. "Paul's good on keyboards, and he writes great songs."

"Which neither of you can sing!" Starshine remarked. "Shove up a bit, Laura."

"Yeah, we need a decent vocalist," said Steve, retrieving the ignition key from under the dash. "I don't suppose *you* can sing, Laura?"

"Yes, actually," she said.

They all stared at her.

"It's true!" she insisted. "That's what I've been doing for my living this past year. I don't know any current pop, though."

"We'll audition you after the festival," promised

Paul.

Melanie sighed dreamily and rearranged her trailing sleeves. "Do you ever get the feeling that some things are just *meant*?" she said.

"Yes," Paul replied, gazing at Laura. "I do."

He was nothing like Idenion. But he had gentle eyes.

The van revved noisily and roared away into the summer morning.

THE END